CN
CARTOON NETWORK

The AMAZING WORLD OF GUMBALL
TUNNEL KINGDOM

created by **BEN BOCQUELET**

script by **MEGAN BRENNAN**

art by **KATE SHERRON**

colors by **CHARLOTTE "CHIKUTO" HARRISON**

with **MEG CASEY & NIMALI ABEYRATNE**

letters by **MIKE FIORENTINO**

cover by **JENNA AYOUB**

designer **CHELSEA ROBERTS**

assistant editor **MICHAEL MOCCIO**

editor **WHITNEY LEOPARD**

with special thanks to **MARISA MARIONAKIS, JANET NO, CURTIS LELASH, CONRAD MONTGOMERY,** and the wonderful folks at **CARTOON NETWORK.**

D0126914

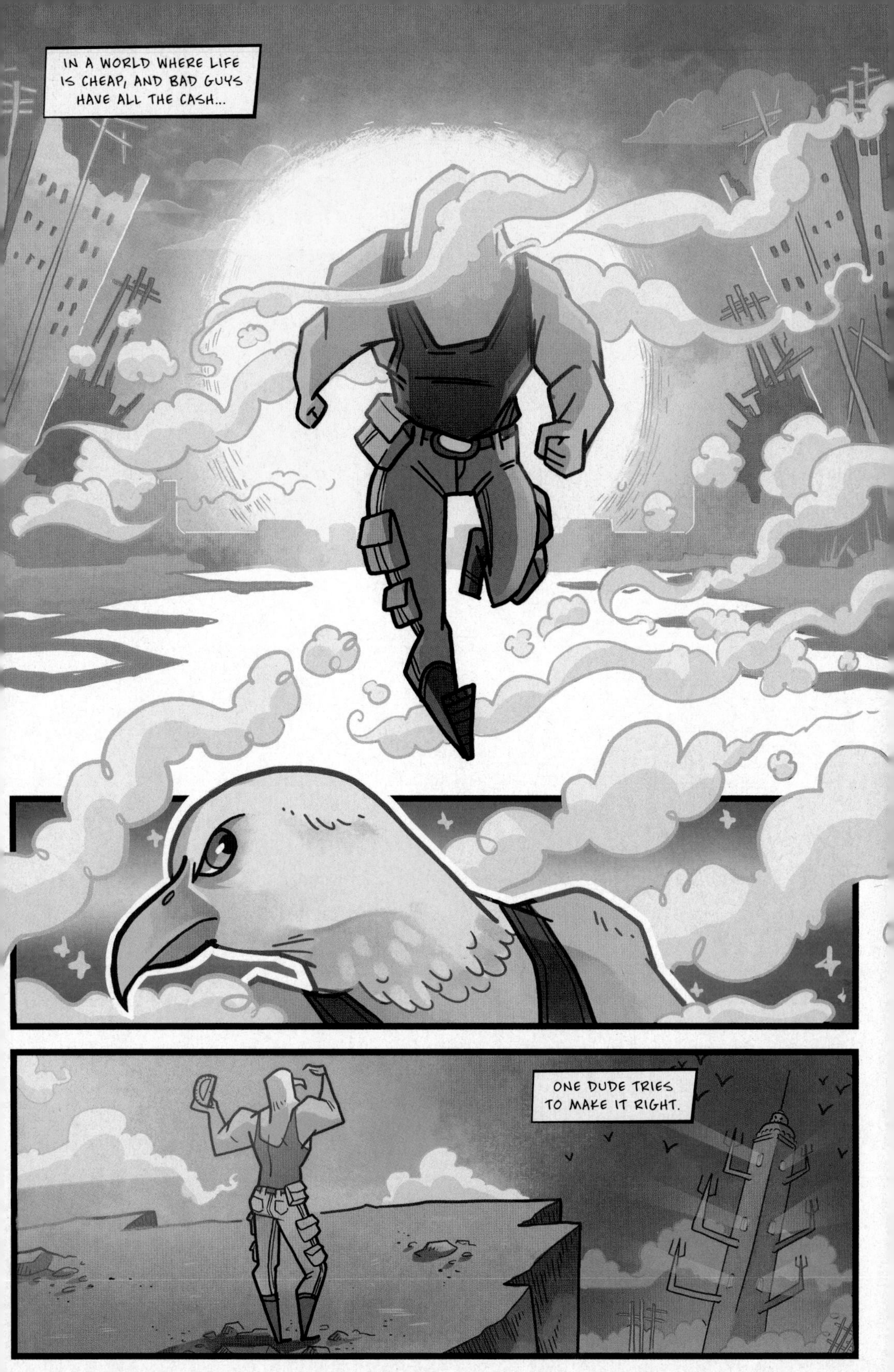
IN A WORLD WHERE LIFE IS CHEAP, AND BAD GUYS HAVE ALL THE CASH...
ONE DUDE TRIES TO MAKE IT RIGHT.

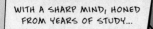

WITH A SHARP MIND, HONED FROM YEARS OF STUDY...

...AND A BODY THAT CAN FIGHT GOOD.

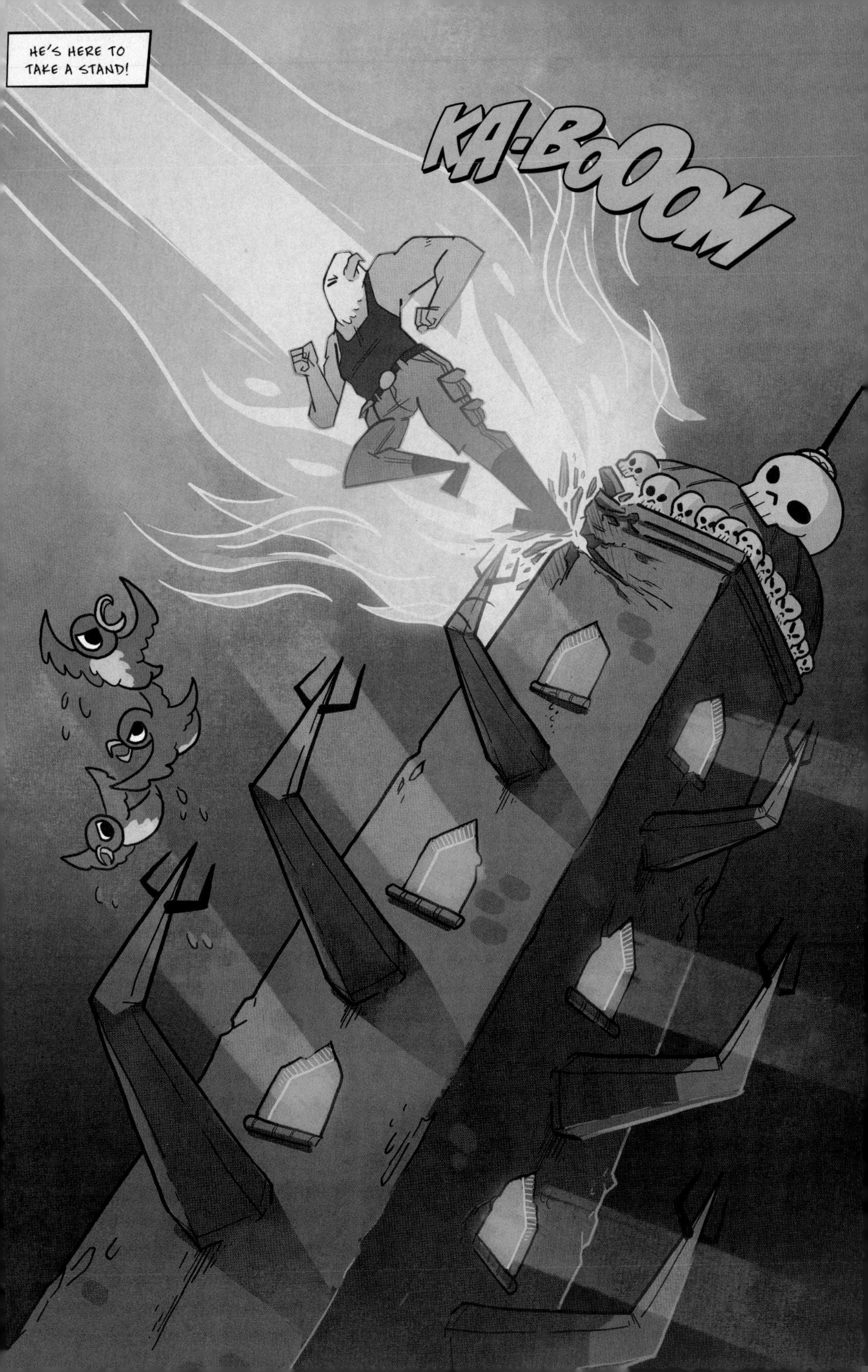
HE'S HERE TO TAKE A STAND!
KA-BOOOOM

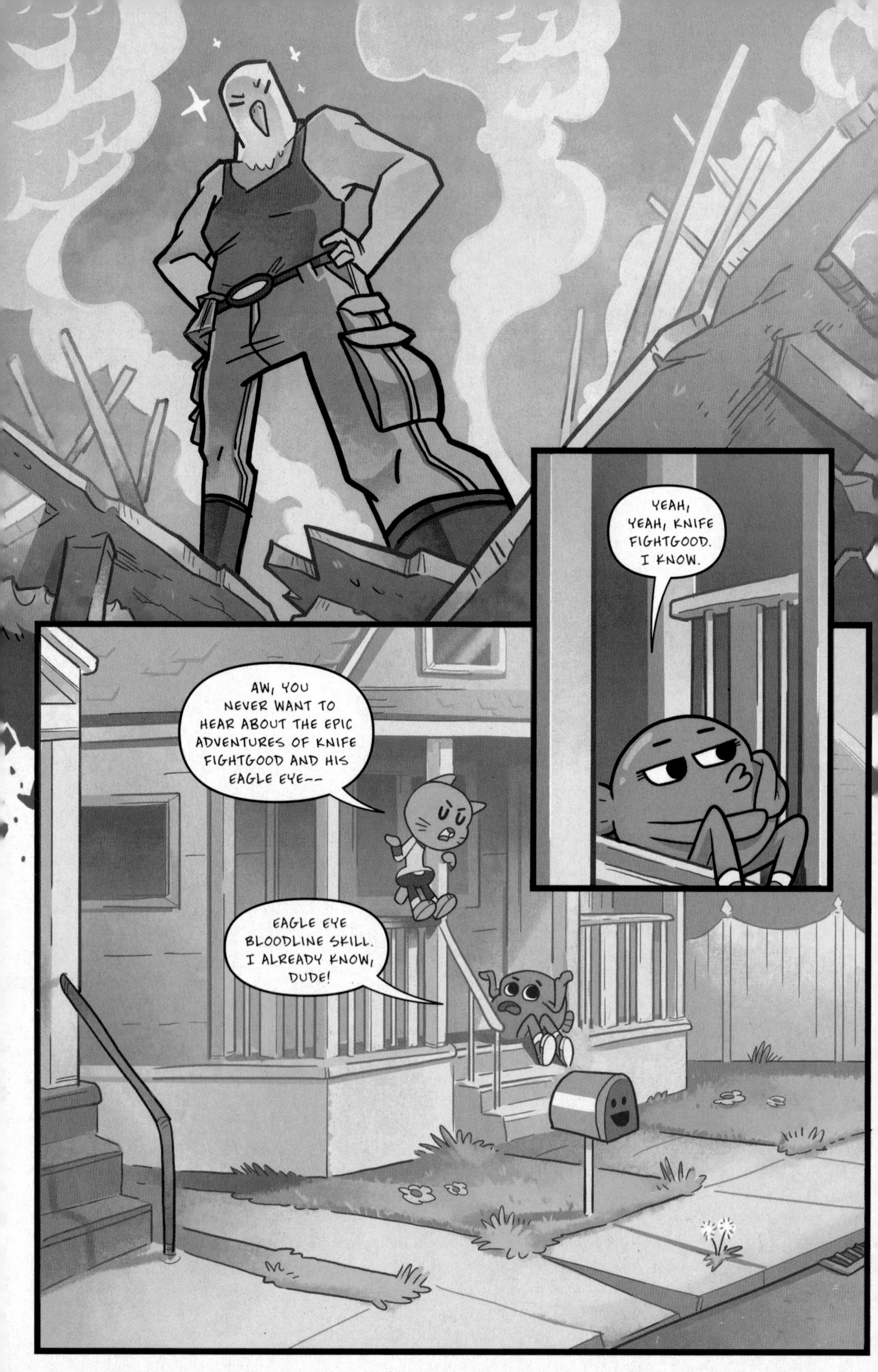
YEAH, YEAH, KNIFE FIGHTGOOD. I KNOW.
AW, YOU NEVER WANT TO HEAR ABOUT THE EPIC ADVENTURES OF KNIFE FIGHTGOOD AND HIS EAGLE EYE--
EAGLE EYE BLOODLINE SKILL. I ALREADY KNOW, DUDE!

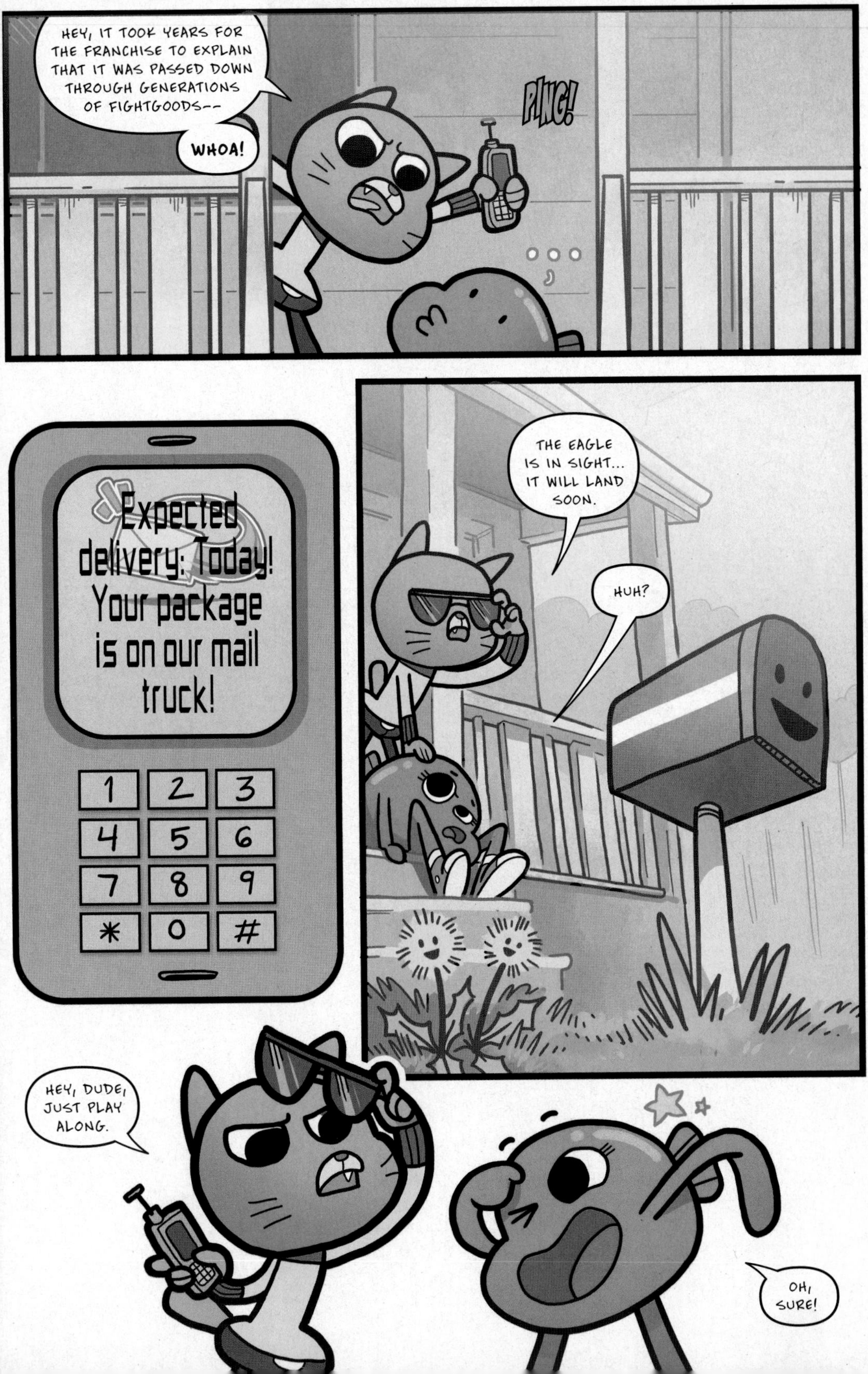

HEY, IT TOOK YEARS FOR THE FRANCHISE TO EXPLAIN THAT IT WAS PASSED DOWN THROUGH GENERATIONS OF FIGHTGOODS--
WHOA!
PING!
...
Expected delivery: Today! Your package is on our mail truck!
1 2 3
4 5 6
7 8 9
* 0 #
THE EAGLE IS IN SIGHT... IT WILL LAND SOON.
HUH?
HEY, DUDE, JUST PLAY ALONG.
OH, SURE!

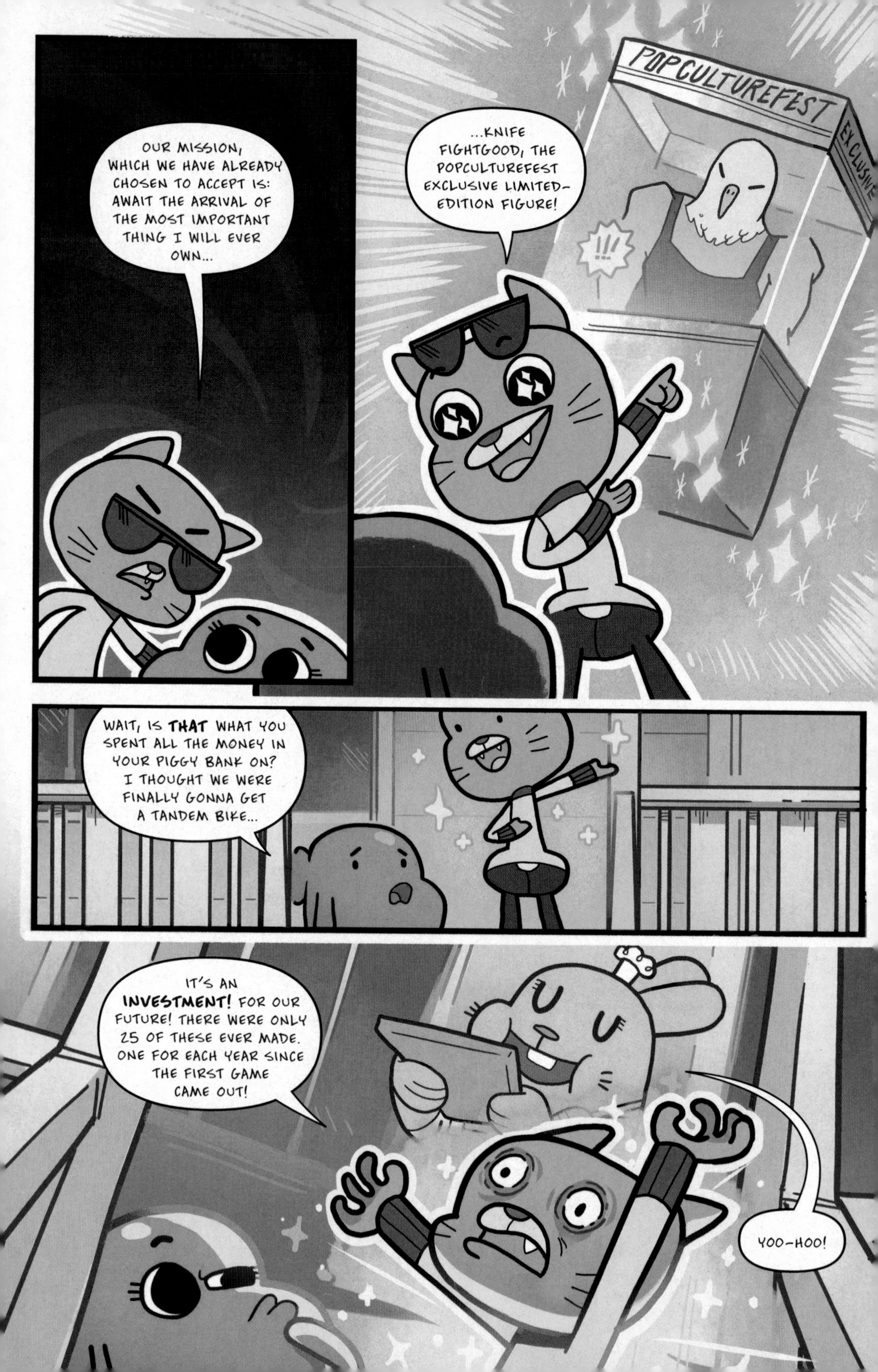
OUR MISSION, WHICH WE HAVE ALREADY CHOSEN TO ACCEPT IS: AWAIT THE ARRIVAL OF THE MOST IMPORTANT THING I WILL EVER OWN...
...KNIFE FIGHTGOOD, THE POPCULTUREFEST EXCLUSIVE LIMITED-EDITION FIGURE!
POPCULTUREFEST
EXCLUSIVE
!!!
WAIT, IS **THAT** WHAT YOU SPENT ALL THE MONEY IN YOUR PIGGY BANK ON? I THOUGHT WE WERE FINALLY GONNA GET A TANDEM BIKE...
IT'S AN **INVESTMENT!** FOR OUR FUTURE! THERE WERE ONLY 25 OF THESE EVER MADE. ONE FOR EACH YEAR SINCE THE FIRST GAME CAME OUT!
YOO-HOO!

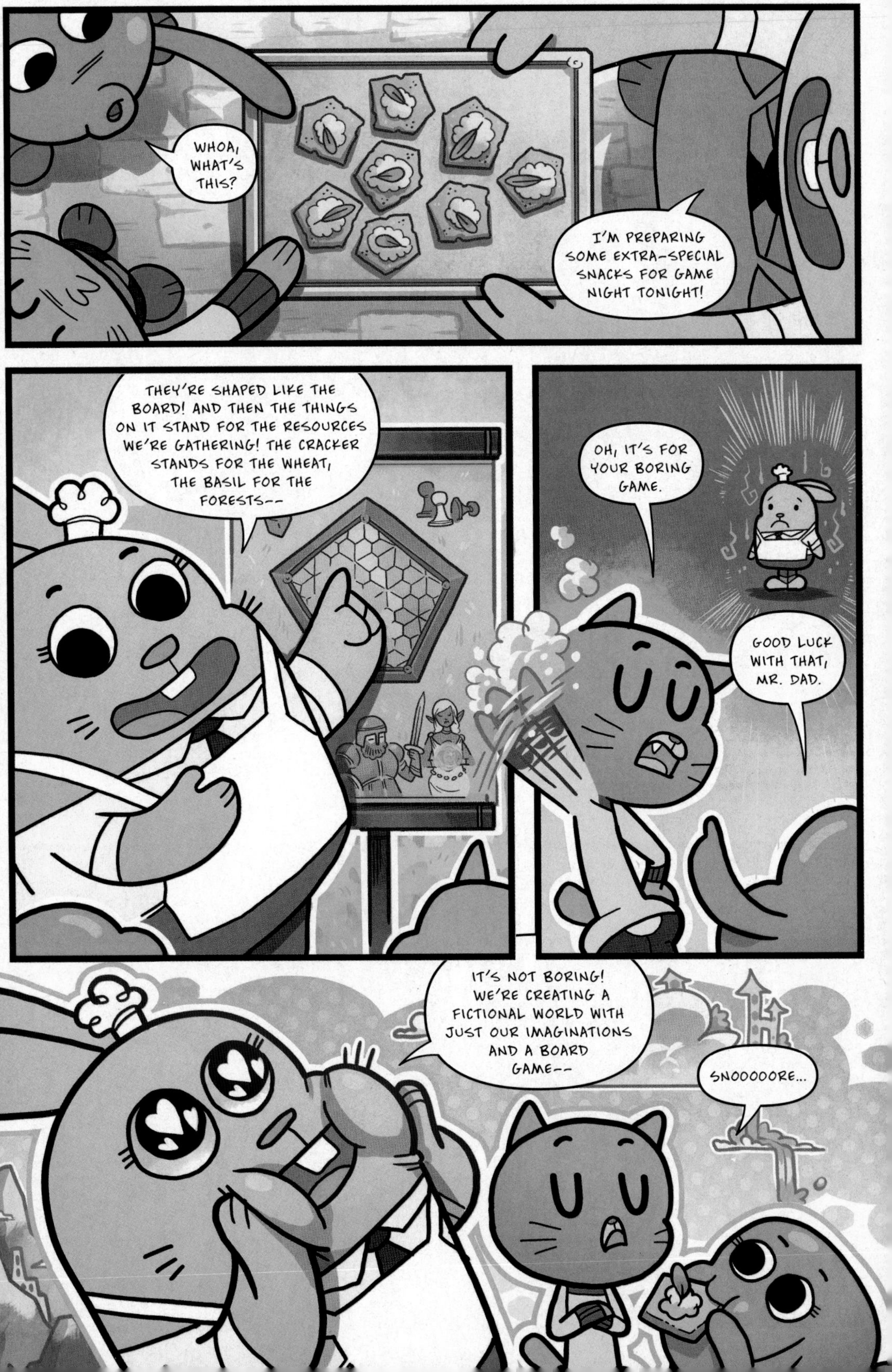
WHOA, WHAT'S THIS?
I'M PREPARING SOME EXTRA-SPECIAL SNACKS FOR GAME NIGHT TONIGHT!
THEY'RE SHAPED LIKE THE BOARD! AND THEN THE THINGS ON IT STAND FOR THE RESOURCES WE'RE GATHERING! THE CRACKER STANDS FOR THE WHEAT, THE BASIL FOR THE FORESTS--
OH, IT'S FOR YOUR BORING GAME.
GOOD LUCK WITH THAT, MR. DAD.
IT'S NOT BORING! WE'RE CREATING A FICTIONAL WORLD WITH JUST OUR IMAGINATIONS AND A BOARD GAME--
SNOOOOORE...

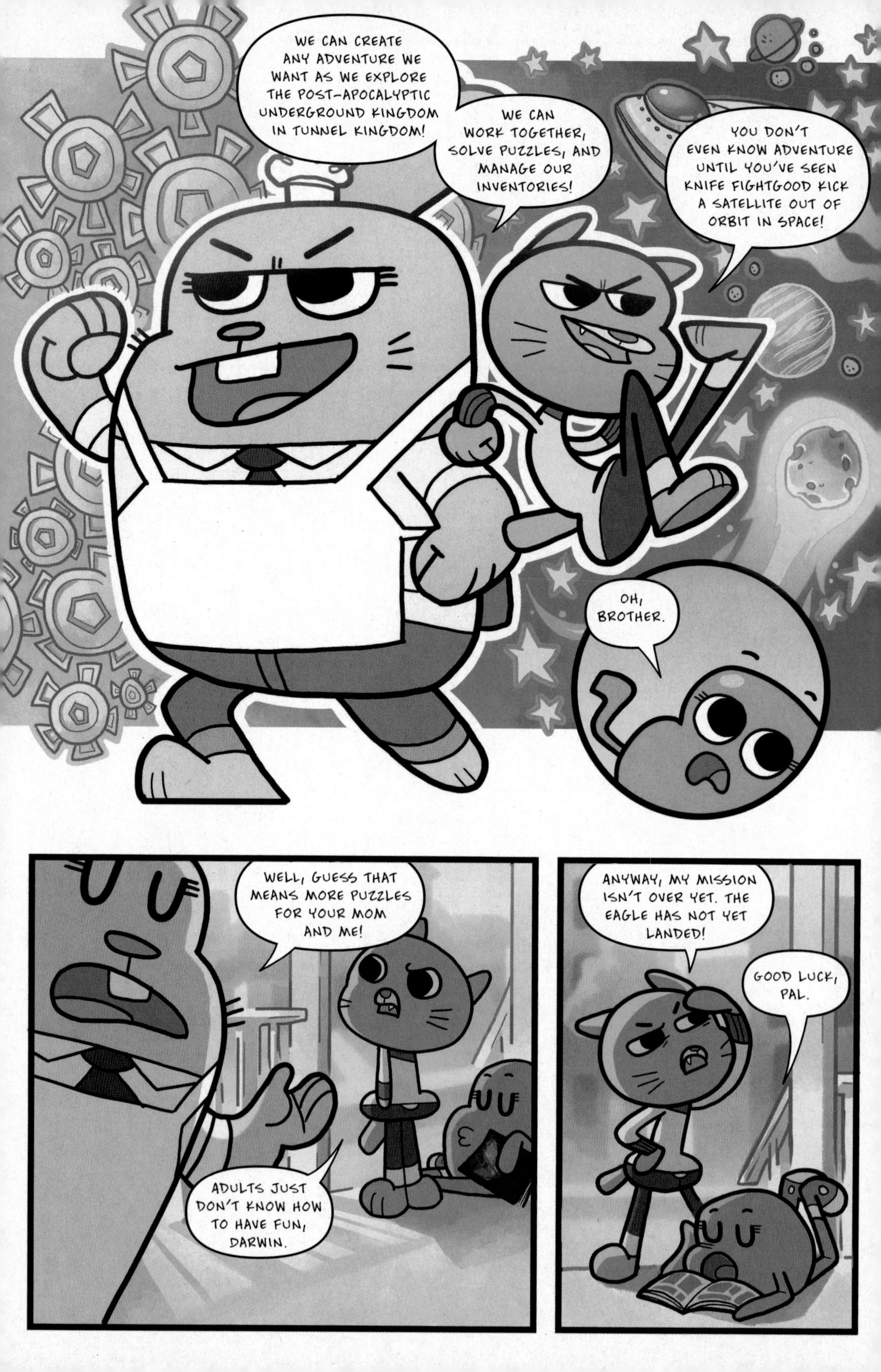
WE CAN CREATE ANY ADVENTURE WE WANT AS WE EXPLORE THE POST-APOCALYPTIC UNDERGROUND KINGDOM IN TUNNEL KINGDOM!
WE CAN WORK TOGETHER, SOLVE PUZZLES, AND MANAGE OUR INVENTORIES!
YOU DON'T EVEN KNOW ADVENTURE UNTIL YOU'VE SEEN KNIFE FIGHTGOOD KICK A SATELLITE OUT OF ORBIT IN SPACE!
OH, BROTHER.
WELL, GUESS THAT MEANS MORE PUZZLES FOR YOUR MOM AND ME!
ADULTS JUST DON'T KNOW HOW TO HAVE FUN, DARWIN.
ANYWAY, MY MISSION ISN'T OVER YET. THE EAGLE HAS NOT YET LANDED!
GOOD LUCK, PAL.

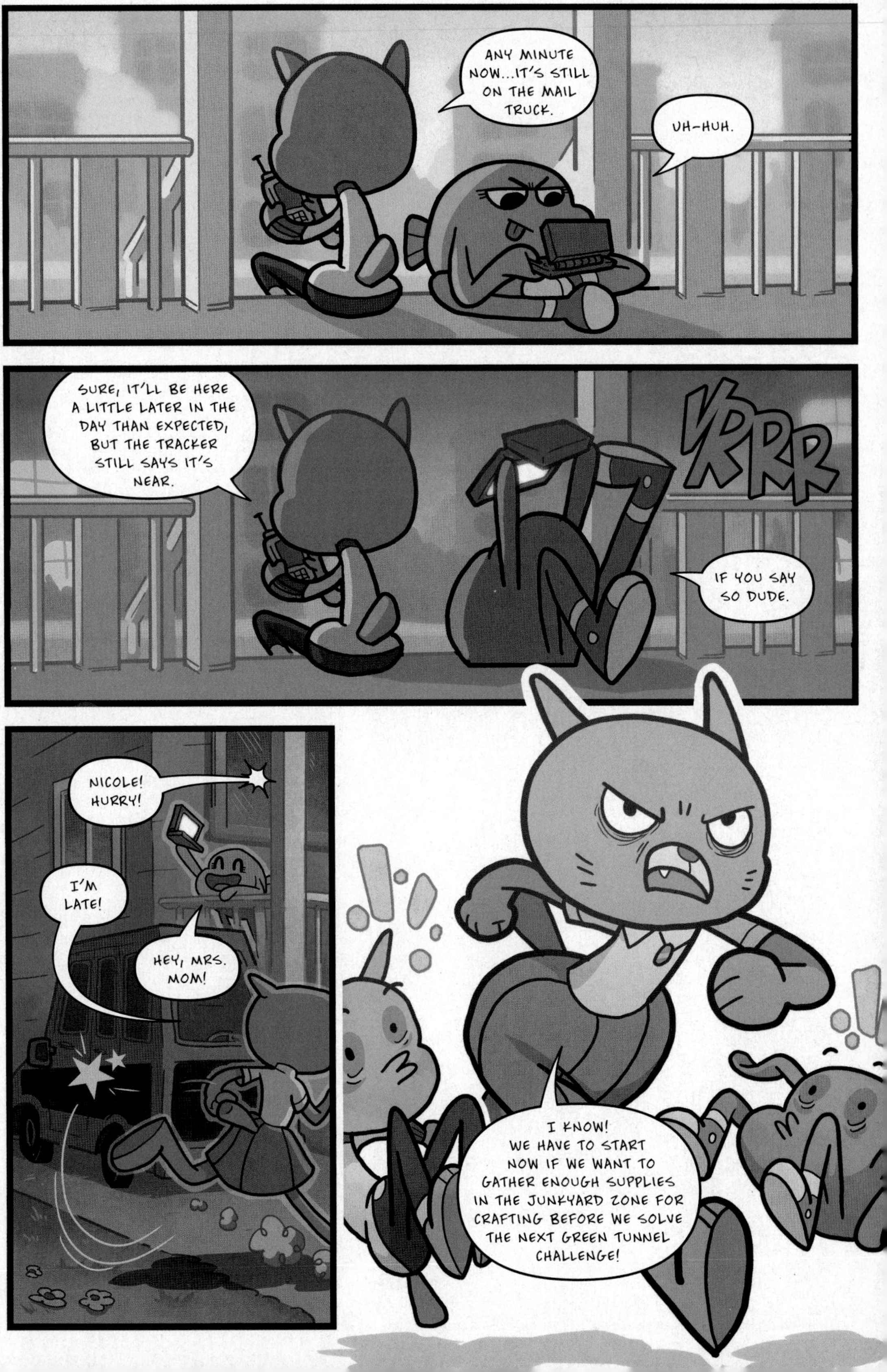
ANY MINUTE NOW...IT'S STILL ON THE MAIL TRUCK.
UH-HUH.
SURE, IT'LL BE HERE A LITTLE LATER IN THE DAY THAN EXPECTED, BUT THE TRACKER STILL SAYS IT'S NEAR.
VRRR
IF YOU SAY SO DUDE.
NICOLE! HURRY!
I'M LATE!
HEY, MRS. MOM!
I KNOW! WE HAVE TO START NOW IF WE WANT TO GATHER ENOUGH SUPPLIES IN THE JUNKYARD ZONE FOR CRAFTING BEFORE WE SOLVE THE NEXT GREEN TUNNEL CHALLENGE!

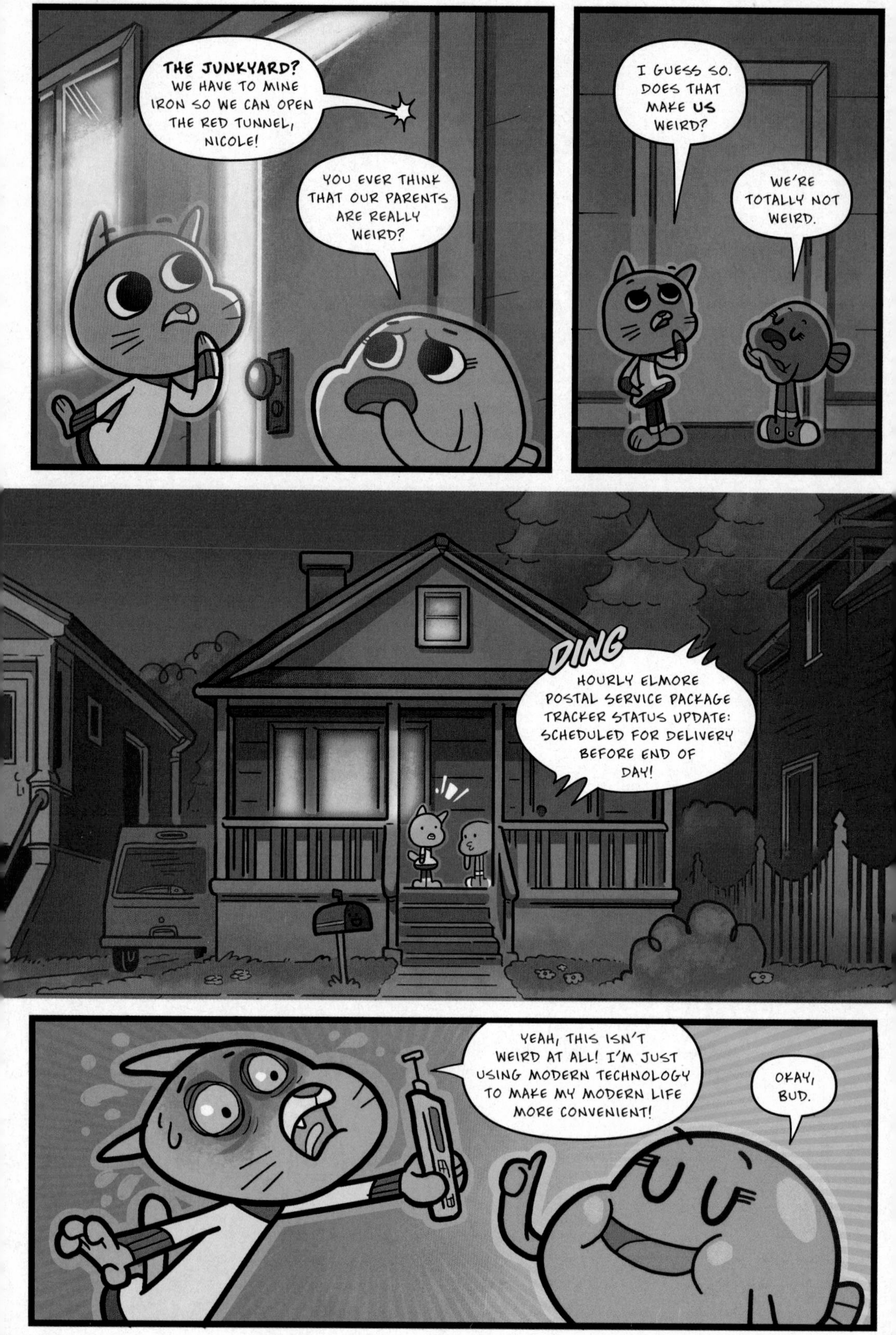
THE JUNKYARD? WE HAVE TO MINE IRON SO WE CAN OPEN THE RED TUNNEL, NICOLE!
YOU EVER THINK THAT OUR PARENTS ARE REALLY WEIRD?
I GUESS SO. DOES THAT MAKE US WEIRD?
WE'RE TOTALLY NOT WEIRD.
DING
HOURLY ELMORE POSTAL SERVICE PACKAGE TRACKER STATUS UPDATE: SCHEDULED FOR DELIVERY BEFORE END OF DAY!
YEAH, THIS ISN'T WEIRD AT ALL! I'M JUST USING MODERN TECHNOLOGY TO MAKE MY MODERN LIFE MORE CONVENIENT!
OKAY, BUD.

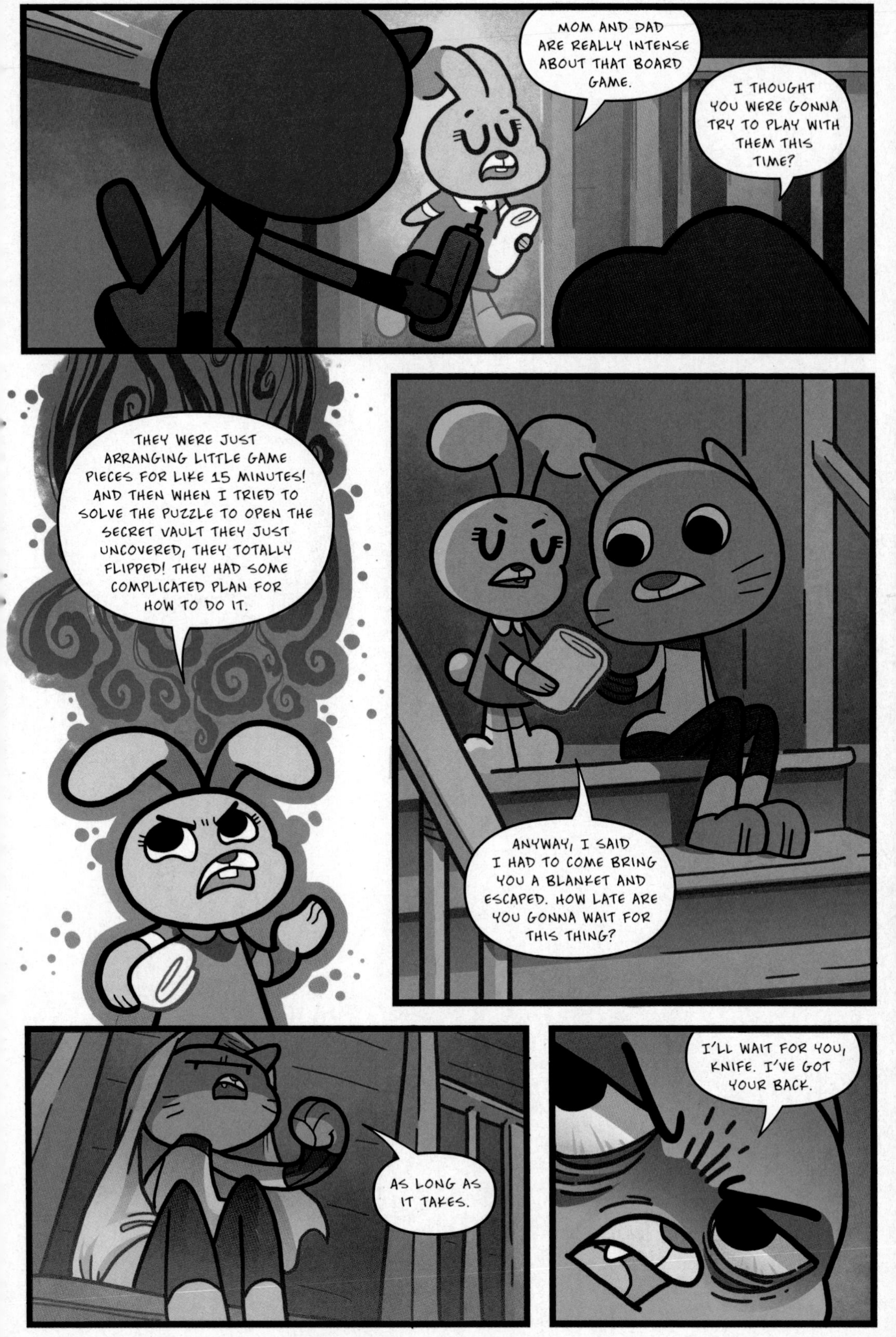
MOM AND DAD ARE REALLY INTENSE ABOUT THAT BOARD GAME.
I THOUGHT YOU WERE GONNA TRY TO PLAY WITH THEM THIS TIME?
THEY WERE JUST ARRANGING LITTLE GAME PIECES FOR LIKE 15 MINUTES! AND THEN WHEN I TRIED TO SOLVE THE PUZZLE TO OPEN THE SECRET VAULT THEY JUST UNCOVERED, THEY TOTALLY FLIPPED! THEY HAD SOME COMPLICATED PLAN FOR HOW TO DO IT.
ANYWAY, I SAID I HAD TO COME BRING YOU A BLANKET AND ESCAPED. HOW LATE ARE YOU GONNA WAIT FOR THIS THING?
AS LONG AS IT TAKES.
I'LL WAIT FOR YOU, KNIFE. I'VE GOT YOUR BACK.

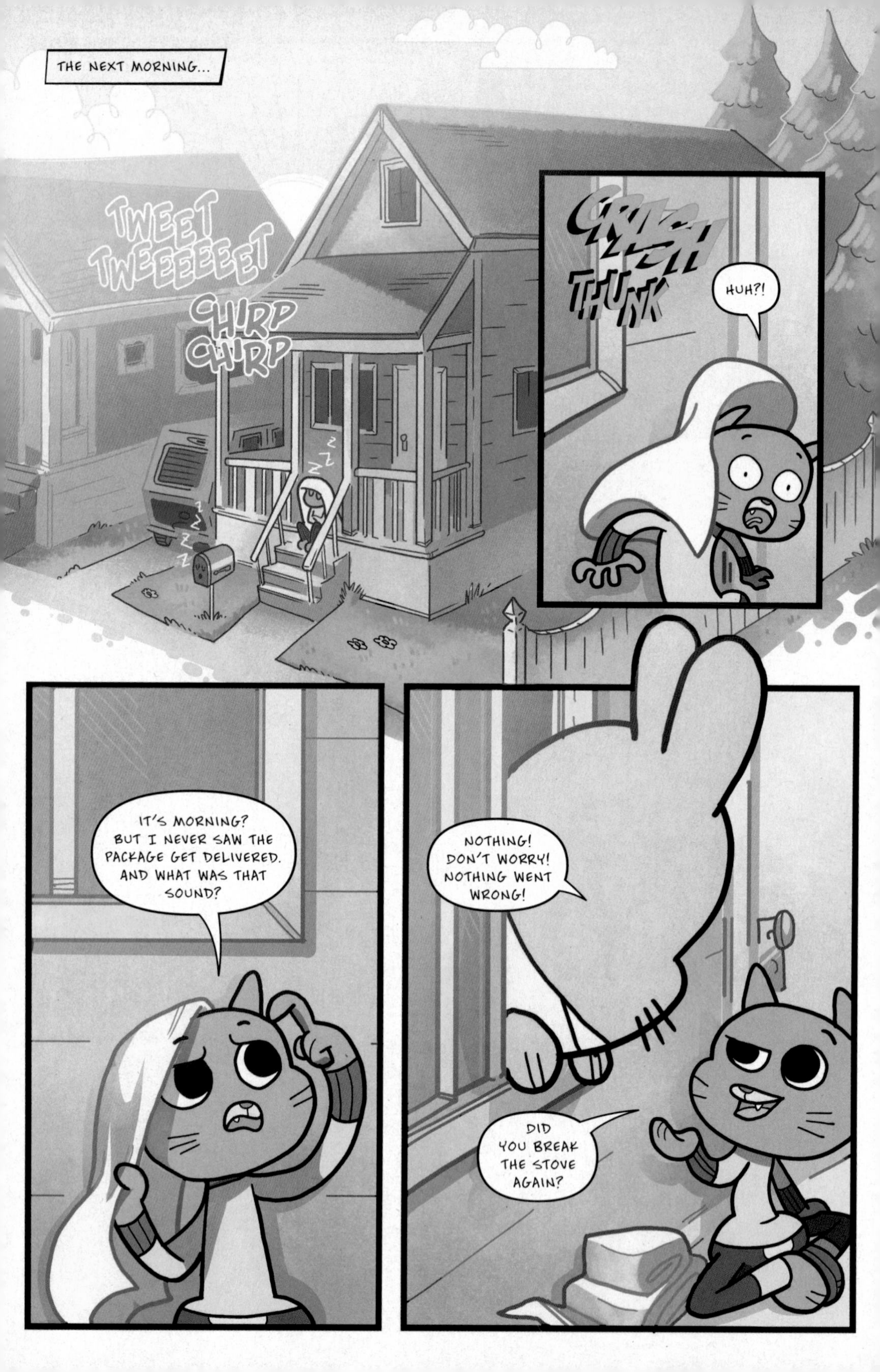
THE NEXT MORNING...
TWEET TWEEEEEET
CHIRP CHIRP
CRUSH
THUNK
HUH?!
IT'S MORNING? BUT I NEVER SAW THE PACKAGE GET DELIVERED. AND WHAT WAS THAT SOUND?
NOTHING! DON'T WORRY! NOTHING WENT WRONG!
DID YOU BREAK THE STOVE AGAIN?

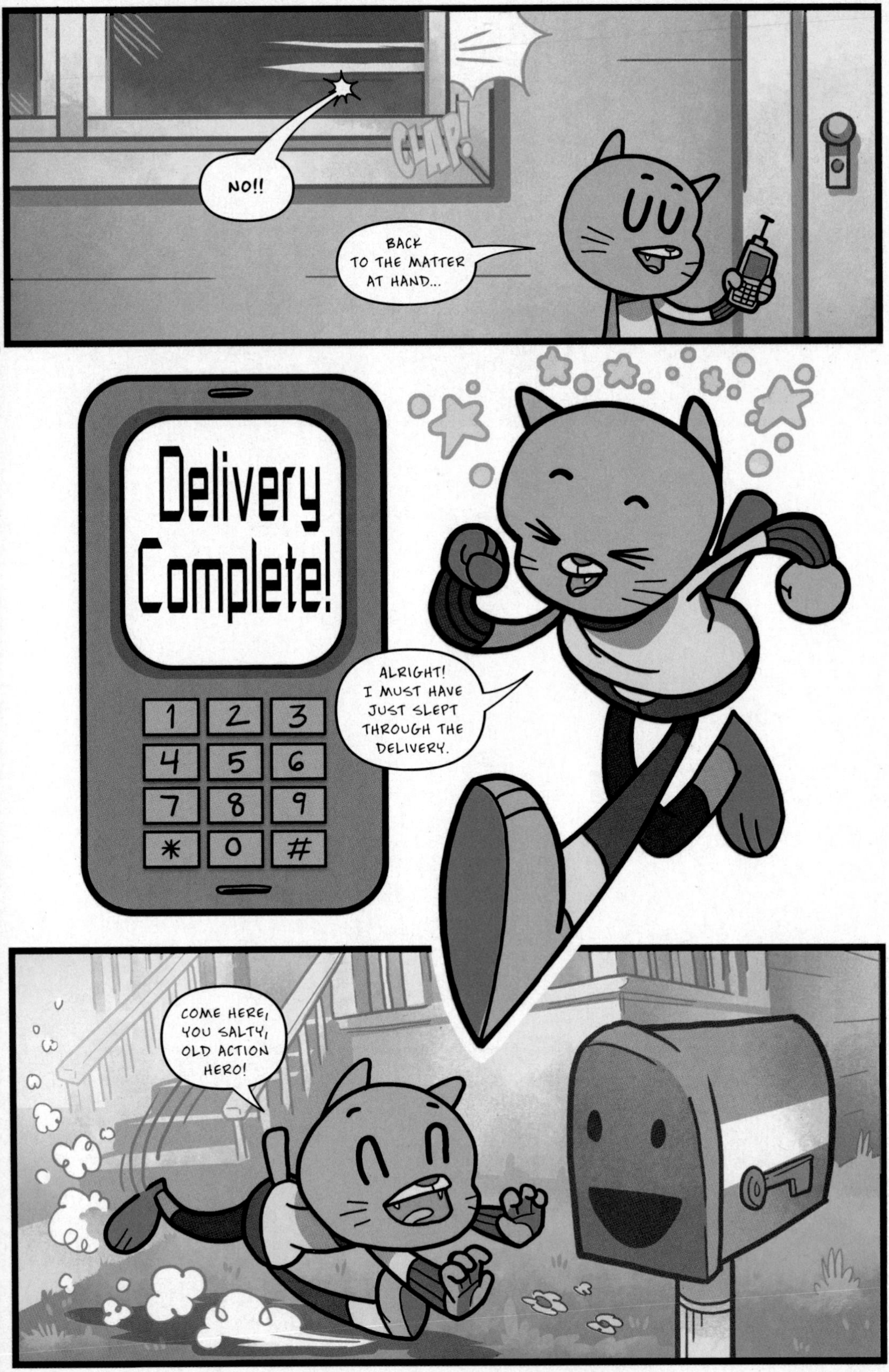
NO!!
CLAP!
BACK TO THE MATTER AT HAND...
Delivery Complete!
1 2 3 4 5 6 7 8 9 * 0 #
ALRIGHT! I MUST HAVE JUST SLEPT THROUGH THE DELIVERY.
COME HERE, YOU SALTY, OLD ACTION HERO!

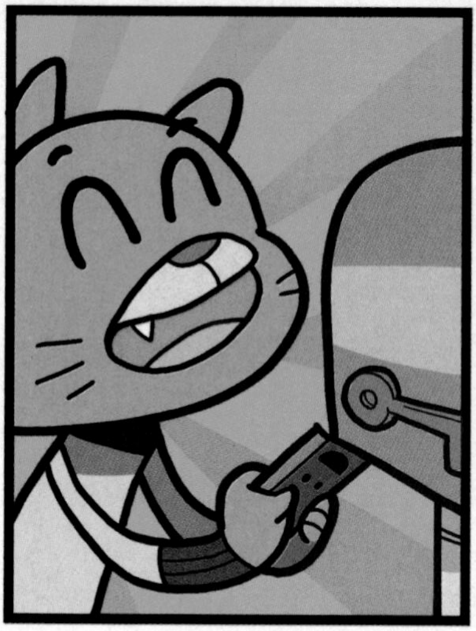
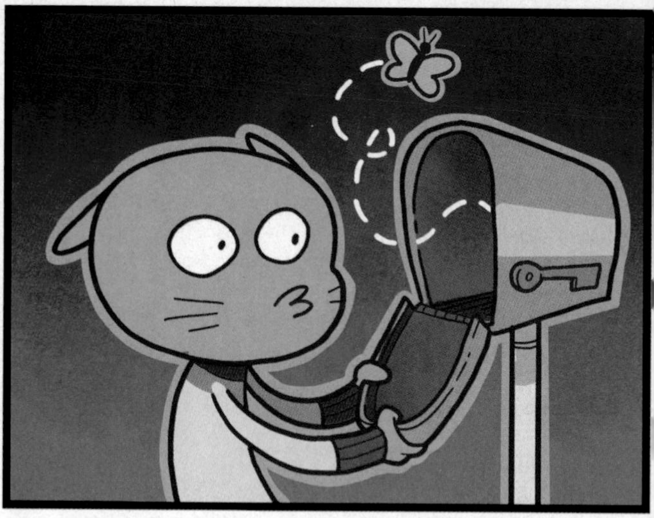
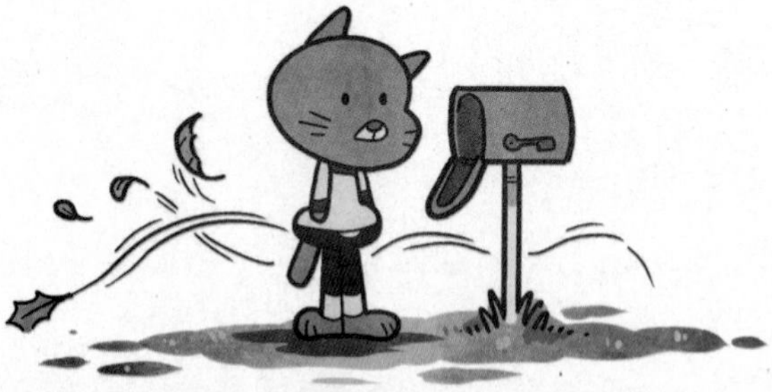
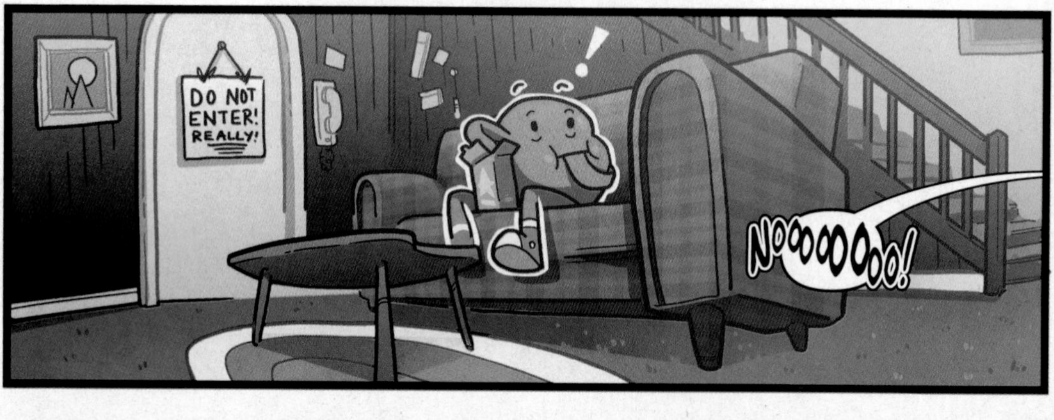
DO NOT ENTER! REALLY!
NOOOOOOOO!

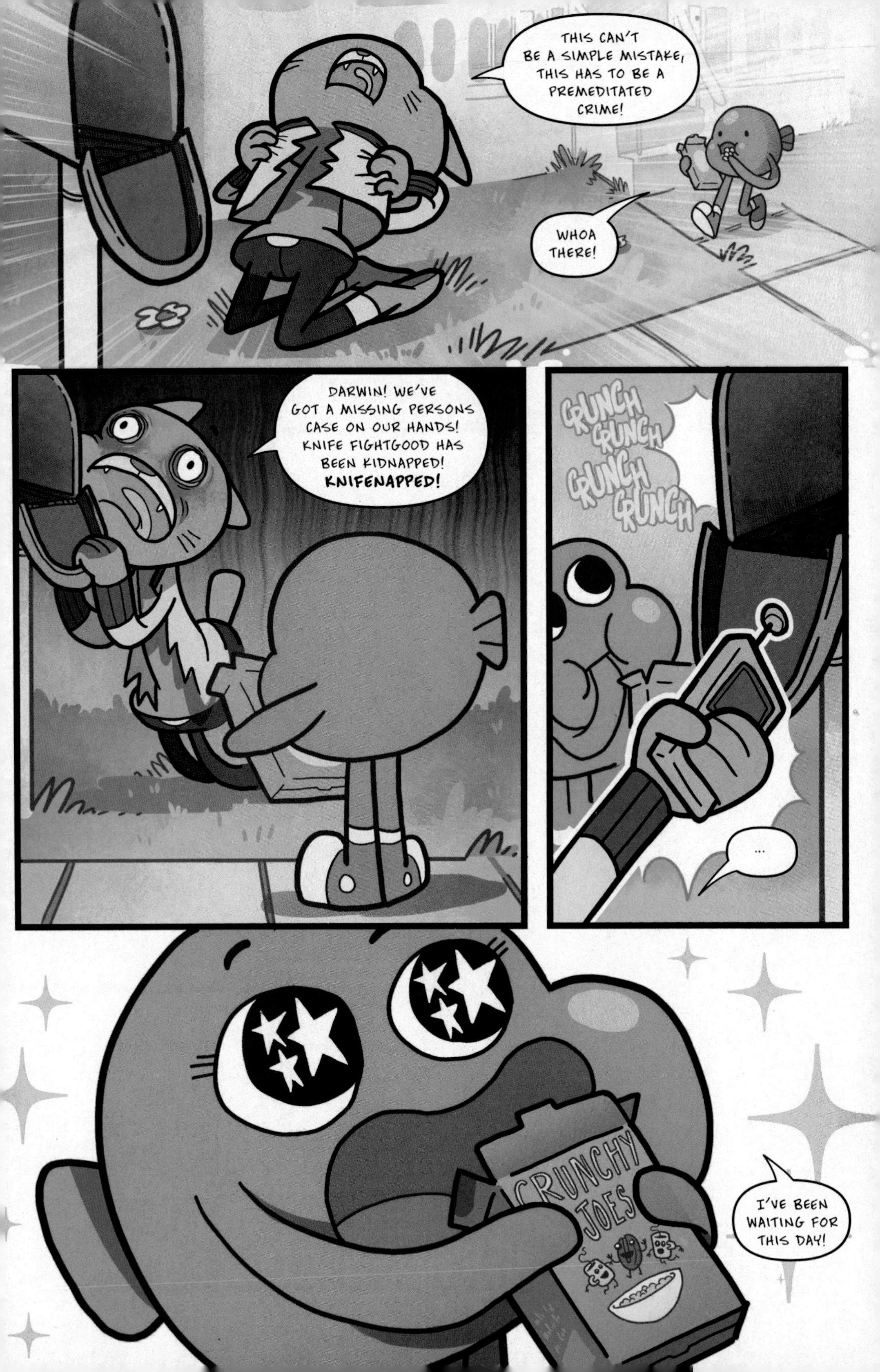
THIS CAN'T BE A SIMPLE MISTAKE, THIS HAS TO BE A PREMEDITATED CRIME!
WHOA THERE!
DARWIN! WE'VE GOT A MISSING PERSONS CASE ON OUR HANDS! KNIFE FIGHTGOOD HAS BEEN KIDNAPPED! **KNIFENAPPED!**
CRUNCH CRUNCH CRUNCH CRUNCH
...
CRUNCHY JOES
I'VE BEEN WAITING FOR THIS DAY!

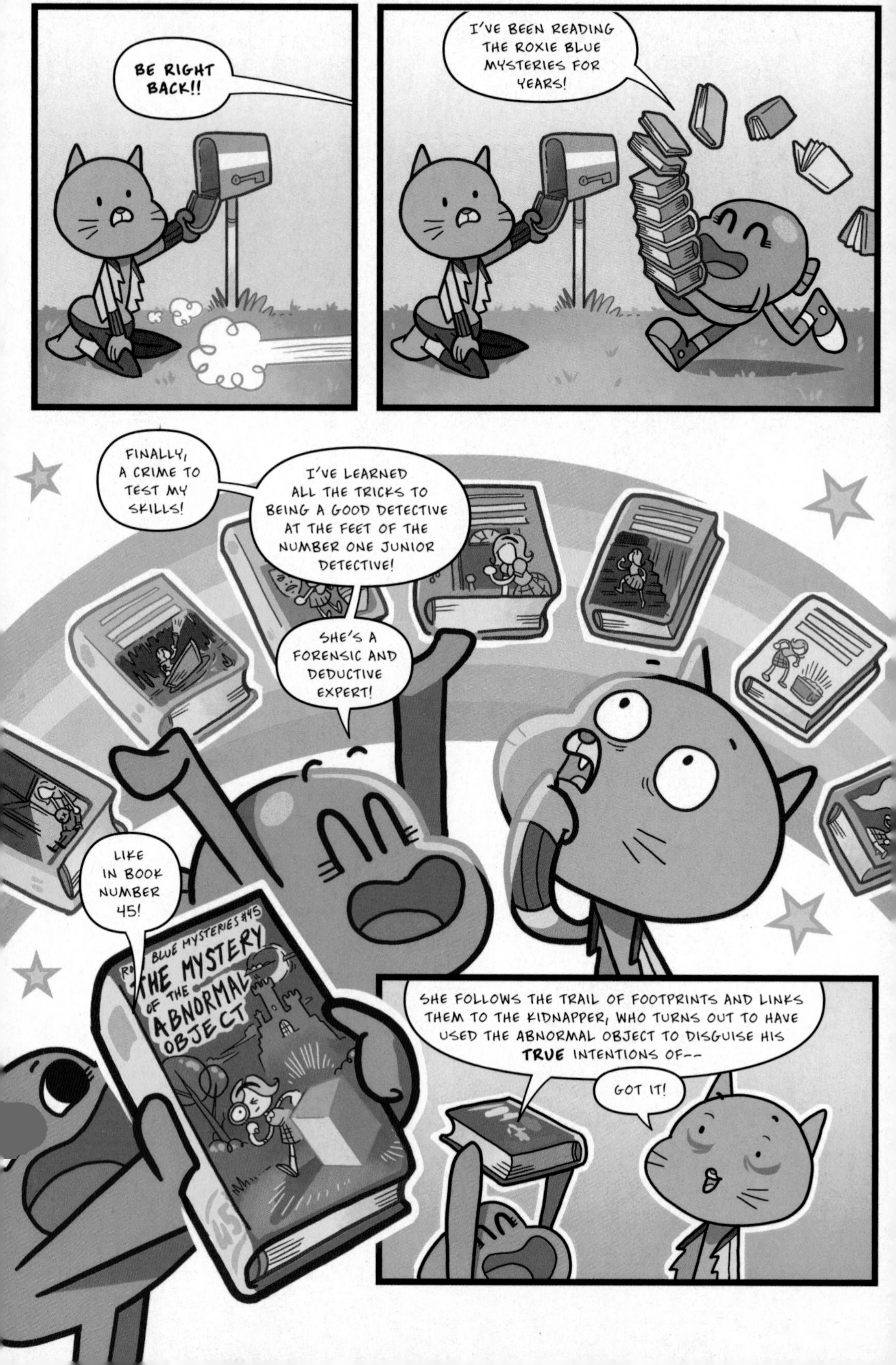
BE RIGHT BACK!!
I'VE BEEN READING THE ROXIE BLUE MYSTERIES FOR YEARS!
FINALLY, A CRIME TO TEST MY SKILLS!
I'VE LEARNED ALL THE TRICKS TO BEING A GOOD DETECTIVE AT THE FEET OF THE NUMBER ONE JUNIOR DETECTIVE!
SHE'S A FORENSIC AND DEDUCTIVE EXPERT!
LIKE IN BOOK NUMBER 45!
BLUE MYSTERIES #45
THE MYSTERY OF THE ABNORMAL OBJECT
45
SHE FOLLOWS THE TRAIL OF FOOTPRINTS AND LINKS THEM TO THE KIDNAPPER, WHO TURNS OUT TO HAVE USED THE ABNORMAL OBJECT TO DISGUISE HIS TRUE INTENTIONS OF--
GOT IT!

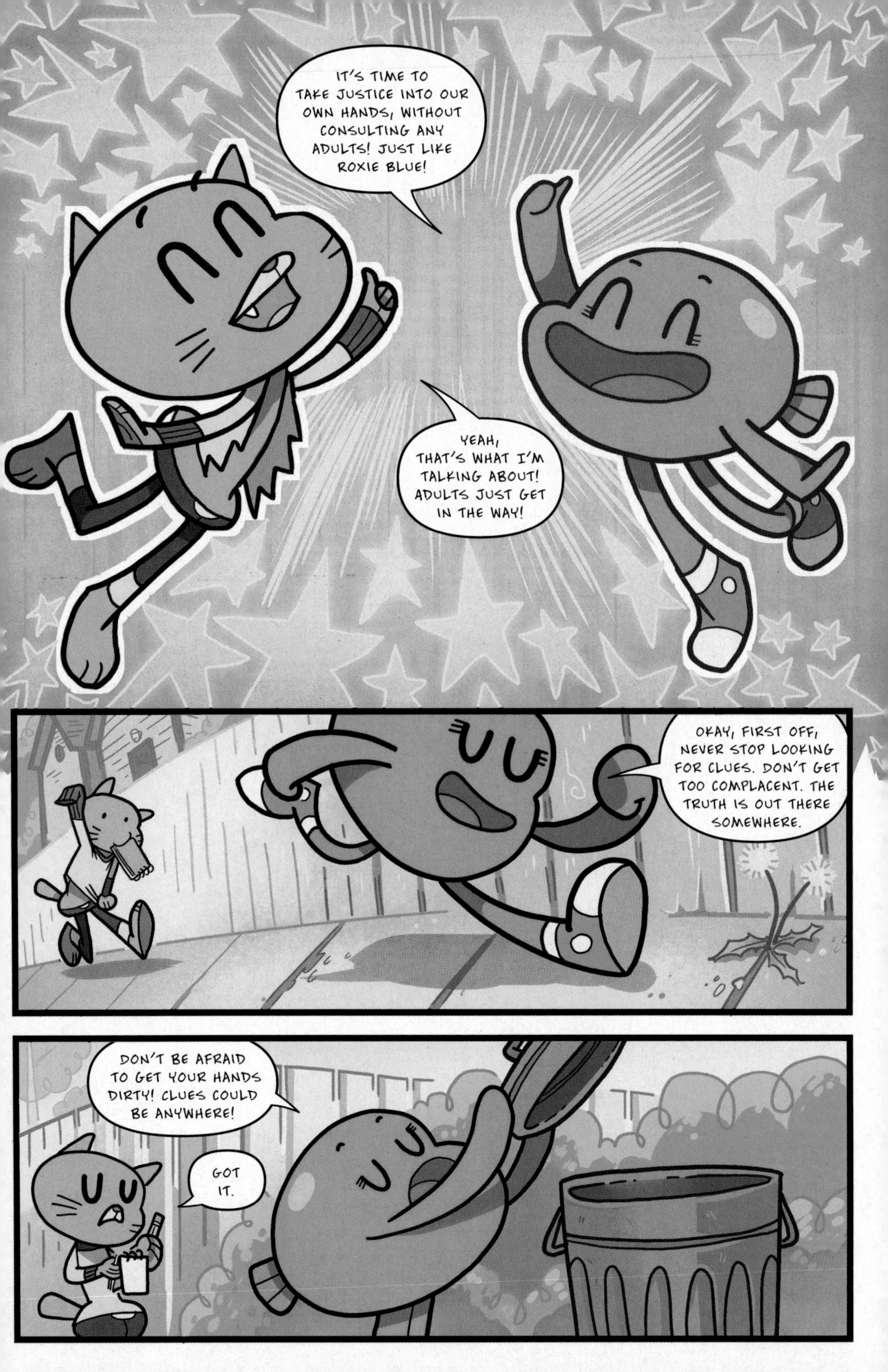
IT'S TIME TO TAKE JUSTICE INTO OUR OWN HANDS, WITHOUT CONSULTING ANY ADULTS! JUST LIKE ROXIE BLUE!
YEAH, THAT'S WHAT I'M TALKING ABOUT! ADULTS JUST GET IN THE WAY!
OKAY, FIRST OFF, NEVER STOP LOOKING FOR CLUES. DON'T GET TOO COMPLACENT. THE TRUTH IS OUT THERE SOMEWHERE.
DON'T BE AFRAID TO GET YOUR HANDS DIRTY! CLUES COULD BE ANYWHERE!
GOT IT.

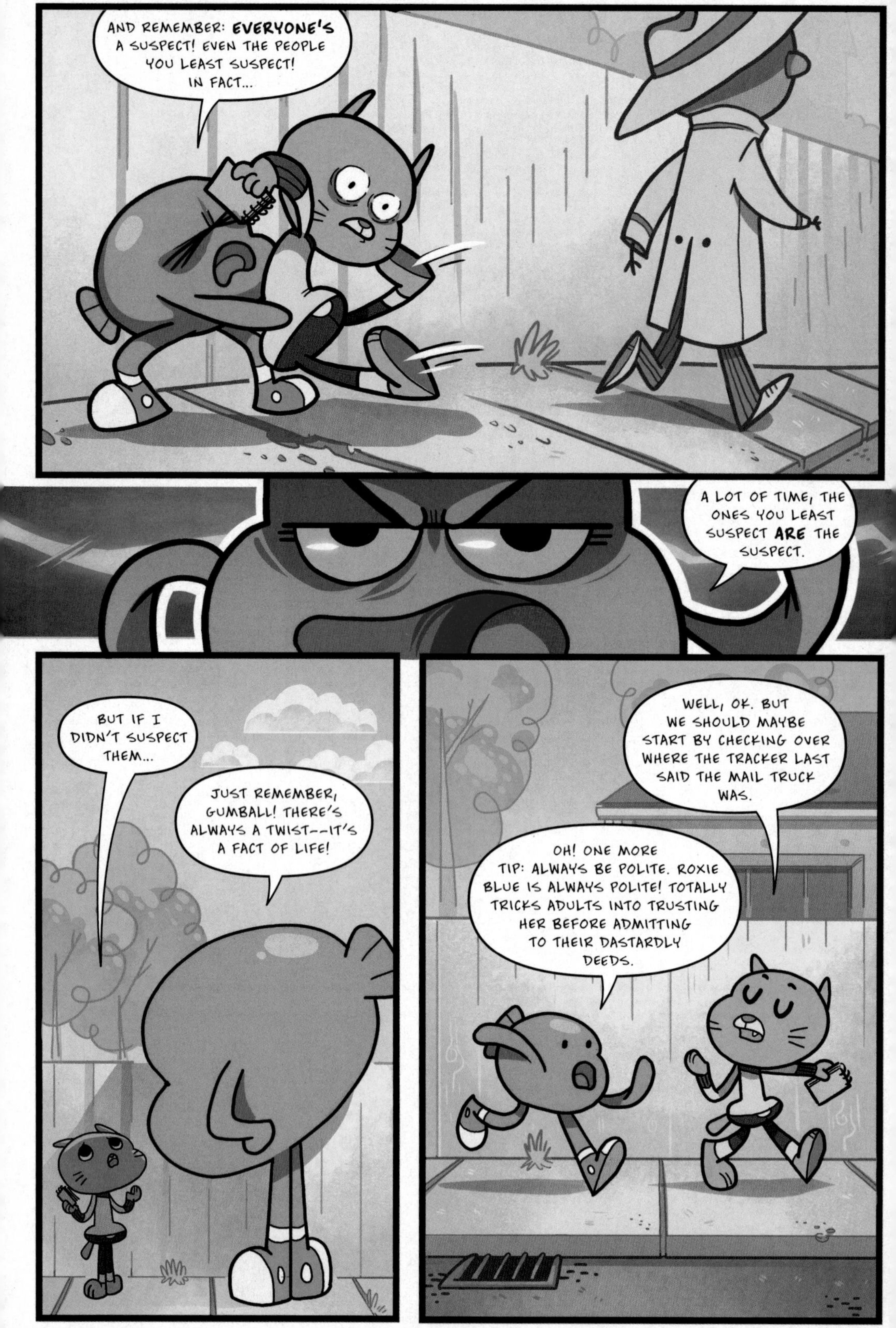
AND REMEMBER: **EVERYONE'S** A SUSPECT! EVEN THE PEOPLE YOU LEAST SUSPECT! IN FACT...
A LOT OF TIME, THE ONES YOU LEAST SUSPECT **ARE** THE SUSPECT.
BUT IF I DIDN'T SUSPECT THEM...
JUST REMEMBER, GUMBALL! THERE'S ALWAYS A TWIST--IT'S A FACT OF LIFE!
WELL, OK. BUT WE SHOULD MAYBE START BY CHECKING OVER WHERE THE TRACKER LAST SAID THE MAIL TRUCK WAS.
OH! ONE MORE TIP: ALWAYS BE POLITE. ROXIE BLUE IS ALWAYS POLITE! TOTALLY TRICKS ADULTS INTO TRUSTING HER BEFORE ADMITTING TO THEIR DASTARDLY DEEDS.

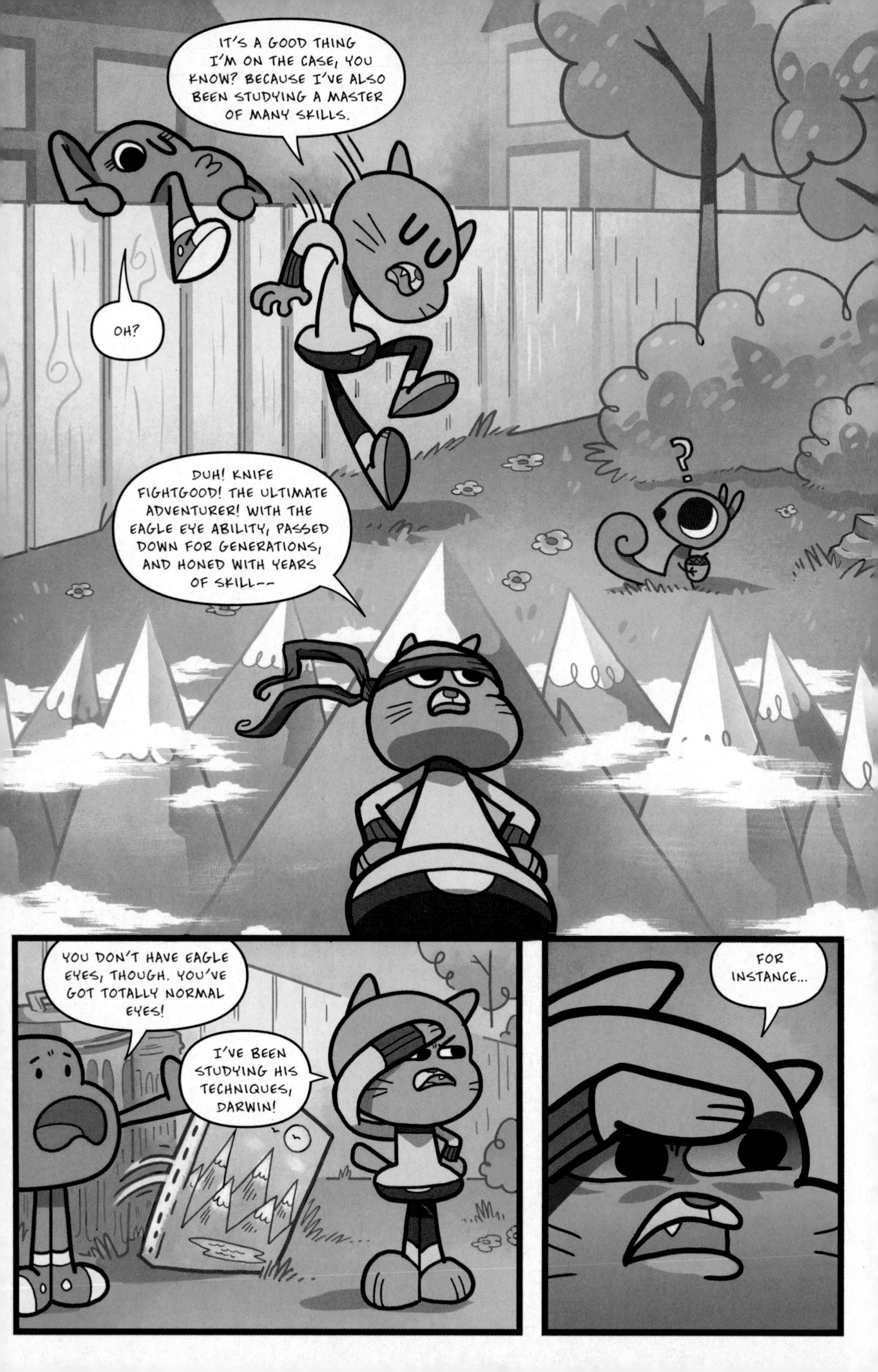
IT'S A GOOD THING I'M ON THE CASE, YOU KNOW? BECAUSE I'VE ALSO BEEN STUDYING A MASTER OF MANY SKILLS.
OH?
DUH! KNIFE FIGHTGOOD! THE ULTIMATE ADVENTURER! WITH THE EAGLE EYE ABILITY, PASSED DOWN FOR GENERATIONS, AND HONED WITH YEARS OF SKILL--
?
YOU DON'T HAVE EAGLE EYES, THOUGH. YOU'VE GOT TOTALLY NORMAL EYES!
I'VE BEEN STUDYING HIS TECHNIQUES, DARWIN!
FOR INSTANCE...

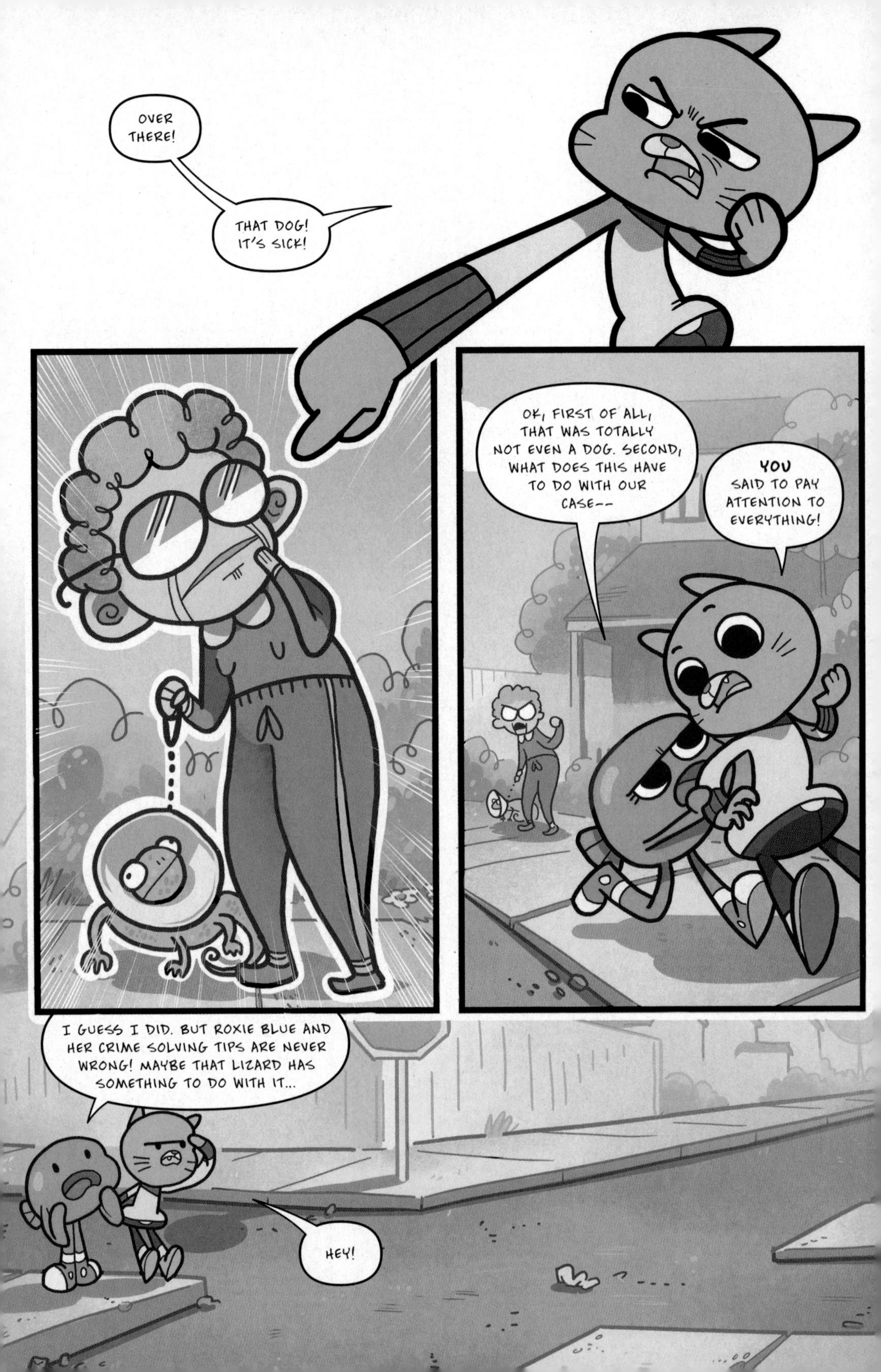
OVER THERE!
THAT DOG! IT'S SICK!
OK, FIRST OF ALL, THAT WAS TOTALLY NOT EVEN A DOG. SECOND, WHAT DOES THIS HAVE TO DO WITH OUR CASE--
YOU SAID TO PAY ATTENTION TO EVERYTHING!
I GUESS I DID. BUT ROXIE BLUE AND HER CRIME SOLVING TIPS ARE NEVER WRONG! MAYBE THAT LIZARD HAS SOMETHING TO DO WITH IT...
HEY!

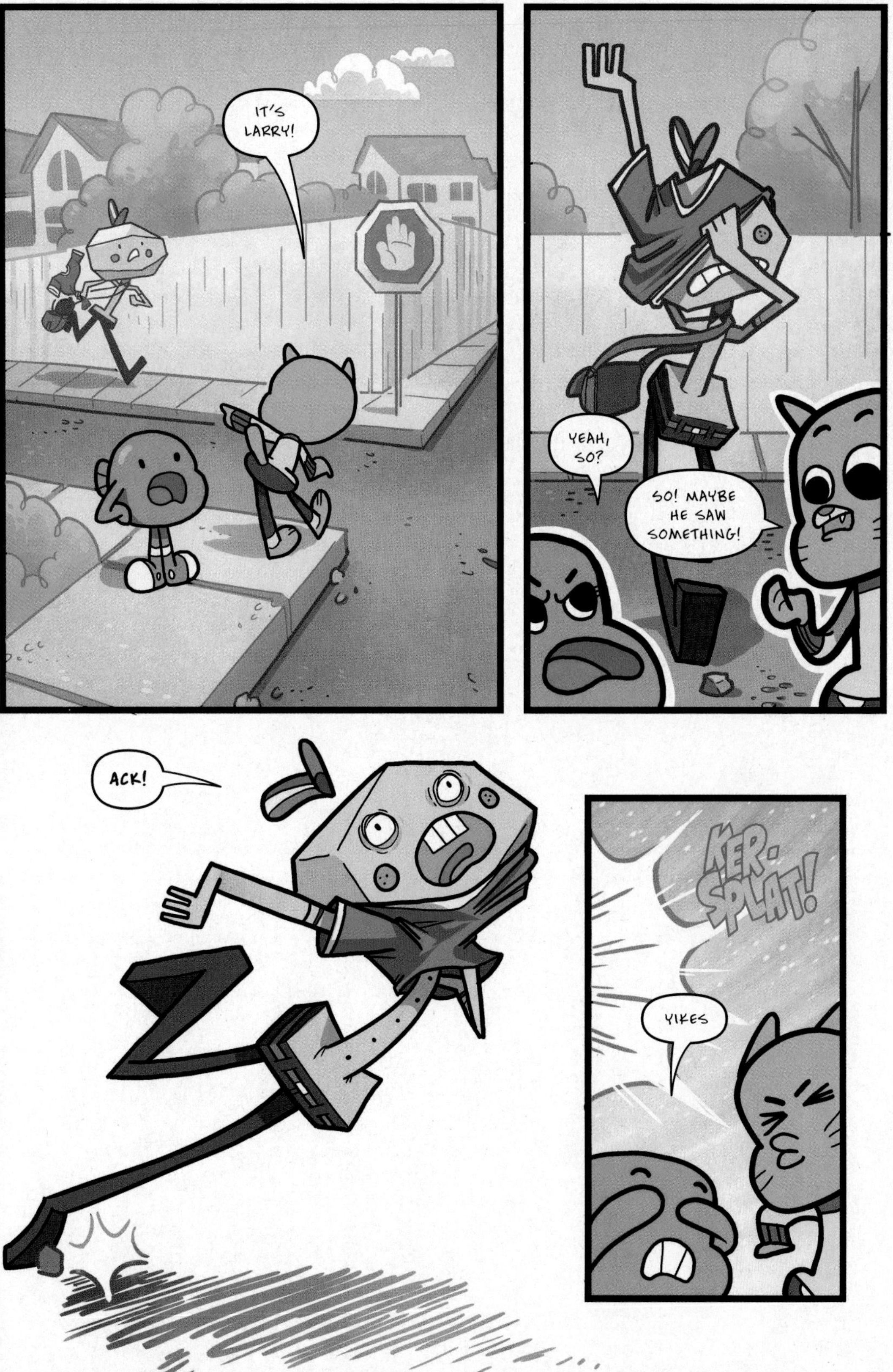
IT'S LARRY!
YEAH, SO?
SO! MAYBE HE SAW SOMETHING!
ACK!
KER-SPLAT!
YIKES

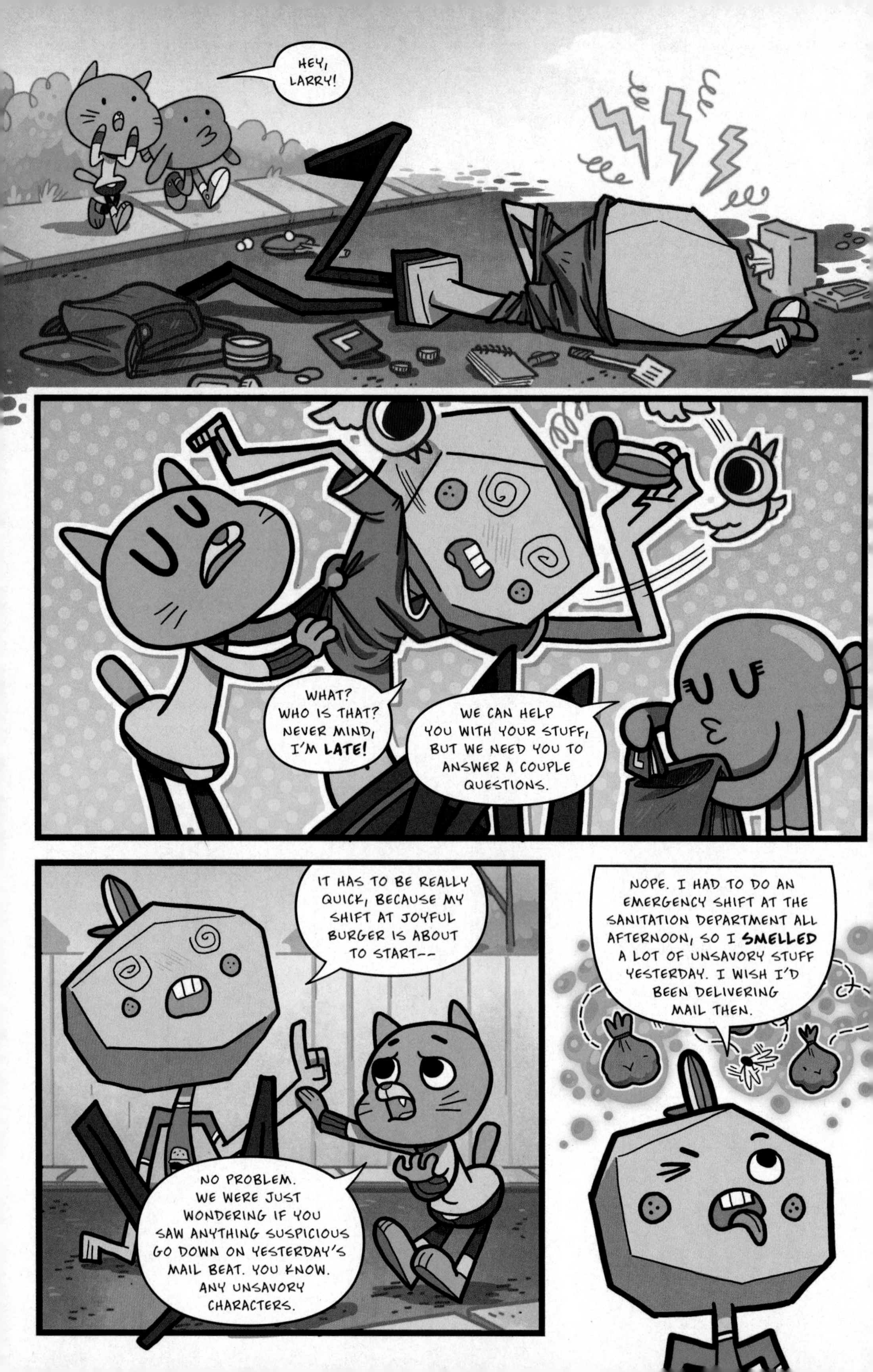
HEY, LARRY!
WHAT? WHO IS THAT? NEVER MIND, I'M **LATE!**
WE CAN HELP YOU WITH YOUR STUFF, BUT WE NEED YOU TO ANSWER A COUPLE QUESTIONS.
IT HAS TO BE REALLY QUICK, BECAUSE MY SHIFT AT JOYFUL BURGER IS ABOUT TO START--
NO PROBLEM. WE WERE JUST WONDERING IF YOU SAW ANYTHING SUSPICIOUS GO DOWN ON YESTERDAY'S MAIL BEAT. YOU KNOW. ANY UNSAVORY CHARACTERS.
NOPE. I HAD TO DO AN EMERGENCY SHIFT AT THE SANITATION DEPARTMENT ALL AFTERNOON, SO I **SMELLED** A LOT OF UNSAVORY STUFF YESTERDAY. I WISH I'D BEEN DELIVERING MAIL THEN.

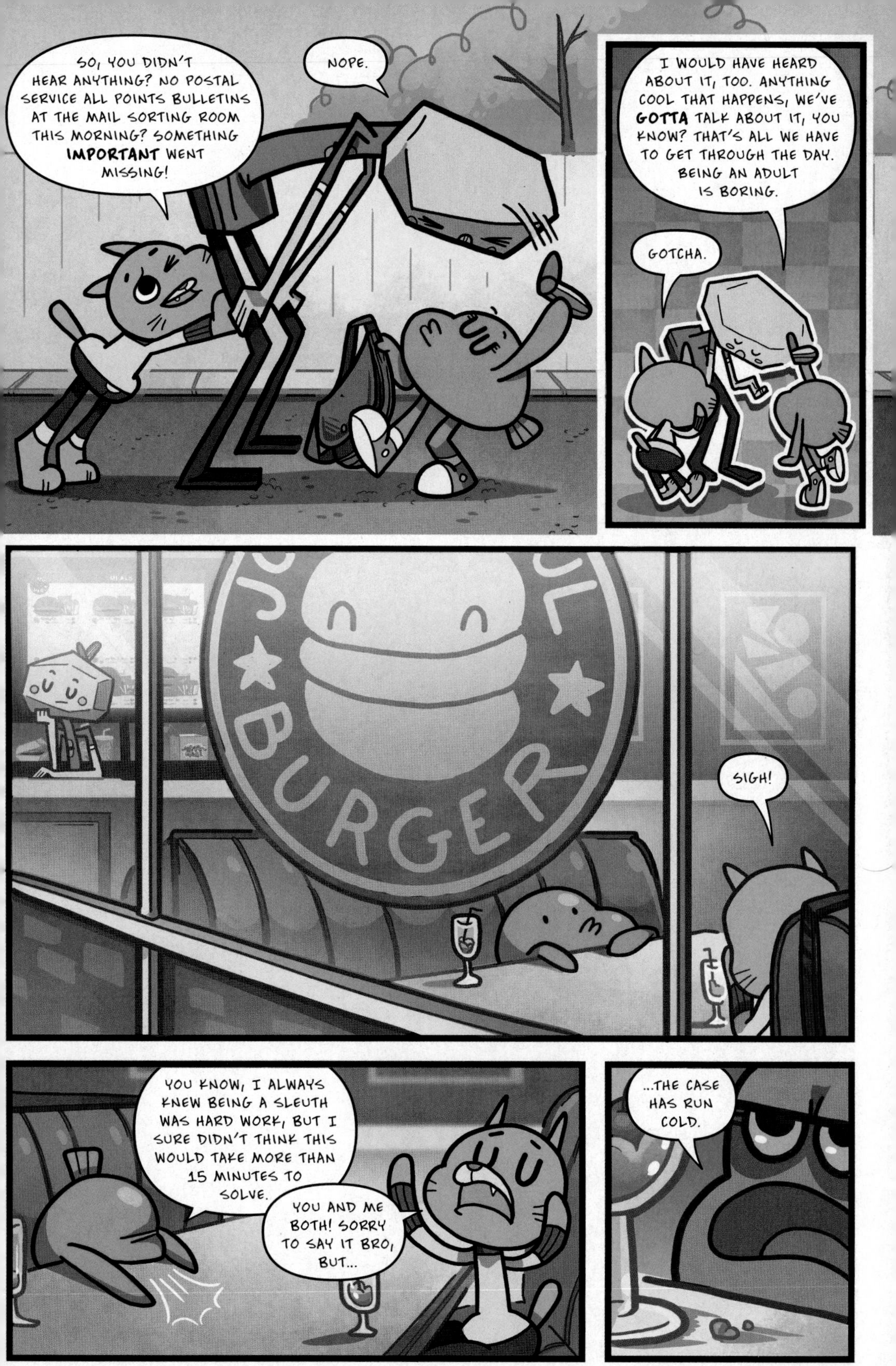

SO, YOU DIDN'T HEAR ANYTHING? NO POSTAL SERVICE ALL POINTS BULLETINS AT THE MAIL SORTING ROOM THIS MORNING? SOMETHING **IMPORTANT** WENT MISSING!
NOPE.
I WOULD HAVE HEARD ABOUT IT, TOO. ANYTHING COOL THAT HAPPENS, WE'VE **GOTTA** TALK ABOUT IT, YOU KNOW? THAT'S ALL WE HAVE TO GET THROUGH THE DAY. BEING AN ADULT IS BORING.
GOTCHA.
BURGER
SIGH!
YOU KNOW, I ALWAYS KNEW BEING A SLEUTH WAS HARD WORK, BUT I SURE DIDN'T THINK THIS WOULD TAKE MORE THAN 15 MINUTES TO SOLVE.
YOU AND ME BOTH! SORRY TO SAY IT BRO, BUT...
...THE CASE HAS RUN COLD.

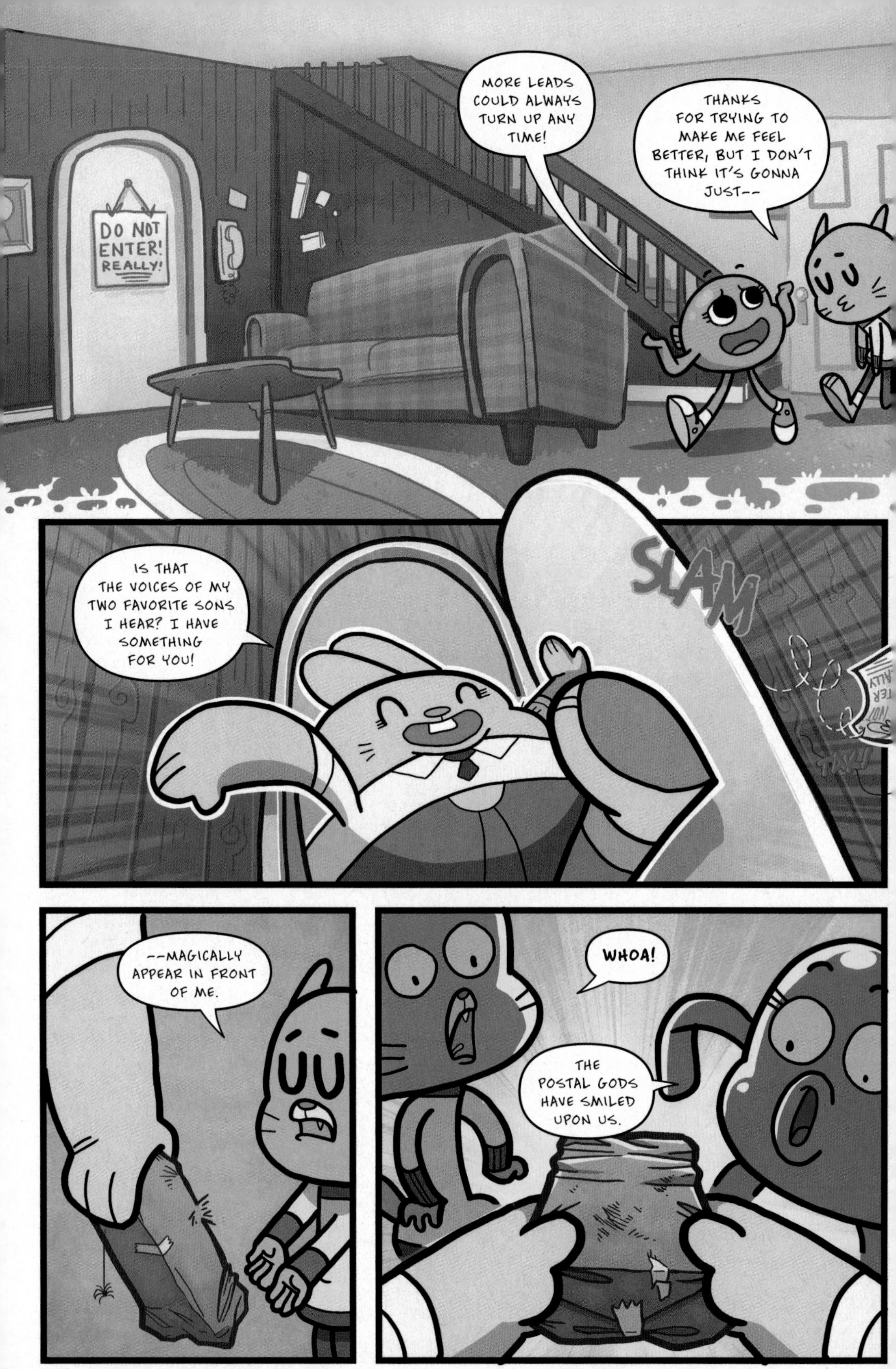
DO NOT ENTER! REALLY!
MORE LEADS COULD ALWAYS TURN UP ANY TIME!
THANKS FOR TRYING TO MAKE ME FEEL BETTER, BUT I DON'T THINK IT'S GONNA JUST--
SLAM
IS THAT THE VOICES OF MY TWO FAVORITE SONS I HEAR? I HAVE SOMETHING FOR YOU!
--MAGICALLY APPEAR IN FRONT OF ME.
WHOA!
THE POSTAL GODS HAVE SMILED UPON US.

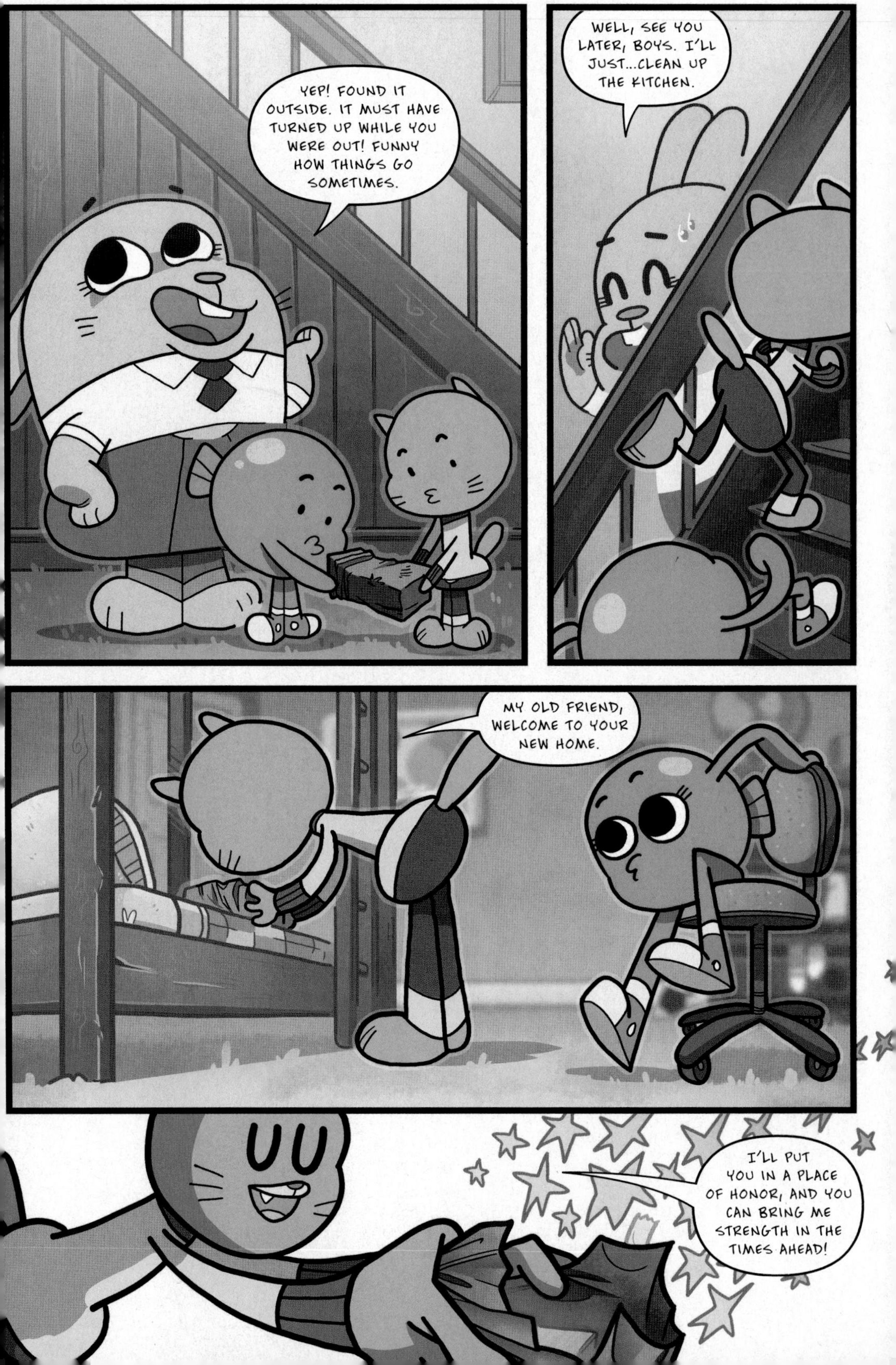
YEP! FOUND IT OUTSIDE. IT MUST HAVE TURNED UP WHILE YOU WERE OUT! FUNNY HOW THINGS GO SOMETIMES.
WELL, SEE YOU LATER, BOYS. I'LL JUST...CLEAN UP THE KITCHEN.
MY OLD FRIEND, WELCOME TO YOUR NEW HOME.
I'LL PUT YOU IN A PLACE OF HONOR, AND YOU CAN BRING ME STRENGTH IN THE TIMES AHEAD!

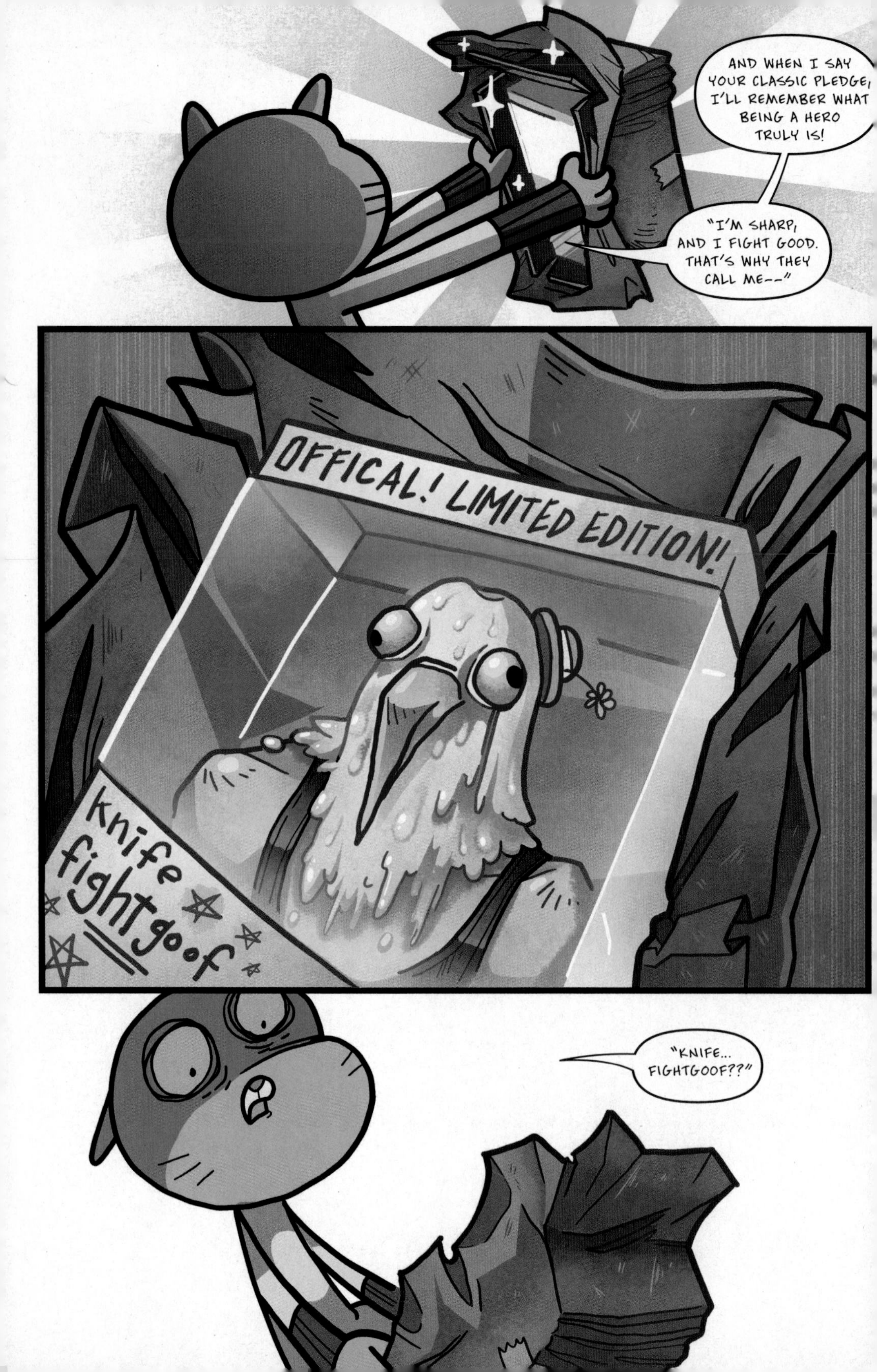
AND WHEN I SAY YOUR CLASSIC PLEDGE, I'LL REMEMBER WHAT BEING A HERO TRULY IS!
"I'M SHARP, AND I FIGHT GOOD. THAT'S WHY THEY CALL ME--"
OFFICAL! LIMITED EDITION!
knife fightgoof
"KNIFE... FIGHTGOOF??"

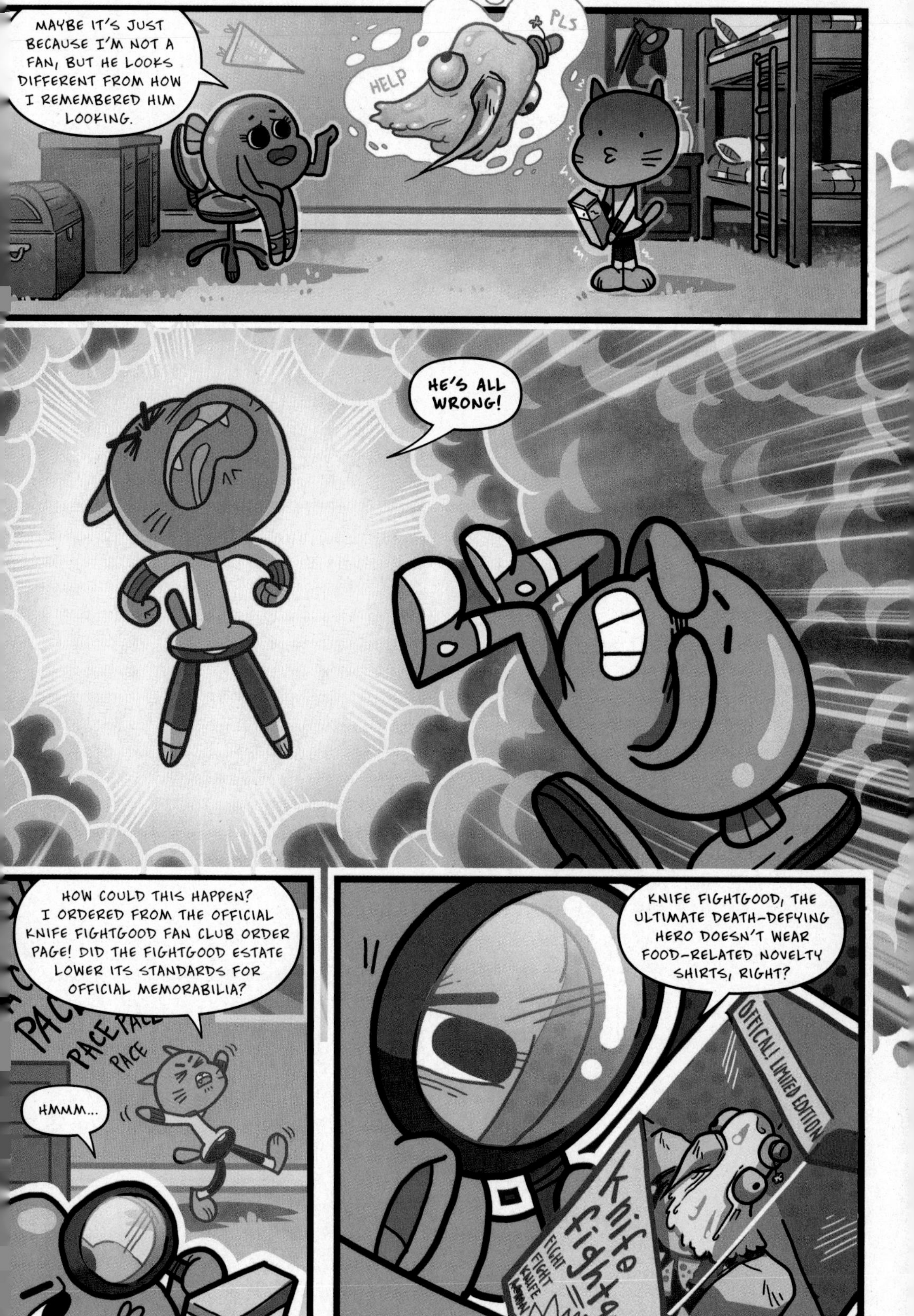

MAYBE IT'S JUST BECAUSE I'M NOT A FAN, BUT HE LOOKS DIFFERENT FROM HOW I REMEMBERED HIM LOOKING.
HELP
PLS
HE'S ALL WRONG!
HOW COULD THIS HAPPEN? I ORDERED FROM THE OFFICIAL KNIFE FIGHTGOOD FAN CLUB ORDER PAGE! DID THE FIGHTGOOD ESTATE LOWER ITS STANDARDS FOR OFFICIAL MEMORABILIA?
PACE PACE PACE
HMMM...
KNIFE FIGHTGOOD, THE ULTIMATE DEATH-DEFYING HERO DOESN'T WEAR FOOD-RELATED NOVELTY SHIRTS, RIGHT?
OFFICAL! LIMITED EDITION
knife fightgood
FIGHT
FIGHT
KNIFE

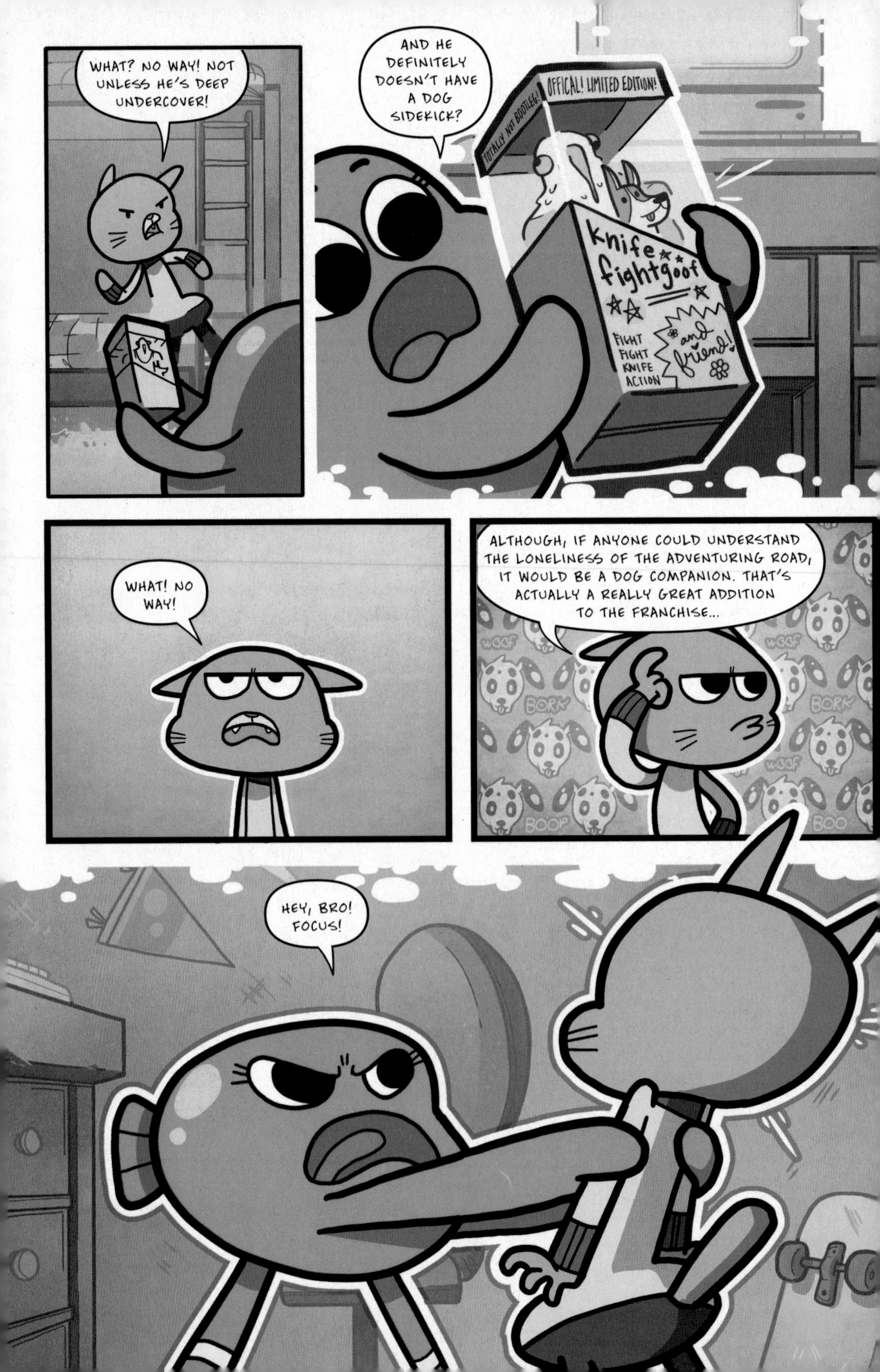
WHAT? NO WAY! NOT UNLESS HE'S DEEP UNDERCOVER!
AND HE DEFINITELY DOESN'T HAVE A DOG SIDEKICK?
OFFICAL! LIMITED EDITION!
TOTALLY NOT BOOTLEG!
knife fightgoof
and friend!
FIGHT FIGHT KNIFE ACTION
WHAT! NO WAY!
ALTHOUGH, IF ANYONE COULD UNDERSTAND THE LONELINESS OF THE ADVENTURING ROAD, IT WOULD BE A DOG COMPANION. THAT'S ACTUALLY A REALLY GREAT ADDITION TO THE FRANCHISE...
WOOF
BORK
BOOP
HEY, BRO! FOCUS!

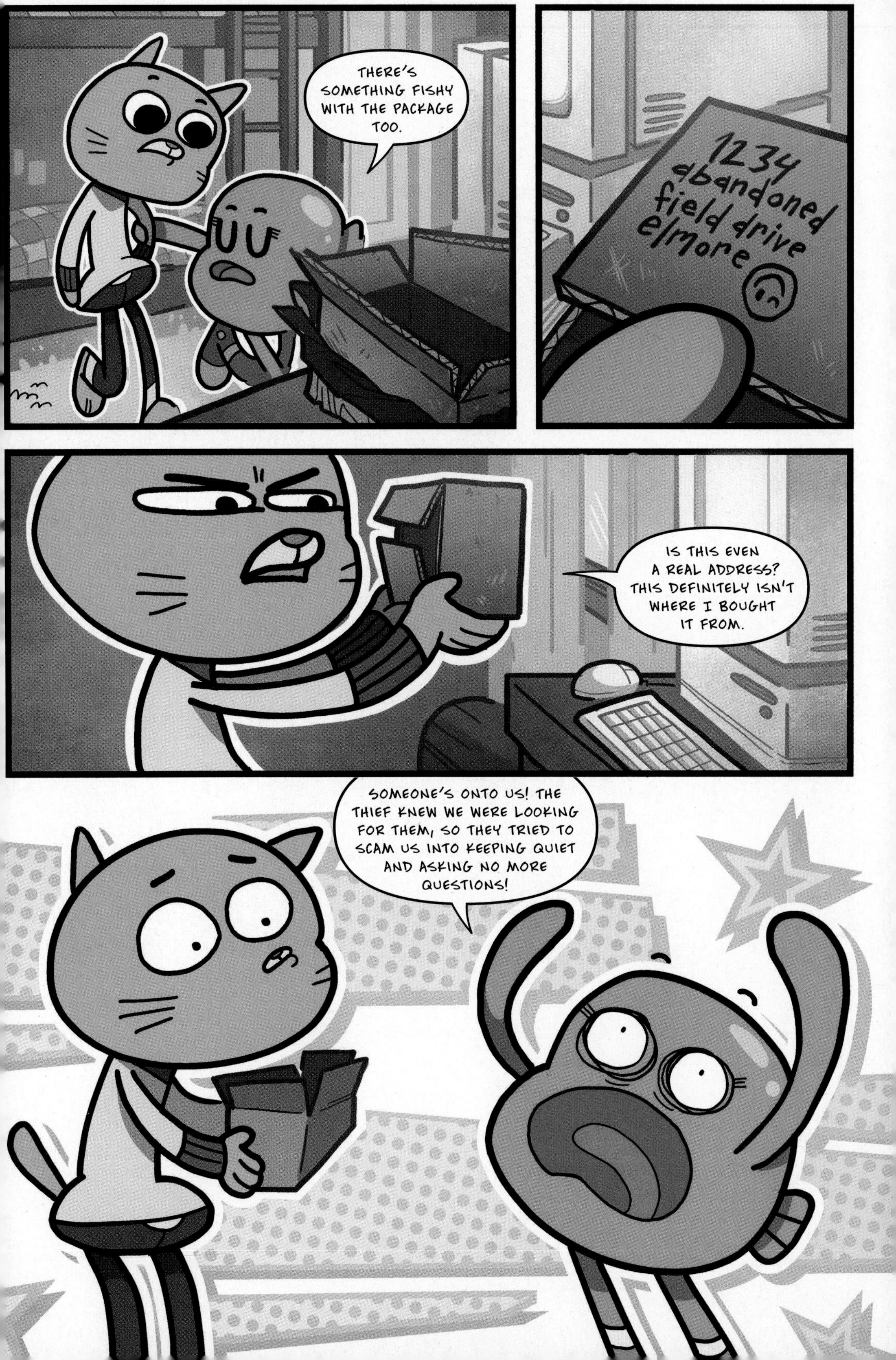
THERE'S SOMETHING FISHY WITH THE PACKAGE TOO.
1234 abandoned field drive elmore
IS THIS EVEN A REAL ADDRESS? THIS DEFINITELY ISN'T WHERE I BOUGHT IT FROM.
SOMEONE'S ONTO US! THE THIEF KNEW WE WERE LOOKING FOR THEM, SO THEY TRIED TO SCAM US INTO KEEPING QUIET AND ASKING NO MORE QUESTIONS!

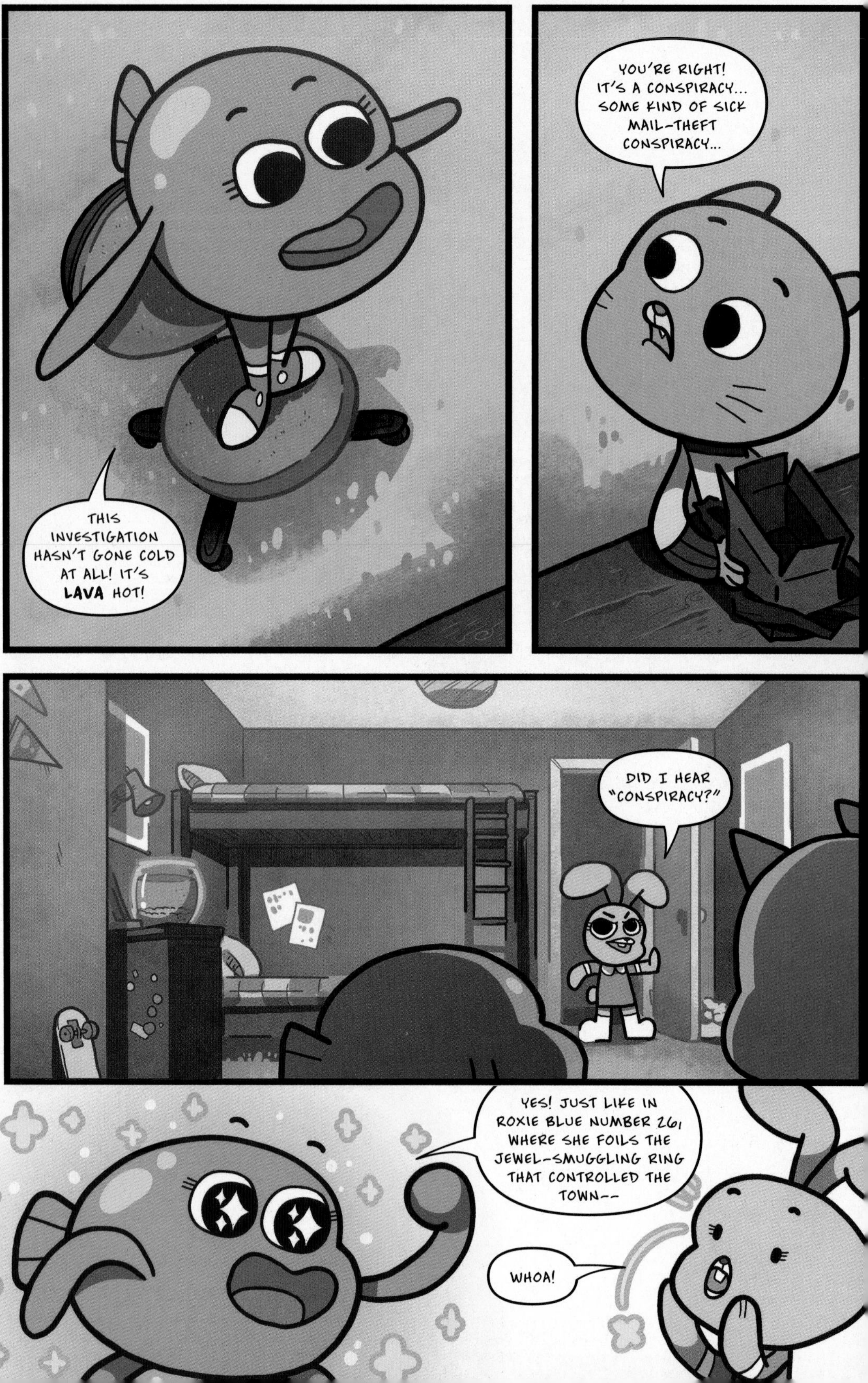
THIS INVESTIGATION HASN'T GONE COLD AT ALL! IT'S LAVA HOT!
YOU'RE RIGHT! IT'S A CONSPIRACY... SOME KIND OF SICK MAIL-THEFT CONSPIRACY...
DID I HEAR "CONSPIRACY?"
YES! JUST LIKE IN ROXIE BLUE NUMBER 26, WHERE SHE FOILS THE JEWEL-SMUGGLING RING THAT CONTROLLED THE TOWN--
WHOA!

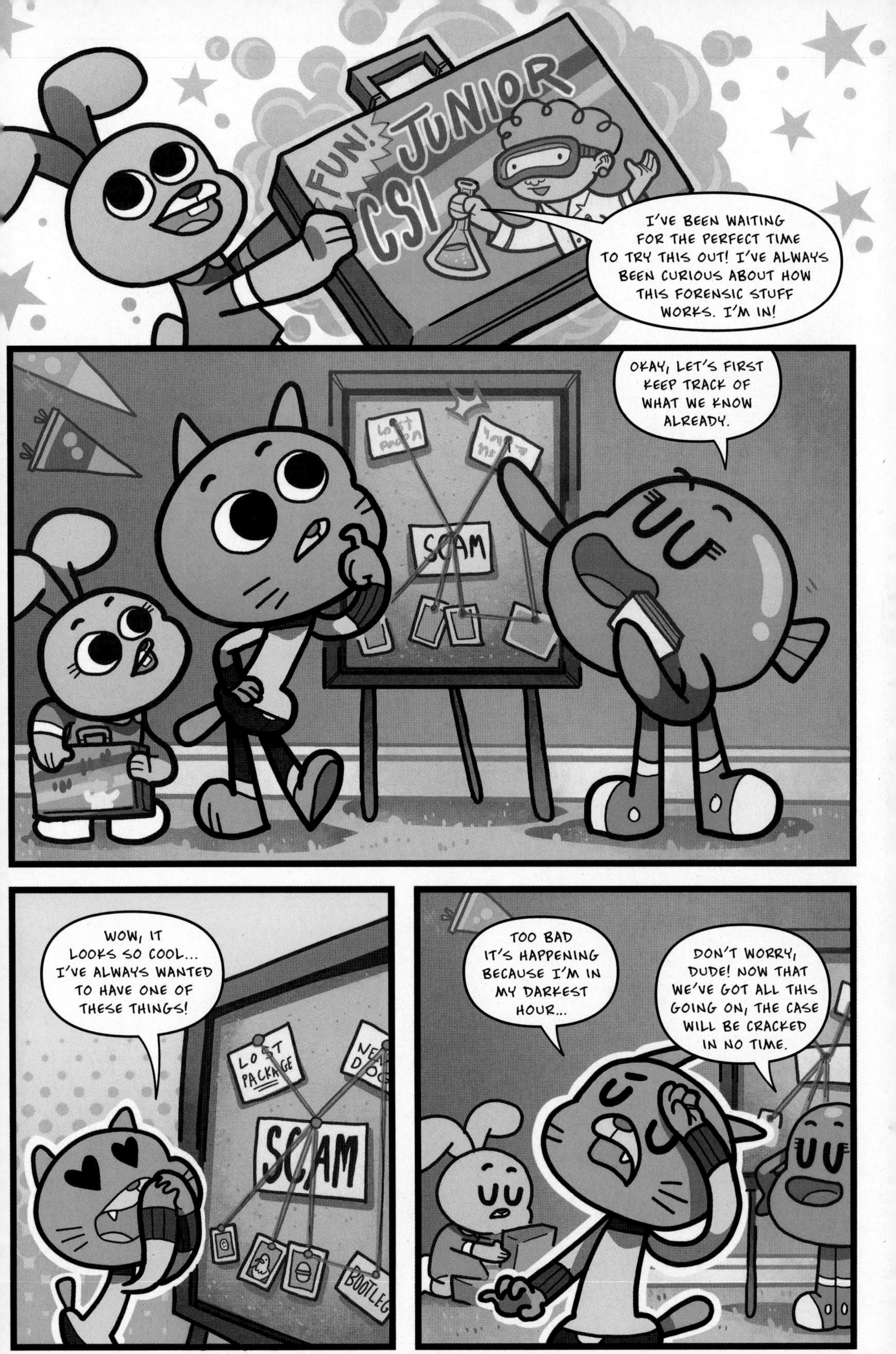
FUN!
JUNIOR
CSI
I'VE BEEN WAITING FOR THE PERFECT TIME TO TRY THIS OUT! I'VE ALWAYS BEEN CURIOUS ABOUT HOW THIS FORENSIC STUFF WORKS. I'M IN!
OKAY, LET'S FIRST KEEP TRACK OF WHAT WE KNOW ALREADY.
SCAM
WOW, IT LOOKS SO COOL... I'VE ALWAYS WANTED TO HAVE ONE OF THESE THINGS!
LOST PACKAGE
SCAM
BOOTLEG
TOO BAD IT'S HAPPENING BECAUSE I'M IN MY DARKEST HOUR...
DON'T WORRY, DUDE! NOW THAT WE'VE GOT ALL THIS GOING ON, THE CASE WILL BE CRACKED IN NO TIME.

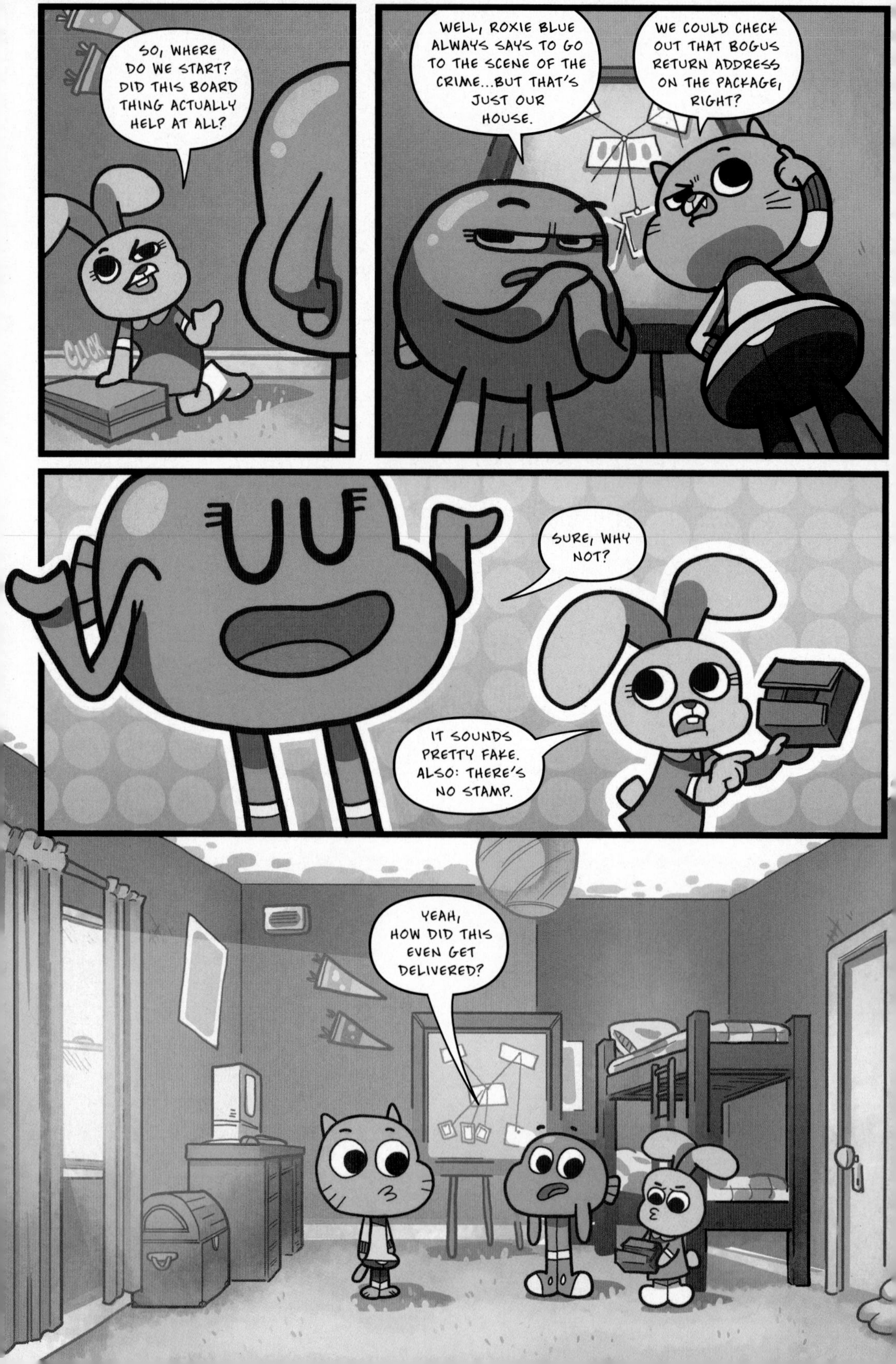
SO, WHERE DO WE START? DID THIS BOARD THING ACTUALLY HELP AT ALL?
CLICK
WELL, ROXIE BLUE ALWAYS SAYS TO GO TO THE SCENE OF THE CRIME...BUT THAT'S JUST OUR HOUSE.
WE COULD CHECK OUT THAT BOGUS RETURN ADDRESS ON THE PACKAGE, RIGHT?
SURE, WHY NOT?
IT SOUNDS PRETTY FAKE. ALSO: THERE'S NO STAMP.
YEAH, HOW DID THIS EVEN GET DELIVERED?

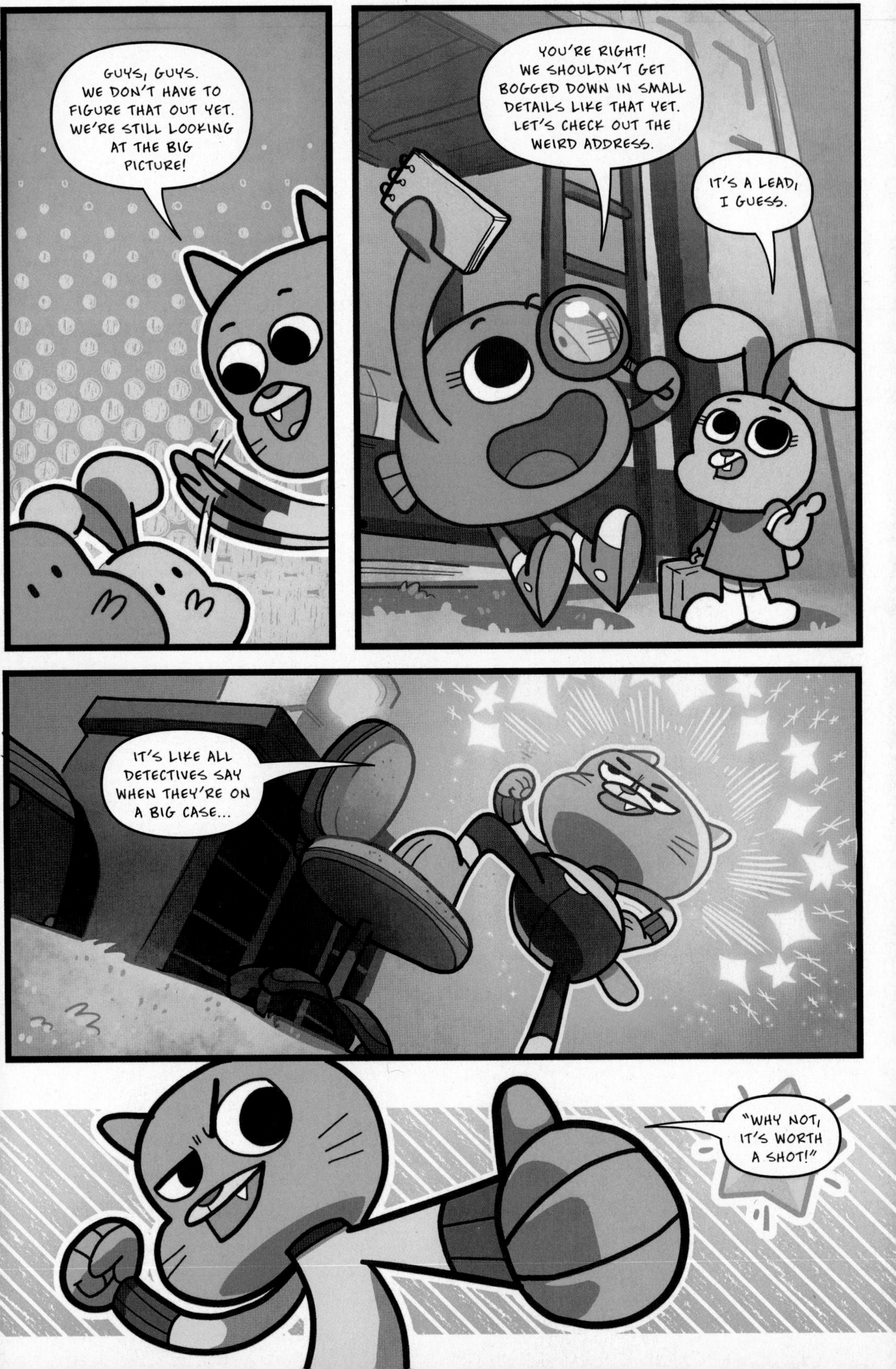
GUYS, GUYS. WE DON'T HAVE TO FIGURE THAT OUT YET. WE'RE STILL LOOKING AT THE BIG PICTURE!
YOU'RE RIGHT! WE SHOULDN'T GET BOGGED DOWN IN SMALL DETAILS LIKE THAT YET. LET'S CHECK OUT THE WEIRD ADDRESS.
IT'S A LEAD, I GUESS.
IT'S LIKE ALL DETECTIVES SAY WHEN THEY'RE ON A BIG CASE...
"WHY NOT, IT'S WORTH A SHOT!"

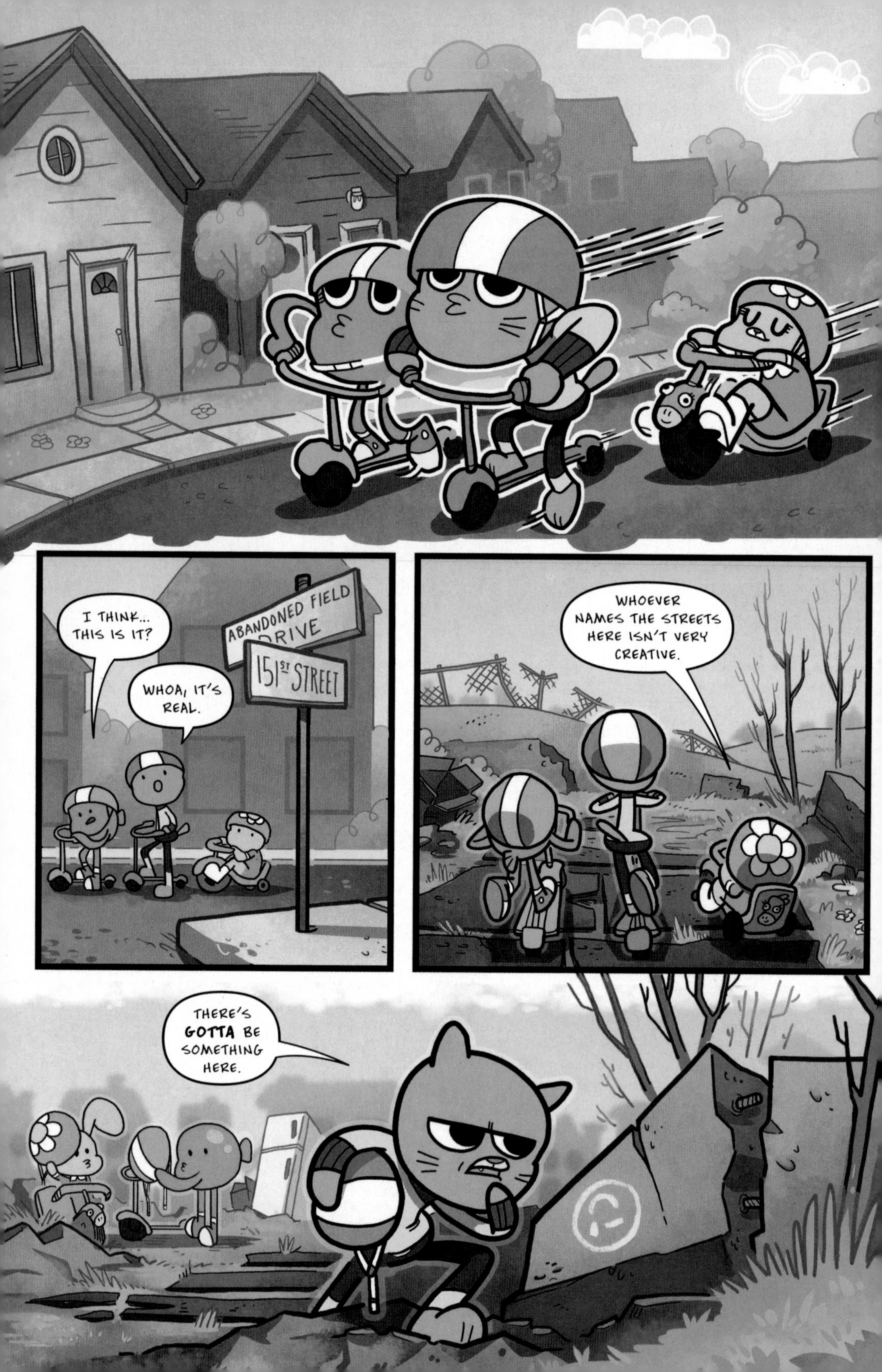
I THINK... THIS IS IT?
ABANDONED FIELD DRIVE
151ST STREET
WHOA, IT'S REAL.
WHOEVER NAMES THE STREETS HERE ISN'T VERY CREATIVE.
THERE'S **GOTTA** BE SOMETHING HERE.

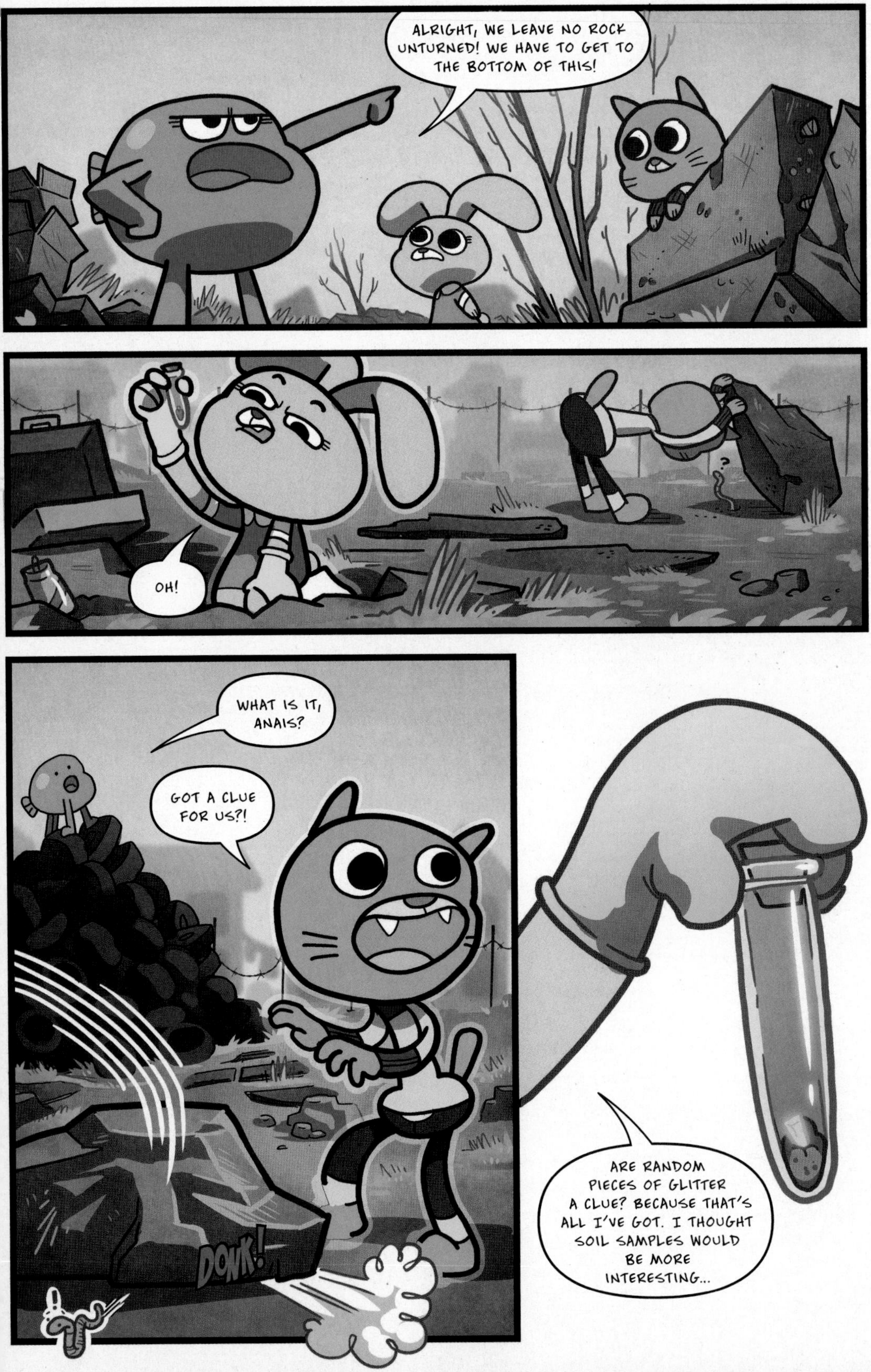
ALRIGHT, WE LEAVE NO ROCK UNTURNED! WE HAVE TO GET TO THE BOTTOM OF THIS!
OH!
WHAT IS IT, ANAIS?
GOT A CLUE FOR US?!
ARE RANDOM PIECES OF GLITTER A CLUE? BECAUSE THAT'S ALL I'VE GOT. I THOUGHT SOIL SAMPLES WOULD BE MORE INTERESTING...
DONK!

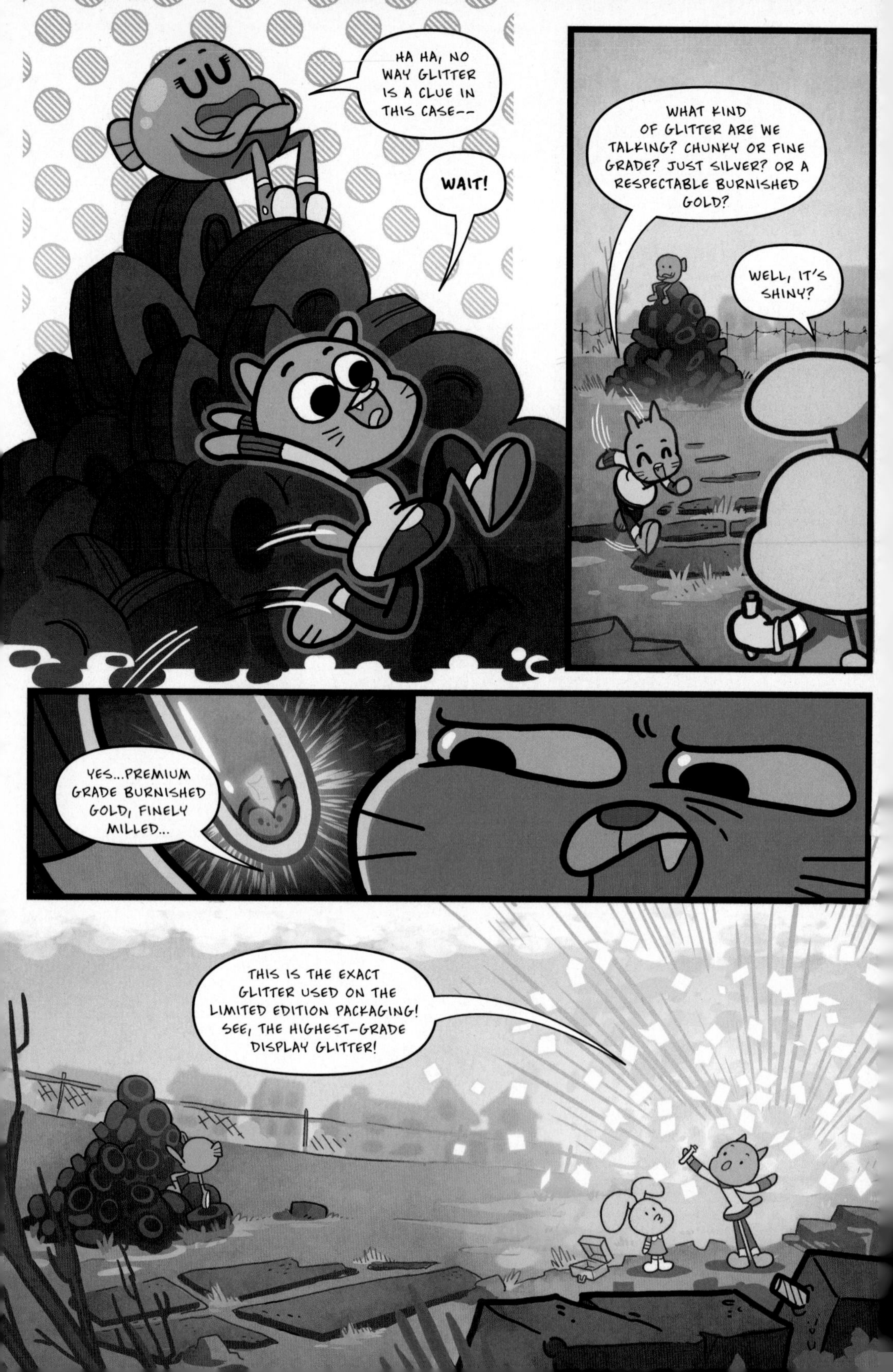
HA HA, NO WAY GLITTER IS A CLUE IN THIS CASE--
WAIT!
WHAT KIND OF GLITTER ARE WE TALKING? CHUNKY OR FINE GRADE? JUST SILVER? OR A RESPECTABLE BURNISHED GOLD?
WELL, IT'S SHINY?
YES...PREMIUM GRADE BURNISHED GOLD, FINELY MILLED...
THIS IS THE EXACT GLITTER USED ON THE LIMITED EDITION PACKAGING! SEE, THE HIGHEST-GRADE DISPLAY GLITTER!

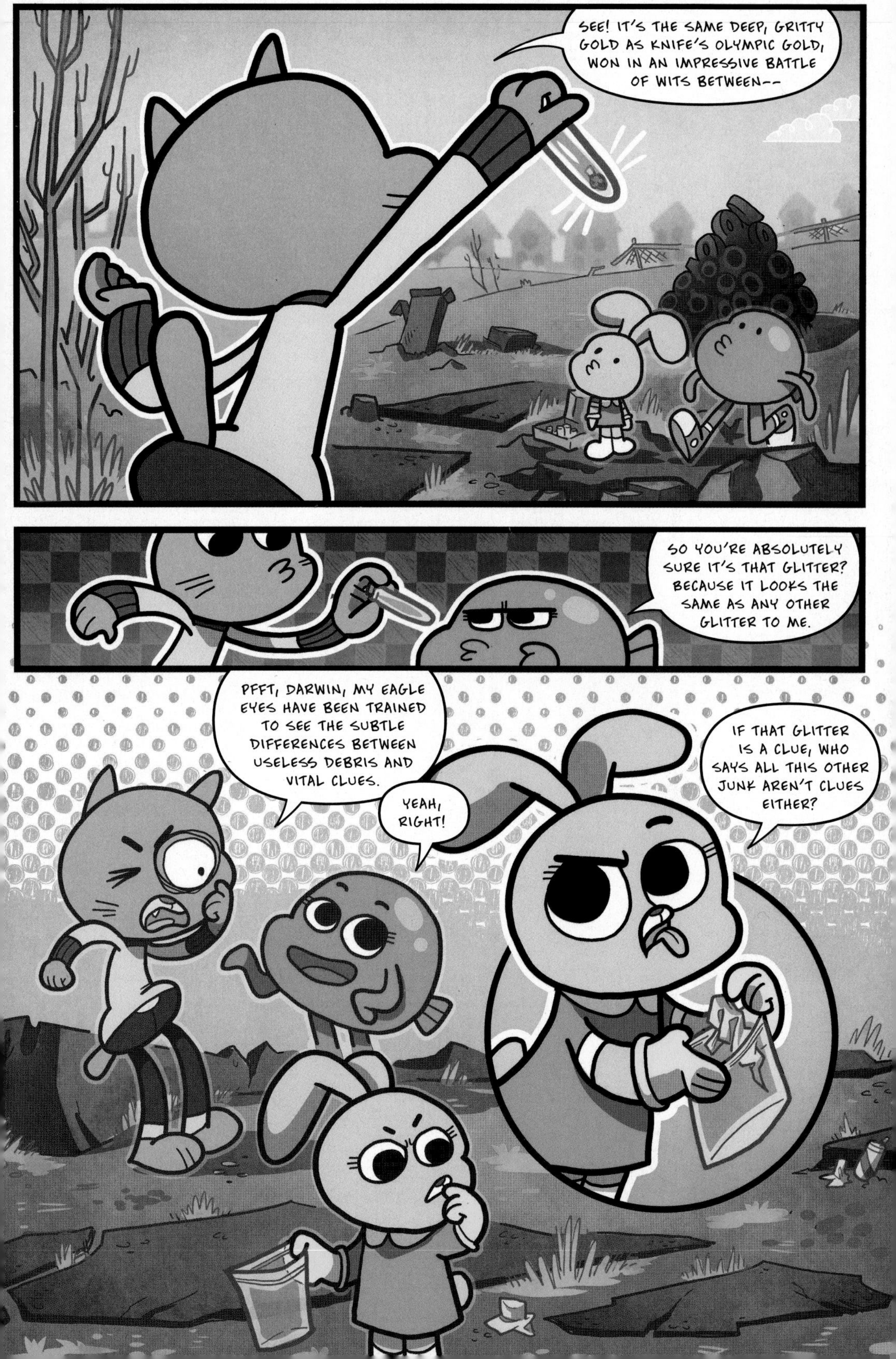
SEE! IT'S THE SAME DEEP, GRITTY GOLD AS KNIFE'S OLYMPIC GOLD, WON IN AN IMPRESSIVE BATTLE OF WITS BETWEEN--
SO YOU'RE ABSOLUTELY SURE IT'S THAT GLITTER? BECAUSE IT LOOKS THE SAME AS ANY OTHER GLITTER TO ME.
PFFT, DARWIN, MY EAGLE EYES HAVE BEEN TRAINED TO SEE THE SUBTLE DIFFERENCES BETWEEN USELESS DEBRIS AND VITAL CLUES.
YEAH, RIGHT!
IF THAT GLITTER IS A CLUE, WHO SAYS ALL THIS OTHER JUNK AREN'T CLUES EITHER?

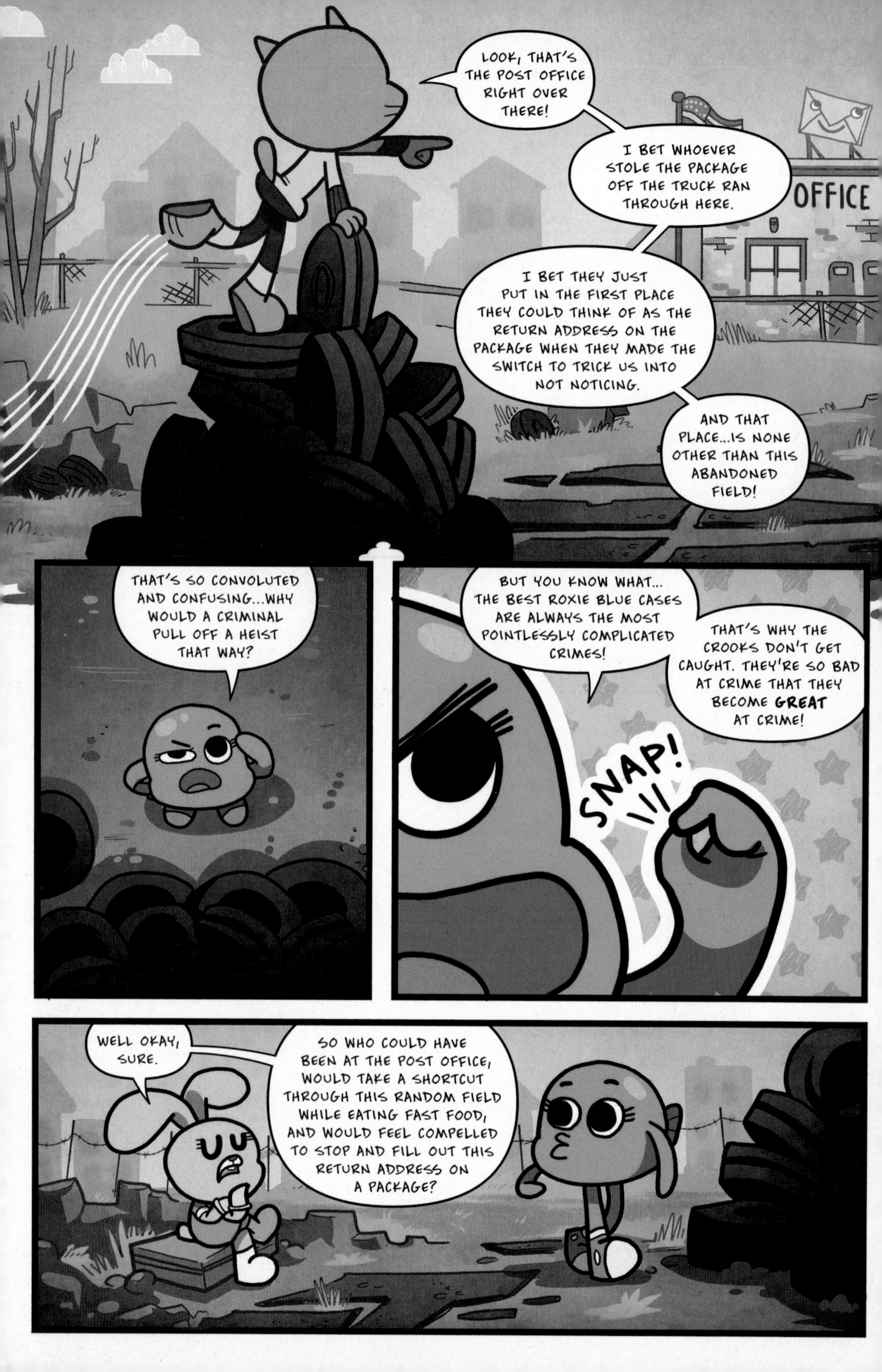

LOOK, THAT'S THE POST OFFICE RIGHT OVER THERE!
I BET WHOEVER STOLE THE PACKAGE OFF THE TRUCK RAN THROUGH HERE.
OFFICE
I BET THEY JUST PUT IN THE FIRST PLACE THEY COULD THINK OF AS THE RETURN ADDRESS ON THE PACKAGE WHEN THEY MADE THE SWITCH TO TRICK US INTO NOT NOTICING.
AND THAT PLACE...IS NONE OTHER THAN THIS ABANDONED FIELD!
THAT'S SO CONVOLUTED AND CONFUSING...WHY WOULD A CRIMINAL PULL OFF A HEIST THAT WAY?
BUT YOU KNOW WHAT... THE BEST ROXIE BLUE CASES ARE ALWAYS THE MOST POINTLESSLY COMPLICATED CRIMES!
THAT'S WHY THE CROOKS DON'T GET CAUGHT. THEY'RE SO BAD AT CRIME THAT THEY BECOME **GREAT** AT CRIME!
SNAP!
WELL OKAY, SURE.
SO WHO COULD HAVE BEEN AT THE POST OFFICE, WOULD TAKE A SHORTCUT THROUGH THIS RANDOM FIELD WHILE EATING FAST FOOD, AND WOULD FEEL COMPELLED TO STOP AND FILL OUT THIS RETURN ADDRESS ON A PACKAGE?

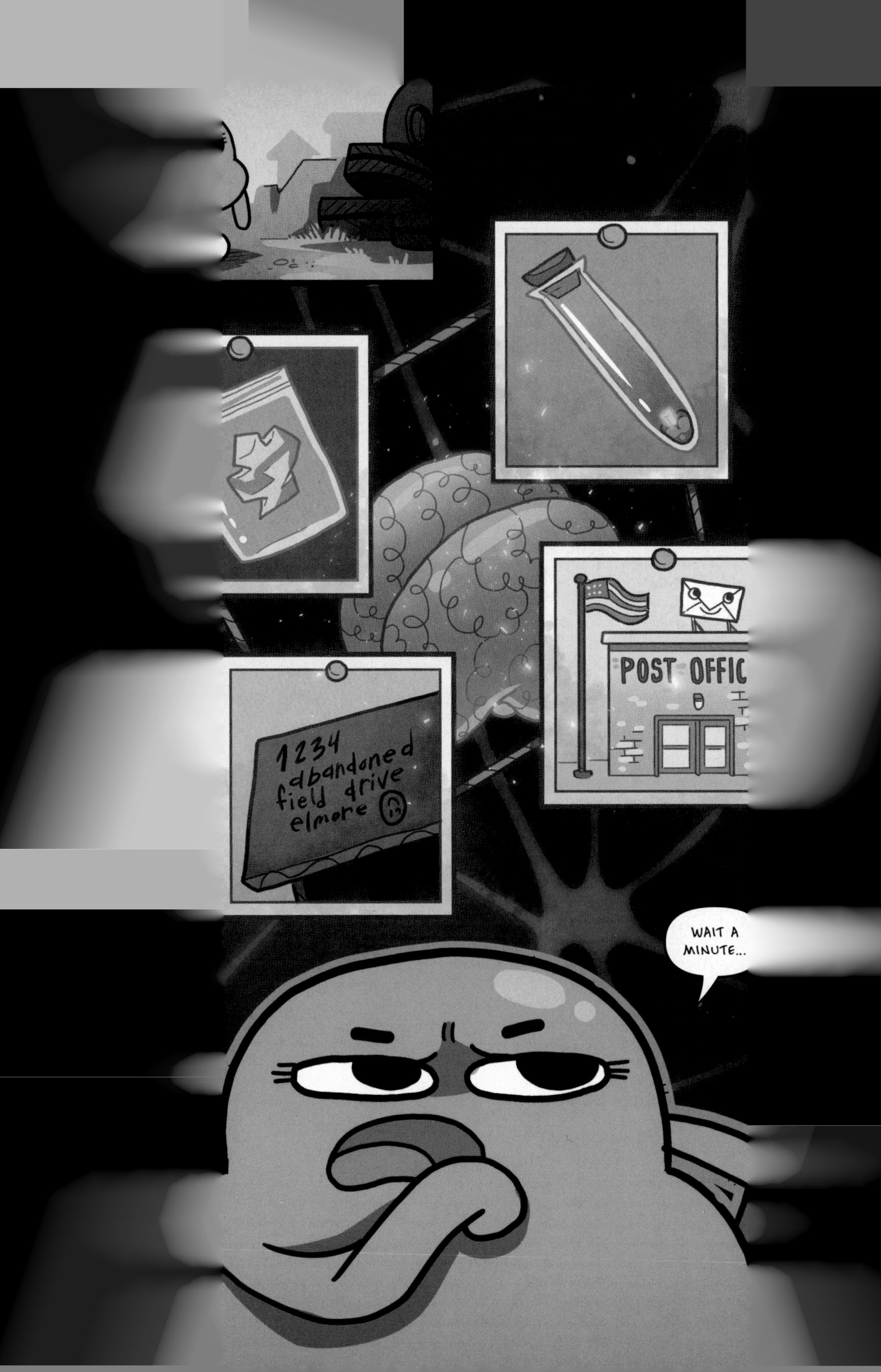
POST OFFIC
1234 abandoned field drive elmore
WAIT A MINUTE...

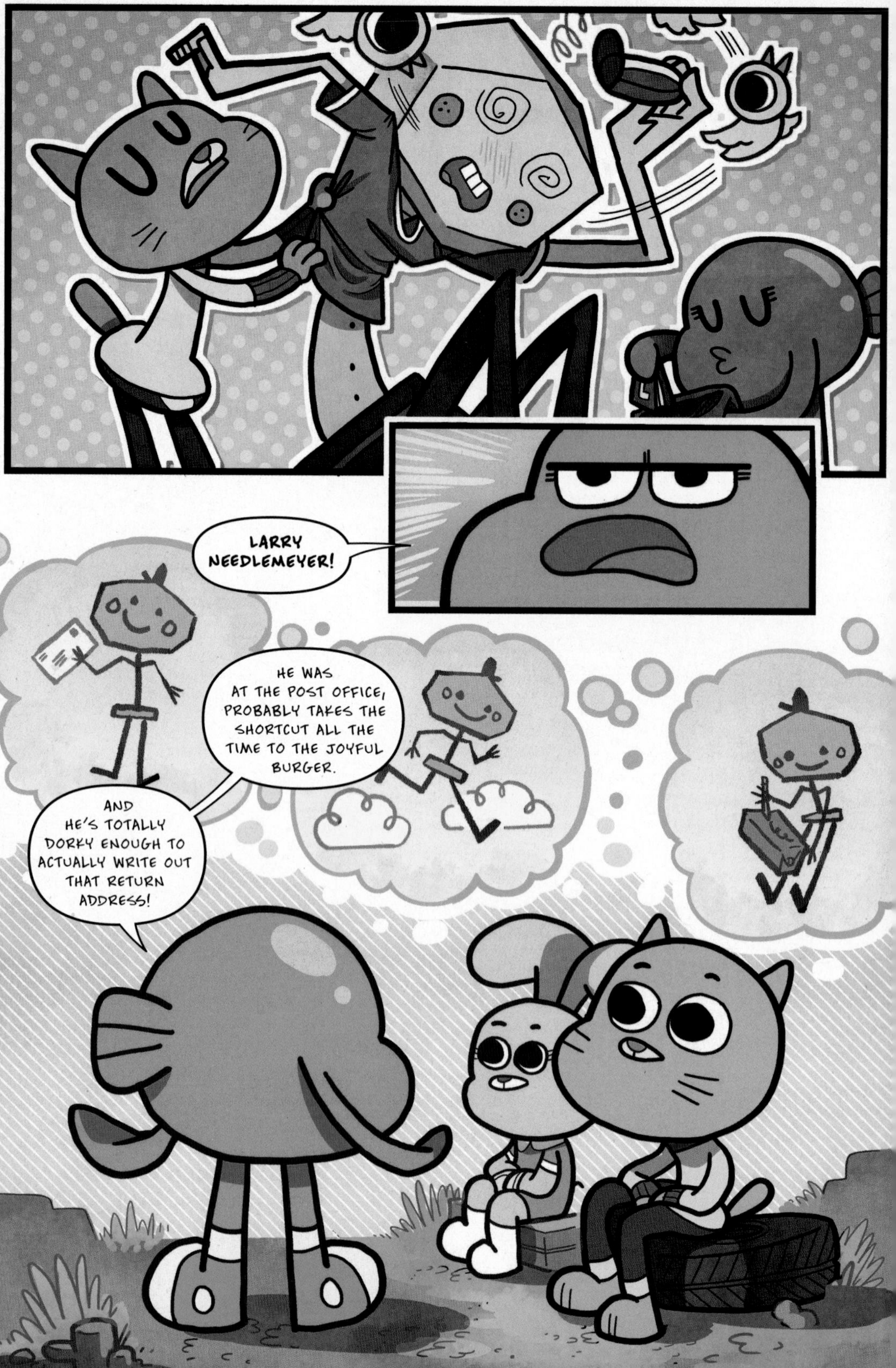
LARRY NEEDLEMEYER!
HE WAS AT THE POST OFFICE, PROBABLY TAKES THE SHORTCUT ALL THE TIME TO THE JOYFUL BURGER.
AND HE'S TOTALLY DORKY ENOUGH TO ACTUALLY WRITE OUT THAT RETURN ADDRESS!

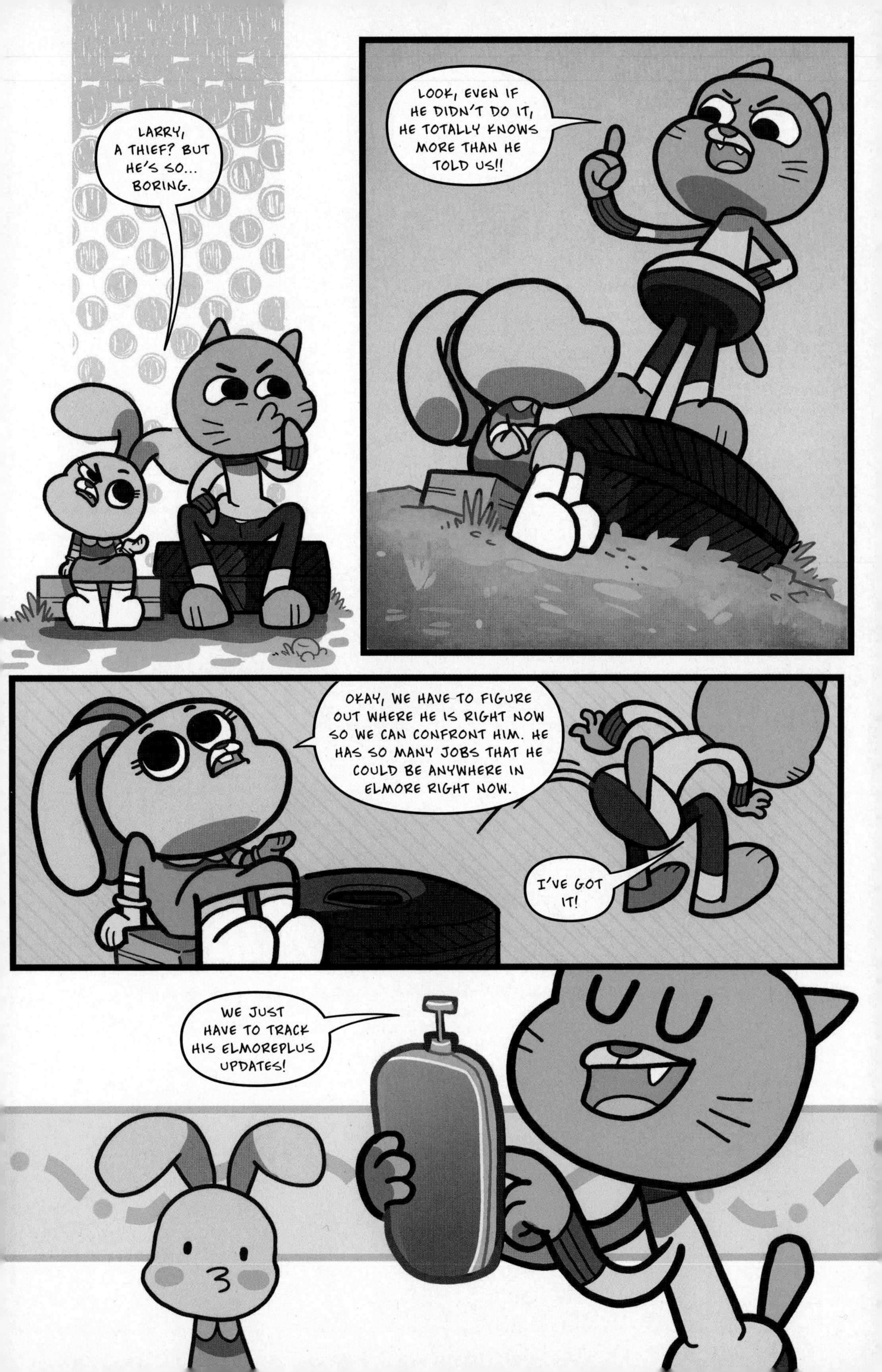
LARRY, A THIEF? BUT HE'S SO... BORING.
LOOK, EVEN IF HE DIDN'T DO IT, HE TOTALLY KNOWS MORE THAN HE TOLD US!!
OKAY, WE HAVE TO FIGURE OUT WHERE HE IS RIGHT NOW SO WE CAN CONFRONT HIM. HE HAS SO MANY JOBS THAT HE COULD BE ANYWHERE IN ELMORE RIGHT NOW.
I'VE GOT IT!
WE JUST HAVE TO TRACK HIS ELMOREPLUS UPDATES!

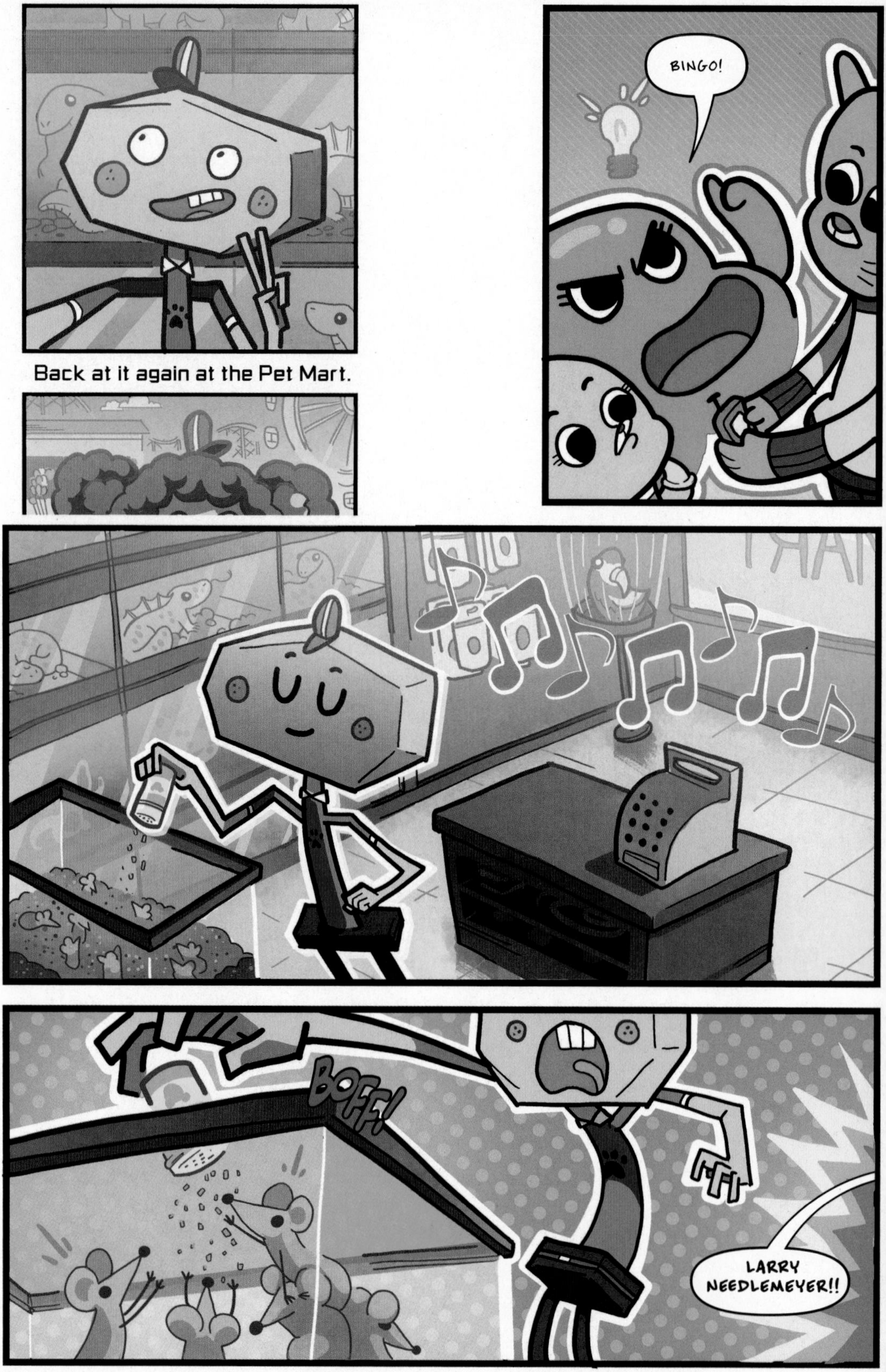
Back at it again at the Pet Mart.
BINGO!
BOFF!
LARRY NEEDLEMEYER!!

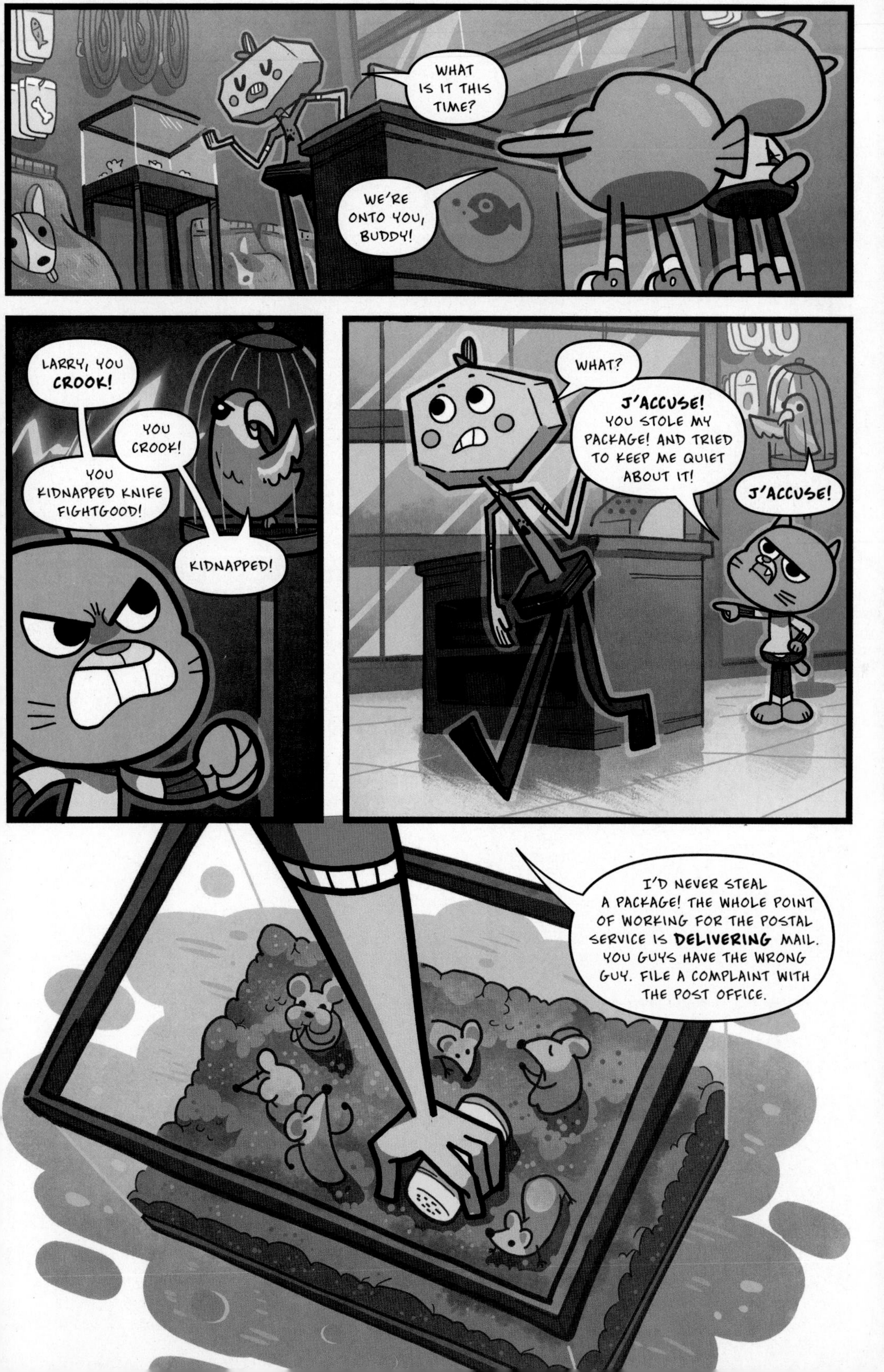
WHAT IS IT THIS TIME?
WE'RE ONTO YOU, BUDDY!
LARRY, YOU **CROOK!**
YOU CROOK!
YOU KIDNAPPED KNIFE FIGHTGOOD!
KIDNAPPED!
WHAT?
J'ACCUSE! YOU STOLE MY PACKAGE! AND TRIED TO KEEP ME QUIET ABOUT IT!
J'ACCUSE!
I'D NEVER STEAL A PACKAGE! THE WHOLE POINT OF WORKING FOR THE POSTAL SERVICE IS **DELIVERING** MAIL. YOU GUYS HAVE THE WRONG GUY. FILE A COMPLAINT WITH THE POST OFFICE.

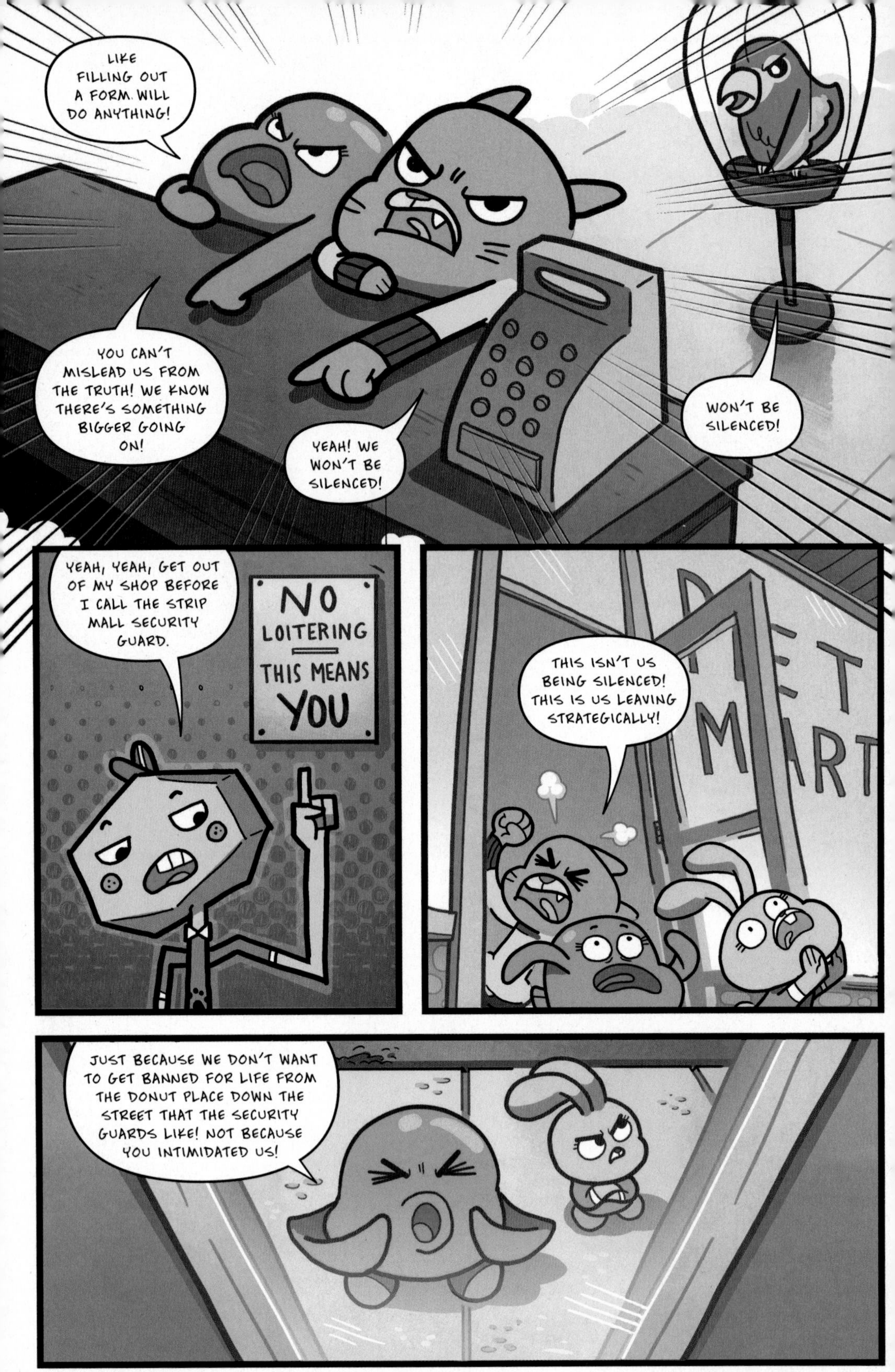
LIKE FILLING OUT A FORM WILL DO ANYTHING!
YOU CAN'T MISLEAD US FROM THE TRUTH! WE KNOW THERE'S SOMETHING BIGGER GOING ON!
YEAH! WE WON'T BE SILENCED!
WON'T BE SILENCED!
YEAH, YEAH, GET OUT OF MY SHOP BEFORE I CALL THE STRIP MALL SECURITY GUARD.
NO LOITERING
THIS MEANS YOU
THIS ISN'T US BEING SILENCED! THIS IS US LEAVING STRATEGICALLY!
JUST BECAUSE WE DON'T WANT TO GET BANNED FOR LIFE FROM THE DONUT PLACE DOWN THE STREET THAT THE SECURITY GUARDS LIKE! NOT BECAUSE YOU INTIMIDATED US!

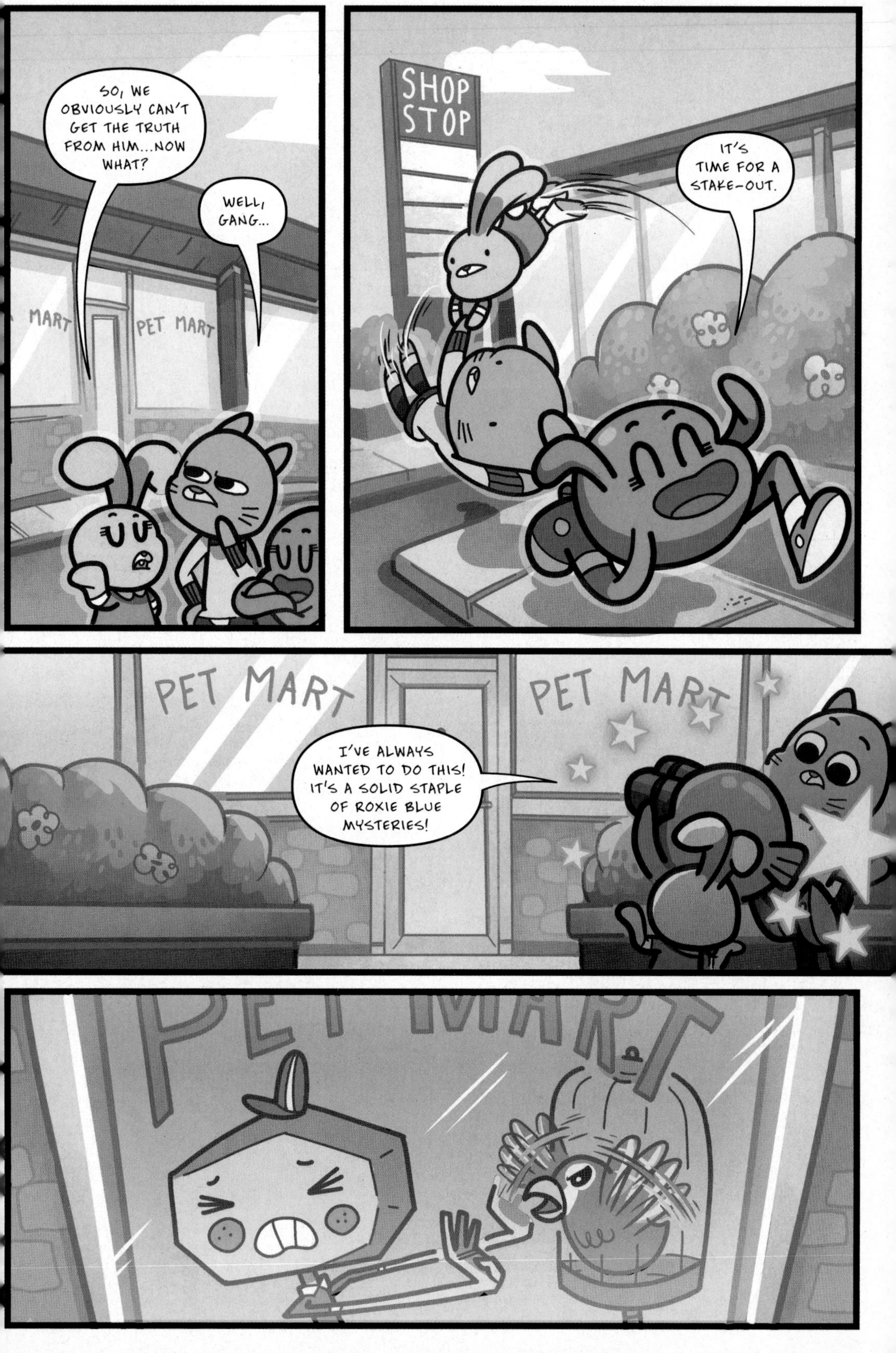
SO, WE OBVIOUSLY CAN'T GET THE TRUTH FROM HIM...NOW WHAT?
WELL, GANG...
MART
PET MART
SHOP STOP
IT'S TIME FOR A STAKE-OUT.
PET MART
PET MART
I'VE ALWAYS WANTED TO DO THIS! IT'S A SOLID STAPLE OF ROXIE BLUE MYSTERIES!
PET MART

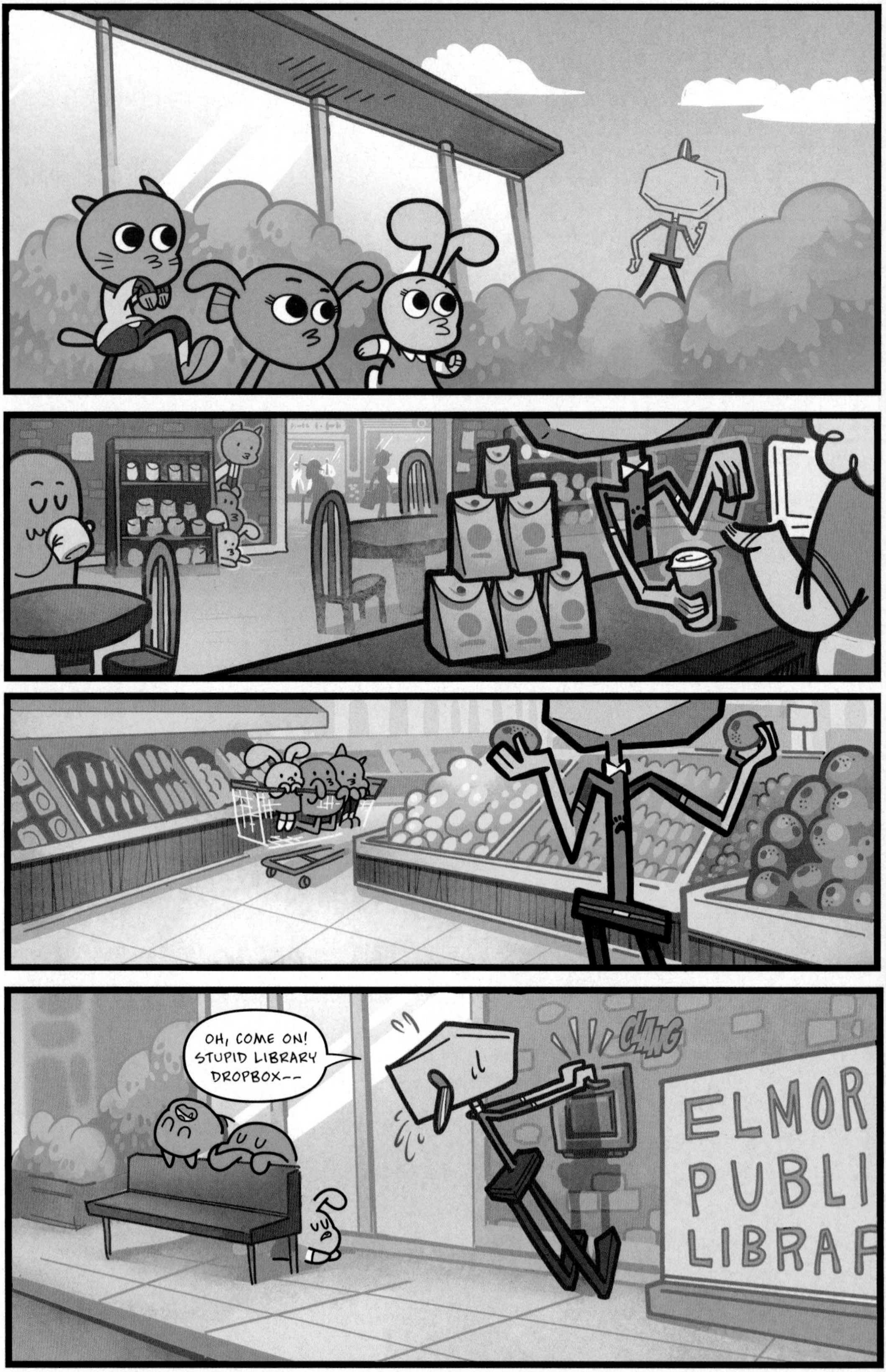
OH, COME ON! STUPID LIBRARY DROPBOX--
CLANG
ELMOR
PUBLI
LIBRAR

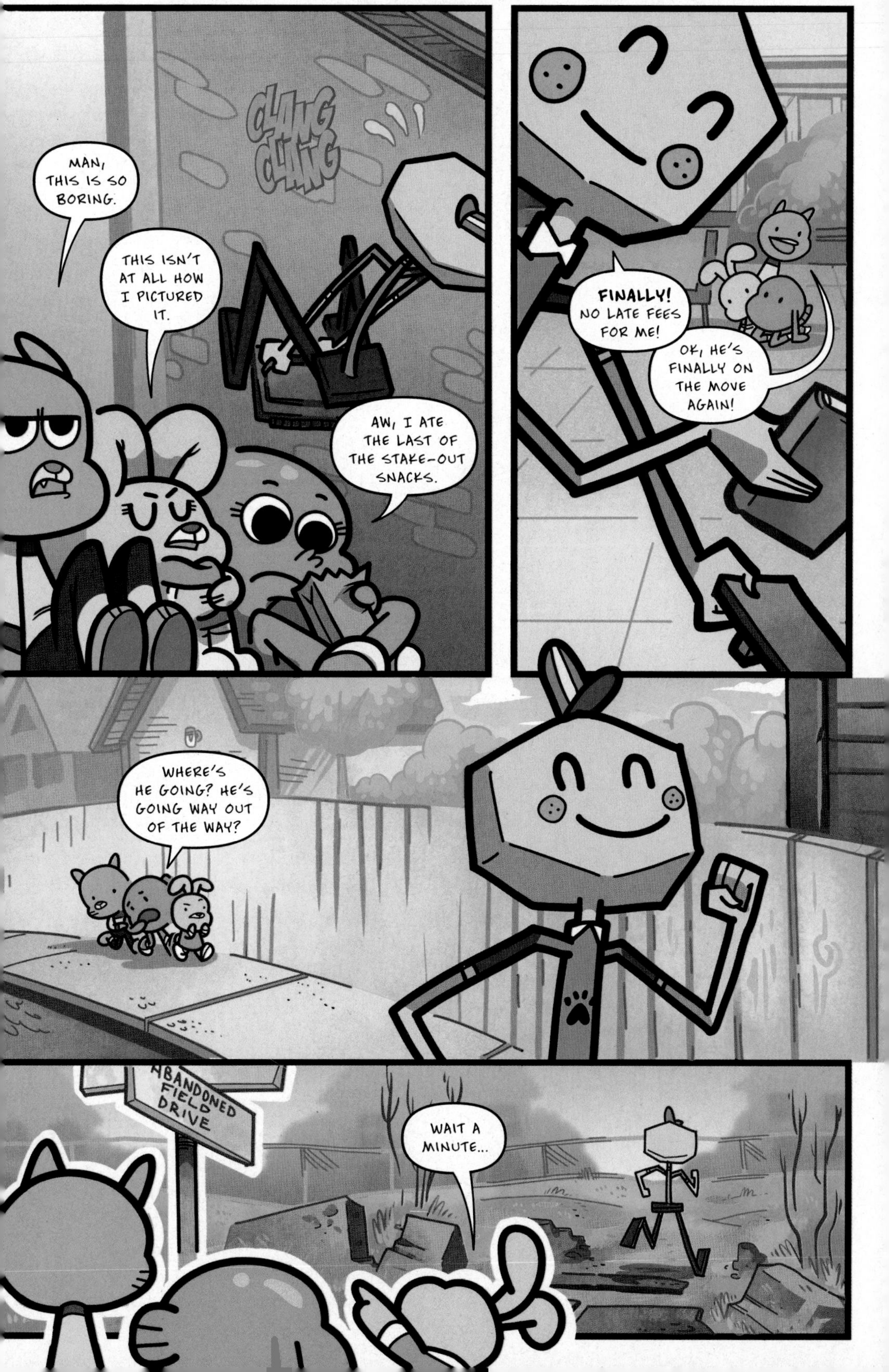
CLANG CLANG
MAN, THIS IS SO BORING.
THIS ISN'T AT ALL HOW I PICTURED IT.
AW, I ATE THE LAST OF THE STAKE-OUT SNACKS.
FINALLY! NO LATE FEES FOR ME!
OK, HE'S FINALLY ON THE MOVE AGAIN!
WHERE'S HE GOING? HE'S GOING WAY OUT OF THE WAY?
ABANDONED FIELD DRIVE
WAIT A MINUTE...

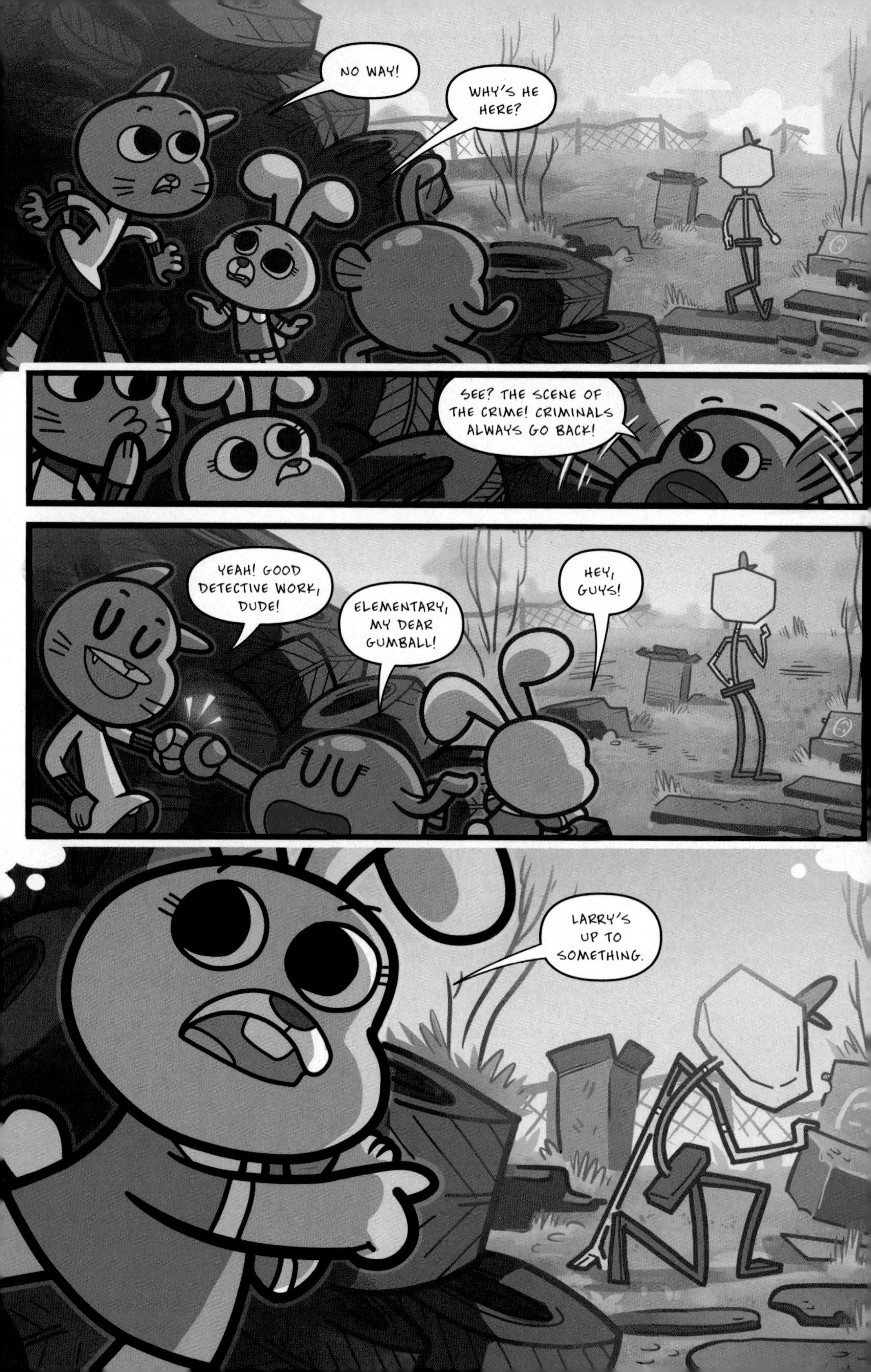
NO WAY!
WHY'S HE HERE?
SEE? THE SCENE OF THE CRIME! CRIMINALS ALWAYS GO BACK!
YEAH! GOOD DETECTIVE WORK, DUDE!
ELEMENTARY, MY DEAR GUMBALL!
HEY, GUYS!
LARRY'S UP TO SOMETHING.

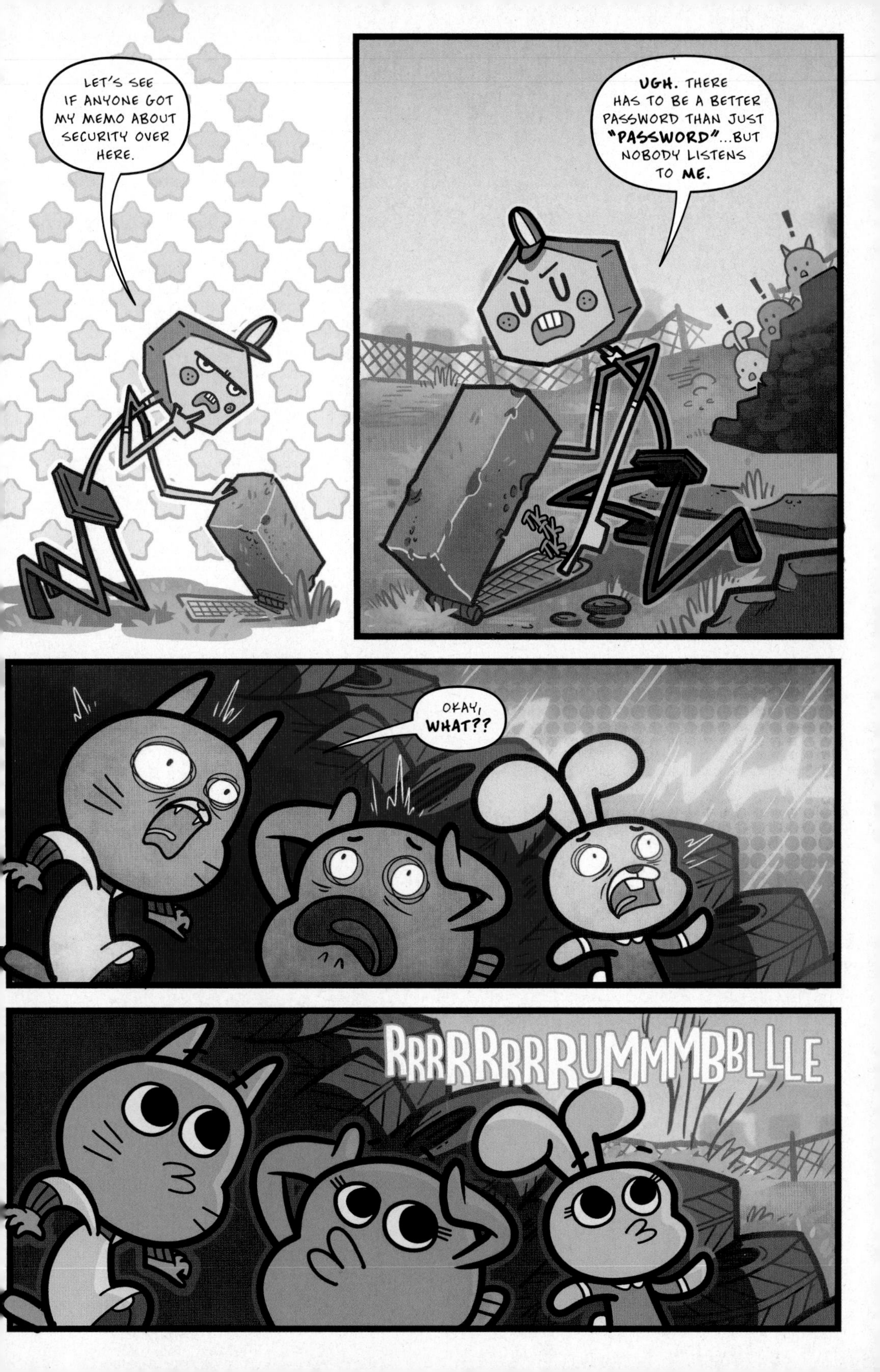
LET'S SEE IF ANYONE GOT MY MEMO ABOUT SECURITY OVER HERE.
UGH. THERE HAS TO BE A BETTER PASSWORD THAN JUST "PASSWORD"...BUT NOBODY LISTENS TO ME.
OKAY, WHAT??
RRRRRRRRUMMMBBLLLE

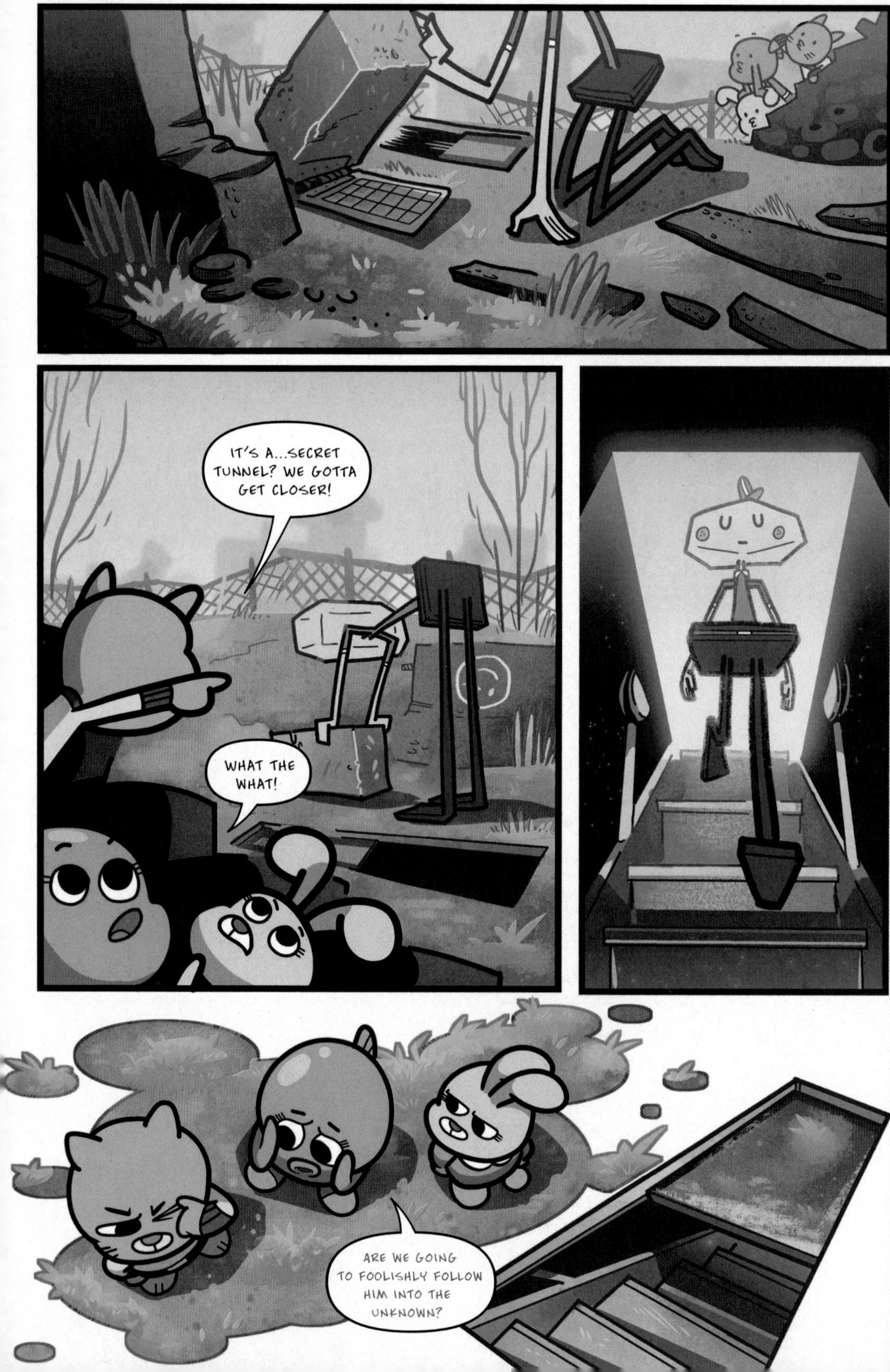
IT'S A...SECRET TUNNEL? WE GOTTA GET CLOSER!
WHAT THE WHAT!
ARE WE GOING TO FOOLISHLY FOLLOW HIM INTO THE UNKNOWN?

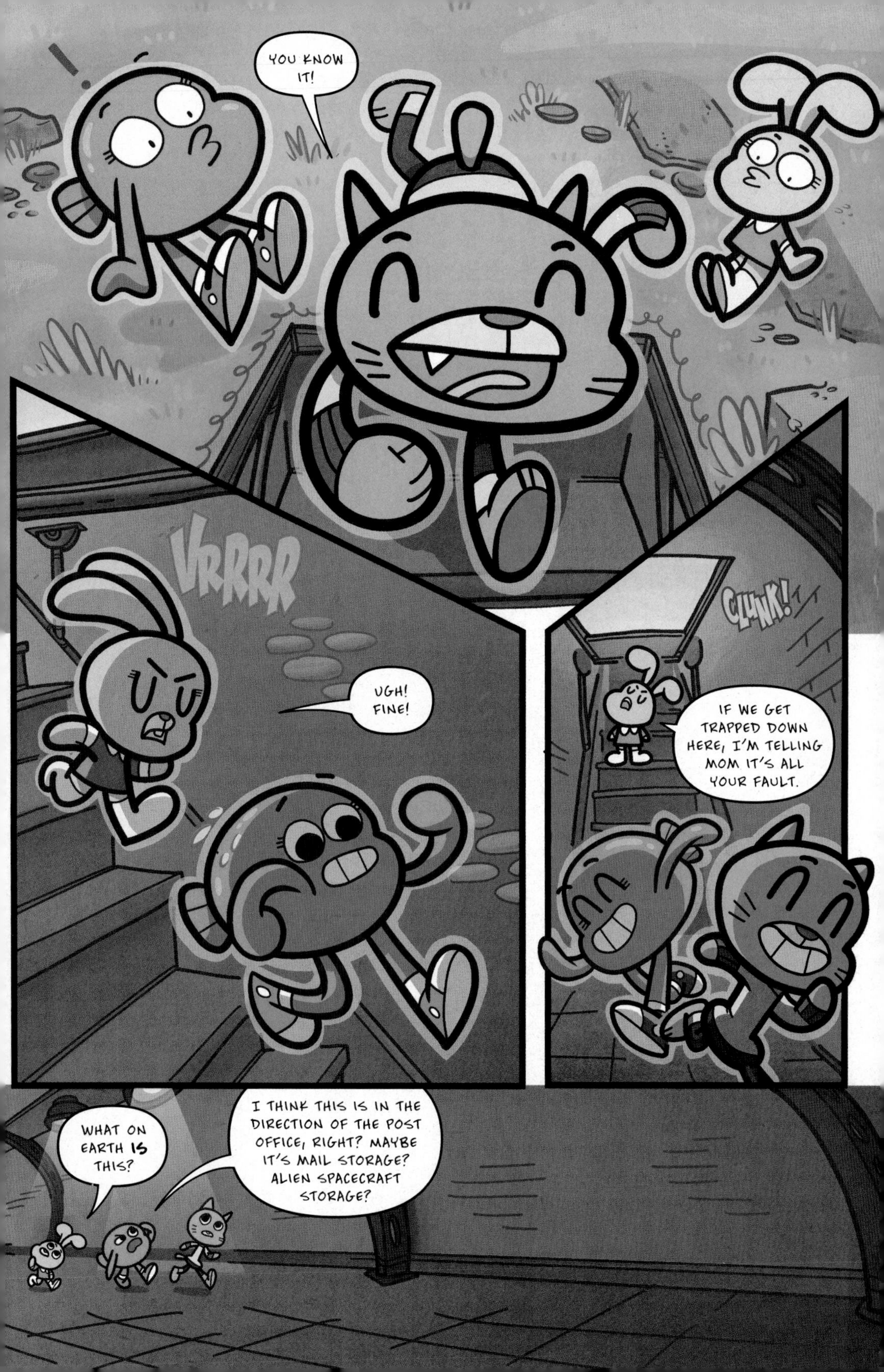
!
YOU KNOW IT!
VRRRR
UGH! FINE!
CLUNK!
IF WE GET TRAPPED DOWN HERE, I'M TELLING MOM IT'S ALL YOUR FAULT.
WHAT ON EARTH IS THIS?
I THINK THIS IS IN THE DIRECTION OF THE POST OFFICE, RIGHT? MAYBE IT'S MAIL STORAGE? ALIEN SPACECRAFT STORAGE?

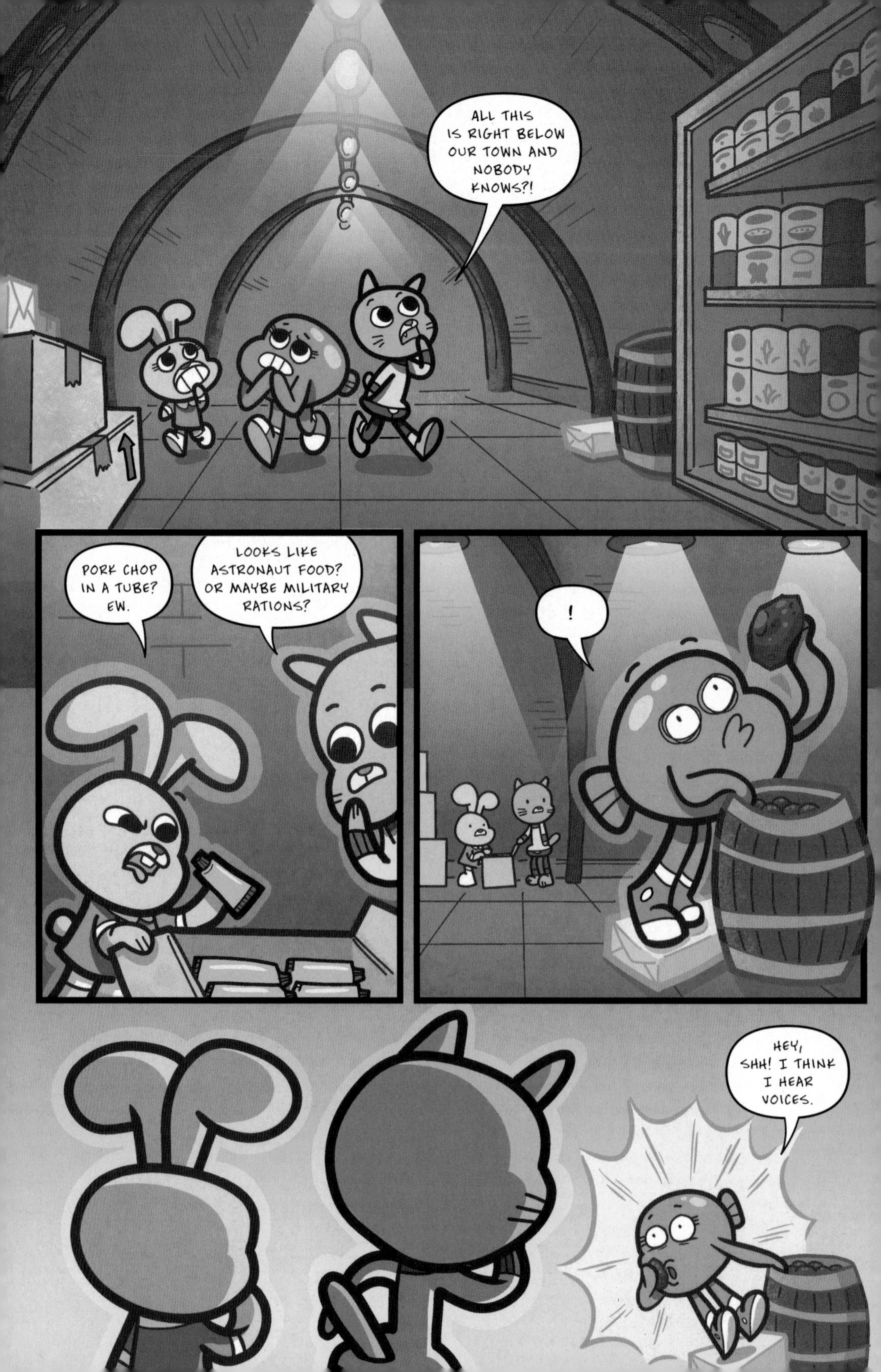
ALL THIS IS RIGHT BELOW OUR TOWN AND NOBODY KNOWS?!
PORK CHOP IN A TUBE? EW.
LOOKS LIKE ASTRONAUT FOOD? OR MAYBE MILITARY RATIONS?
!
HEY, SHH! I THINK I HEAR VOICES.

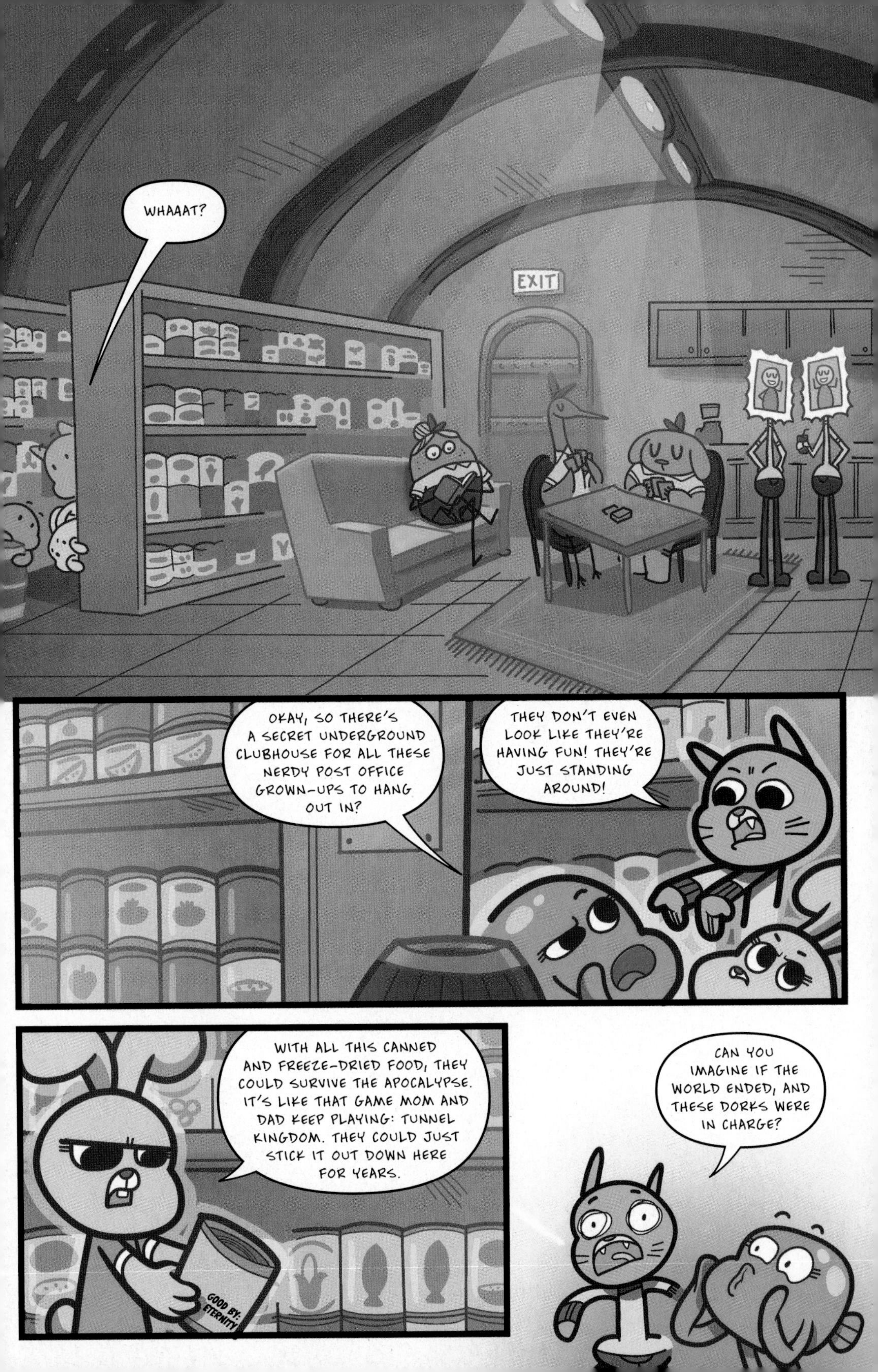
WHAAAT?
EXIT
OKAY, SO THERE'S A SECRET UNDERGROUND CLUBHOUSE FOR ALL THESE NERDY POST OFFICE GROWN-UPS TO HANG OUT IN?
THEY DON'T EVEN LOOK LIKE THEY'RE HAVING FUN! THEY'RE JUST STANDING AROUND!
WITH ALL THIS CANNED AND FREEZE-DRIED FOOD, THEY COULD SURVIVE THE APOCALYPSE. IT'S LIKE THAT GAME MOM AND DAD KEEP PLAYING: TUNNEL KINGDOM. THEY COULD JUST STICK IT OUT DOWN HERE FOR YEARS.
GOOD BY: ETERNITY
CAN YOU IMAGINE IF THE WORLD ENDED, AND THESE DORKS WERE IN CHARGE?

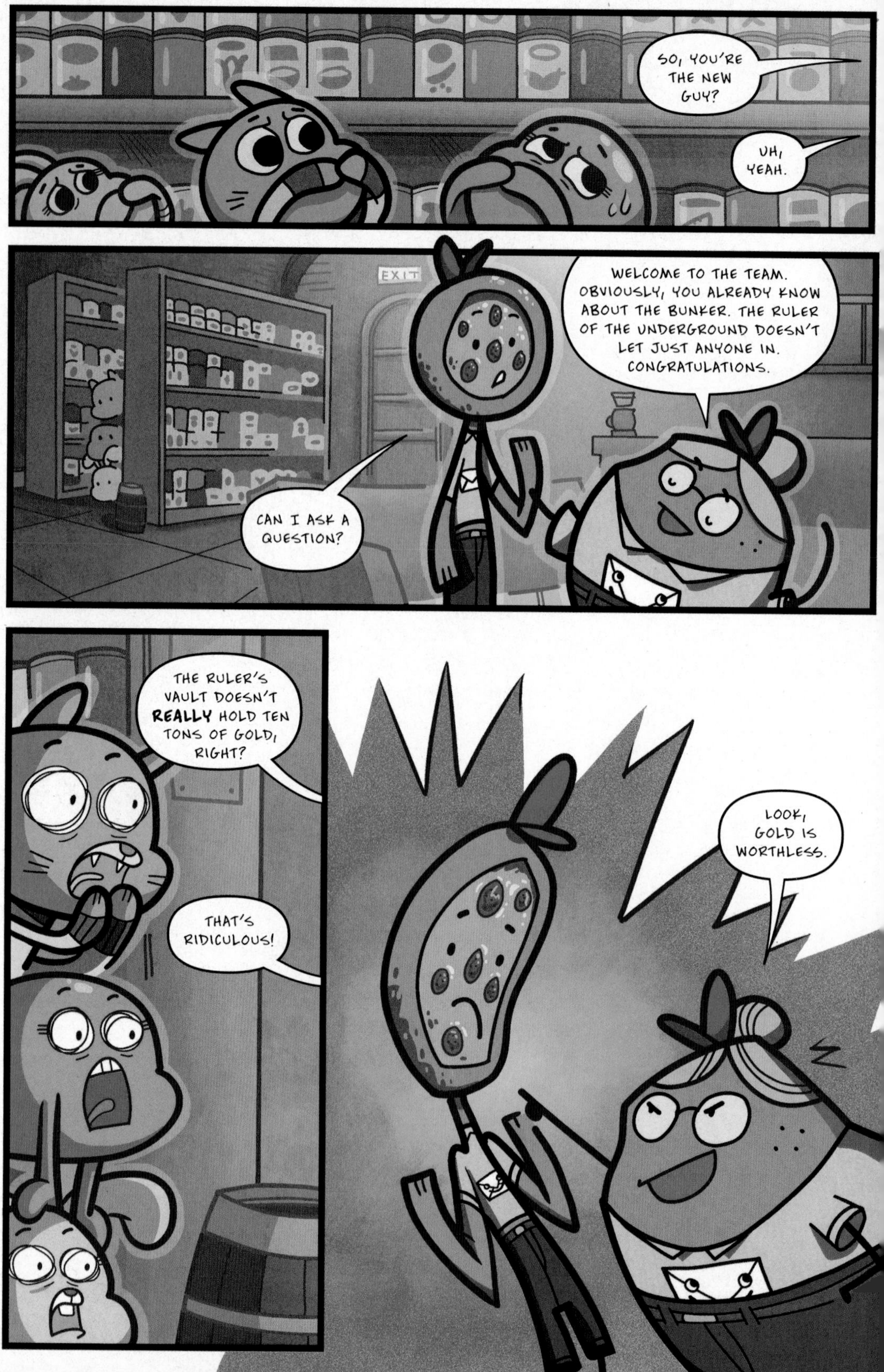
SO, YOU'RE THE NEW GUY?
UH, YEAH.
EXIT
WELCOME TO THE TEAM. OBVIOUSLY, YOU ALREADY KNOW ABOUT THE BUNKER. THE RULER OF THE UNDERGROUND DOESN'T LET JUST ANYONE IN. CONGRATULATIONS.
CAN I ASK A QUESTION?
THE RULER'S VAULT DOESN'T **REALLY** HOLD TEN TONS OF GOLD, RIGHT?
THAT'S RIDICULOUS!
LOOK, GOLD IS WORTHLESS.

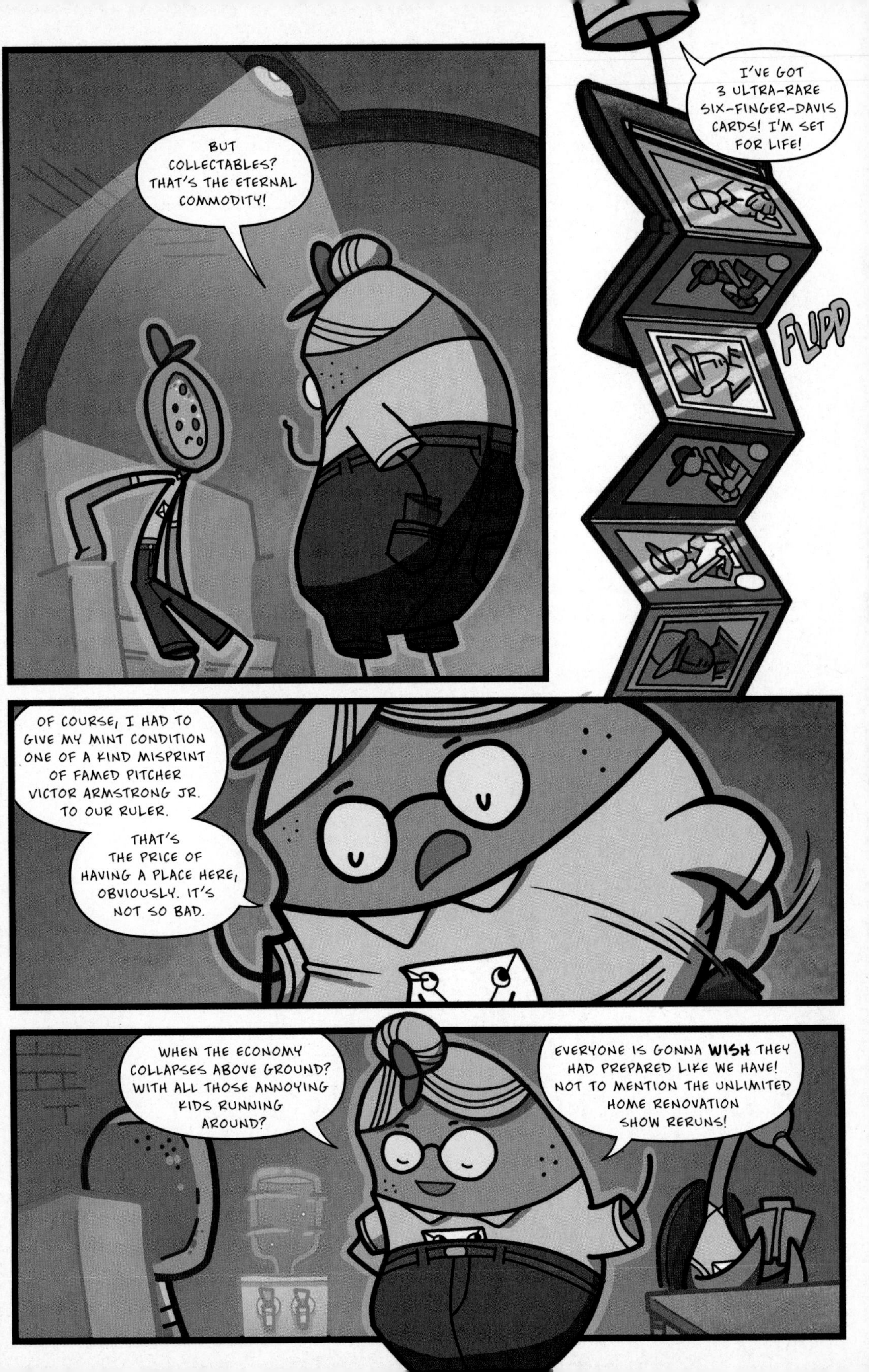
BUT COLLECTABLES? THAT'S THE ETERNAL COMMODITY!
I'VE GOT 3 ULTRA-RARE SIX-FINGER-DAVIS CARDS! I'M SET FOR LIFE!
FLIPP
OF COURSE, I HAD TO GIVE MY MINT CONDITION ONE OF A KIND MISPRINT OF FAMED PITCHER VICTOR ARMSTRONG JR. TO OUR RULER.
THAT'S THE PRICE OF HAVING A PLACE HERE, OBVIOUSLY. IT'S NOT SO BAD.
WHEN THE ECONOMY COLLAPSES ABOVE GROUND? WITH ALL THOSE ANNOYING KIDS RUNNING AROUND?
EVERYONE IS GONNA WISH THEY HAD PREPARED LIKE WE HAVE! NOT TO MENTION THE UNLIMITED HOME RENOVATION SHOW RERUNS!

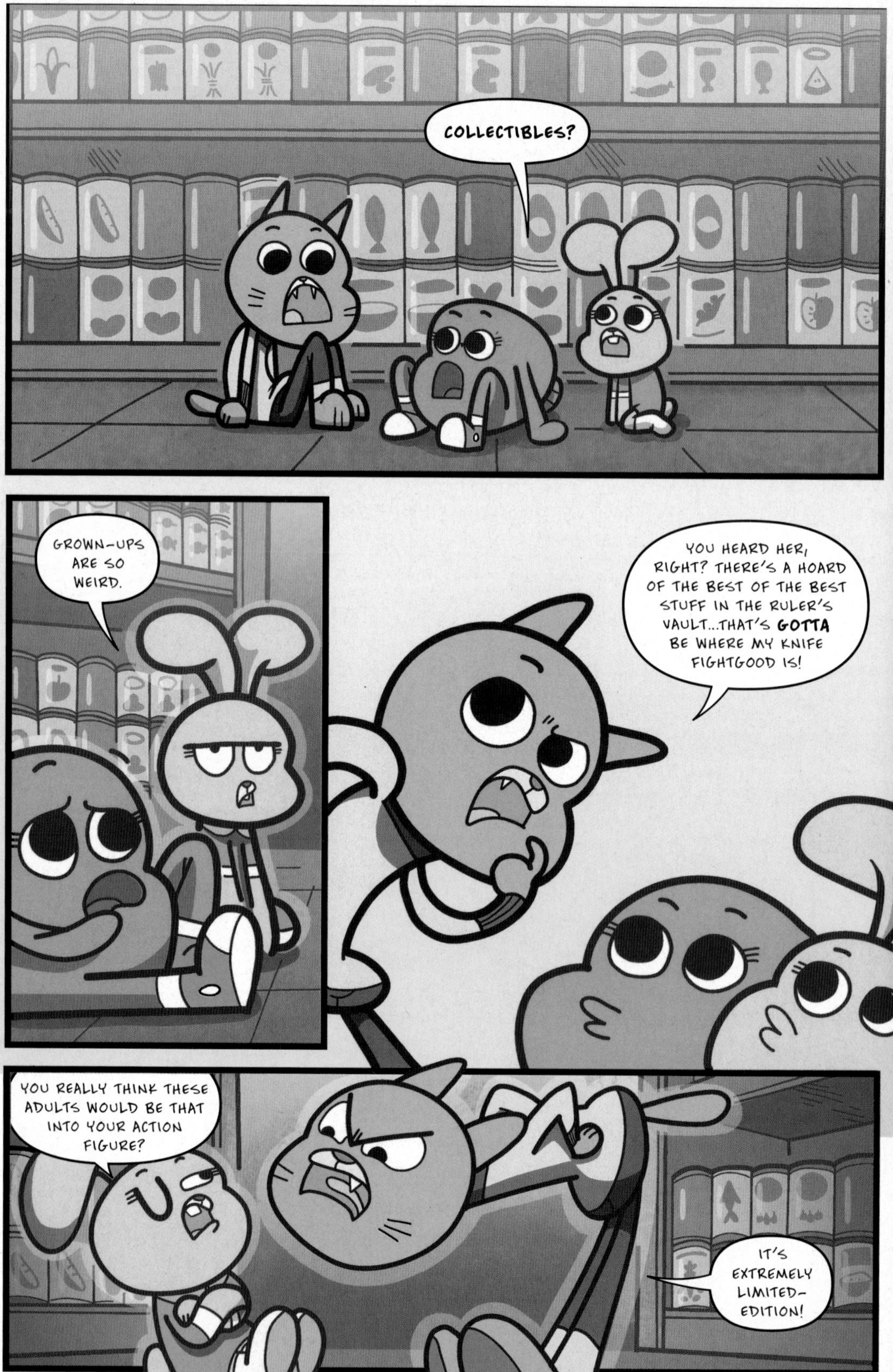
COLLECTIBLES?
GROWN-UPS ARE SO WEIRD.
YOU HEARD HER, RIGHT? THERE'S A HOARD OF THE BEST OF THE BEST STUFF IN THE RULER'S VAULT...THAT'S **GOTTA** BE WHERE MY KNIFE FIGHTGOOD IS!
YOU REALLY THINK THESE ADULTS WOULD BE THAT INTO YOUR ACTION FIGURE?
IT'S EXTREMELY LIMITED-EDITION!

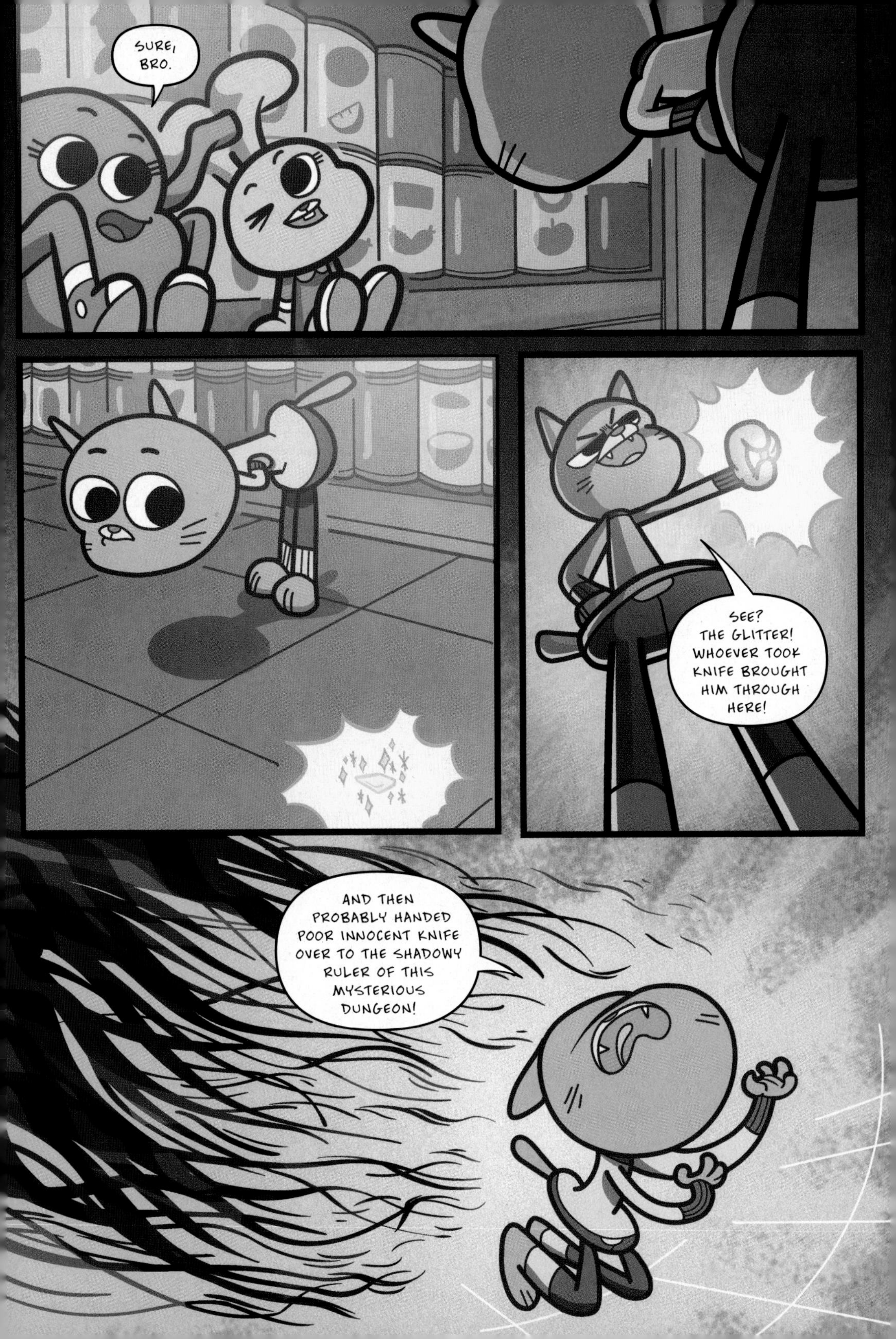
SURE, BRO.
SEE? THE GLITTER! WHOEVER TOOK KNIFE BROUGHT HIM THROUGH HERE!
AND THEN PROBABLY HANDED POOR INNOCENT KNIFE OVER TO THE SHADOWY RULER OF THIS MYSTERIOUS DUNGEON!

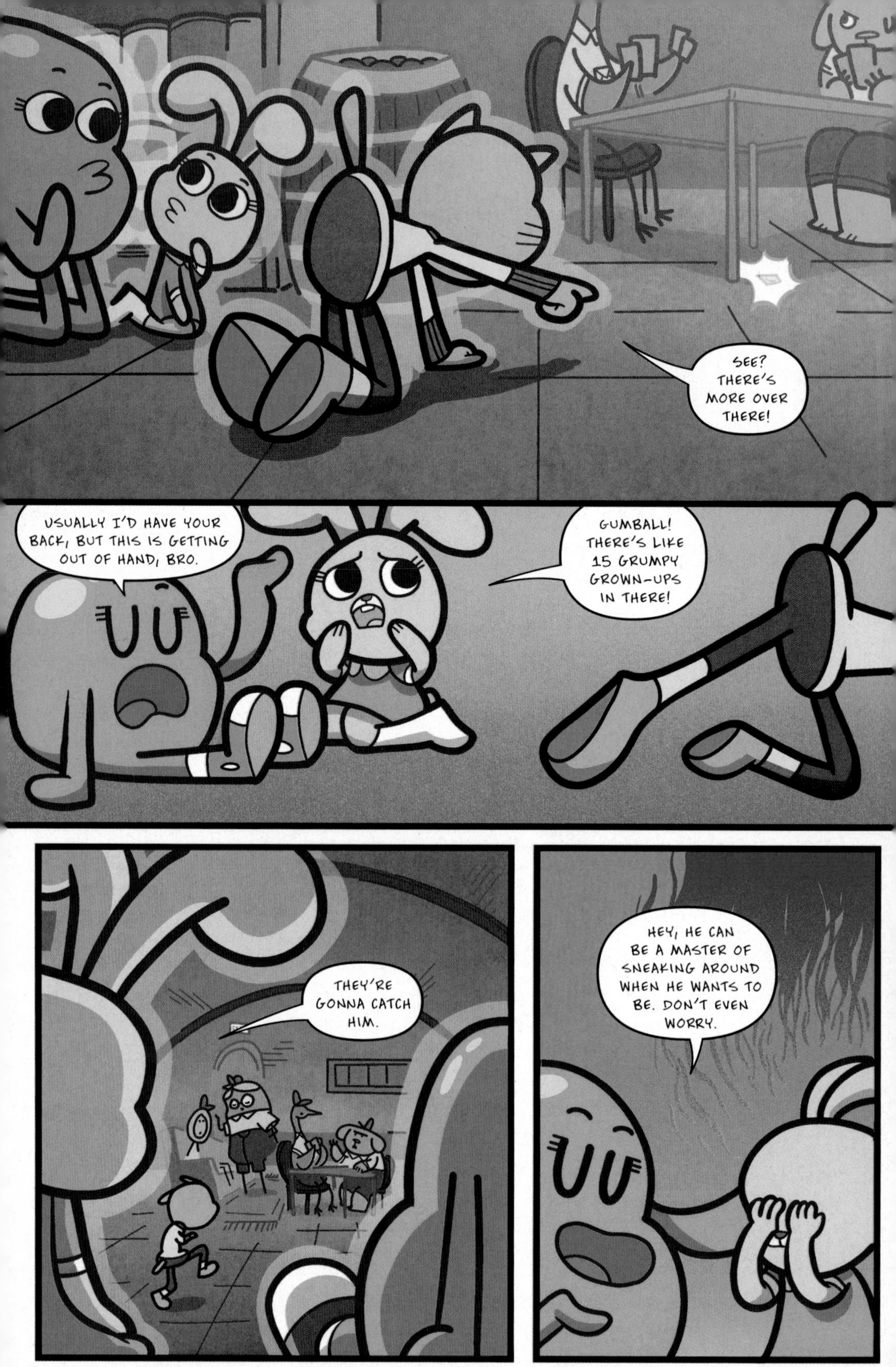
SEE? THERE'S MORE OVER THERE!
USUALLY I'D HAVE YOUR BACK, BUT THIS IS GETTING OUT OF HAND, BRO.
GUMBALL! THERE'S LIKE 15 GRUMPY GROWN-UPS IN THERE!
THEY'RE GONNA CATCH HIM.
HEY, HE CAN BE A MASTER OF SNEAKING AROUND WHEN HE WANTS TO BE. DON'T EVEN WORRY.

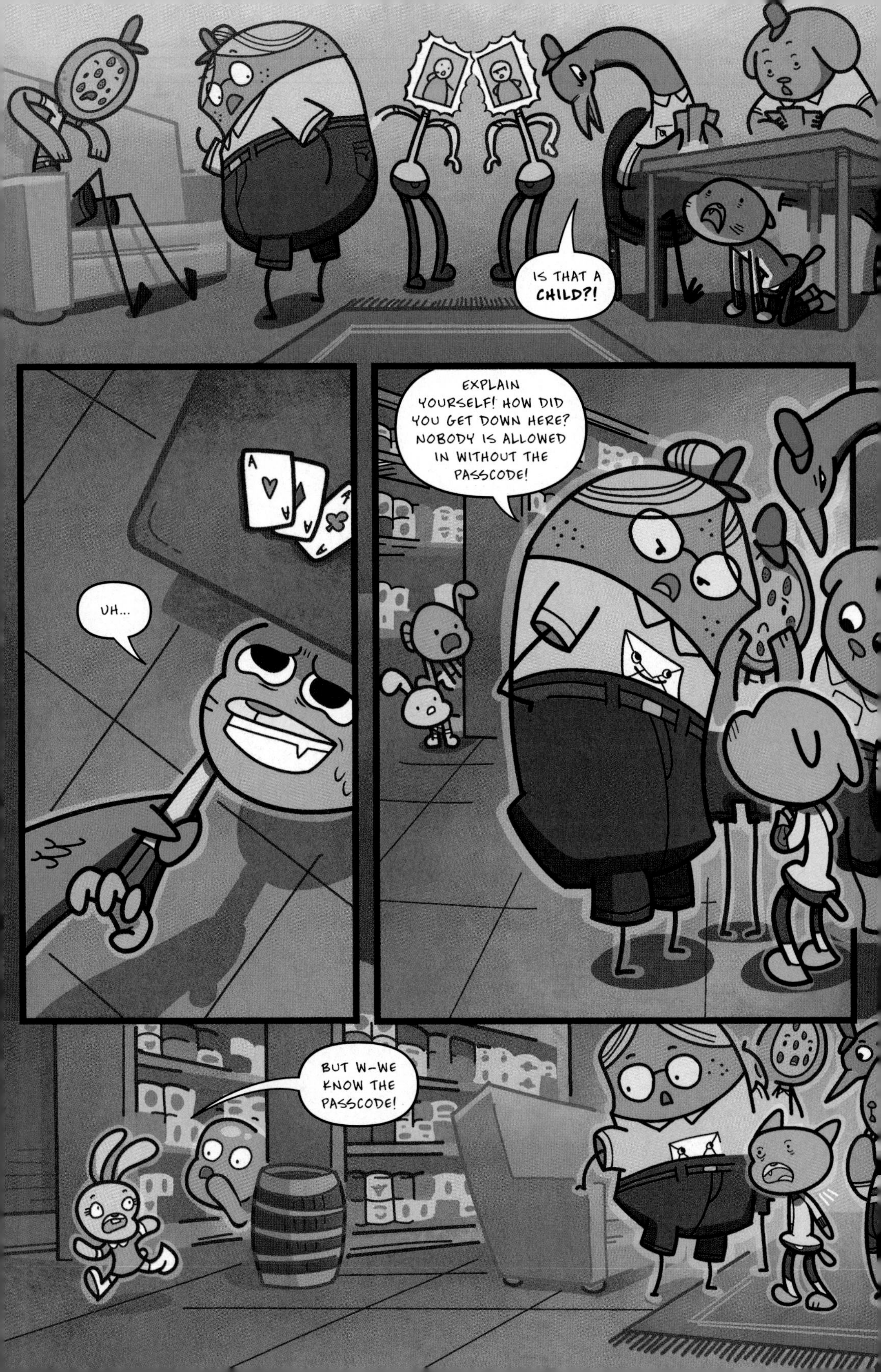

IS THAT A CHILD?!
UH...
EXPLAIN YOURSELF! HOW DID YOU GET DOWN HERE? NOBODY IS ALLOWED IN WITHOUT THE PASSCODE!
BUT W-WE KNOW THE PASSCODE!

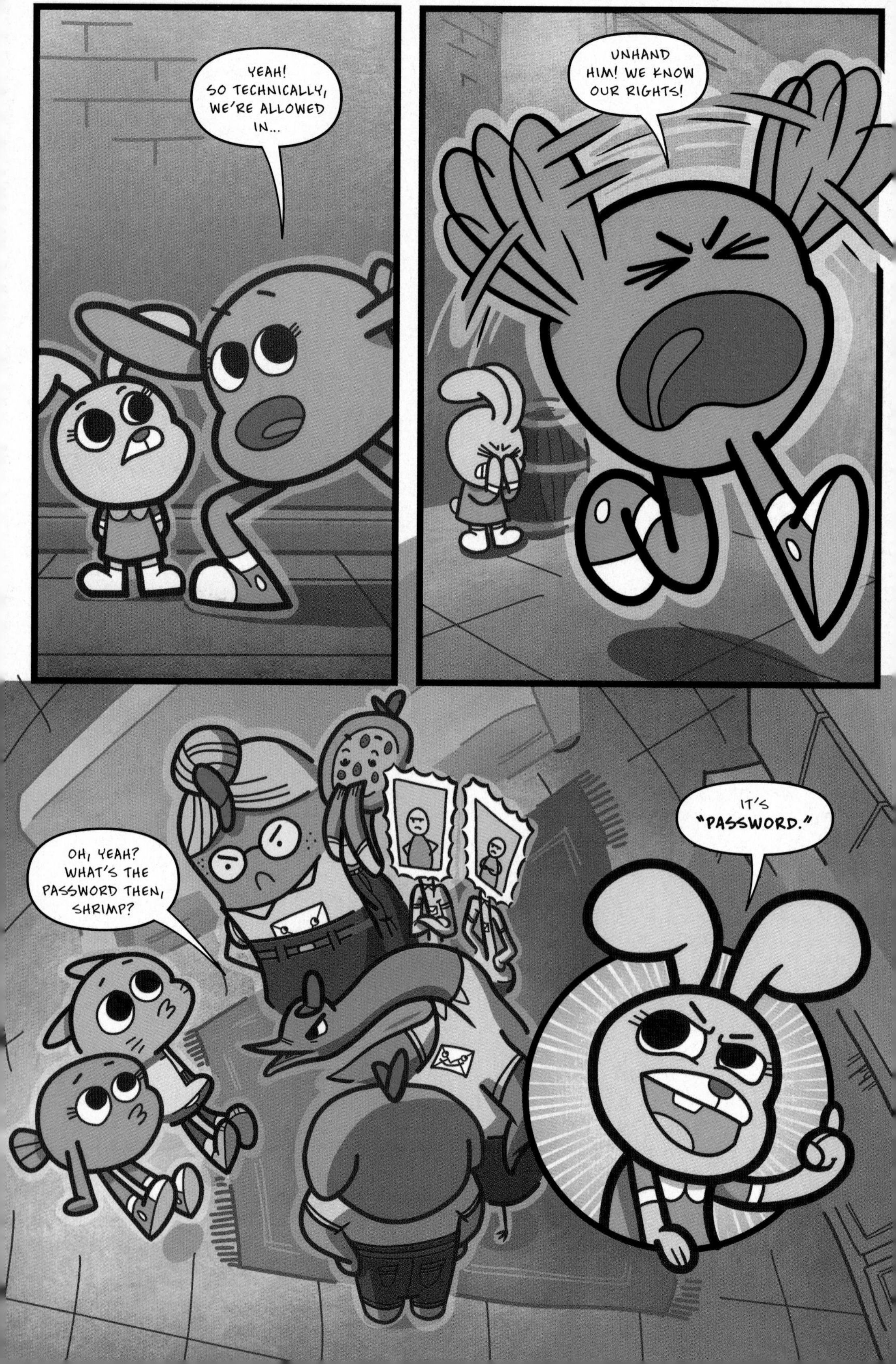
YEAH! SO TECHNICALLY, WE'RE ALLOWED IN...
UNHAND HIM! WE KNOW OUR RIGHTS!
OH, YEAH? WHAT'S THE PASSWORD THEN, SHRIMP?
IT'S "PASSWORD."

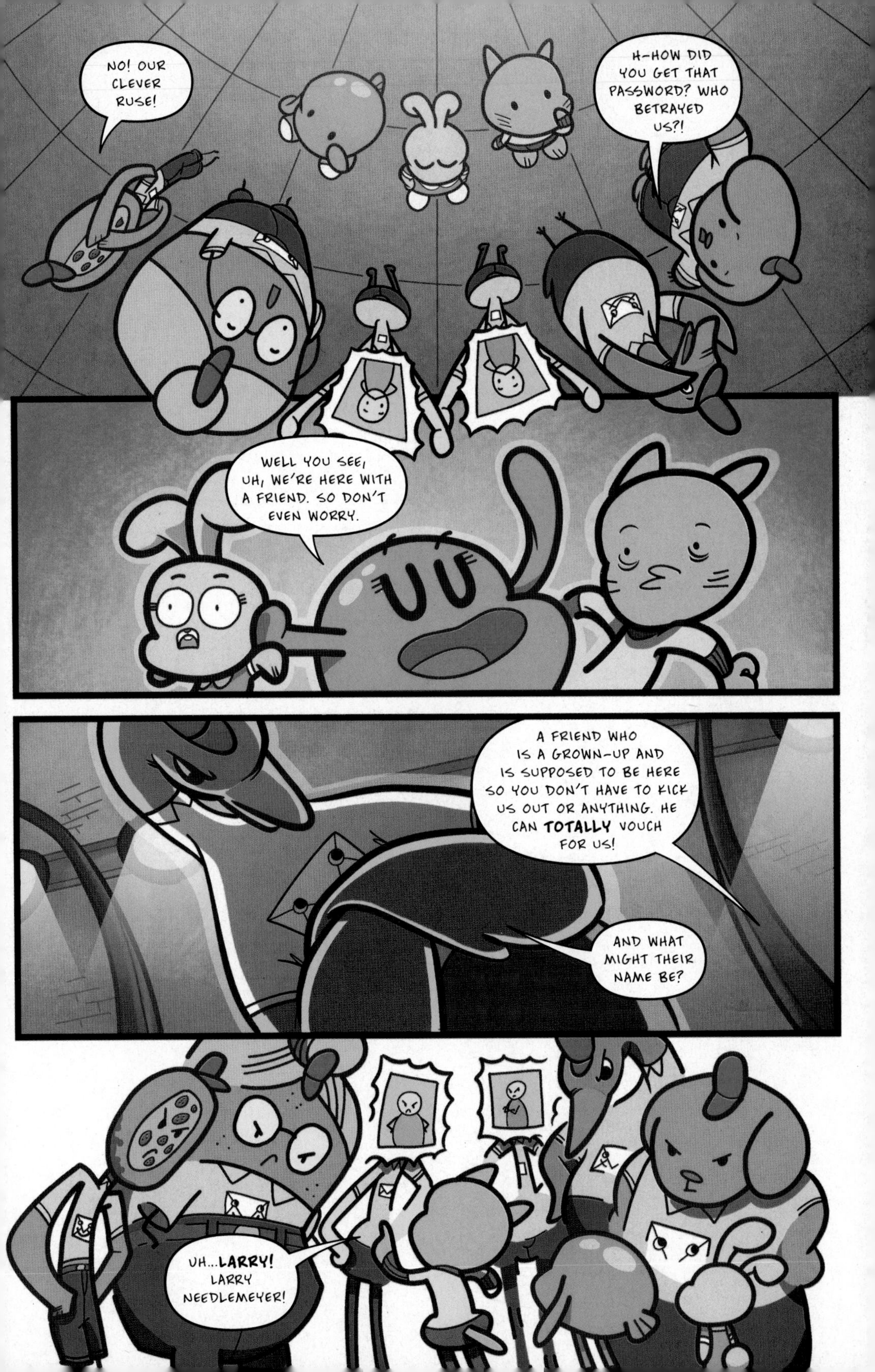
NO! OUR CLEVER RUSE!
H-HOW DID YOU GET THAT PASSWORD? WHO BETRAYED US?!
WELL YOU SEE, UH, WE'RE HERE WITH A FRIEND. SO DON'T EVEN WORRY.
A FRIEND WHO IS A GROWN-UP AND IS SUPPOSED TO BE HERE SO YOU DON'T HAVE TO KICK US OUT OR ANYTHING. HE CAN TOTALLY VOUCH FOR US!
AND WHAT MIGHT THEIR NAME BE?
UH...LARRY! LARRY NEEDLEMEYER!

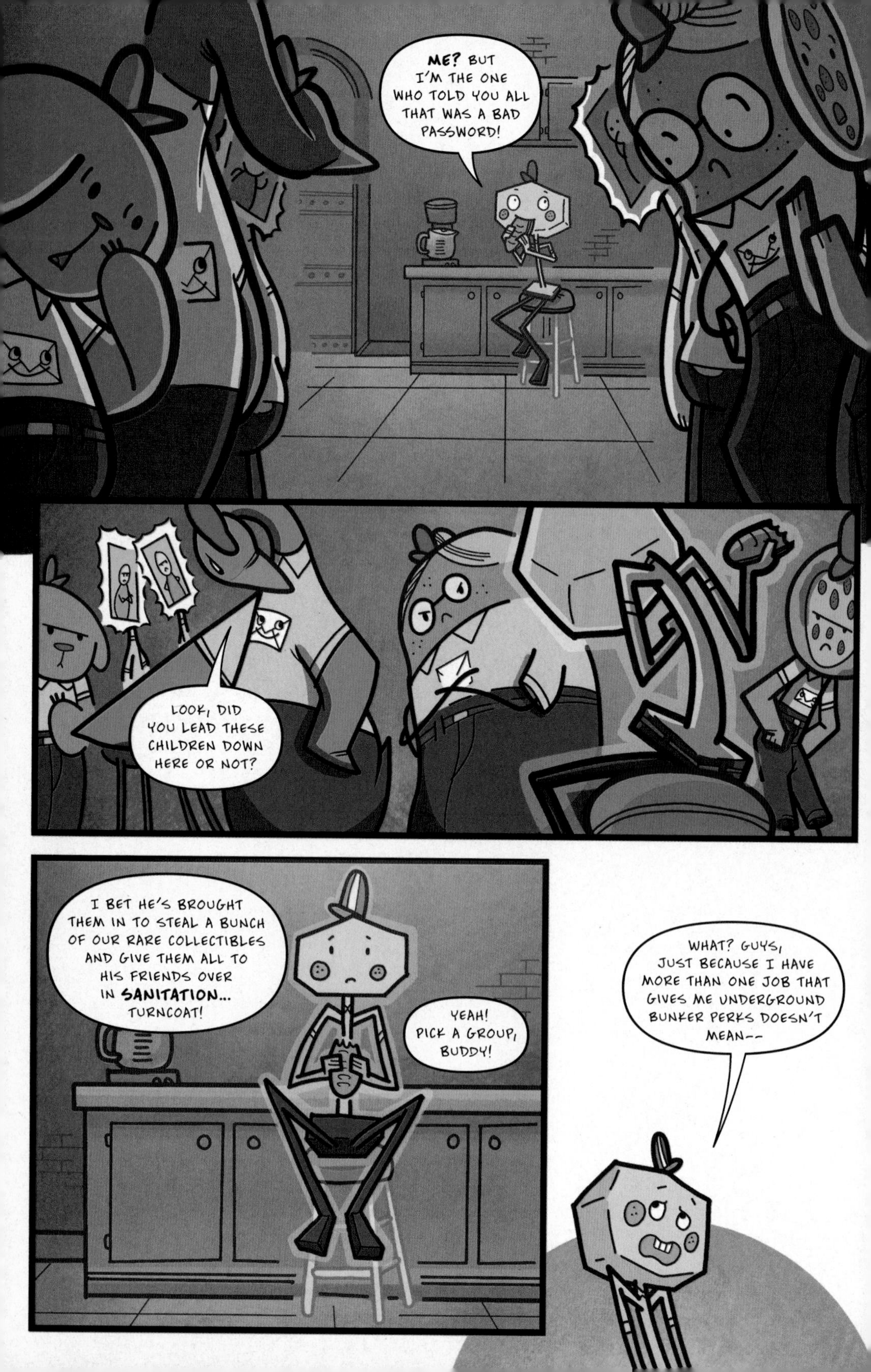
ME? BUT I'M THE ONE WHO TOLD YOU ALL THAT WAS A BAD PASSWORD!
LOOK, DID YOU LEAD THESE CHILDREN DOWN HERE OR NOT?
I BET HE'S BROUGHT THEM IN TO STEAL A BUNCH OF OUR RARE COLLECTIBLES AND GIVE THEM ALL TO HIS FRIENDS OVER IN SANITATION... TURNCOAT!
YEAH! PICK A GROUP, BUDDY!
WHAT? GUYS, JUST BECAUSE I HAVE MORE THAN ONE JOB THAT GIVES ME UNDERGROUND BUNKER PERKS DOESN'T MEAN--

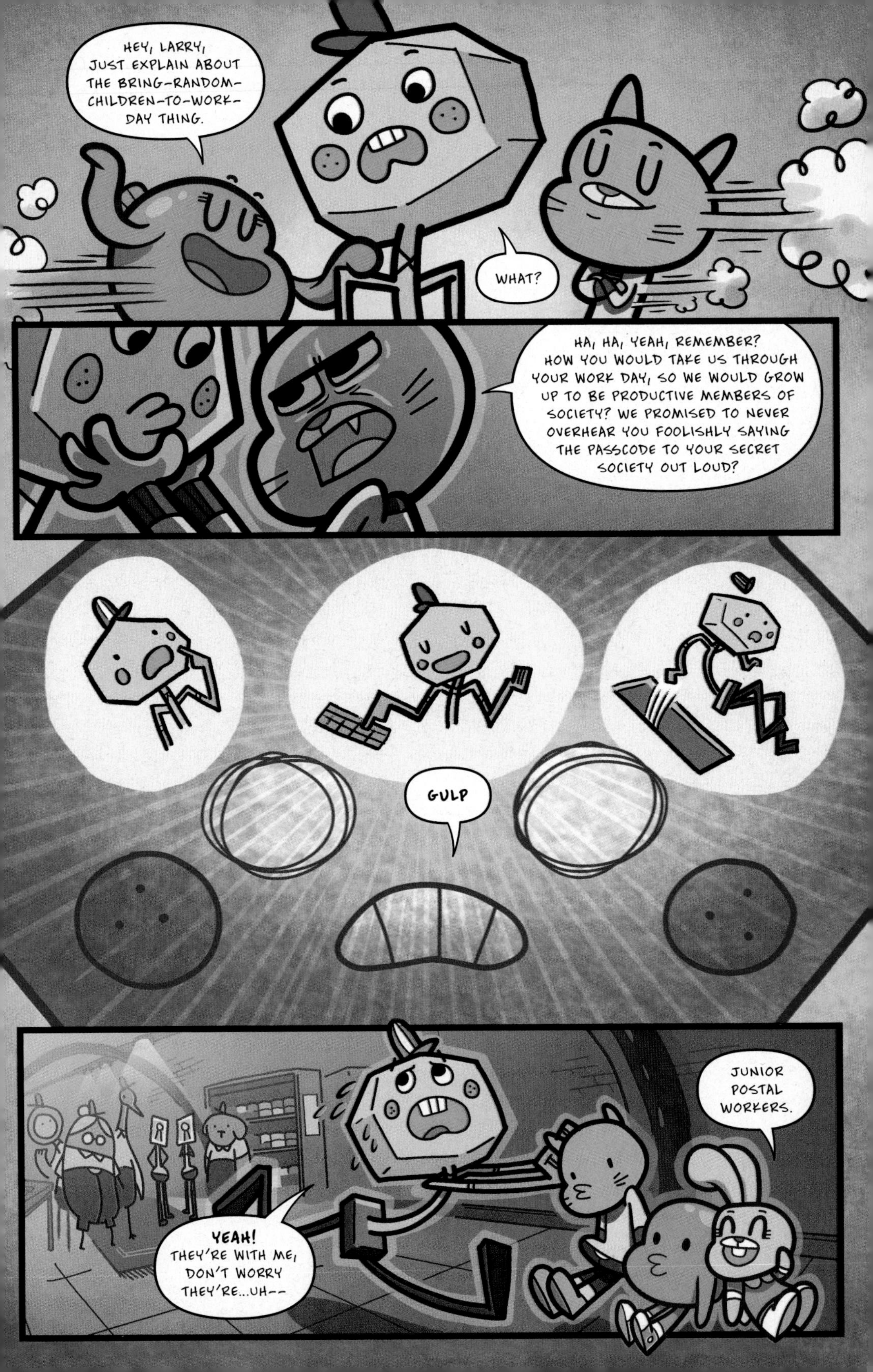
HEY, LARRY, JUST EXPLAIN ABOUT THE BRING-RANDOM-CHILDREN-TO-WORK-DAY THING.
WHAT?
HA, HA, YEAH, REMEMBER? HOW YOU WOULD TAKE US THROUGH YOUR WORK DAY, SO WE WOULD GROW UP TO BE PRODUCTIVE MEMBERS OF SOCIETY? WE PROMISED TO NEVER OVERHEAR YOU FOOLISHLY SAYING THE PASSCODE TO YOUR SECRET SOCIETY OUT LOUD?
GULP
YEAH! THEY'RE WITH ME, DON'T WORRY THEY'RE...UH--
JUNIOR POSTAL WORKERS.

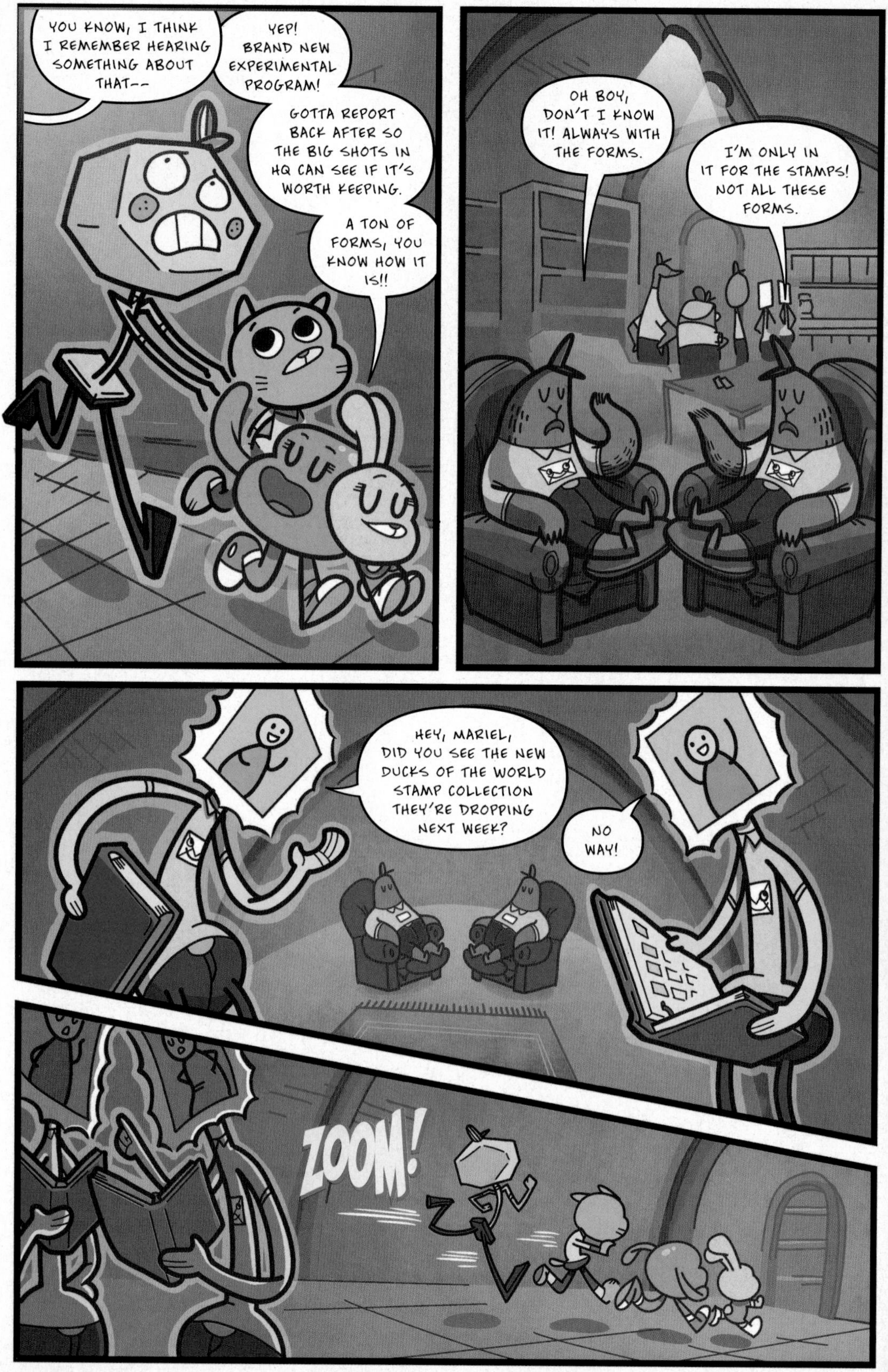

YOU KNOW, I THINK I REMEMBER HEARING SOMETHING ABOUT THAT--
YEP! BRAND NEW EXPERIMENTAL PROGRAM!
GOTTA REPORT BACK AFTER SO THE BIG SHOTS IN HQ CAN SEE IF IT'S WORTH KEEPING.
A TON OF FORMS, YOU KNOW HOW IT IS!!
OH BOY, DON'T I KNOW IT! ALWAYS WITH THE FORMS.
I'M ONLY IN IT FOR THE STAMPS! NOT ALL THESE FORMS.
HEY, MARIEL, DID YOU SEE THE NEW DUCKS OF THE WORLD STAMP COLLECTION THEY'RE DROPPING NEXT WEEK?
NO WAY!
ZOOM!

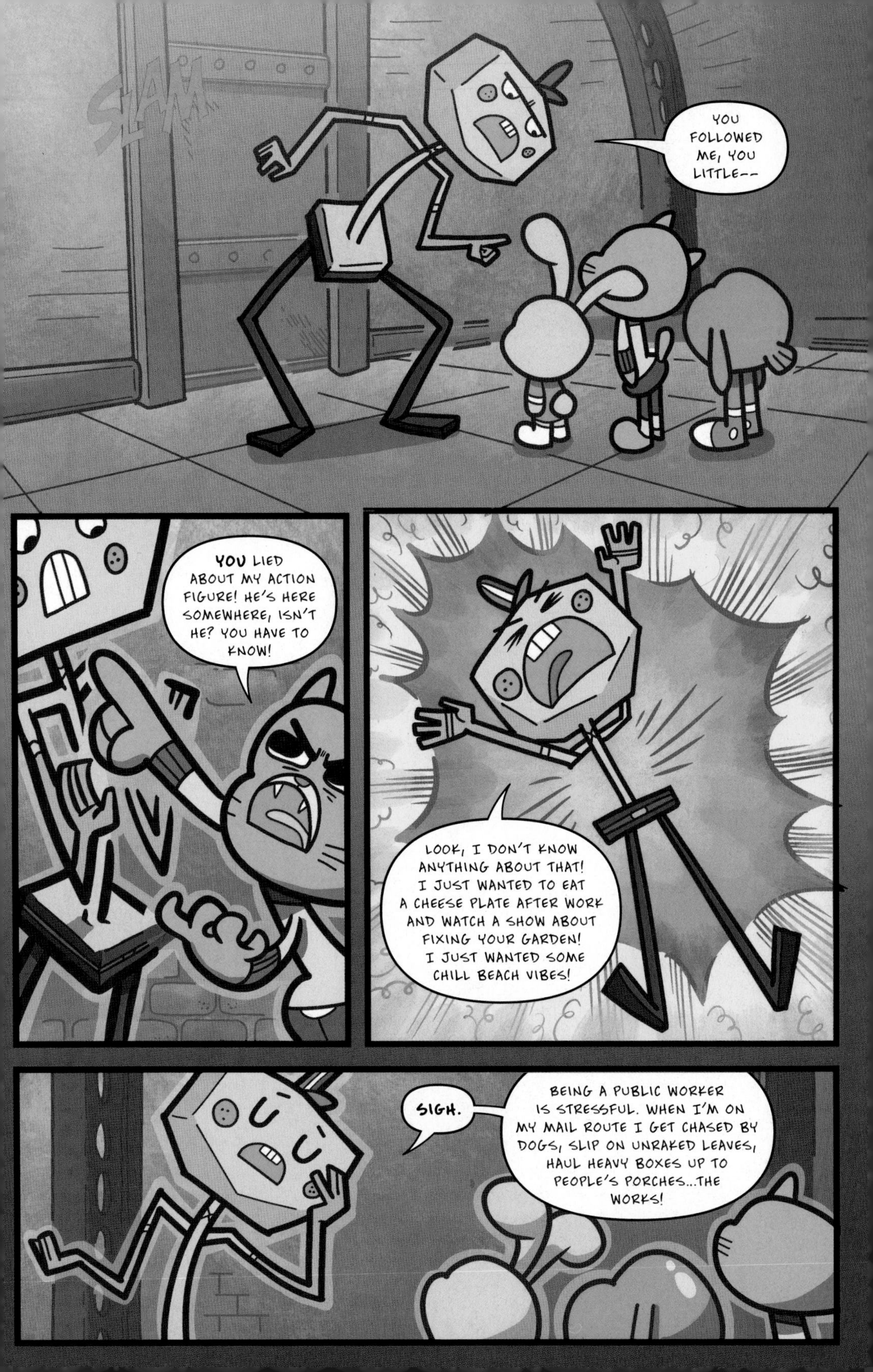
SLAM
YOU FOLLOWED ME, YOU LITTLE--
YOU LIED ABOUT MY ACTION FIGURE! HE'S HERE SOMEWHERE, ISN'T HE? YOU HAVE TO KNOW!
LOOK, I DON'T KNOW ANYTHING ABOUT THAT! I JUST WANTED TO EAT A CHEESE PLATE AFTER WORK AND WATCH A SHOW ABOUT FIXING YOUR GARDEN! I JUST WANTED SOME CHILL BEACH VIBES!
SIGH.
BEING A PUBLIC WORKER IS STRESSFUL. WHEN I'M ON MY MAIL ROUTE I GET CHASED BY DOGS, SLIP ON UNRAKED LEAVES, HAUL HEAVY BOXES UP TO PEOPLE'S PORCHES...THE WORKS!

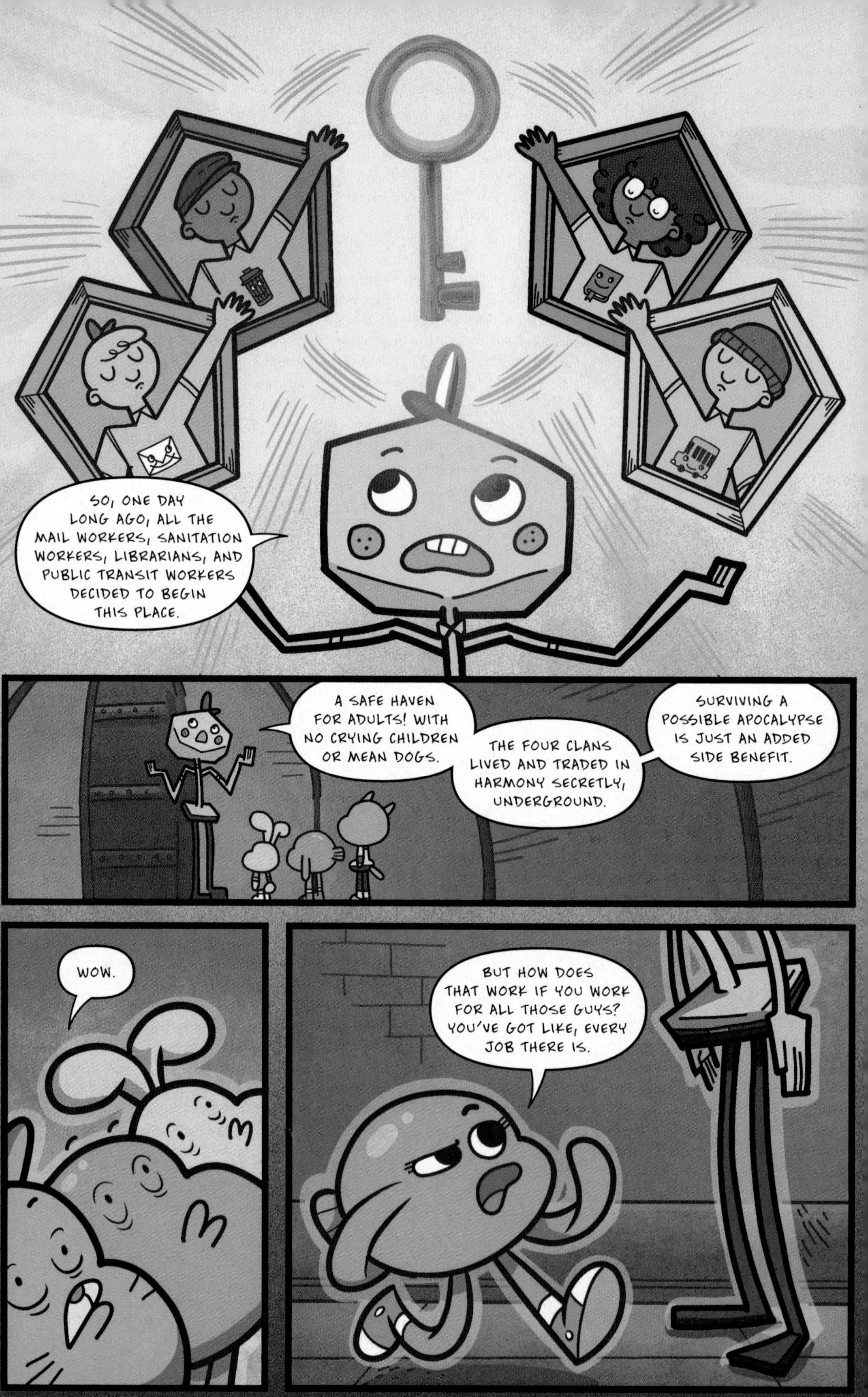
SO, ONE DAY LONG AGO, ALL THE MAIL WORKERS, SANITATION WORKERS, LIBRARIANS, AND PUBLIC TRANSIT WORKERS DECIDED TO BEGIN THIS PLACE.
A SAFE HAVEN FOR ADULTS! WITH NO CRYING CHILDREN OR MEAN DOGS.
THE FOUR CLANS LIVED AND TRADED IN HARMONY SECRETLY, UNDERGROUND.
SURVIVING A POSSIBLE APOCALYPSE IS JUST AN ADDED SIDE BENEFIT.
WOW.
BUT HOW DOES THAT WORK IF YOU WORK FOR ALL THOSE GUYS? YOU'VE GOT LIKE, EVERY JOB THERE IS.

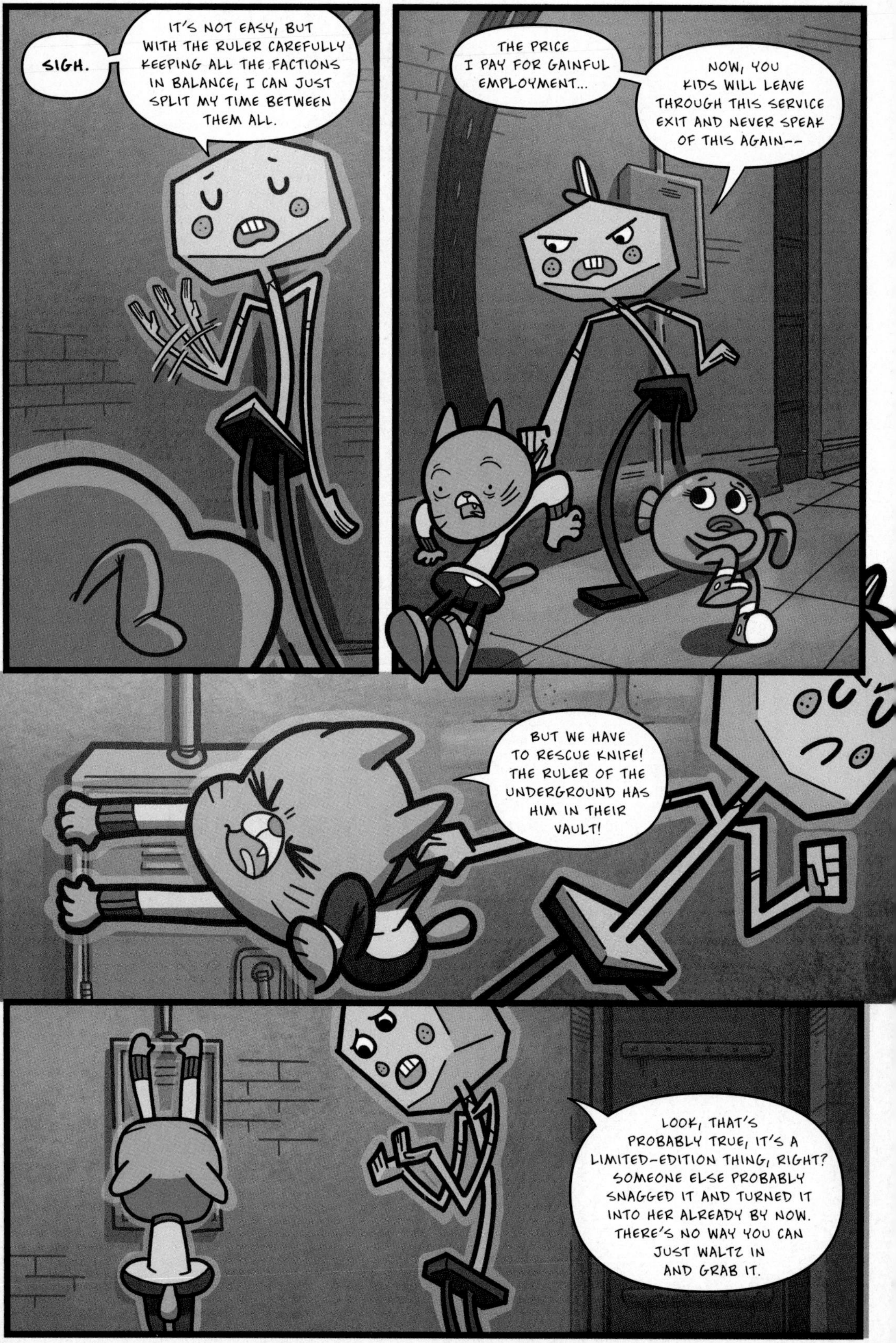
SIGH.
IT'S NOT EASY, BUT WITH THE RULER CAREFULLY KEEPING ALL THE FACTIONS IN BALANCE, I CAN JUST SPLIT MY TIME BETWEEN THEM ALL.
THE PRICE I PAY FOR GAINFUL EMPLOYMENT...
NOW, YOU KIDS WILL LEAVE THROUGH THIS SERVICE EXIT AND NEVER SPEAK OF THIS AGAIN--
BUT WE HAVE TO RESCUE KNIFE! THE RULER OF THE UNDERGROUND HAS HIM IN THEIR VAULT!
LOOK, THAT'S PROBABLY TRUE, IT'S A LIMITED-EDITION THING, RIGHT? SOMEONE ELSE PROBABLY SNAGGED IT AND TURNED IT INTO HER ALREADY BY NOW. THERE'S NO WAY YOU CAN JUST WALTZ IN AND GRAB IT.

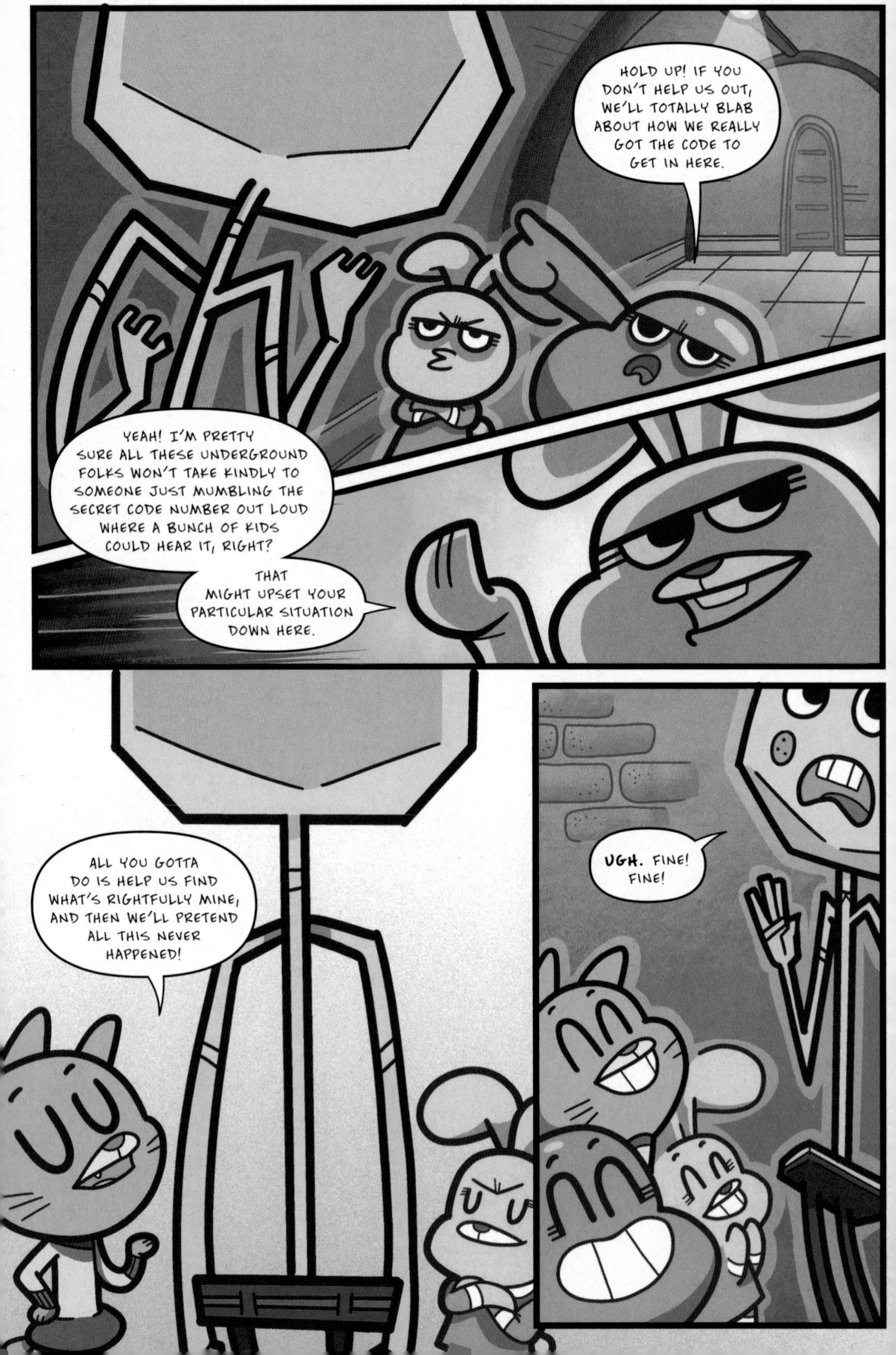
HOLD UP! IF YOU DON'T HELP US OUT, WE'LL TOTALLY BLAB ABOUT HOW WE REALLY GOT THE CODE TO GET IN HERE.
YEAH! I'M PRETTY SURE ALL THESE UNDERGROUND FOLKS WON'T TAKE KINDLY TO SOMEONE JUST MUMBLING THE SECRET CODE NUMBER OUT LOUD WHERE A BUNCH OF KIDS COULD HEAR IT, RIGHT?
THAT MIGHT UPSET YOUR PARTICULAR SITUATION DOWN HERE.
ALL YOU GOTTA DO IS HELP US FIND WHAT'S RIGHTFULLY MINE, AND THEN WE'LL PRETEND ALL THIS NEVER HAPPENED!
UGH. FINE! FINE!

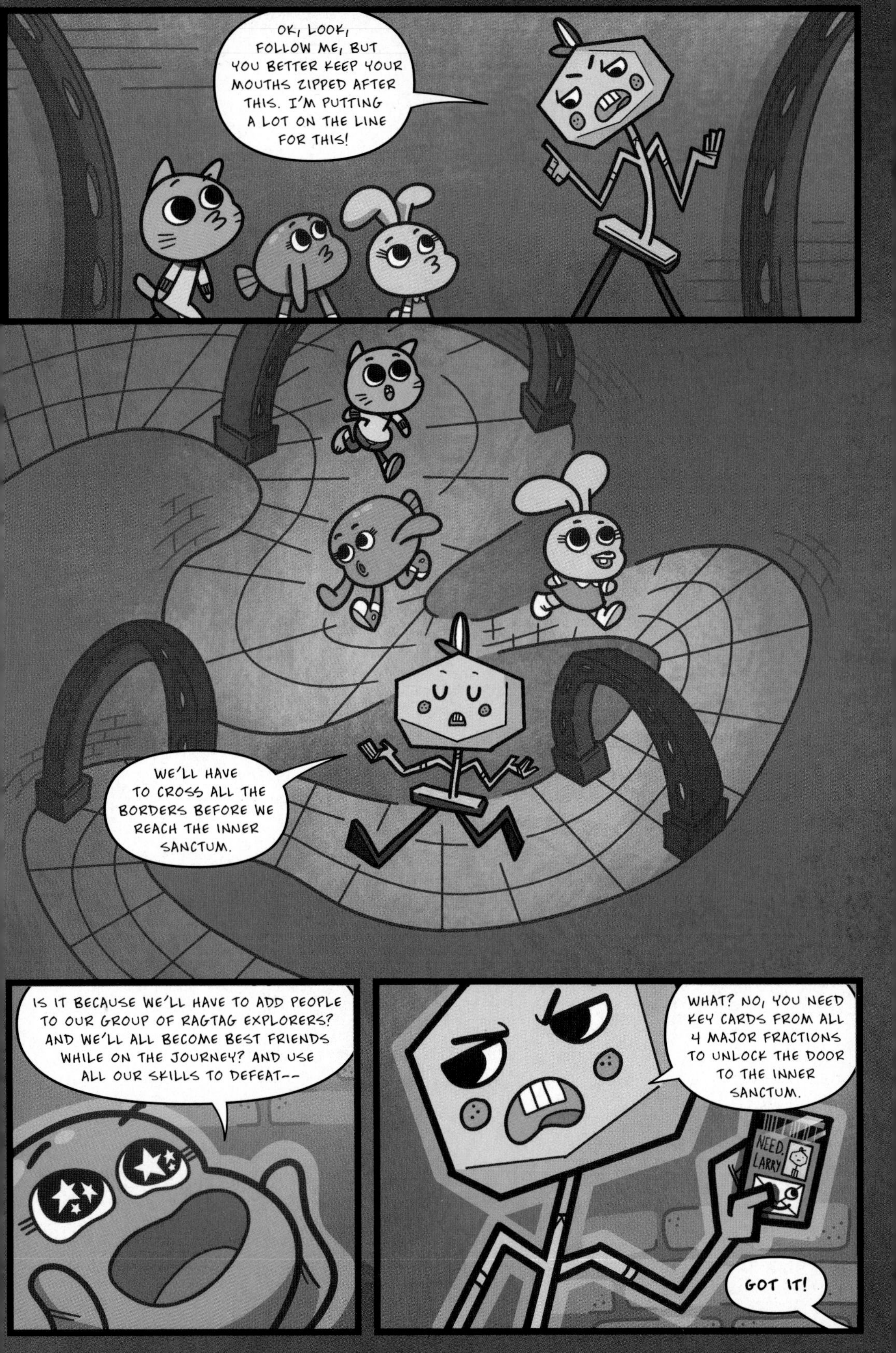
OK, LOOK, FOLLOW ME, BUT YOU BETTER KEEP YOUR MOUTHS ZIPPED AFTER THIS. I'M PUTTING A LOT ON THE LINE FOR THIS!
WE'LL HAVE TO CROSS ALL THE BORDERS BEFORE WE REACH THE INNER SANCTUM.
IS IT BECAUSE WE'LL HAVE TO ADD PEOPLE TO OUR GROUP OF RAGTAG EXPLORERS? AND WE'LL ALL BECOME BEST FRIENDS WHILE ON THE JOURNEY? AND USE ALL OUR SKILLS TO DEFEAT--
WHAT? NO, YOU NEED KEY CARDS FROM ALL 4 MAJOR FRACTIONS TO UNLOCK THE DOOR TO THE INNER SANCTUM.
NEED. LARRY
GOT IT!

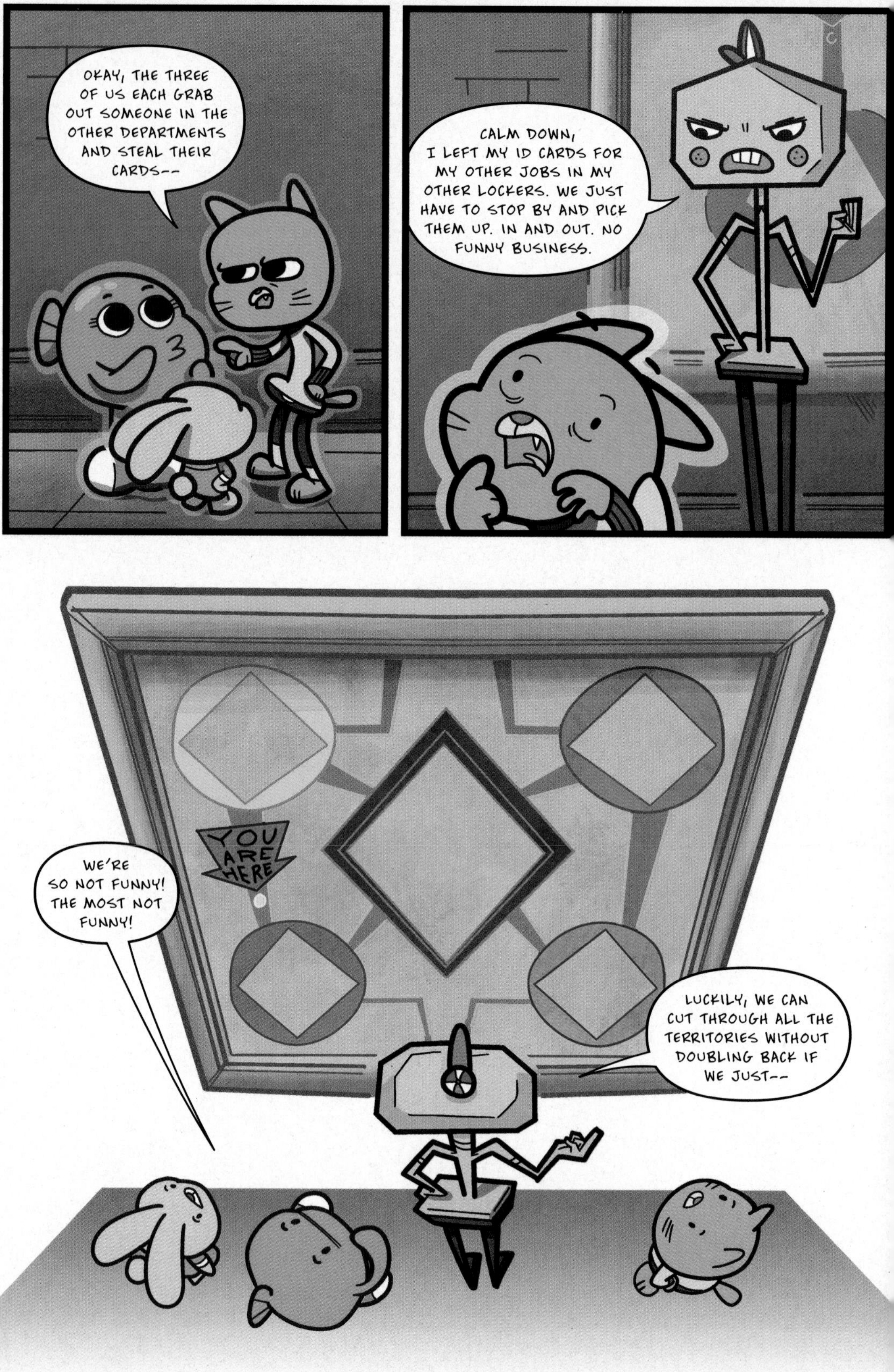
OKAY, THE THREE OF US EACH GRAB OUT SOMEONE IN THE OTHER DEPARTMENTS AND STEAL THEIR CARDS--
CALM DOWN, I LEFT MY ID CARDS FOR MY OTHER JOBS IN MY OTHER LOCKERS. WE JUST HAVE TO STOP BY AND PICK THEM UP. IN AND OUT. NO FUNNY BUSINESS.
YOU ARE HERE
WE'RE SO NOT FUNNY! THE MOST NOT FUNNY!
LUCKILY, WE CAN CUT THROUGH ALL THE TERRITORIES WITHOUT DOUBLING BACK IF WE JUST--

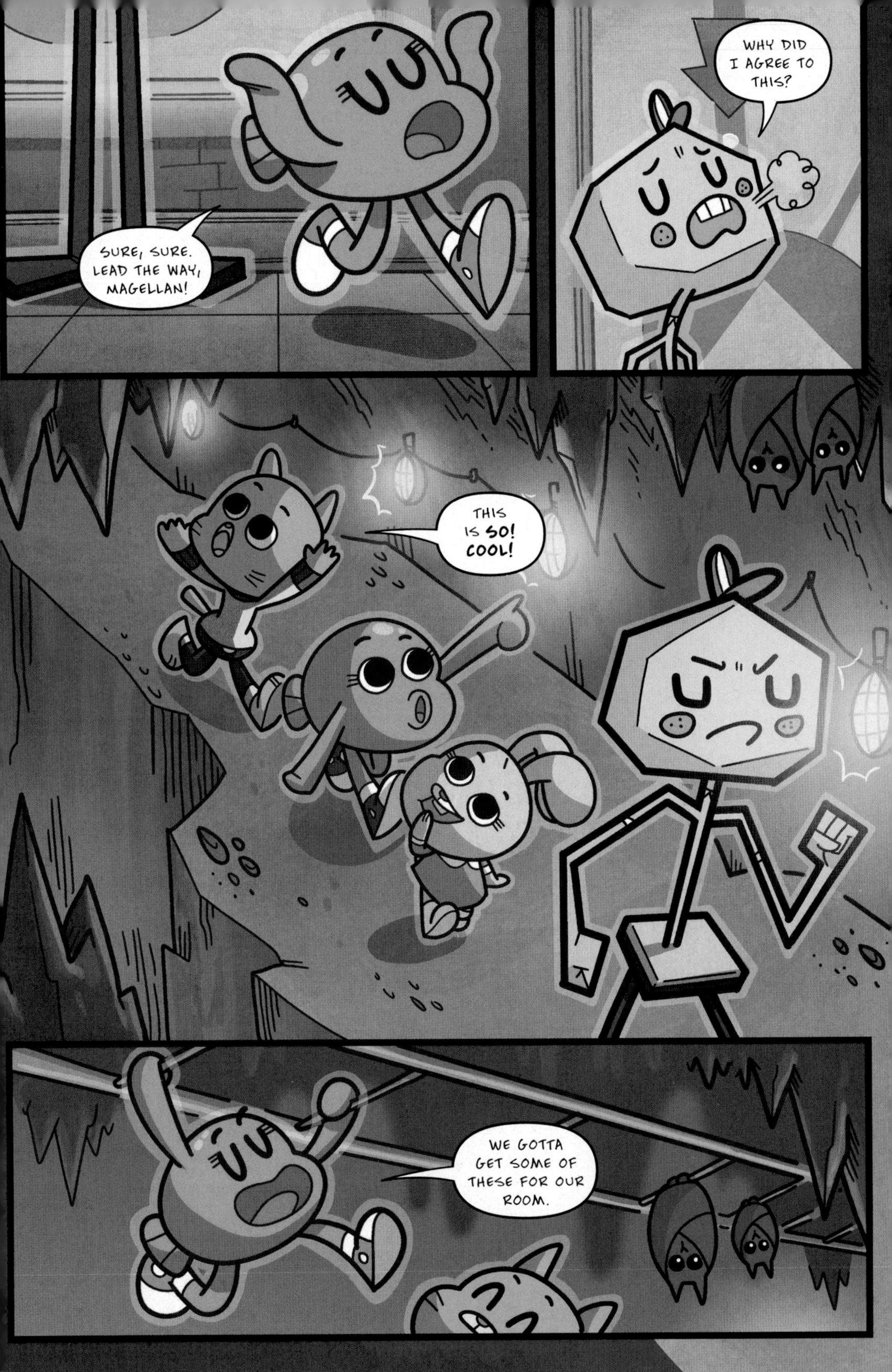
SURE, SURE. LEAD THE WAY, MAGELLAN!
WHY DID I AGREE TO THIS?
THIS IS SO! COOL!
WE GOTTA GET SOME OF THESE FOR OUR ROOM.

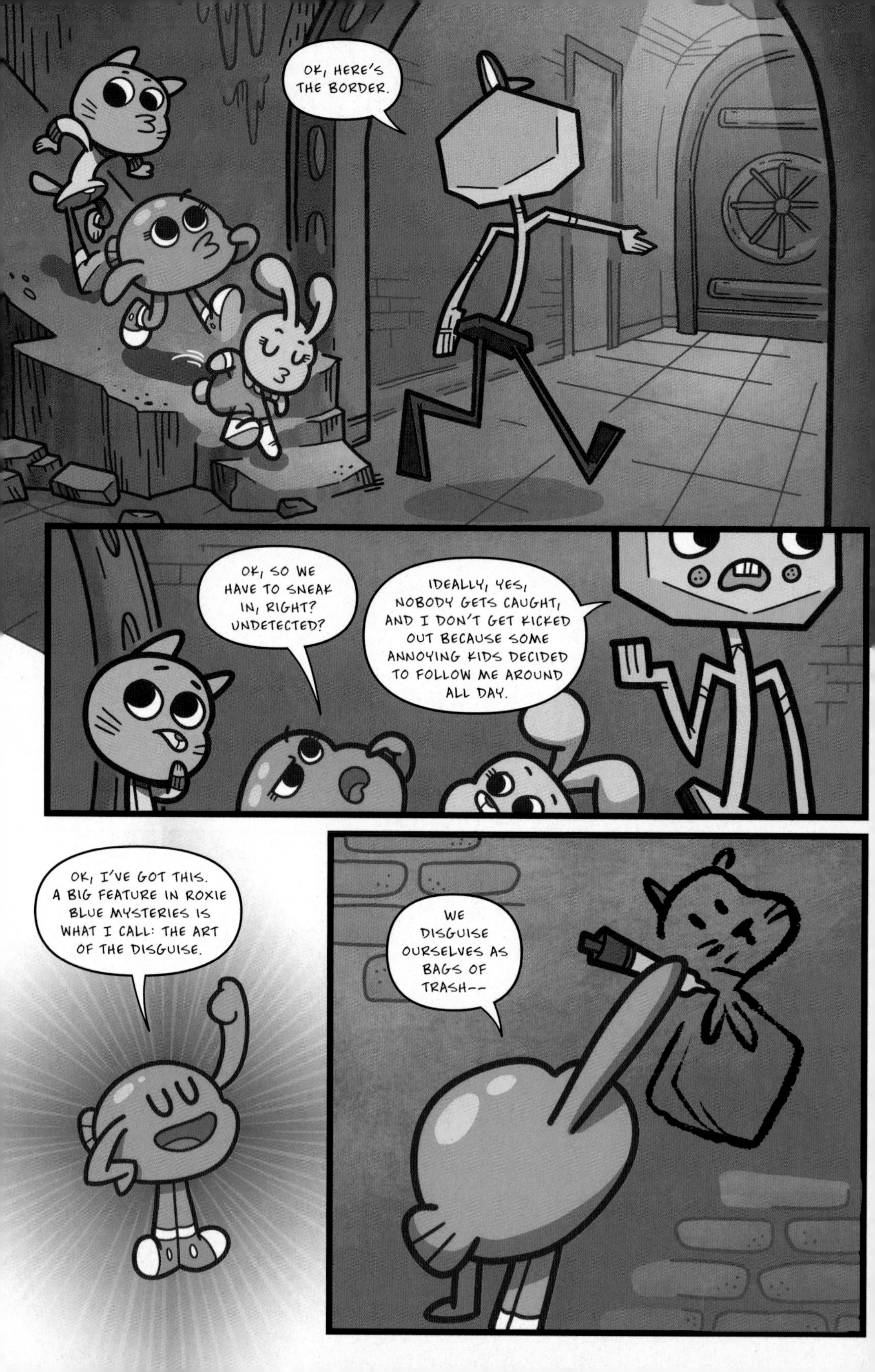

OK, HERE'S THE BORDER.
OK, SO WE HAVE TO SNEAK IN, RIGHT? UNDETECTED?
IDEALLY, YES, NOBODY GETS CAUGHT, AND I DON'T GET KICKED OUT BECAUSE SOME ANNOYING KIDS DECIDED TO FOLLOW ME AROUND ALL DAY.
OK, I'VE GOT THIS. A BIG FEATURE IN ROXIE BLUE MYSTERIES IS WHAT I CALL: THE ART OF THE DISGUISE.
WE DISGUISE OURSELVES AS BAGS OF TRASH--

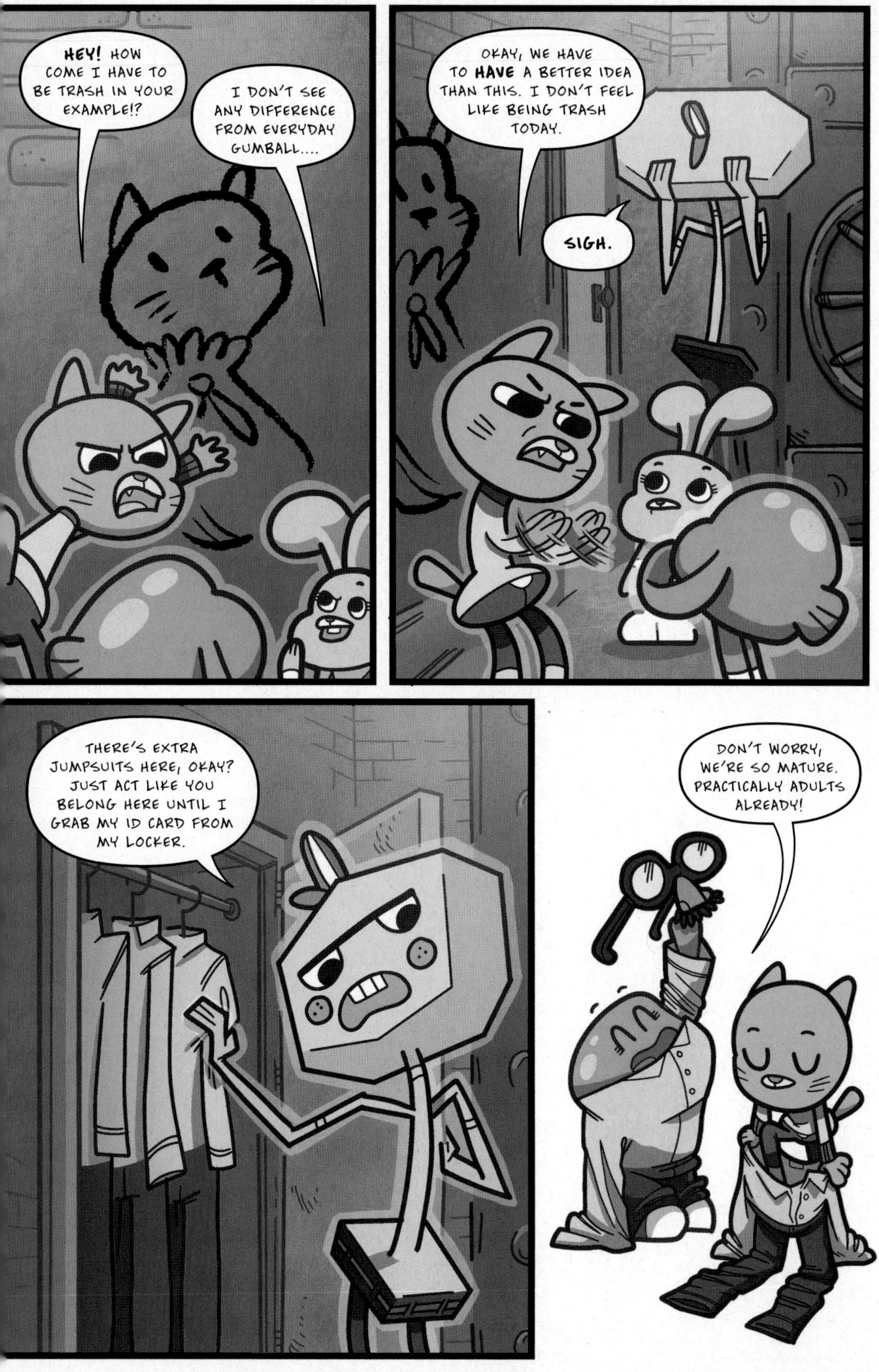
HEY! HOW COME I HAVE TO BE TRASH IN YOUR EXAMPLE!?
I DON'T SEE ANY DIFFERENCE FROM EVERYDAY GUMBALL....
OKAY, WE HAVE TO HAVE A BETTER IDEA THAN THIS. I DON'T FEEL LIKE BEING TRASH TODAY.
SIGH.
THERE'S EXTRA JUMPSUITS HERE, OKAY? JUST ACT LIKE YOU BELONG HERE UNTIL I GRAB MY ID CARD FROM MY LOCKER.
DON'T WORRY, WE'RE SO MATURE. PRACTICALLY ADULTS ALREADY!

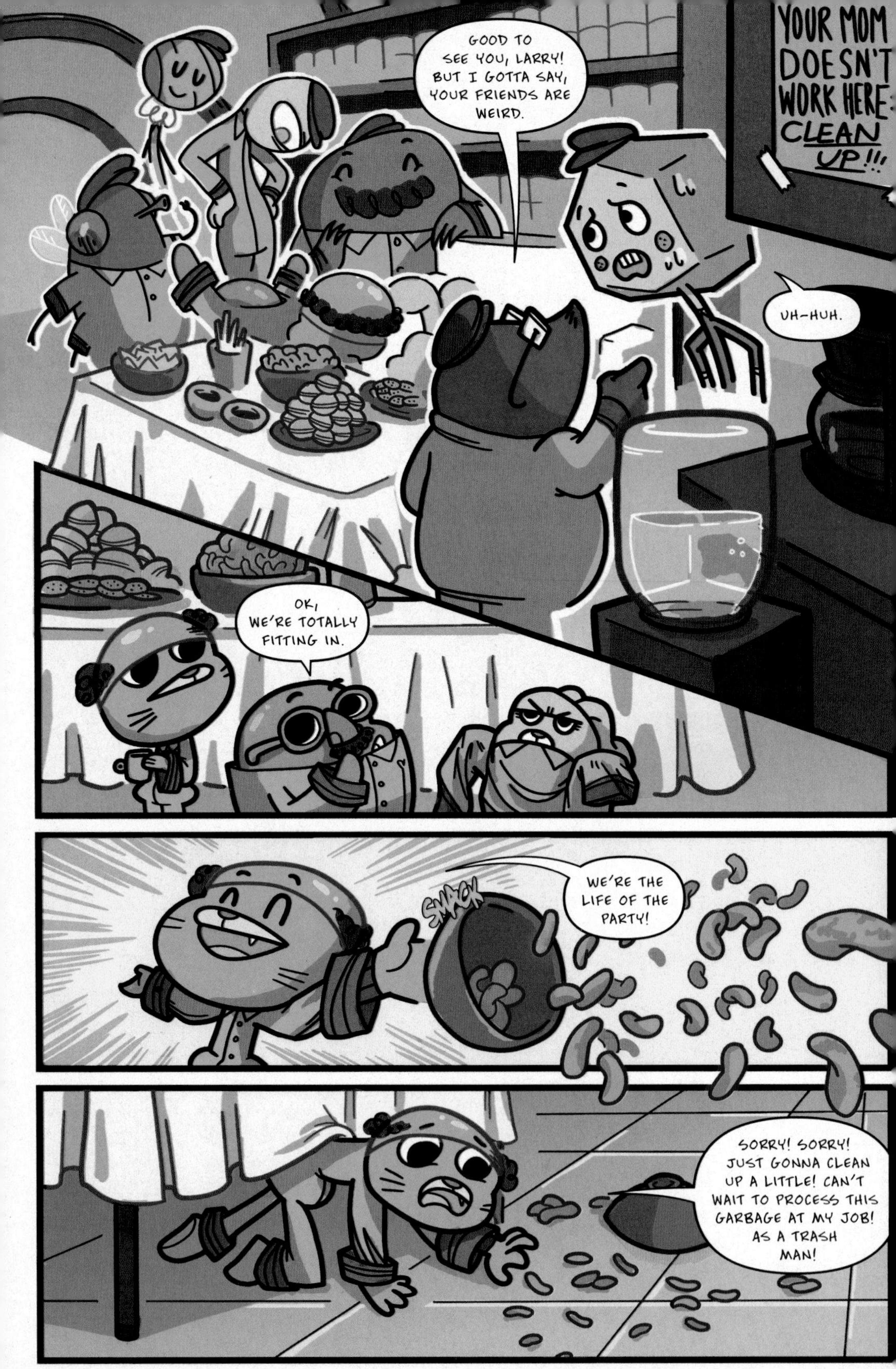
YOUR MOM DOESN'T WORK HERE: CLEAN UP!!!
GOOD TO SEE YOU, LARRY! BUT I GOTTA SAY, YOUR FRIENDS ARE WEIRD.
UH-HUH.
OK, WE'RE TOTALLY FITTING IN.
SMACK
WE'RE THE LIFE OF THE PARTY!
SORRY! SORRY! JUST GONNA CLEAN UP A LITTLE! CAN'T WAIT TO PROCESS THIS GARBAGE AT MY JOB! AS A TRASH MAN!

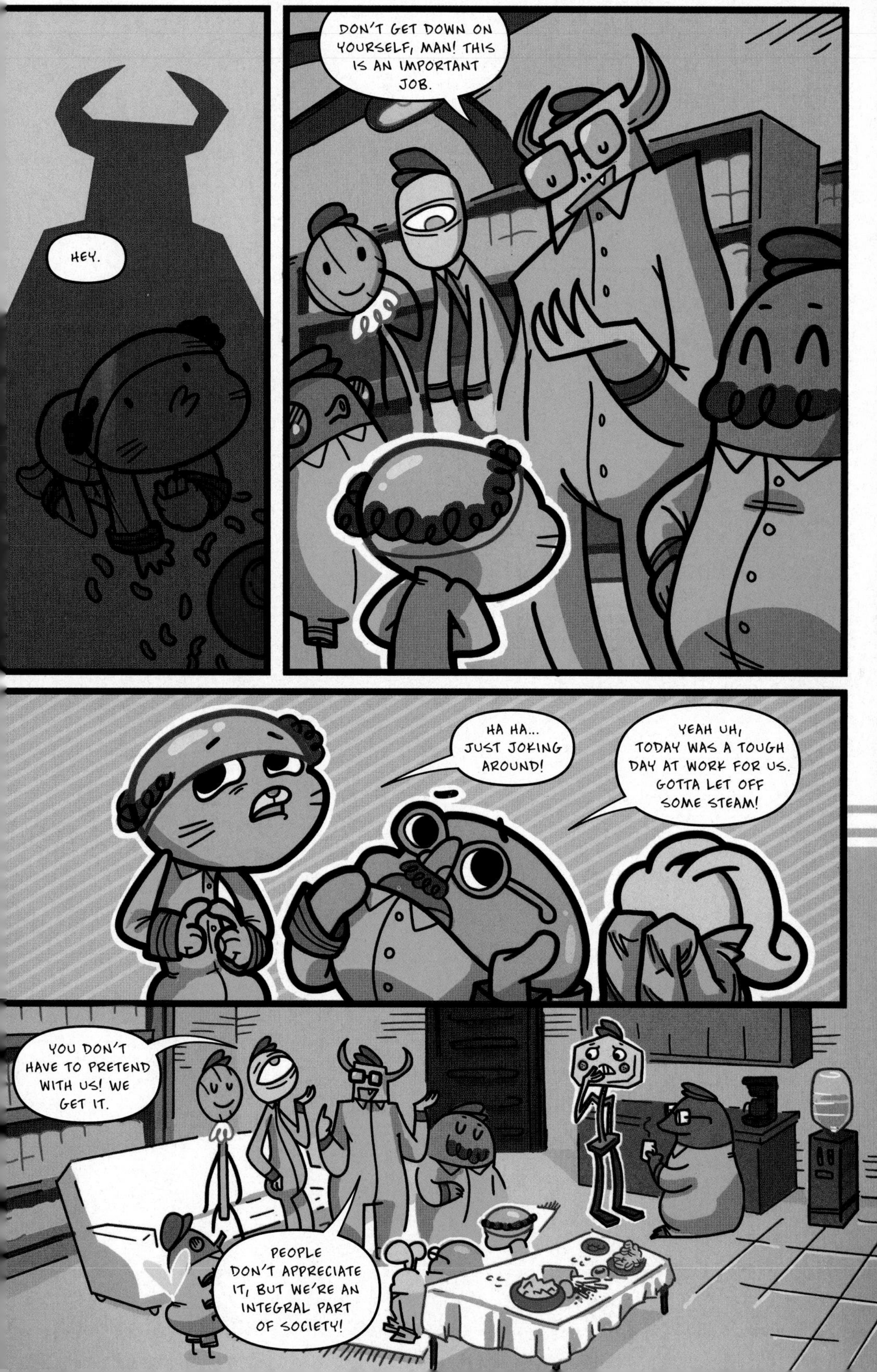
HEY.
DON'T GET DOWN ON YOURSELF, MAN! THIS IS AN IMPORTANT JOB.
HA HA... JUST JOKING AROUND!
YEAH UH, TODAY WAS A TOUGH DAY AT WORK FOR US. GOTTA LET OFF SOME STEAM!
YOU DON'T HAVE TO PRETEND WITH US! WE GET IT.
PEOPLE DON'T APPRECIATE IT, BUT WE'RE AN INTEGRAL PART OF SOCIETY!

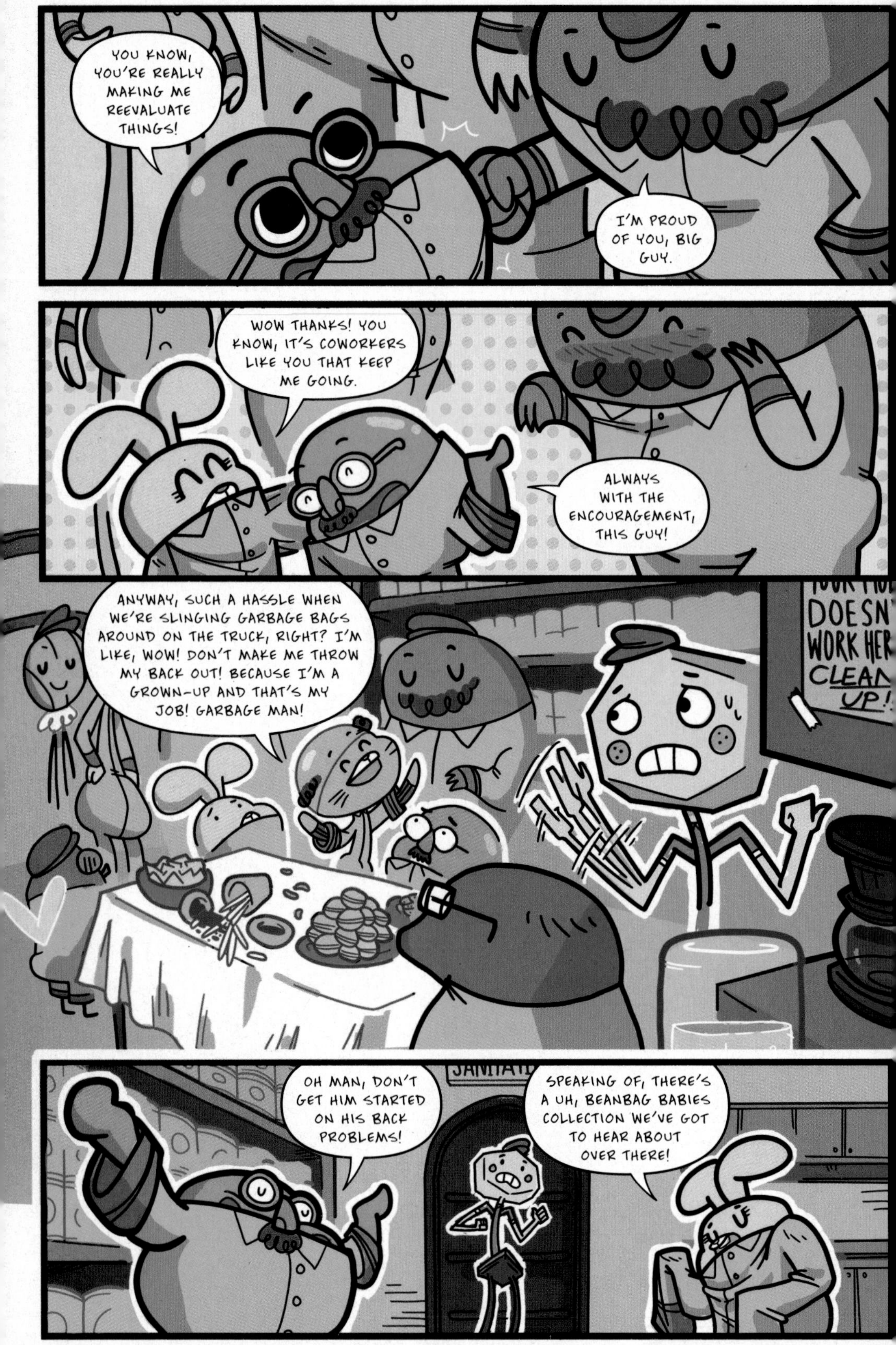
YOU KNOW, YOU'RE REALLY MAKING ME REEVALUATE THINGS!
I'M PROUD OF YOU, BIG GUY.
WOW THANKS! YOU KNOW, IT'S COWORKERS LIKE YOU THAT KEEP ME GOING.
ALWAYS WITH THE ENCOURAGEMENT, THIS GUY!
ANYWAY, SUCH A HASSLE WHEN WE'RE SLINGING GARBAGE BAGS AROUND ON THE TRUCK, RIGHT? I'M LIKE, WOW! DON'T MAKE ME THROW MY BACK OUT! BECAUSE I'M A GROWN-UP AND THAT'S MY JOB! GARBAGE MAN!
DOESN'T WORK HERE CLEAN UP!
OH MAN, DON'T GET HIM STARTED ON HIS BACK PROBLEMS!
SPEAKING OF, THERE'S A UH, BEANBAG BABIES COLLECTION WE'VE GOT TO HEAR ABOUT OVER THERE!

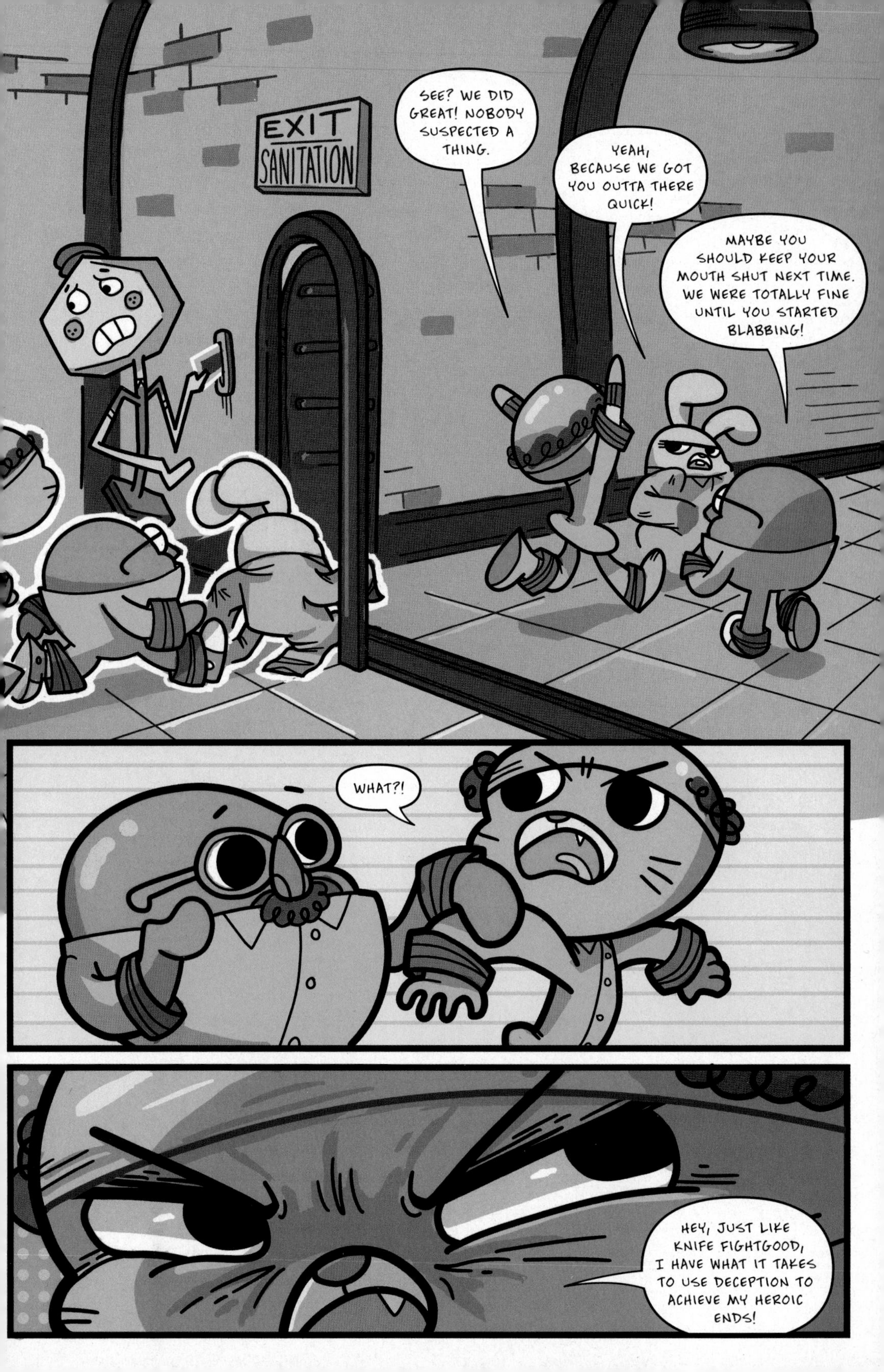
EXIT
SANITATION
SEE? WE DID GREAT! NOBODY SUSPECTED A THING.
YEAH, BECAUSE WE GOT YOU OUTTA THERE QUICK!
MAYBE YOU SHOULD KEEP YOUR MOUTH SHUT NEXT TIME. WE WERE TOTALLY FINE UNTIL YOU STARTED BLABBING!
WHAT?!
HEY, JUST LIKE KNIFE FIGHTGOOD, I HAVE WHAT IT TAKES TO USE DECEPTION TO ACHIEVE MY HEROIC ENDS!

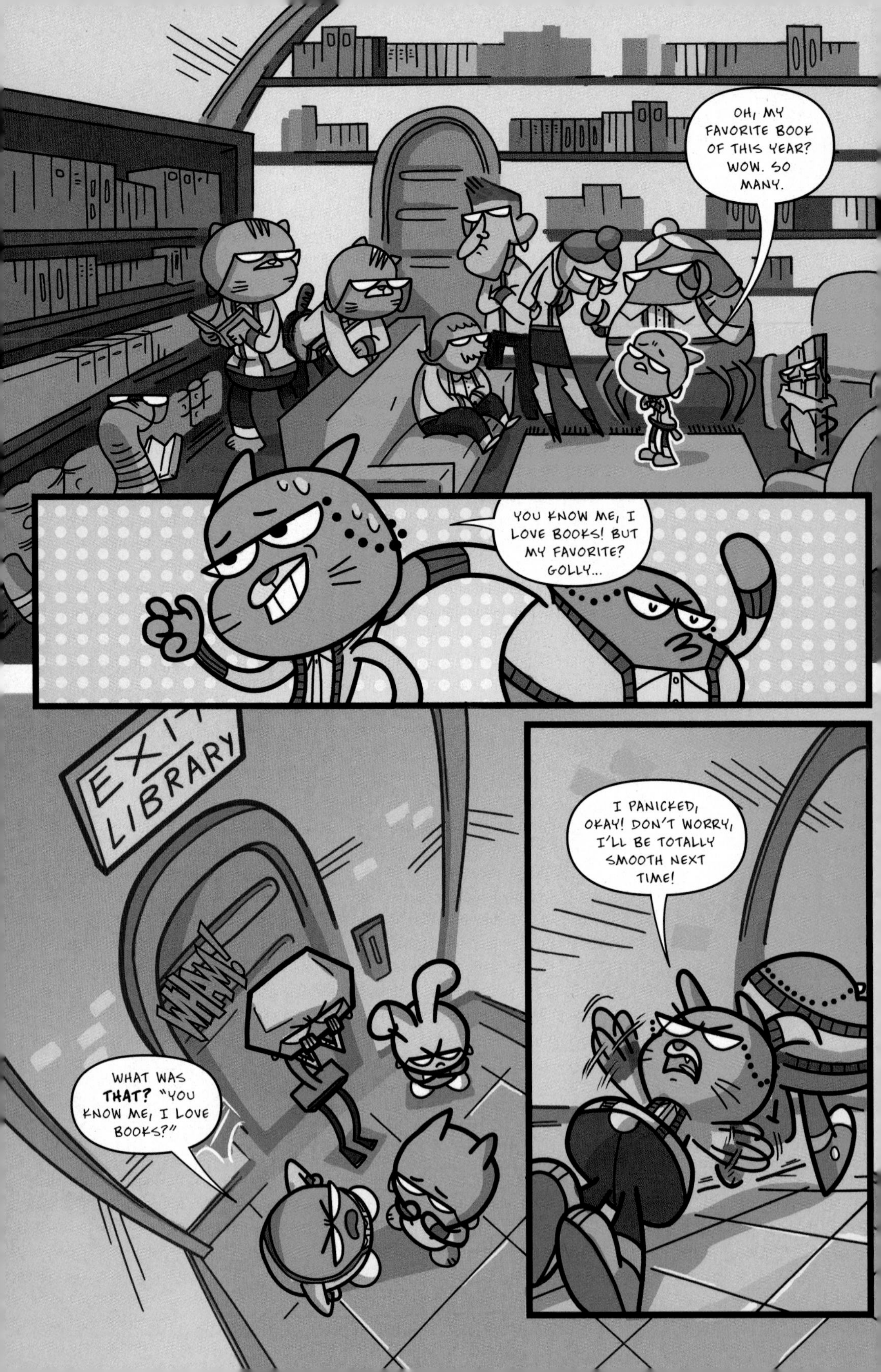
OH, MY FAVORITE BOOK OF THIS YEAR? WOW. SO MANY.
YOU KNOW ME, I LOVE BOOKS! BUT MY FAVORITE? GOLLY...
EXIT LIBRARY
WHAM!
WHAT WAS THAT? "YOU KNOW ME, I LOVE BOOKS?"
I PANICKED, OKAY! DON'T WORRY, I'LL BE TOTALLY SMOOTH NEXT TIME!

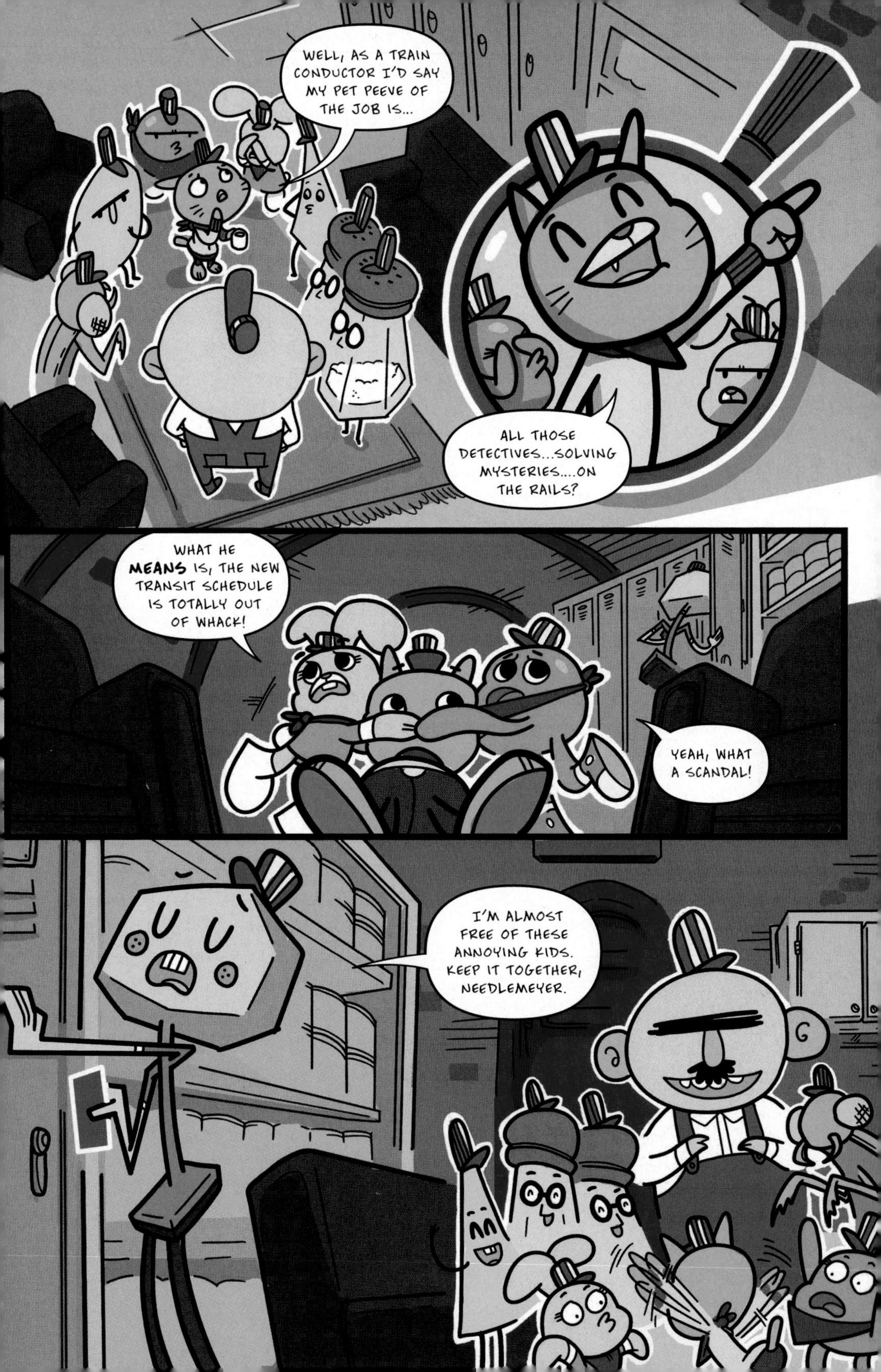
WELL, AS A TRAIN CONDUCTOR I'D SAY MY PET PEEVE OF THE JOB IS...
ALL THOSE DETECTIVES...SOLVING MYSTERIES....ON THE RAILS?
WHAT HE **MEANS** IS, THE NEW TRANSIT SCHEDULE IS TOTALLY OUT OF WHACK!
YEAH, WHAT A SCANDAL!
I'M ALMOST FREE OF THESE ANNOYING KIDS. KEEP IT TOGETHER, NEEDLEMEYER.

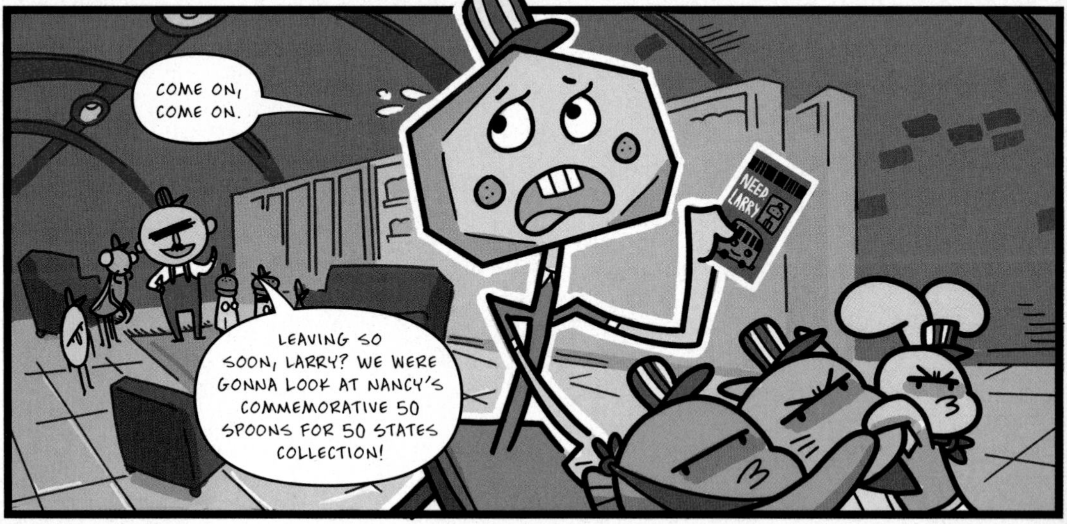
COME ON, COME ON.
NEED LARRY
LEAVING SO SOON, LARRY? WE WERE GONNA LOOK AT NANCY'S COMMEMORATIVE 50 SPOONS FOR 50 STATES COLLECTION!

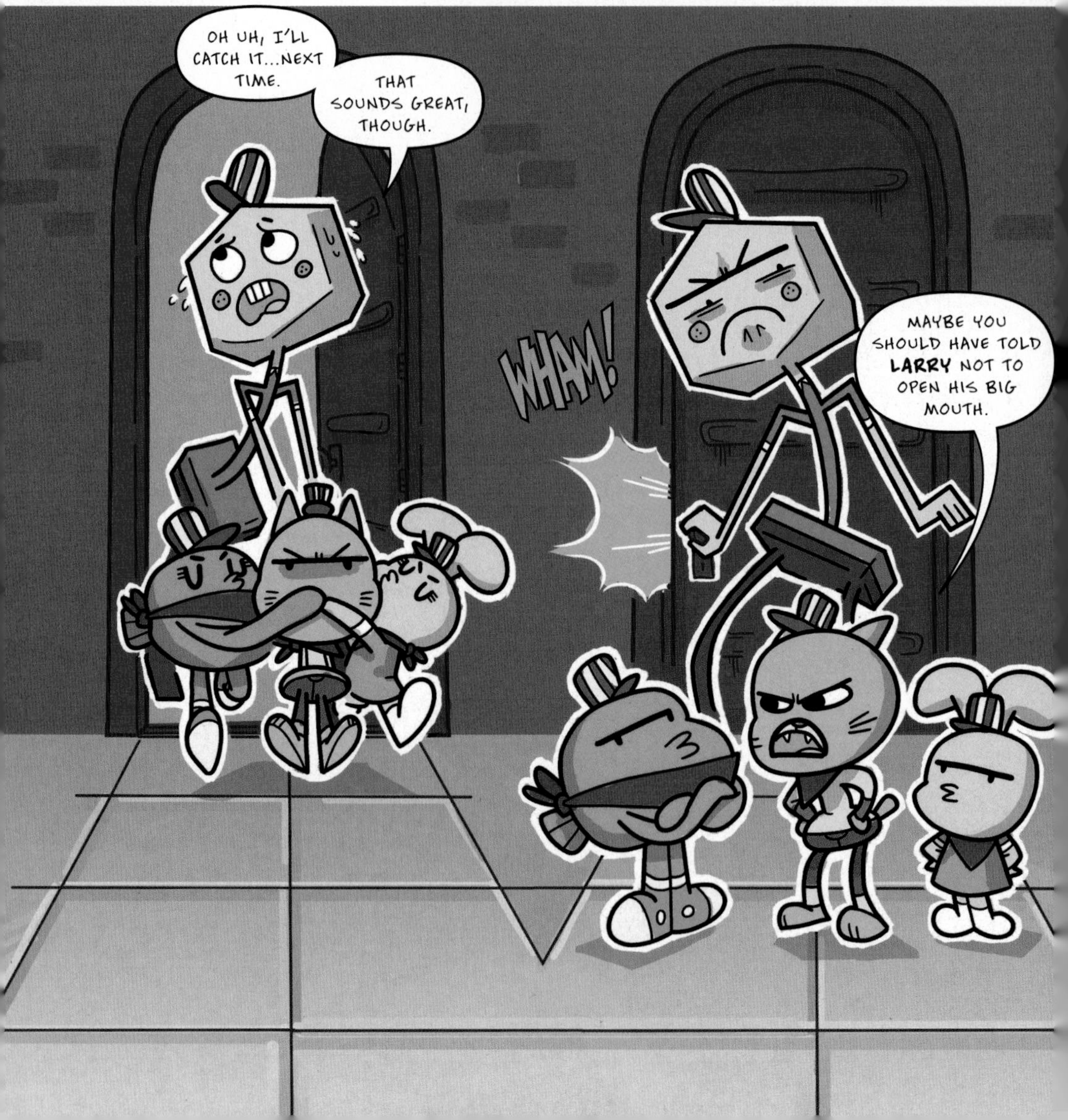
OH UH, I'LL CATCH IT...NEXT TIME.
THAT SOUNDS GREAT, THOUGH.
WHAM!
MAYBE YOU SHOULD HAVE TOLD **LARRY** NOT TO OPEN HIS BIG MOUTH.

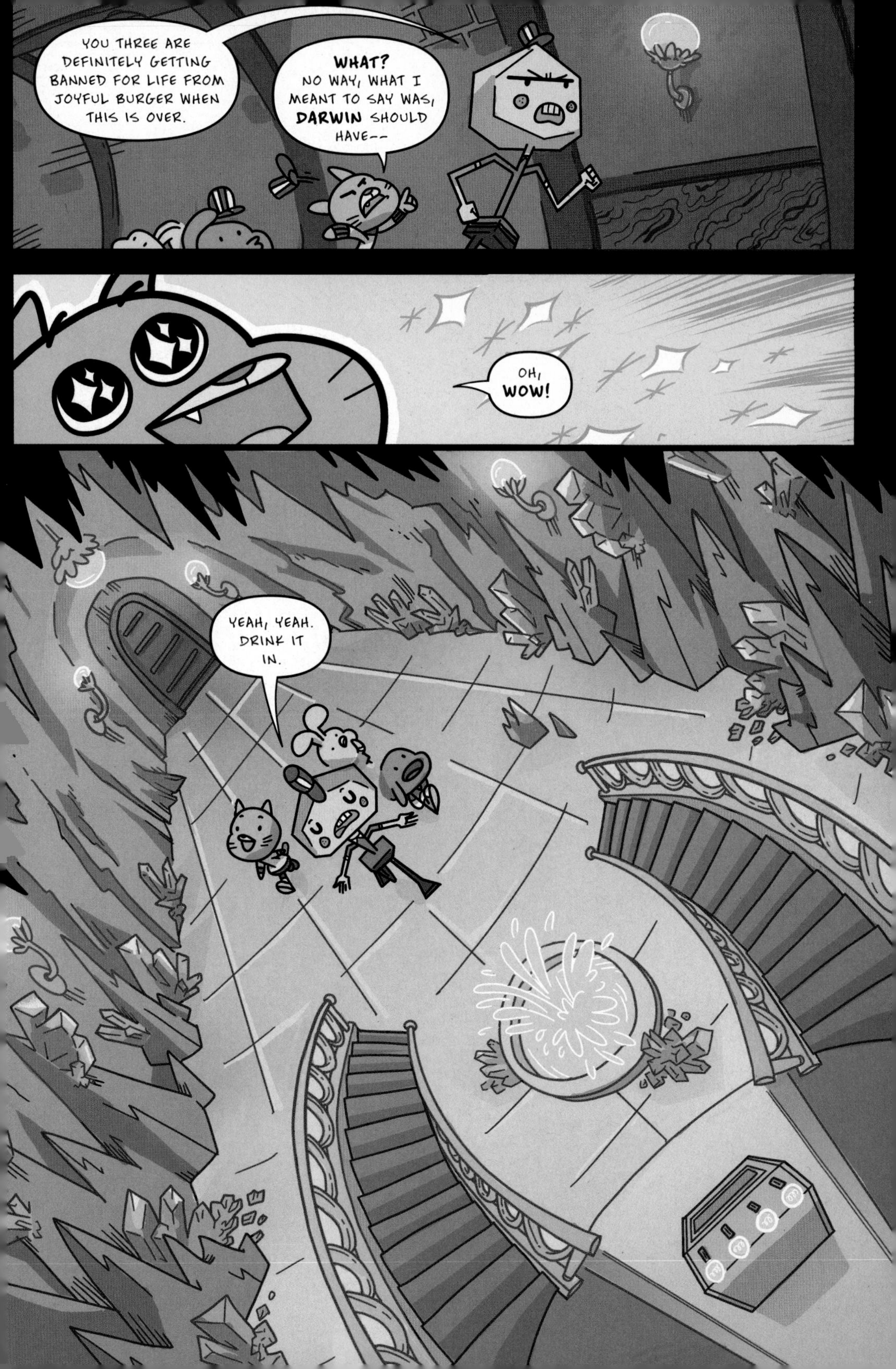
YOU THREE ARE DEFINITELY GETTING BANNED FOR LIFE FROM JOYFUL BURGER WHEN THIS IS OVER.
WHAT? NO WAY, WHAT I MEANT TO SAY WAS, DARWIN SHOULD HAVE--
OH, WOW!
YEAH, YEAH. DRINK IT IN.

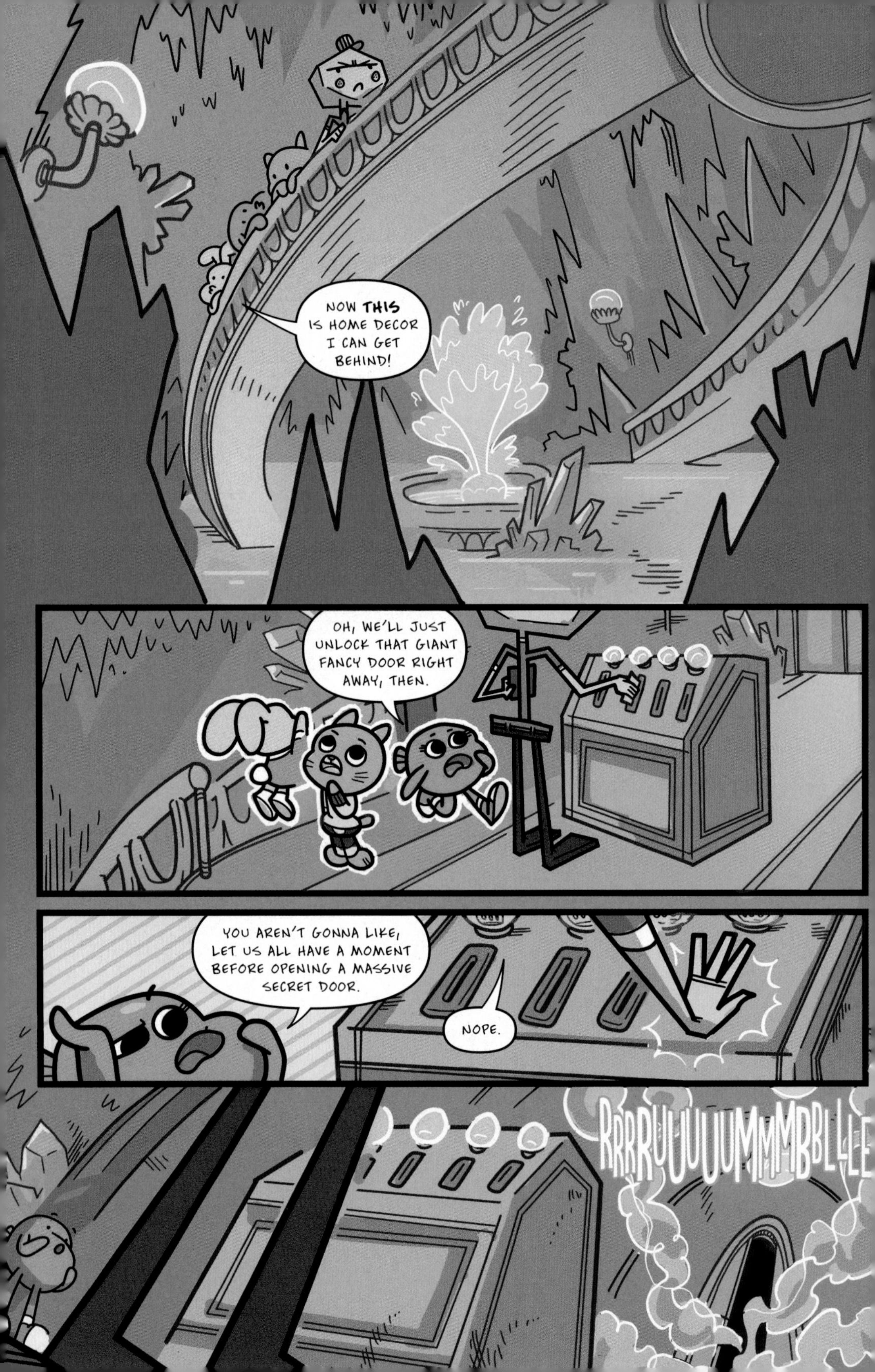
NOW THIS IS HOME DECOR I CAN GET BEHIND!
OH, WE'LL JUST UNLOCK THAT GIANT FANCY DOOR RIGHT AWAY, THEN.
YOU AREN'T GONNA LIKE, LET US ALL HAVE A MOMENT BEFORE OPENING A MASSIVE SECRET DOOR.
NOPE.
RRRRUUUUUMMMBBLLLE

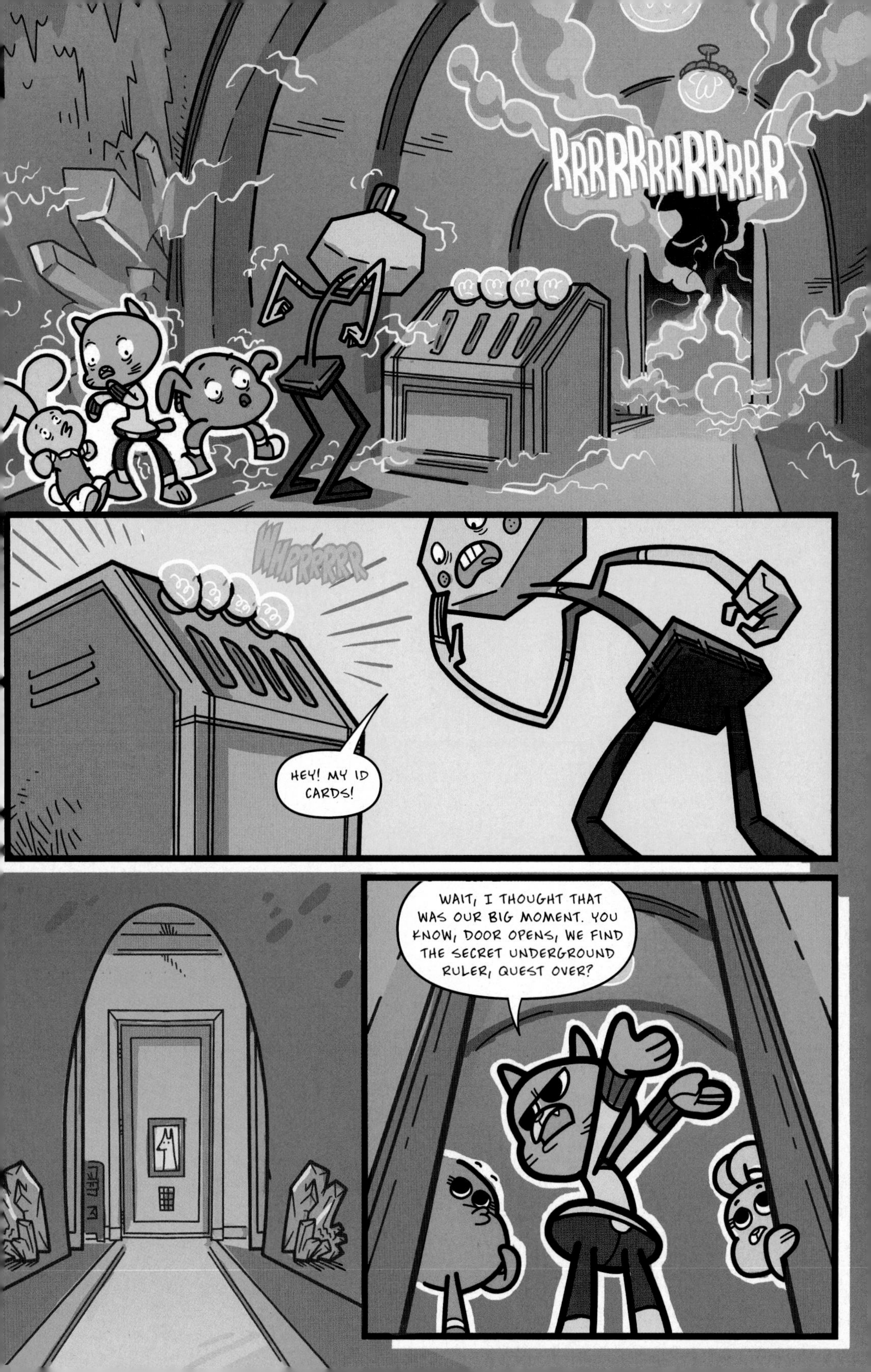
RRRRRRRRRRRRR
WHIRRRRR
HEY! MY ID CARDS!
WAIT, I THOUGHT THAT WAS OUR BIG MOMENT. YOU KNOW, DOOR OPENS, WE FIND THE SECRET UNDERGROUND RULER, QUEST OVER?

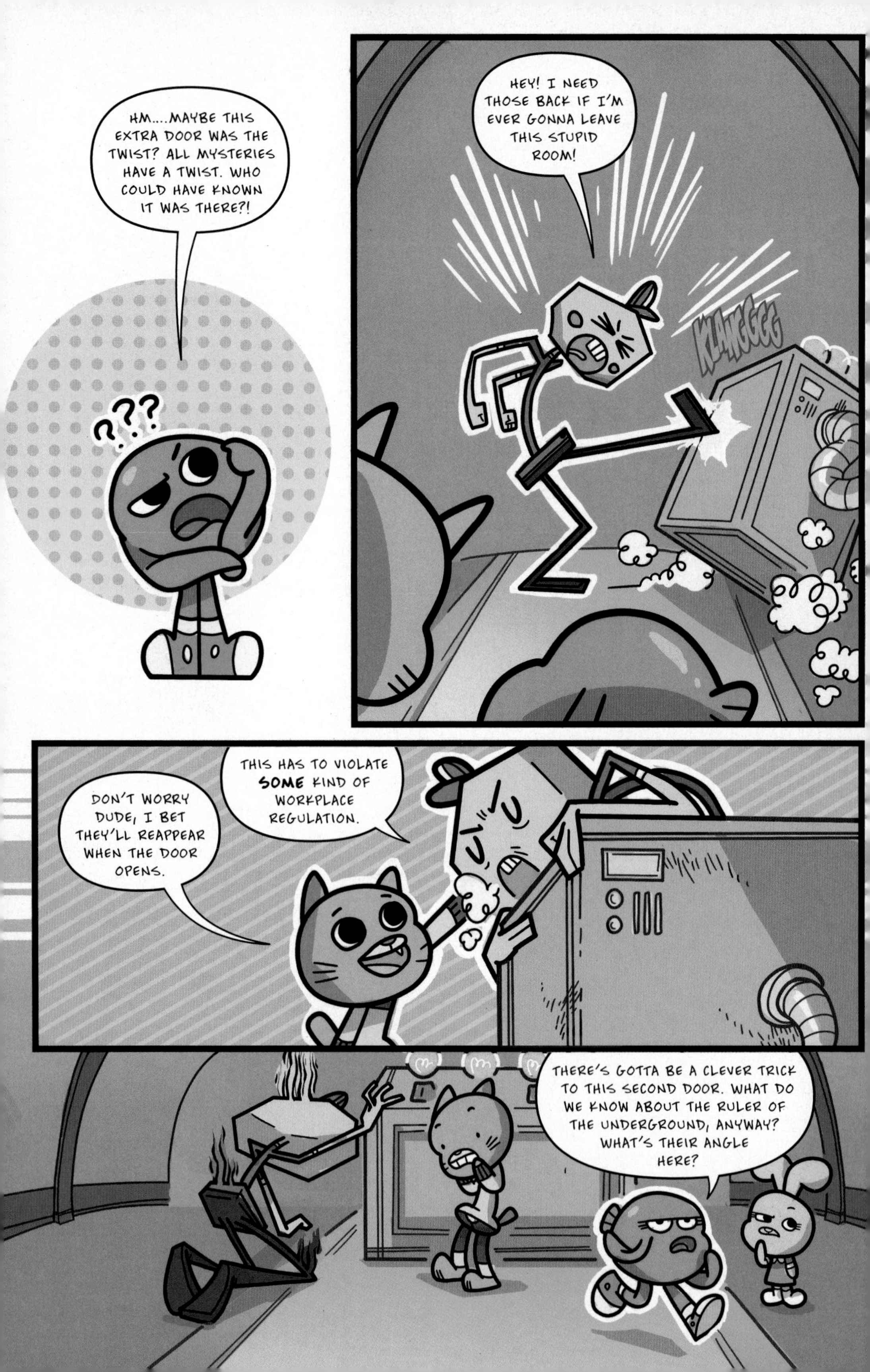
HM....MAYBE THIS EXTRA DOOR WAS THE TWIST? ALL MYSTERIES HAVE A TWIST. WHO COULD HAVE KNOWN IT WAS THERE?!
???
HEY! I NEED THOSE BACK IF I'M EVER GONNA LEAVE THIS STUPID ROOM!
KLANGGGG
DON'T WORRY DUDE, I BET THEY'LL REAPPEAR WHEN THE DOOR OPENS.
THIS HAS TO VIOLATE SOME KIND OF WORKPLACE REGULATION.
THERE'S GOTTA BE A CLEVER TRICK TO THIS SECOND DOOR. WHAT DO WE KNOW ABOUT THE RULER OF THE UNDERGROUND, ANYWAY? WHAT'S THEIR ANGLE HERE?

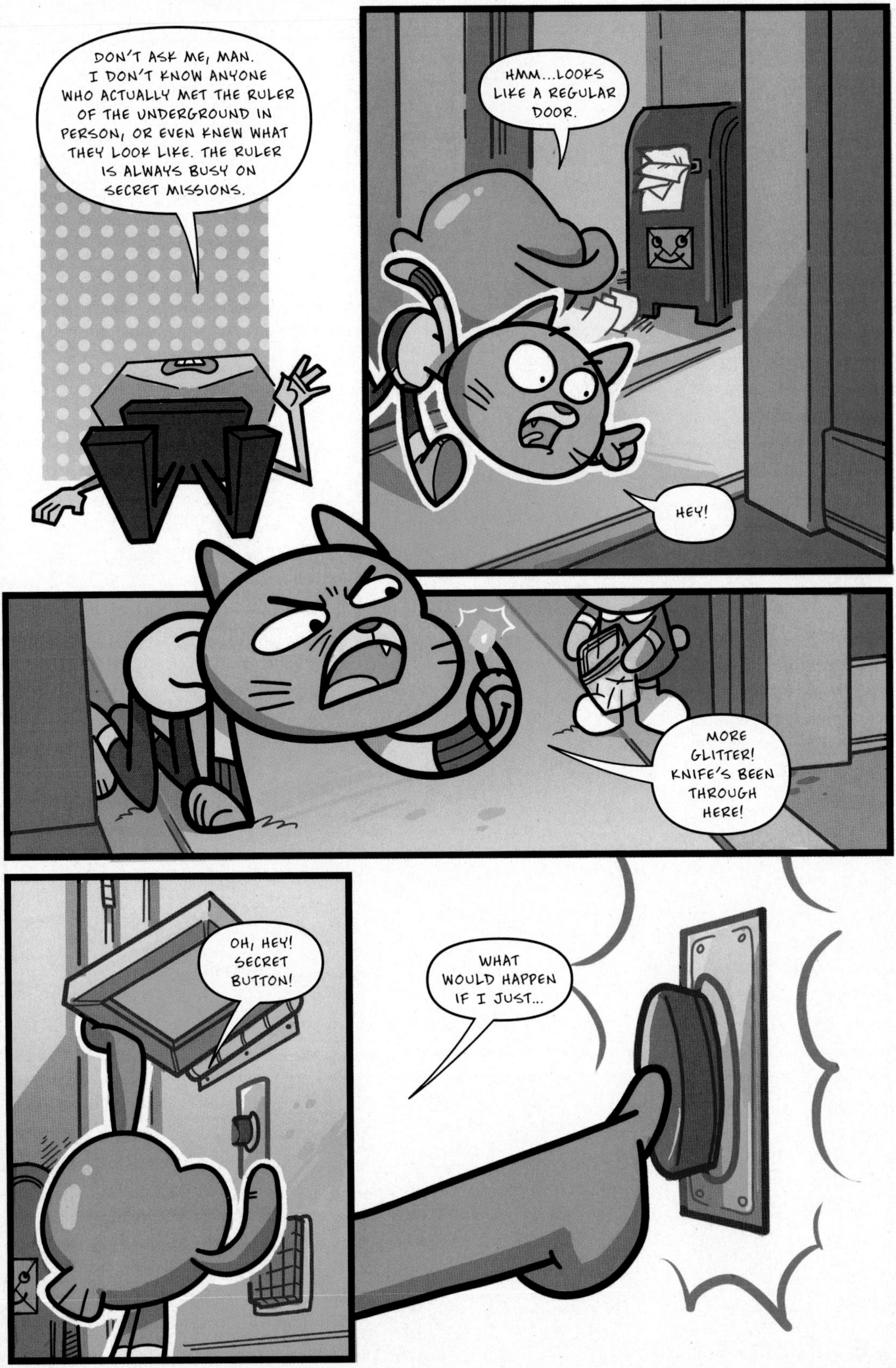
DON'T ASK ME, MAN. I DON'T KNOW ANYONE WHO ACTUALLY MET THE RULER OF THE UNDERGROUND IN PERSON, OR EVEN KNEW WHAT THEY LOOK LIKE. THE RULER IS ALWAYS BUSY ON SECRET MISSIONS.
HMM...LOOKS LIKE A REGULAR DOOR.
HEY!
MORE GLITTER! KNIFE'S BEEN THROUGH HERE!
OH, HEY! SECRET BUTTON!
WHAT WOULD HAPPEN IF I JUST...

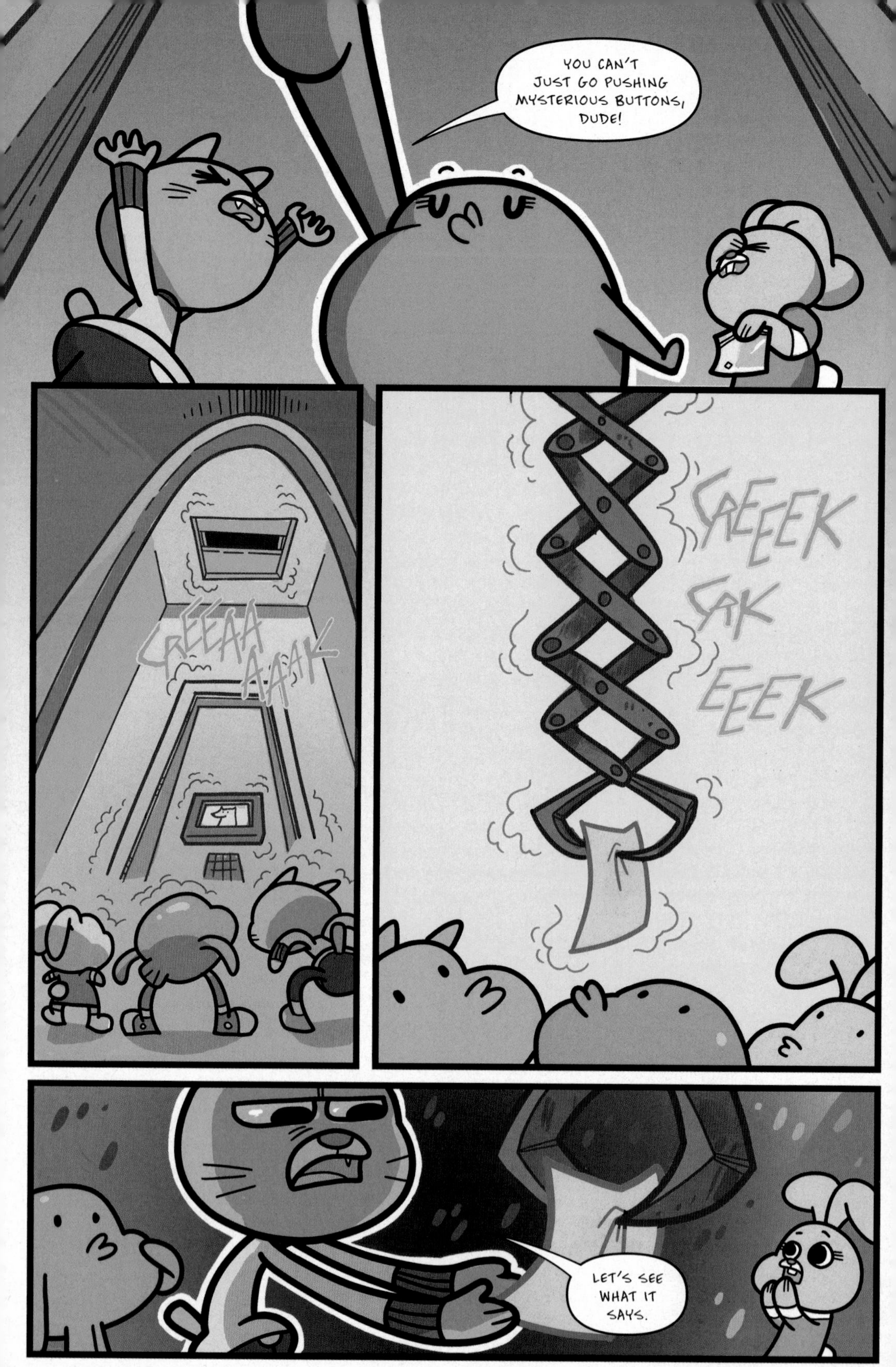
YOU CAN'T JUST GO PUSHING MYSTERIOUS BUTTONS, DUDE!
CREEAA AAAK
CREEEK
CRK
EEEK
LET'S SEE WHAT IT SAYS.

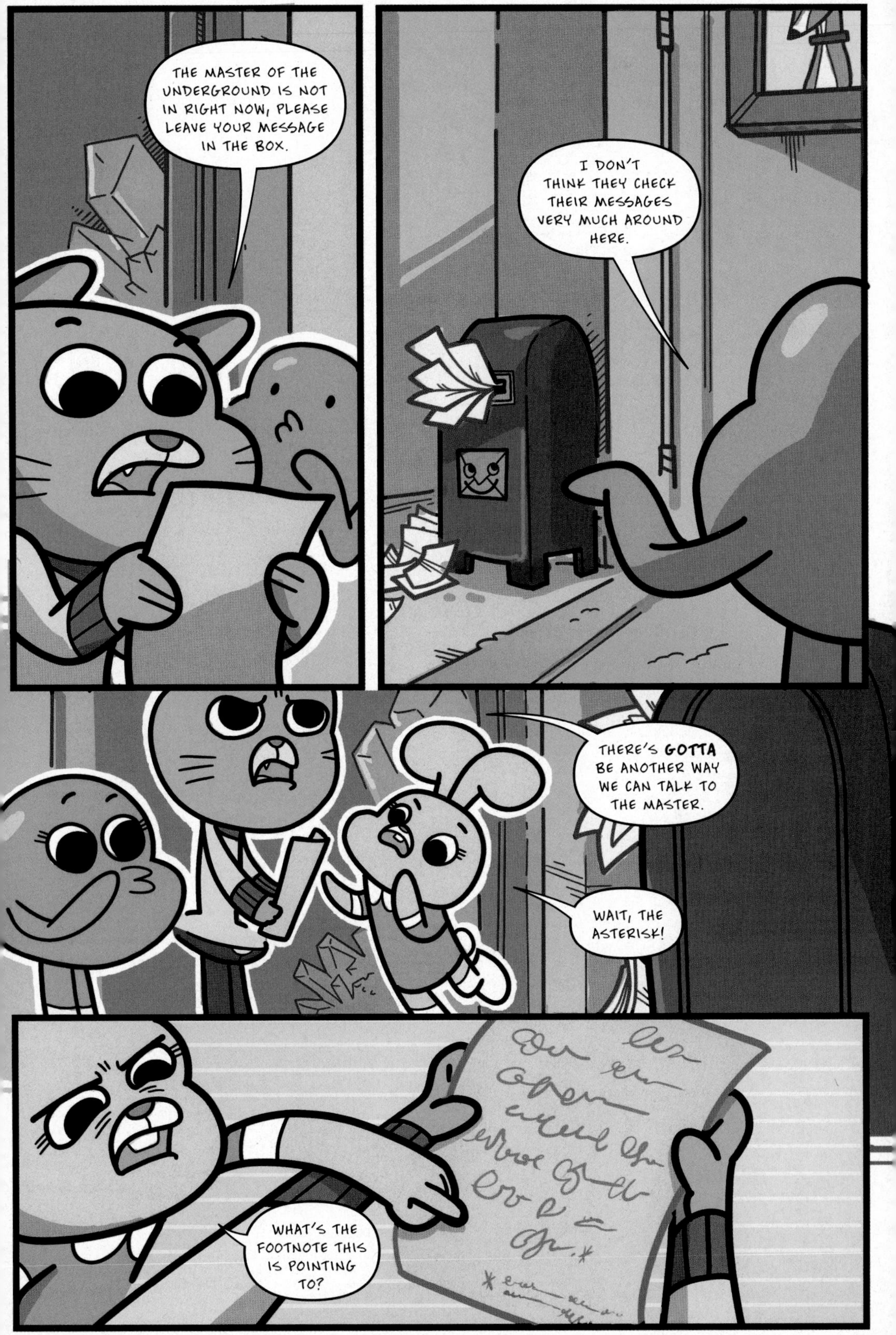
THE MASTER OF THE UNDERGROUND IS NOT IN RIGHT NOW, PLEASE LEAVE YOUR MESSAGE IN THE BOX.
I DON'T THINK THEY CHECK THEIR MESSAGES VERY MUCH AROUND HERE.
THERE'S **GOTTA** BE ANOTHER WAY WE CAN TALK TO THE MASTER.
WAIT, THE ASTERISK!
WHAT'S THE FOOTNOTE THIS IS POINTING TO?

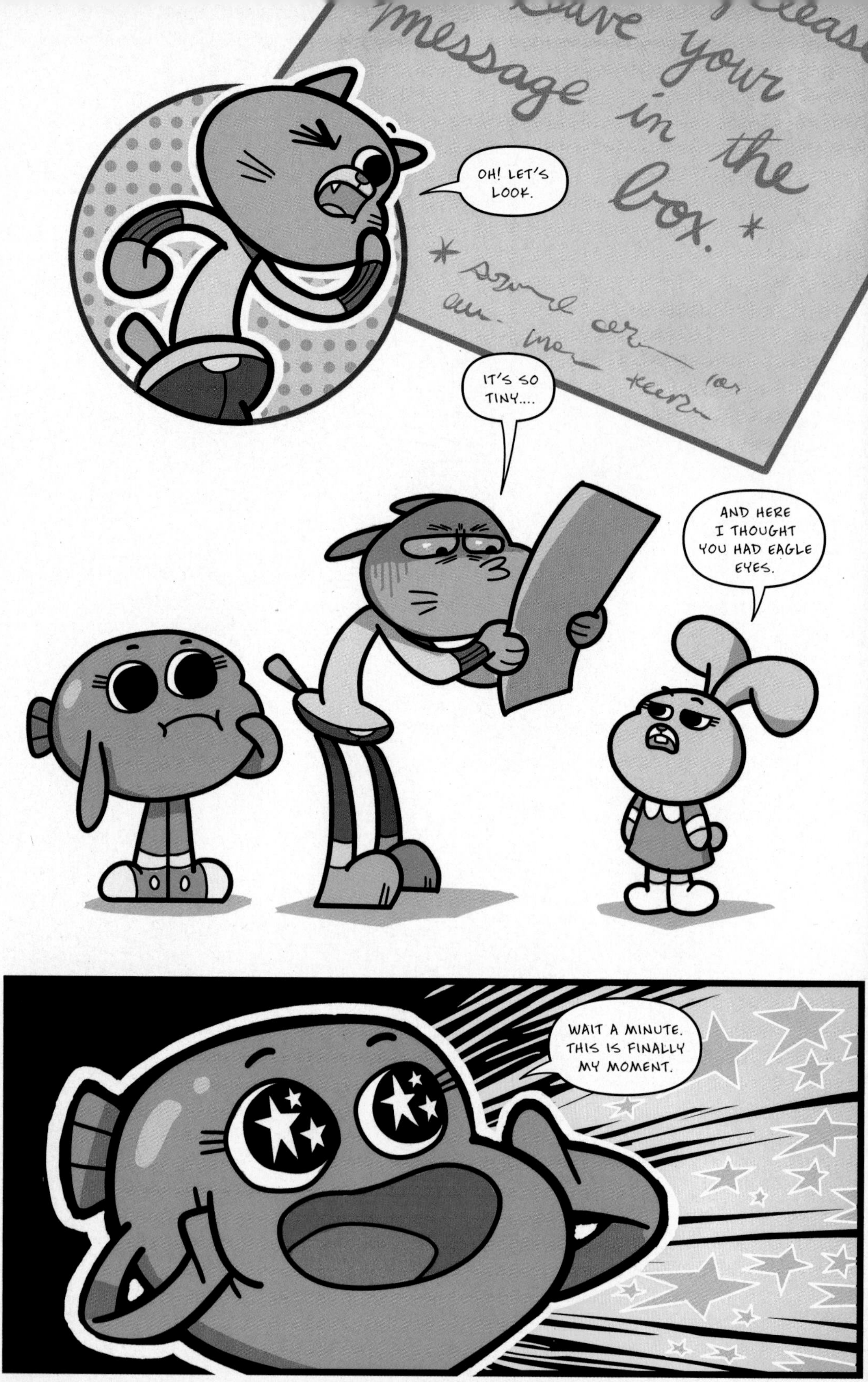

your
message in the
box.
OH! LET'S LOOK.
IT'S SO TINY....
AND HERE I THOUGHT YOU HAD EAGLE EYES.
WAIT A MINUTE. THIS IS FINALLY MY MOMENT.

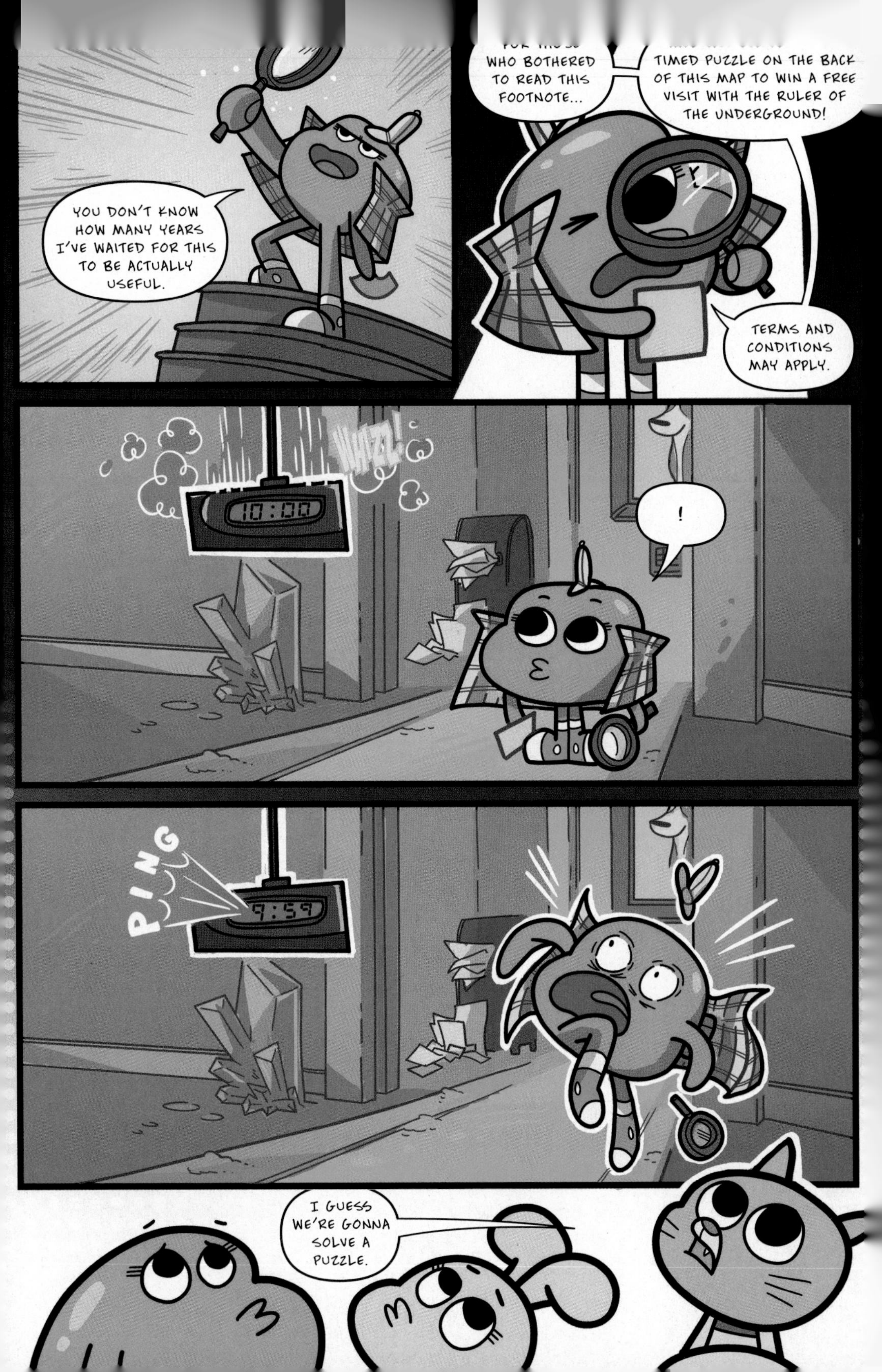
YOU DON'T KNOW HOW MANY YEARS I'VE WAITED FOR THIS TO BE ACTUALLY USEFUL.
WHO BOTHERED TO READ THIS FOOTNOTE...
TIMED PUZZLE ON THE BACK OF THIS MAP TO WIN A FREE VISIT WITH THE RULER OF THE UNDERGROUND!
TERMS AND CONDITIONS MAY APPLY.
WHIZZ!
10:00
!
PING
9:59
I GUESS WE'RE GONNA SOLVE A PUZZLE.

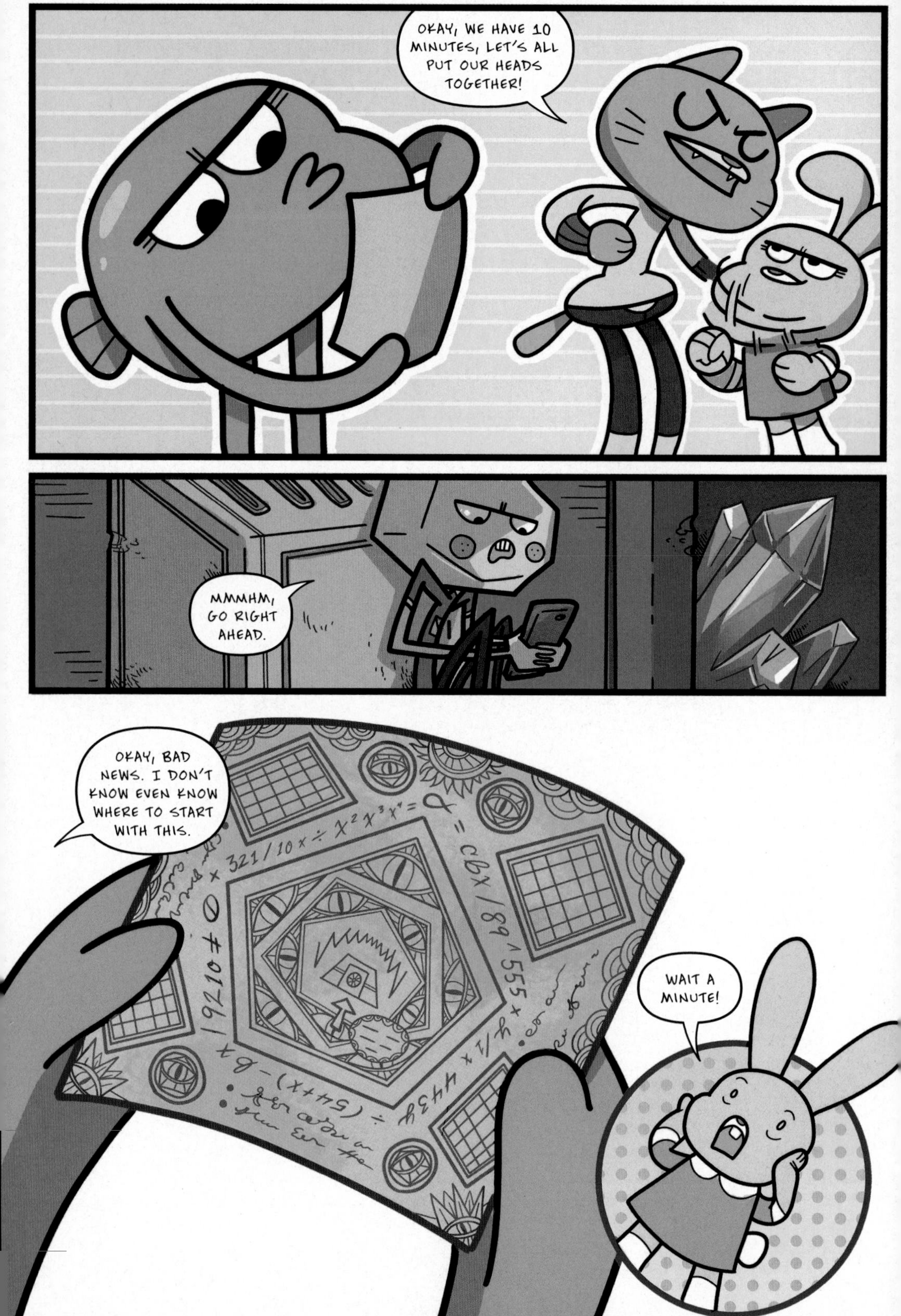
OKAY, WE HAVE 10 MINUTES, LET'S ALL PUT OUR HEADS TOGETHER!
MMMHM, GO RIGHT AHEAD.
OKAY, BAD NEWS. I DON'T KNOW EVEN KNOW WHERE TO START WITH THIS.
WAIT A MINUTE!

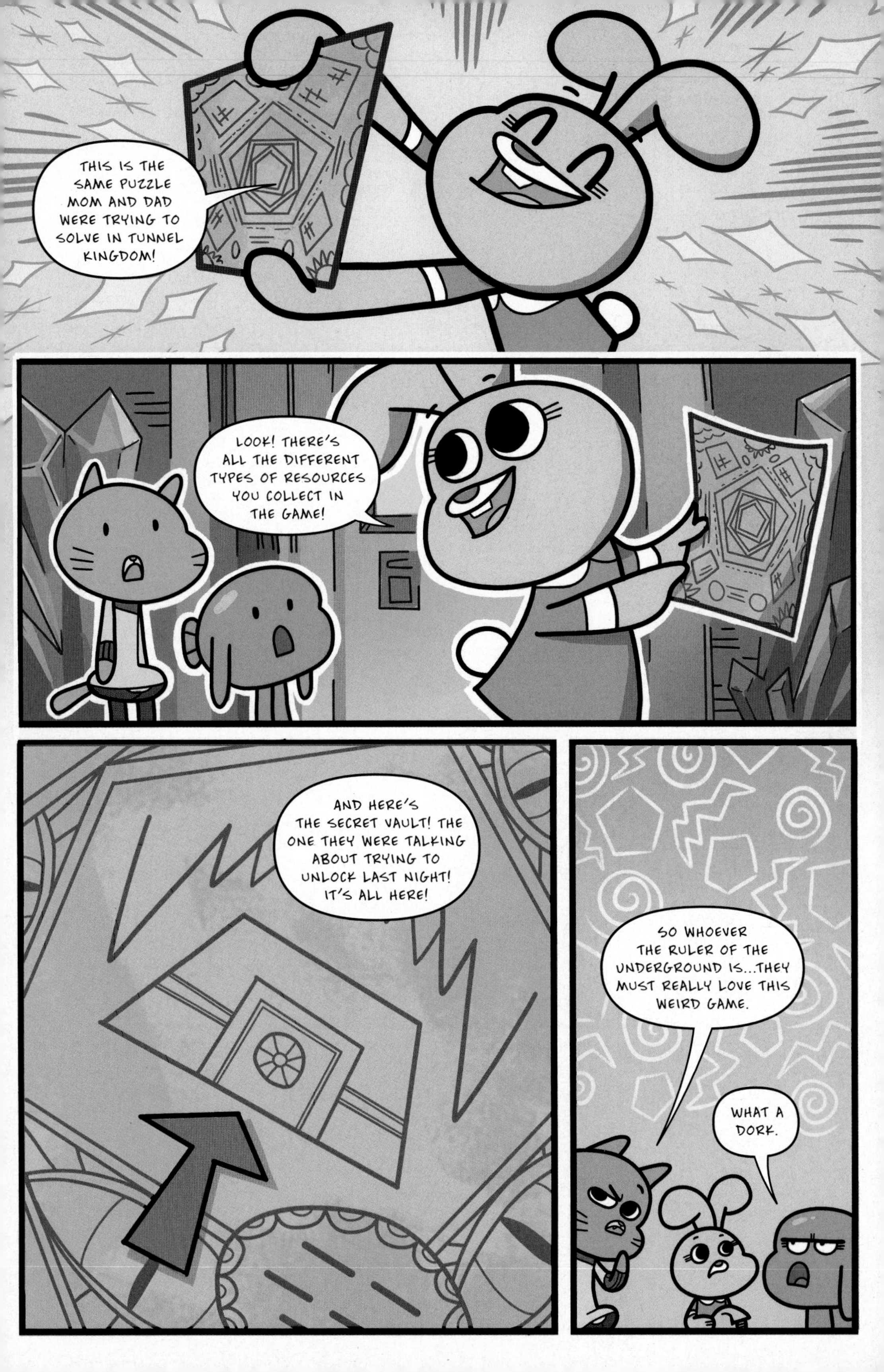
THIS IS THE SAME PUZZLE MOM AND DAD WERE TRYING TO SOLVE IN TUNNEL KINGDOM!
LOOK! THERE'S ALL THE DIFFERENT TYPES OF RESOURCES YOU COLLECT IN THE GAME!
AND HERE'S THE SECRET VAULT! THE ONE THEY WERE TALKING ABOUT TRYING TO UNLOCK LAST NIGHT! IT'S ALL HERE!
SO WHOEVER THE RULER OF THE UNDERGROUND IS...THEY MUST REALLY LOVE THIS WEIRD GAME.
WHAT A DORK.

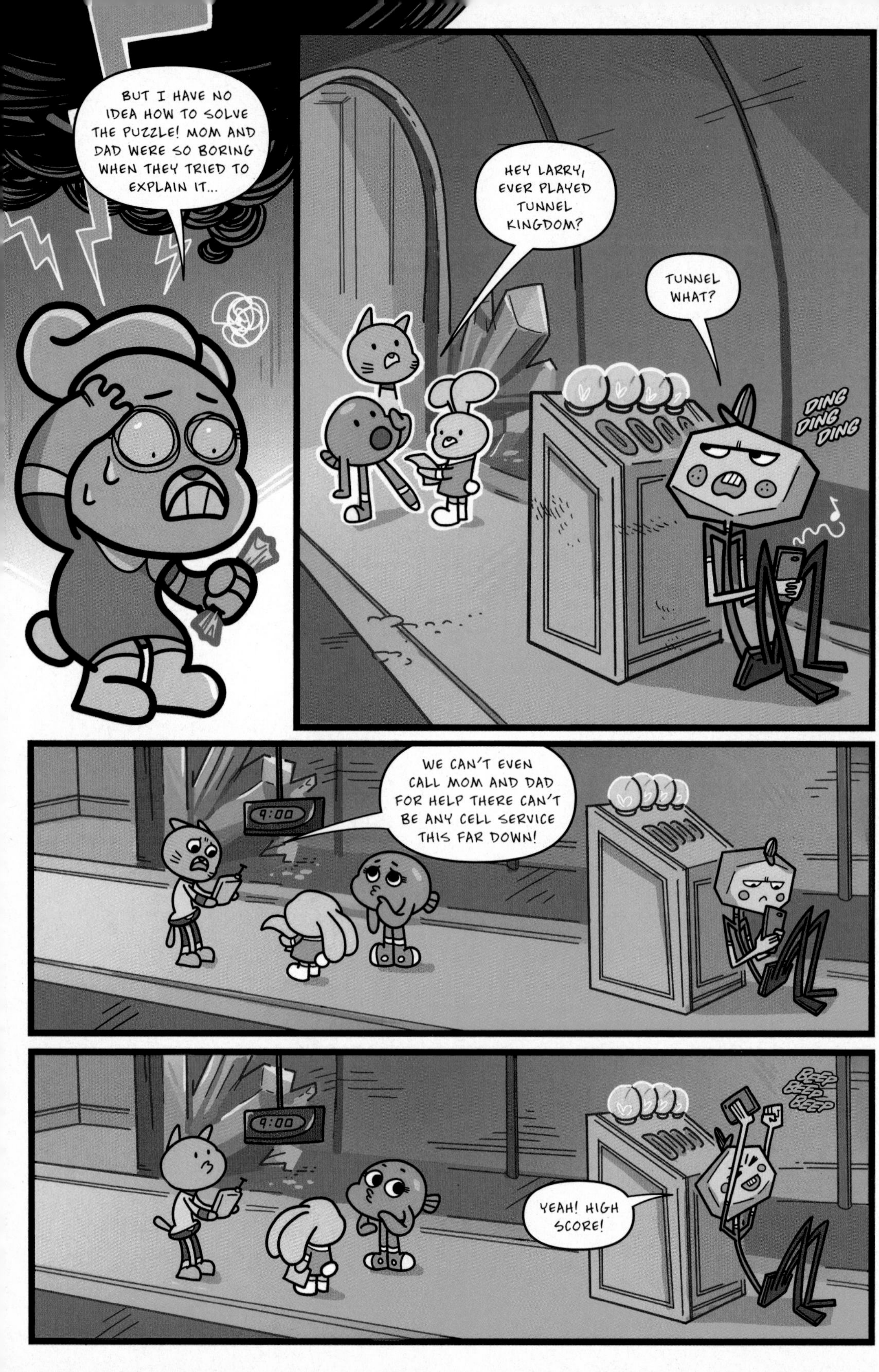
BUT I HAVE NO IDEA HOW TO SOLVE THE PUZZLE! MOM AND DAD WERE SO BORING WHEN THEY TRIED TO EXPLAIN IT...
HEY LARRY, EVER PLAYED TUNNEL KINGDOM?
TUNNEL WHAT?
DING DING DING
WE CAN'T EVEN CALL MOM AND DAD FOR HELP THERE CAN'T BE ANY CELL SERVICE THIS FAR DOWN!
9:00
9:00
BEEP BEEP BEEP
YEAH! HIGH SCORE!

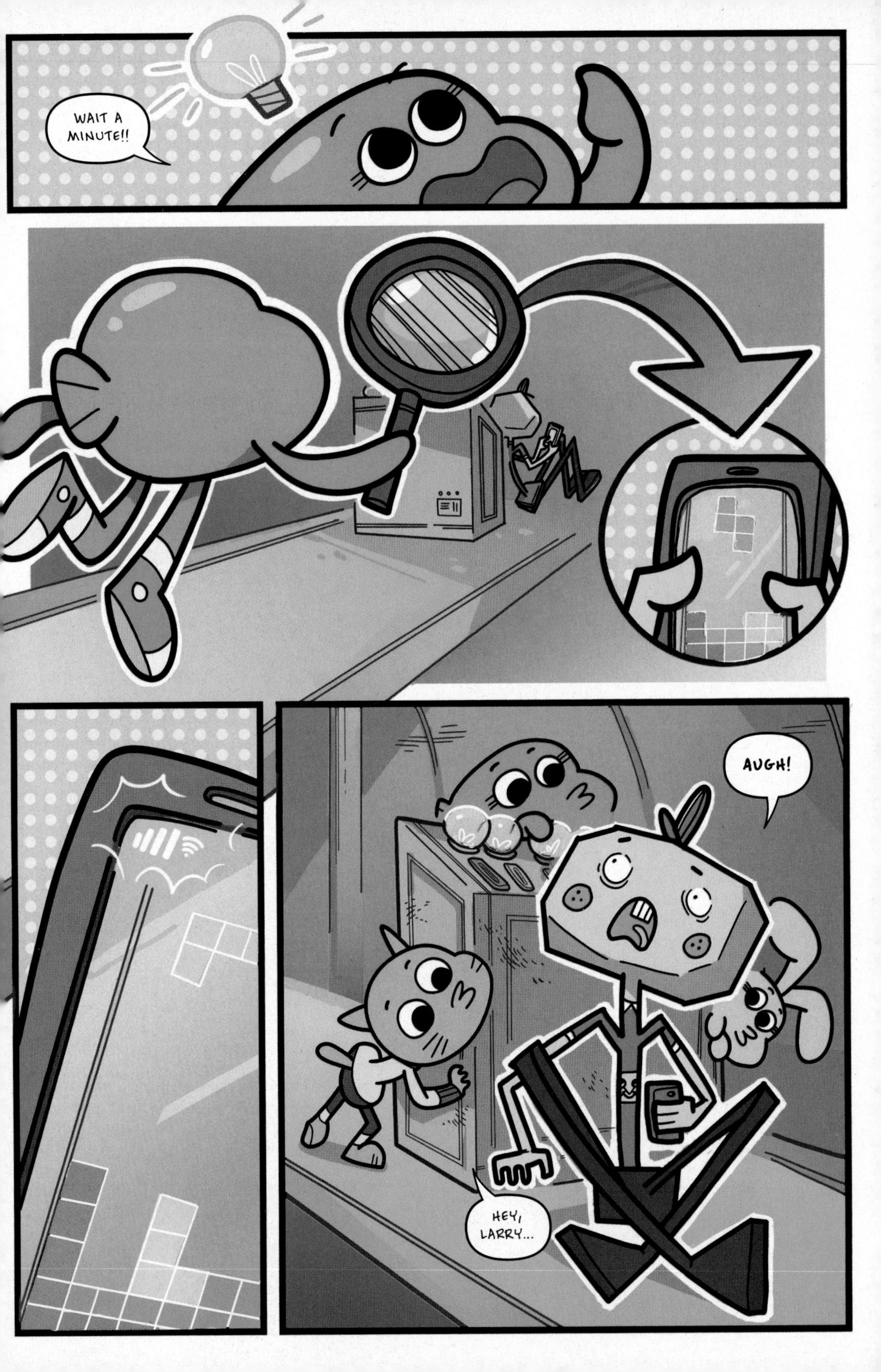
WAIT A MINUTE!!
AUGH!
HEY, LARRY...

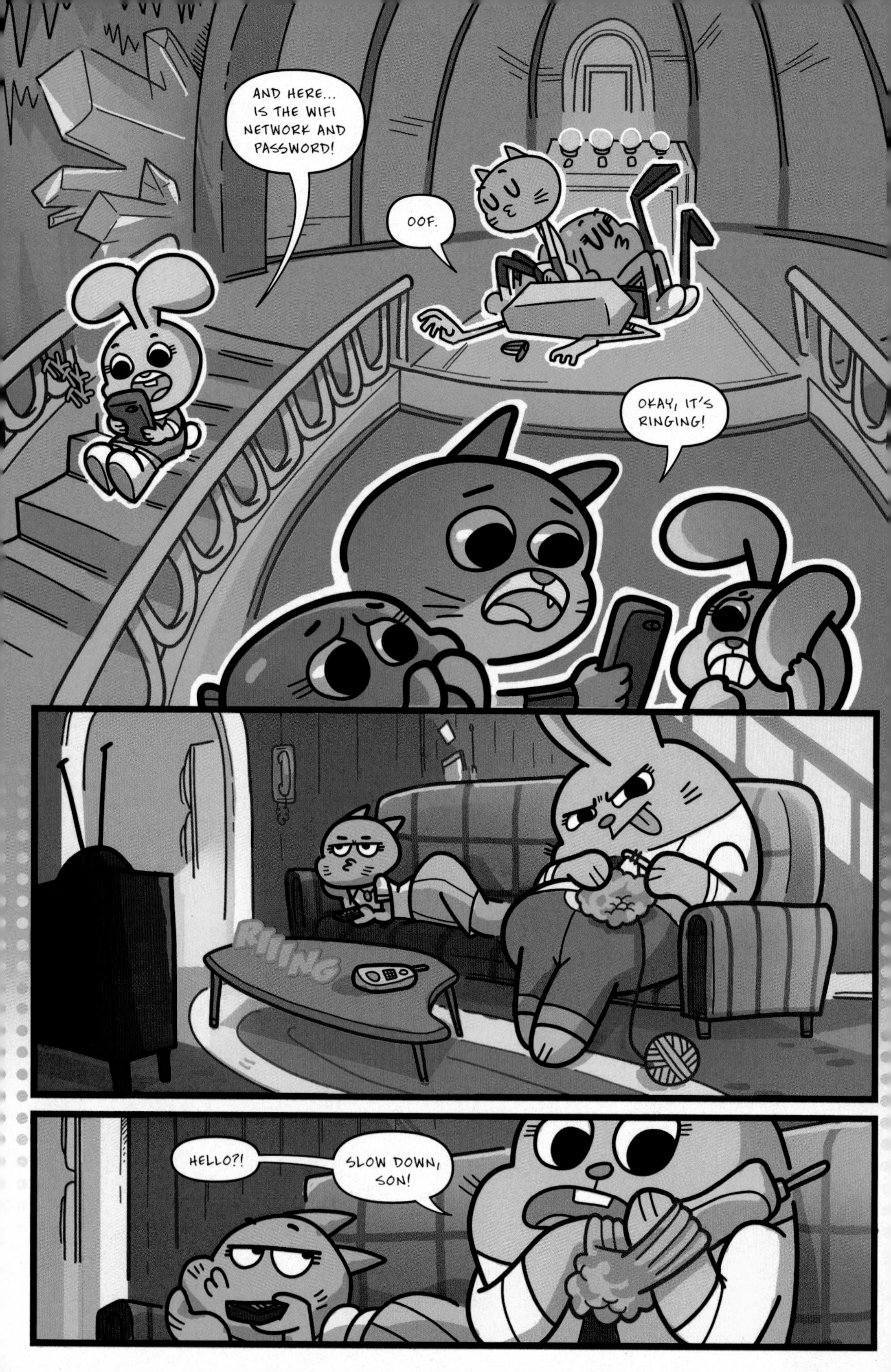
AND HERE... IS THE WIFI NETWORK AND PASSWORD!
OOF.
OKAY, IT'S RINGING!
RIIING
HELLO?!
SLOW DOWN, SON!

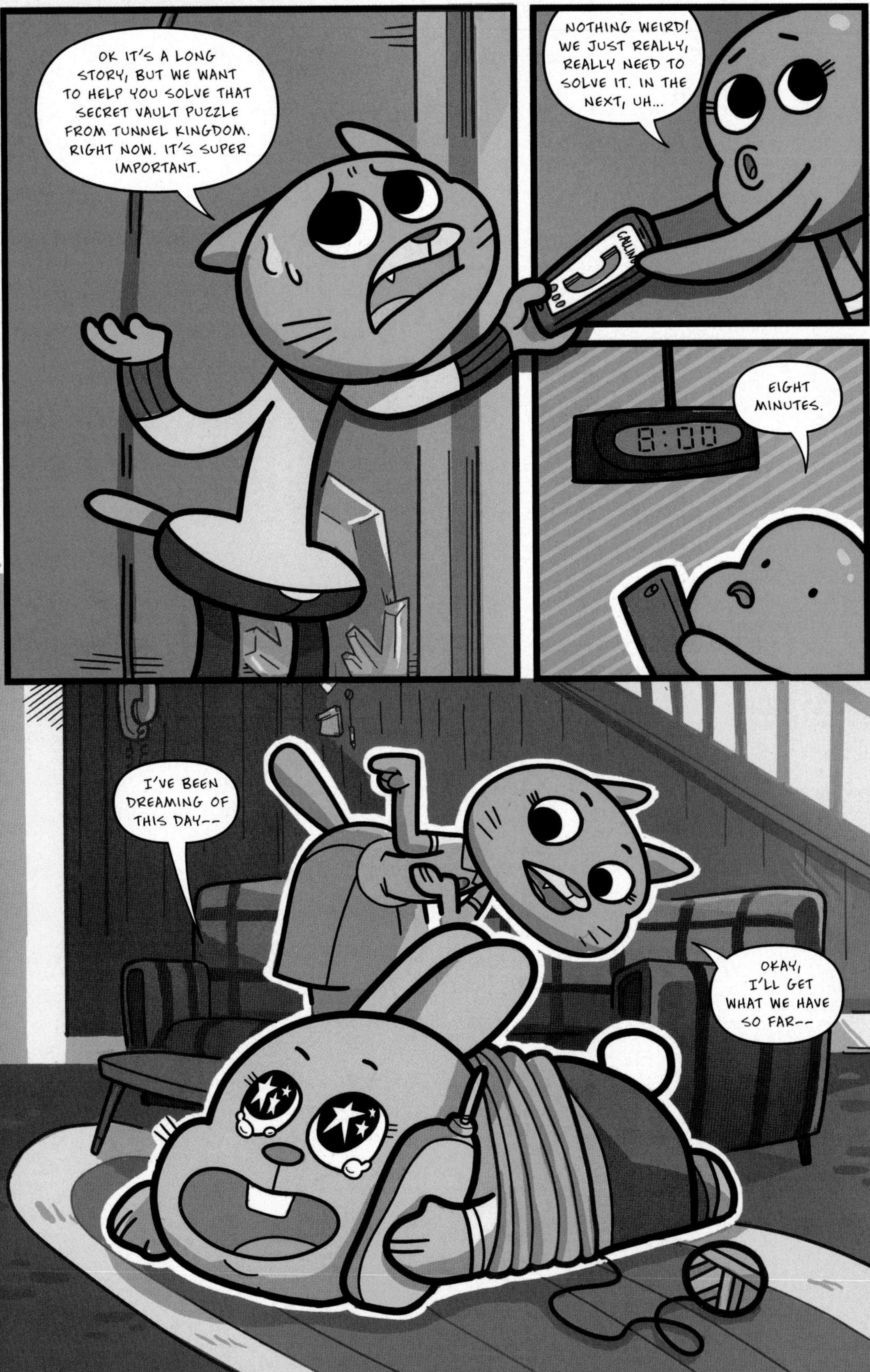
OK IT'S A LONG STORY, BUT WE WANT TO HELP YOU SOLVE THAT SECRET VAULT PUZZLE FROM TUNNEL KINGDOM. RIGHT NOW. IT'S SUPER IMPORTANT.
NOTHING WEIRD! WE JUST REALLY, REALLY NEED TO SOLVE IT. IN THE NEXT, UH...
EIGHT MINUTES.
I'VE BEEN DREAMING OF THIS DAY--
OKAY, I'LL GET WHAT WE HAVE SO FAR--

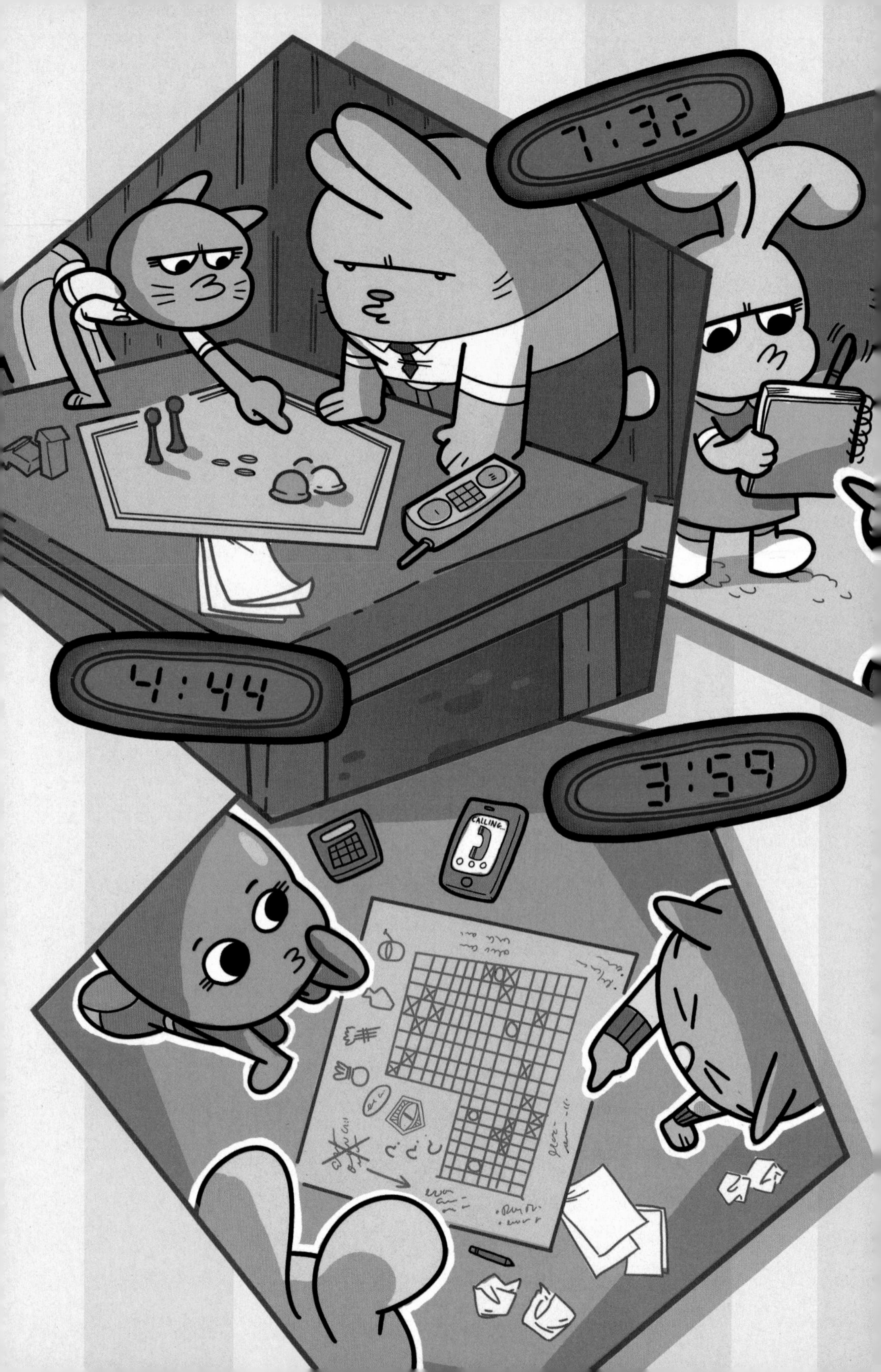
7:32
4:44
3:59
CALLING...

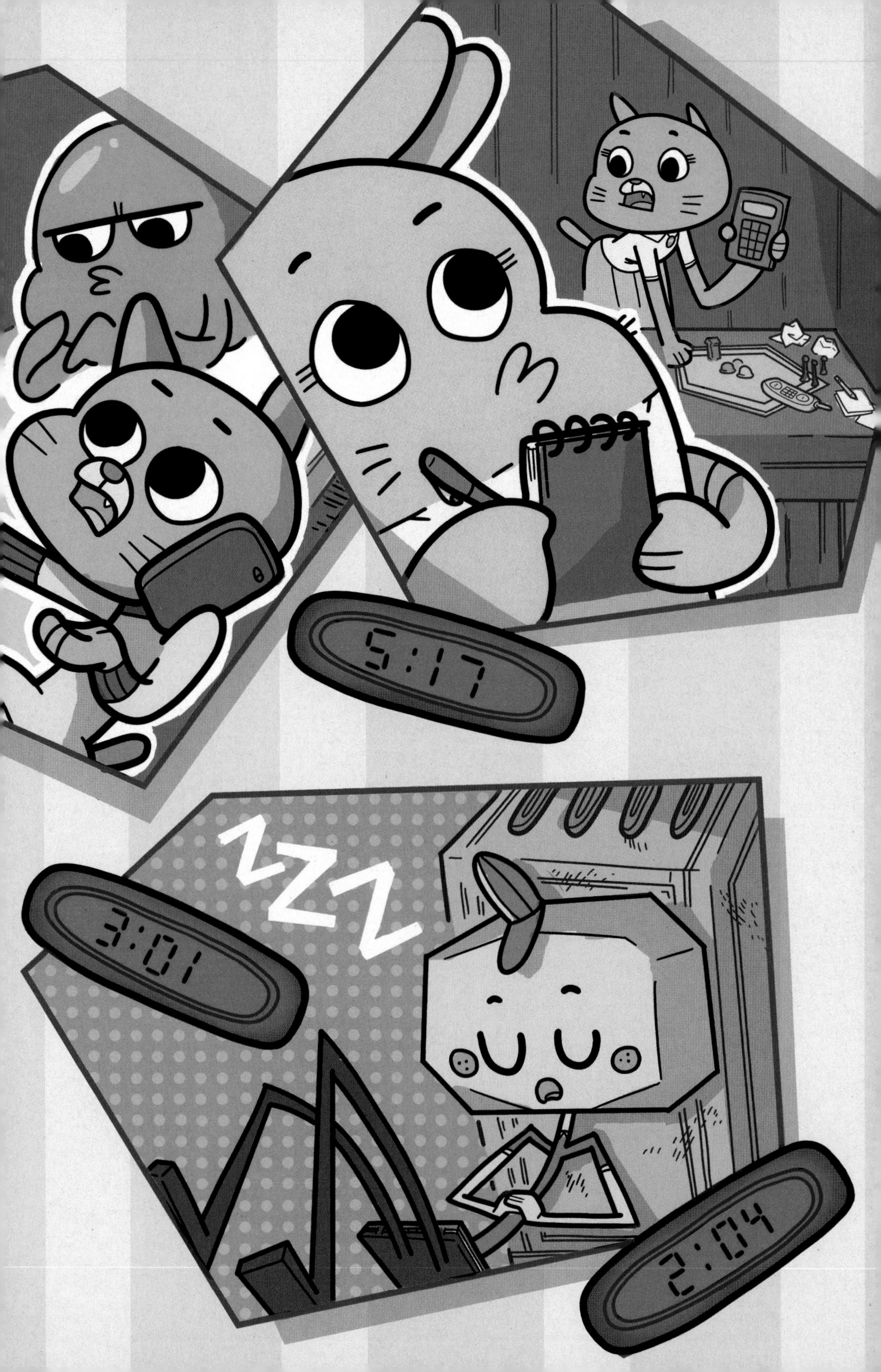
5:17
ZZZ
3:01
2:04

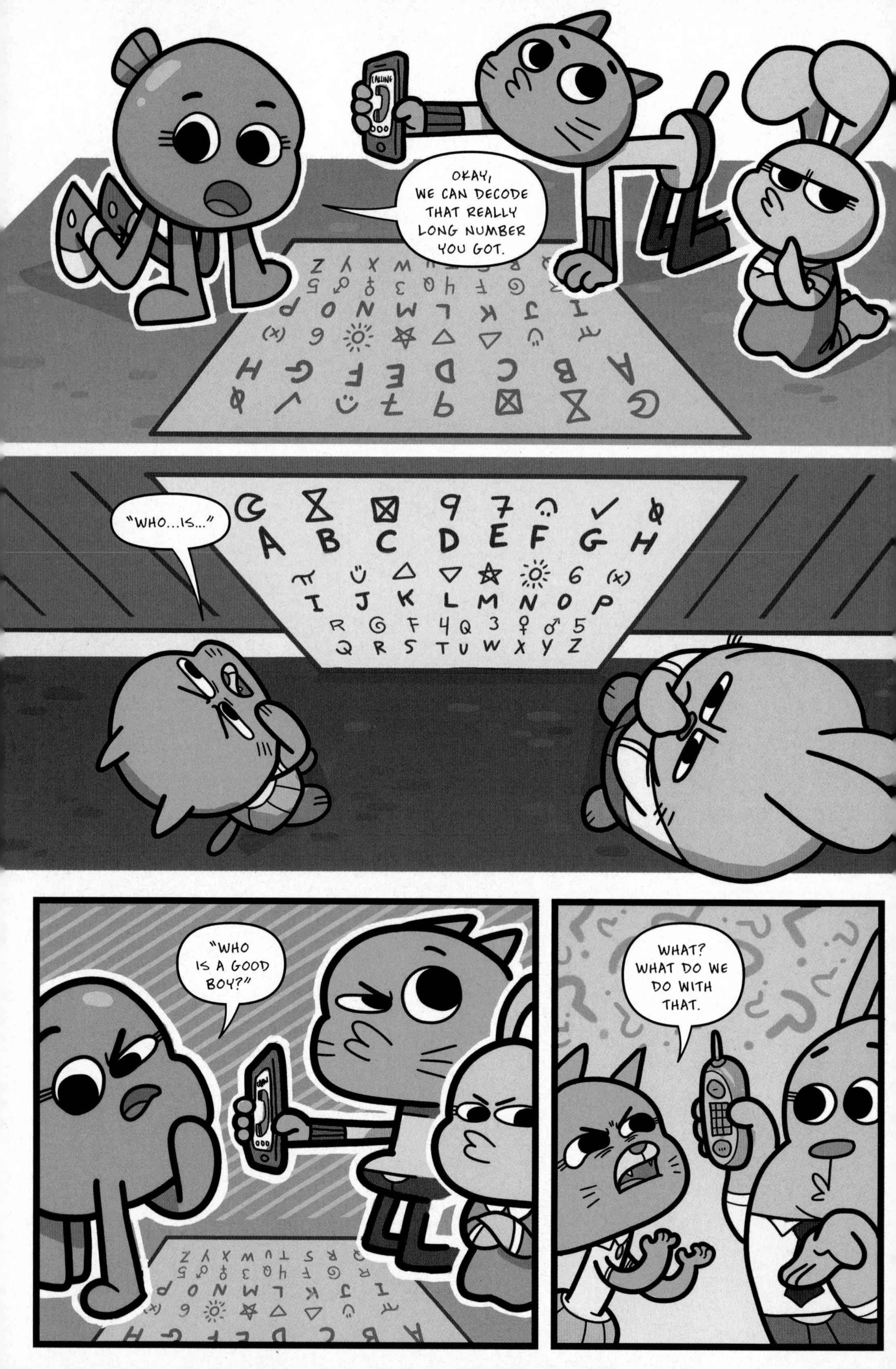
OKAY, WE CAN DECODE THAT REALLY LONG NUMBER YOU GOT.
"WHO...IS..."
A B C D E F G H
I J K L M N O P
Q R S T U W X Y Z
"WHO IS A GOOD BOY?"
WHAT? WHAT DO WE DO WITH THAT.

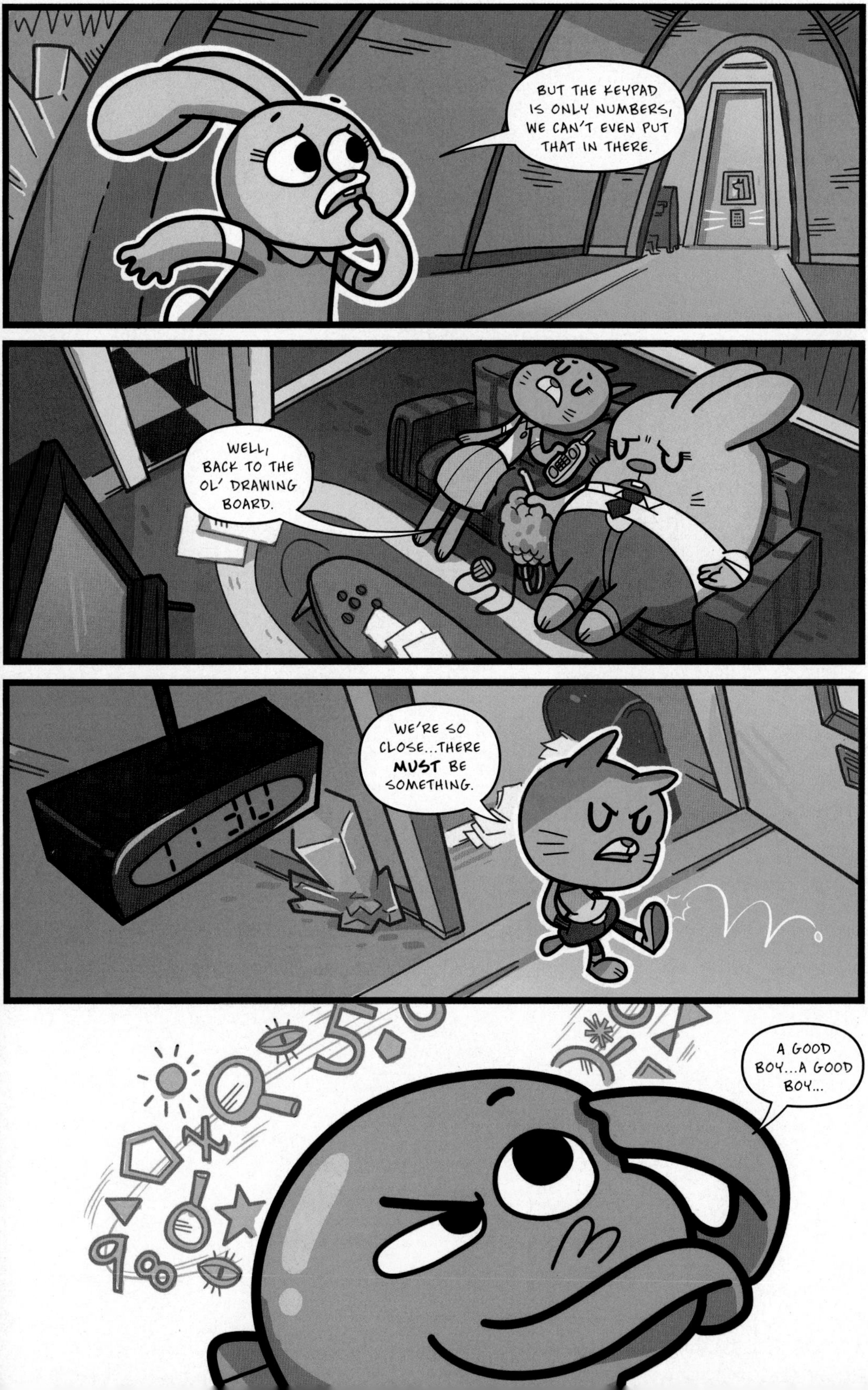
BUT THE KEYPAD IS ONLY NUMBERS, WE CAN'T EVEN PUT THAT IN THERE.
WELL, BACK TO THE OL' DRAWING BOARD.
WE'RE SO CLOSE...THERE **MUST** BE SOMETHING.
A GOOD BOY...A GOOD BOY...

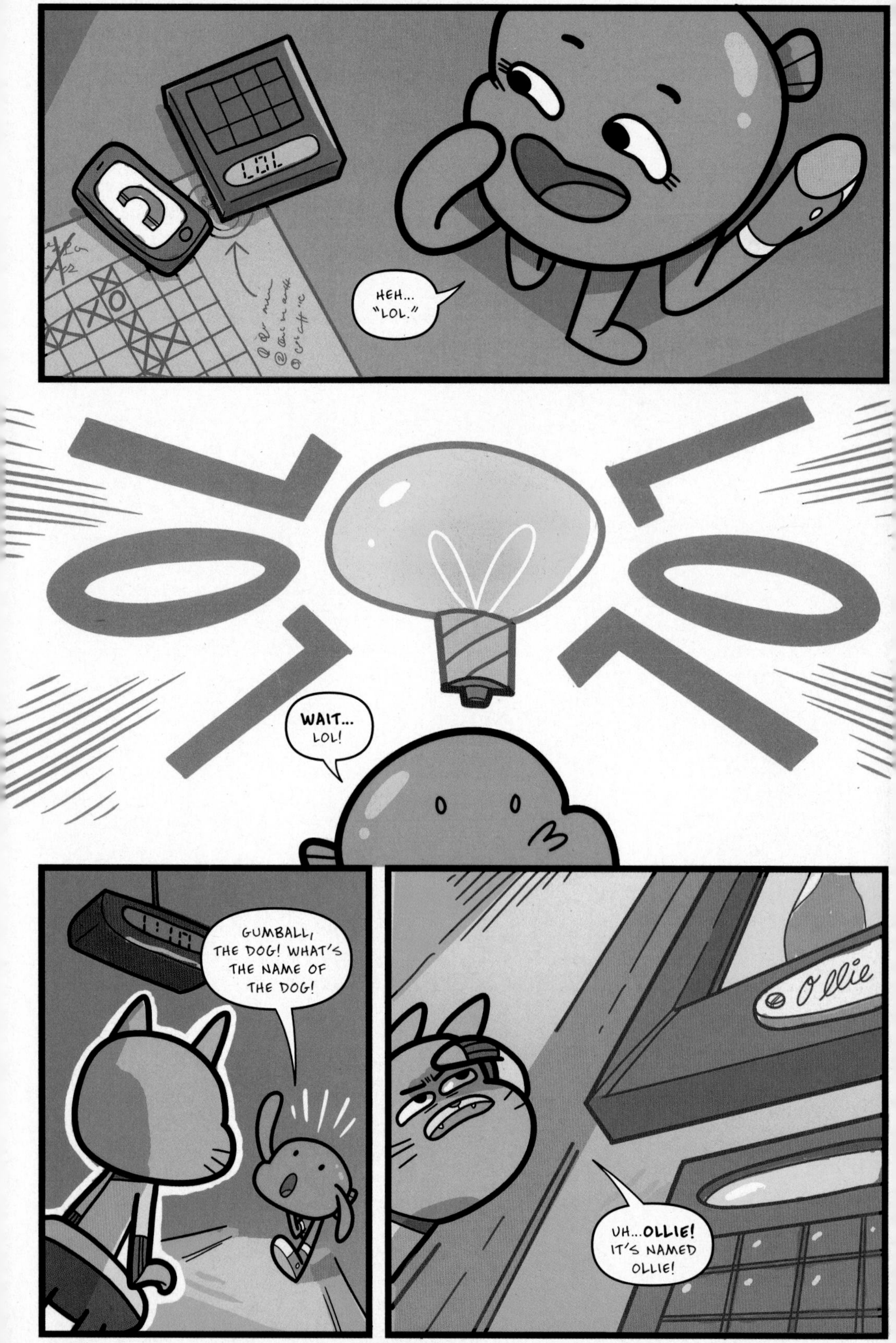
LOL
HEH... "LOL."
LOL
LOL
WAIT... LOL!
GUMBALL, THE DOG! WHAT'S THE NAME OF THE DOG!
Ollie
UH...**OLLIE!** IT'S NAMED OLLIE!

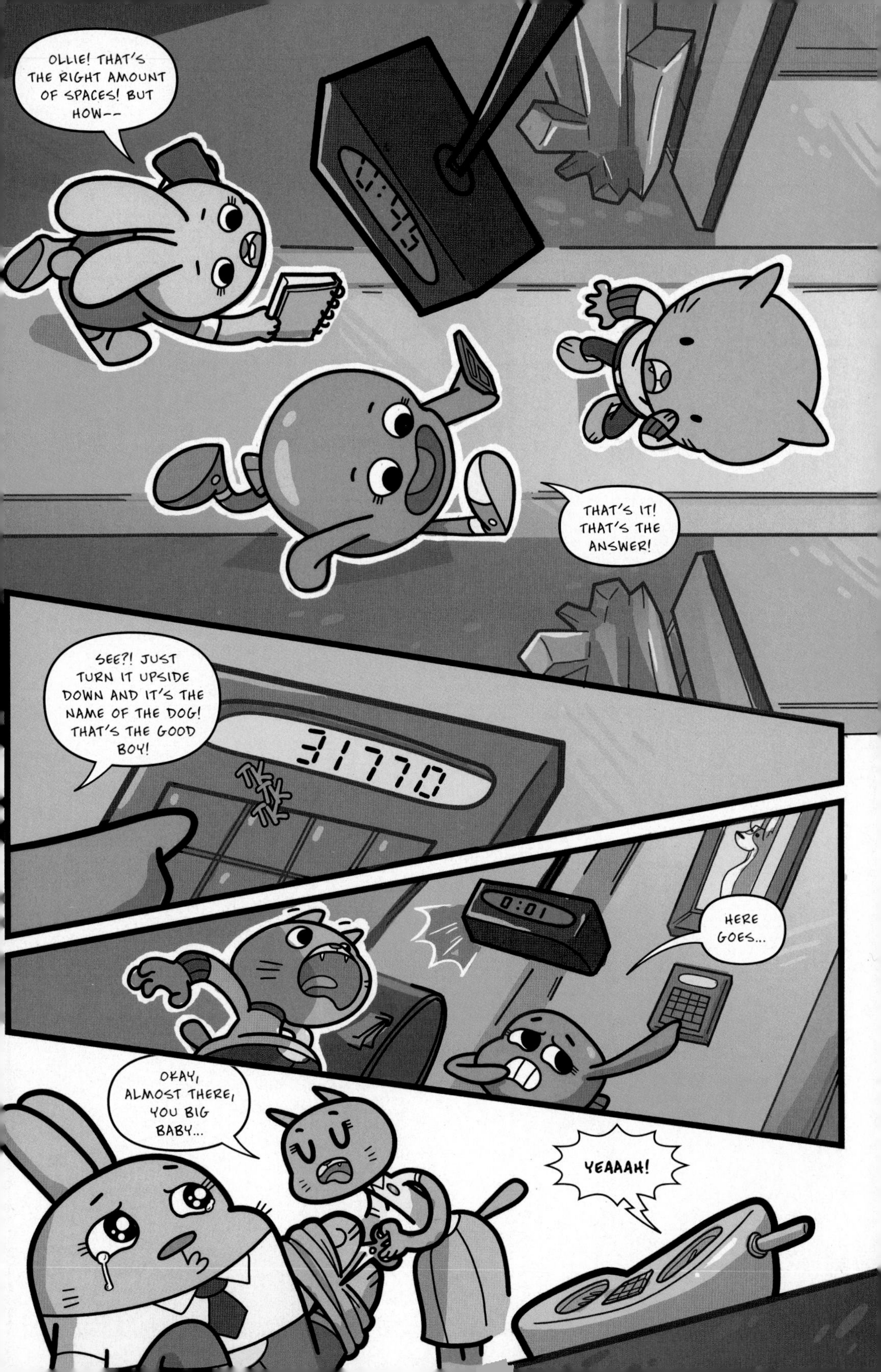
OLLIE! THAT'S THE RIGHT AMOUNT OF SPACES! BUT HOW--
THAT'S IT! THAT'S THE ANSWER!
SEE?! JUST TURN IT UPSIDE DOWN AND IT'S THE NAME OF THE DOG! THAT'S THE GOOD BOY!
31770
0:01
HERE GOES...
OKAY, ALMOST THERE, YOU BIG BABY...
YEAAAH!

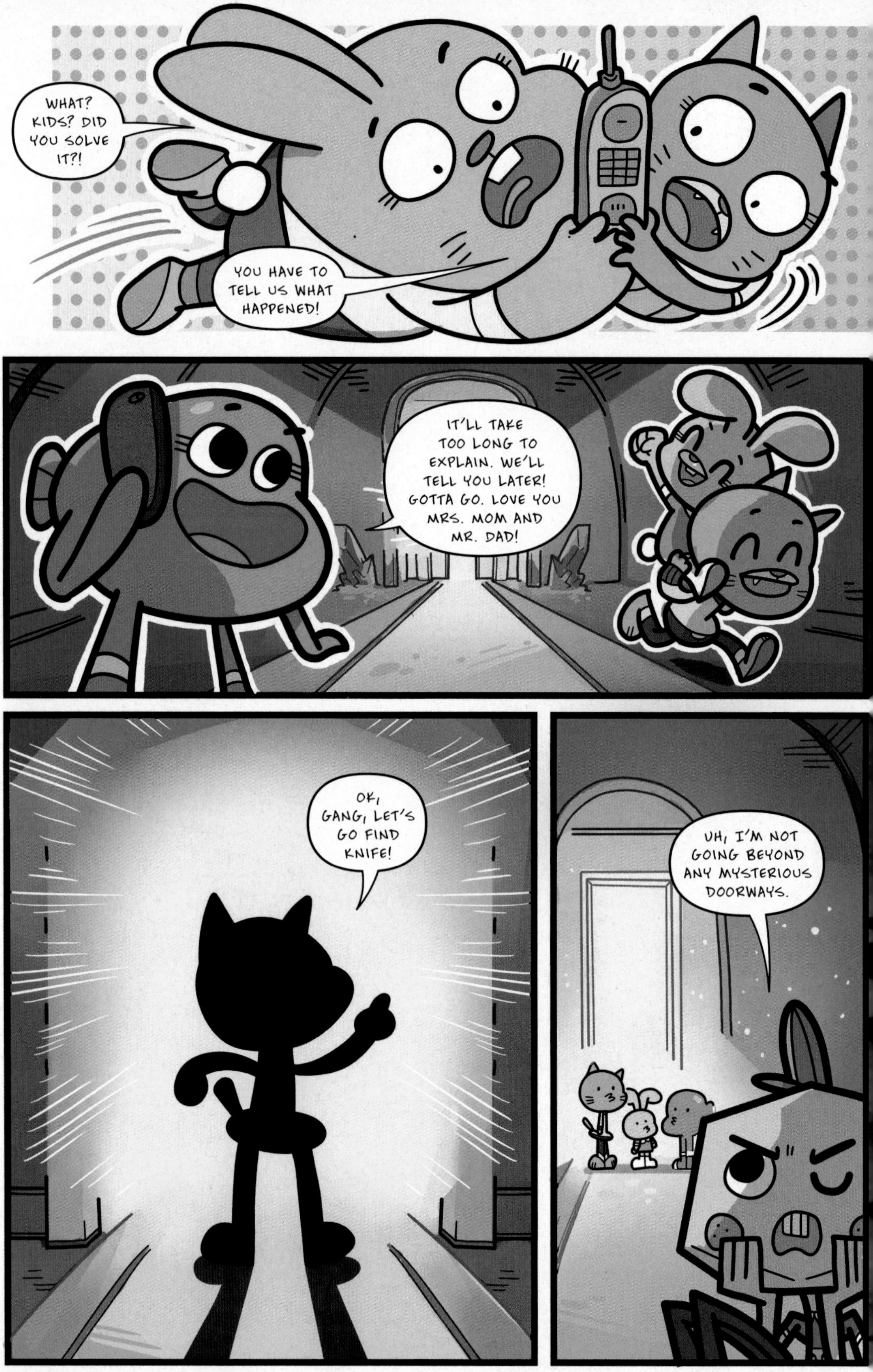
WHAT? KIDS? DID YOU SOLVE IT?!
YOU HAVE TO TELL US WHAT HAPPENED!
IT'LL TAKE TOO LONG TO EXPLAIN. WE'LL TELL YOU LATER! GOTTA GO. LOVE YOU MRS. MOM AND MR. DAD!
OK, GANG, LET'S GO FIND KNIFE!
UH, I'M NOT GOING BEYOND ANY MYSTERIOUS DOORWAYS.

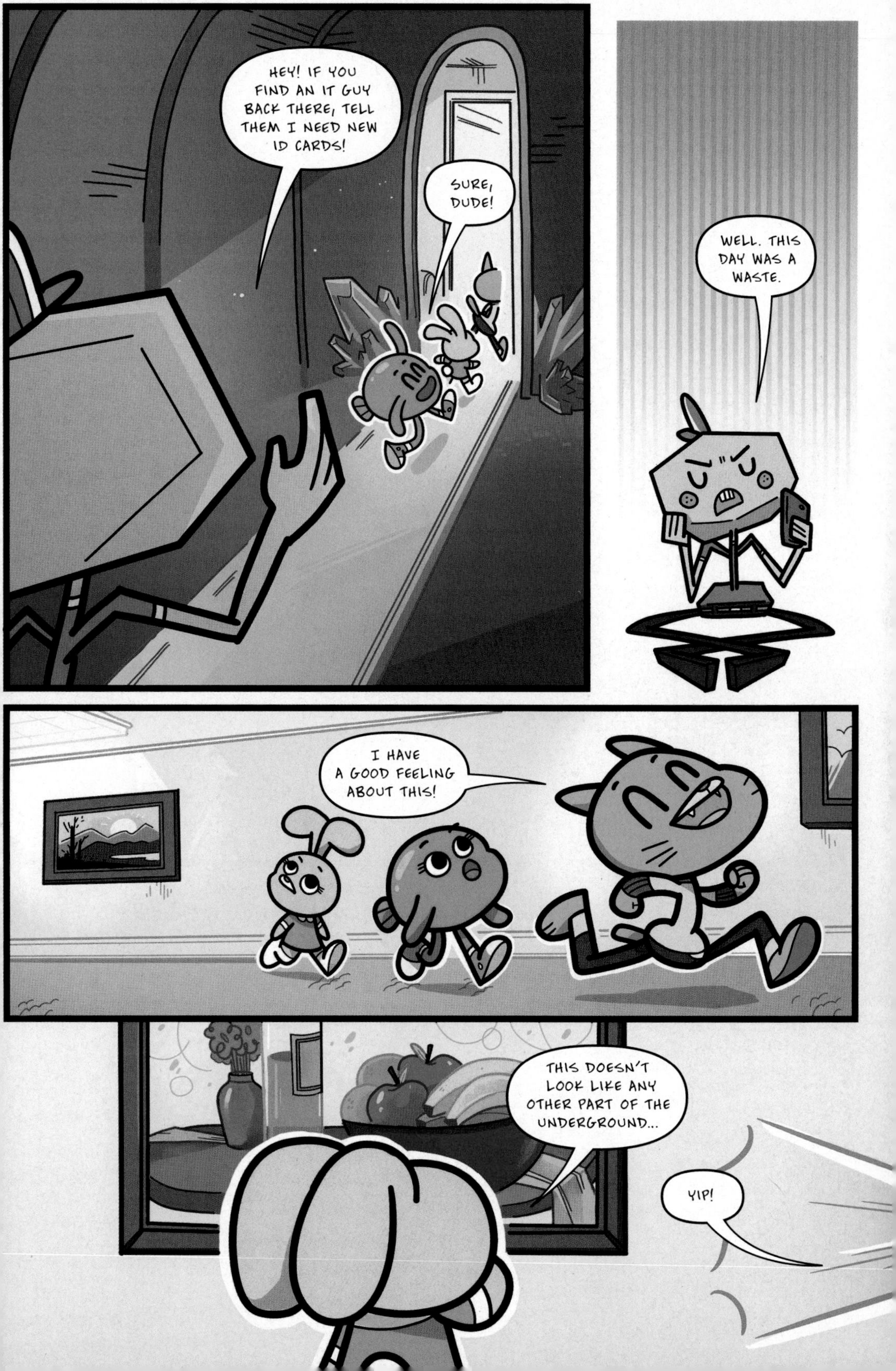
HEY! IF YOU FIND AN IT GUY BACK THERE, TELL THEM I NEED NEW ID CARDS!
SURE, DUDE!
WELL. THIS DAY WAS A WASTE.
I HAVE A GOOD FEELING ABOUT THIS!
THIS DOESN'T LOOK LIKE ANY OTHER PART OF THE UNDERGROUND...
YIP!

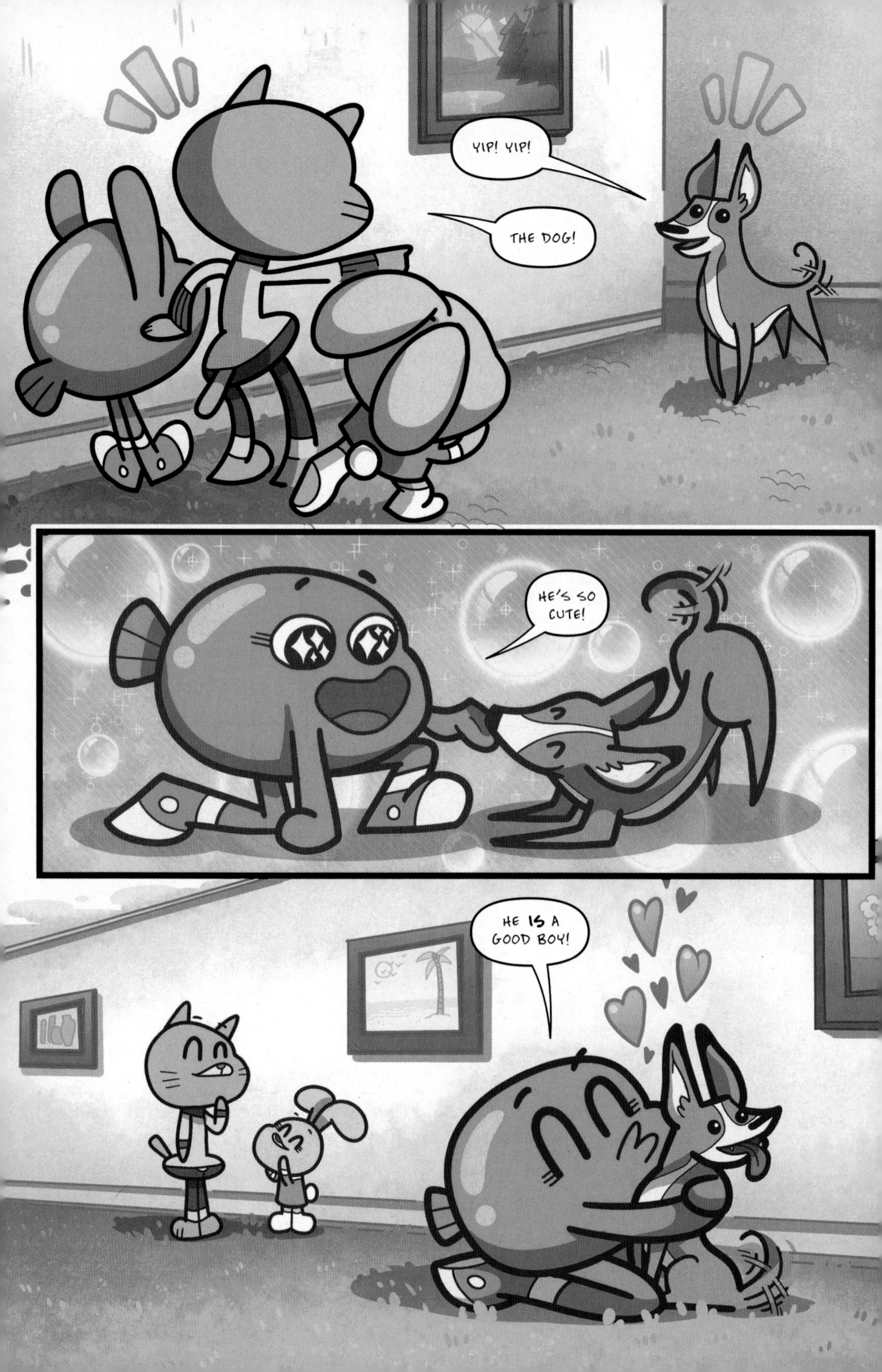
YIP! YIP!
THE DOG!
HE'S SO CUTE!
HE IS A GOOD BOY!

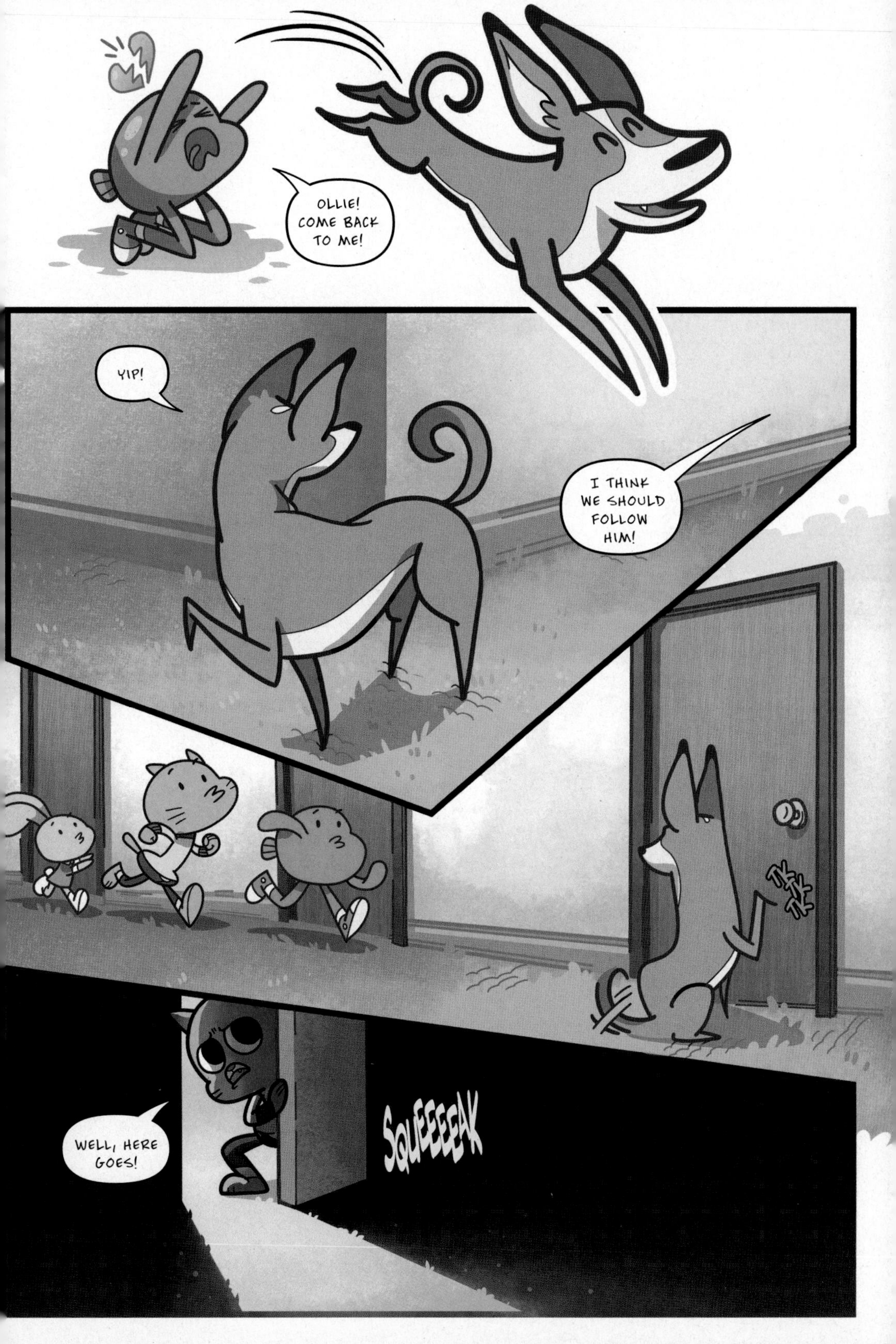
OLLIE! COME BACK TO ME!
YIP!
I THINK WE SHOULD FOLLOW HIM!
TK TK
WELL, HERE GOES!
SQUEEEEAK

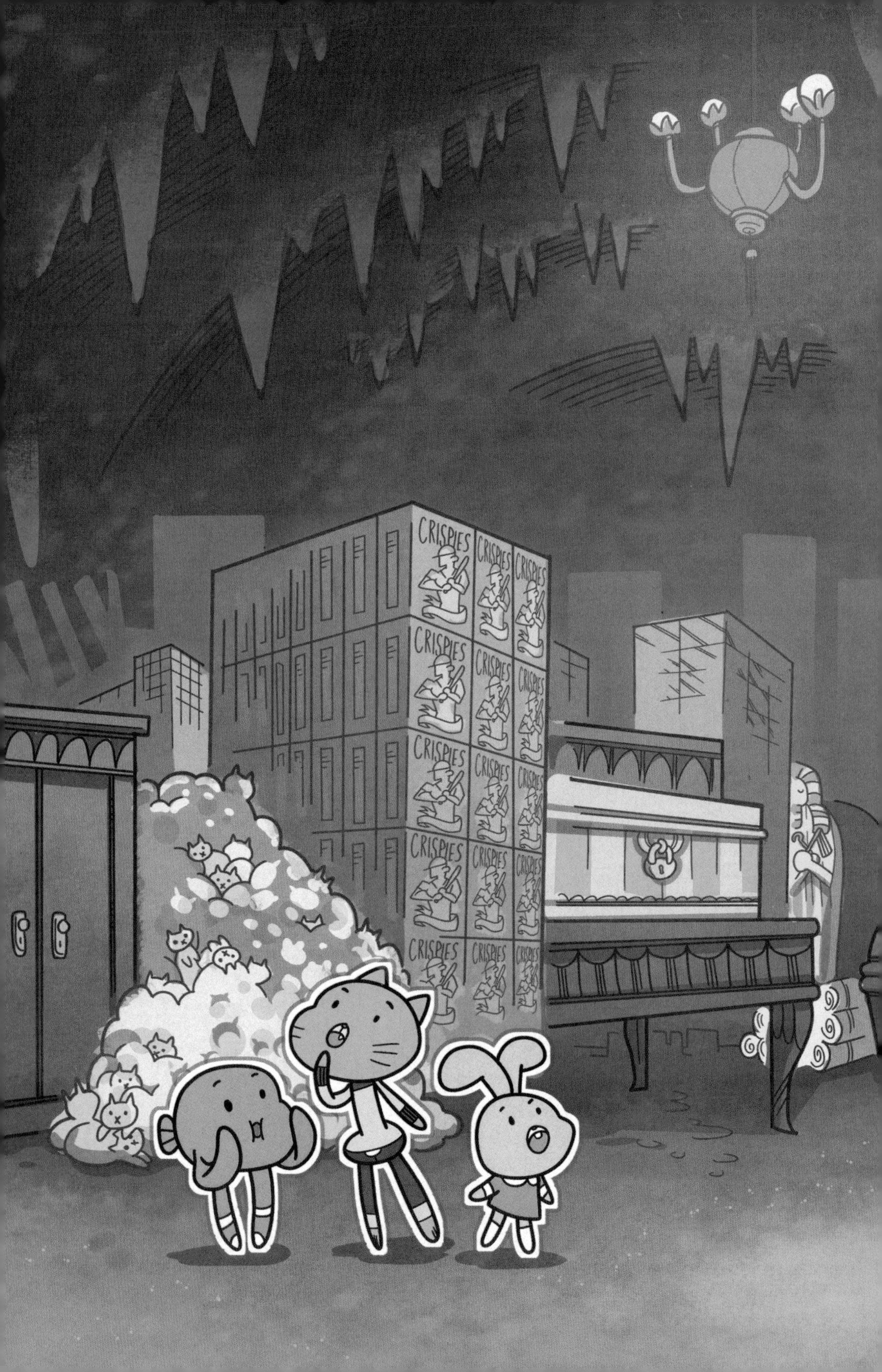
CRISPIES

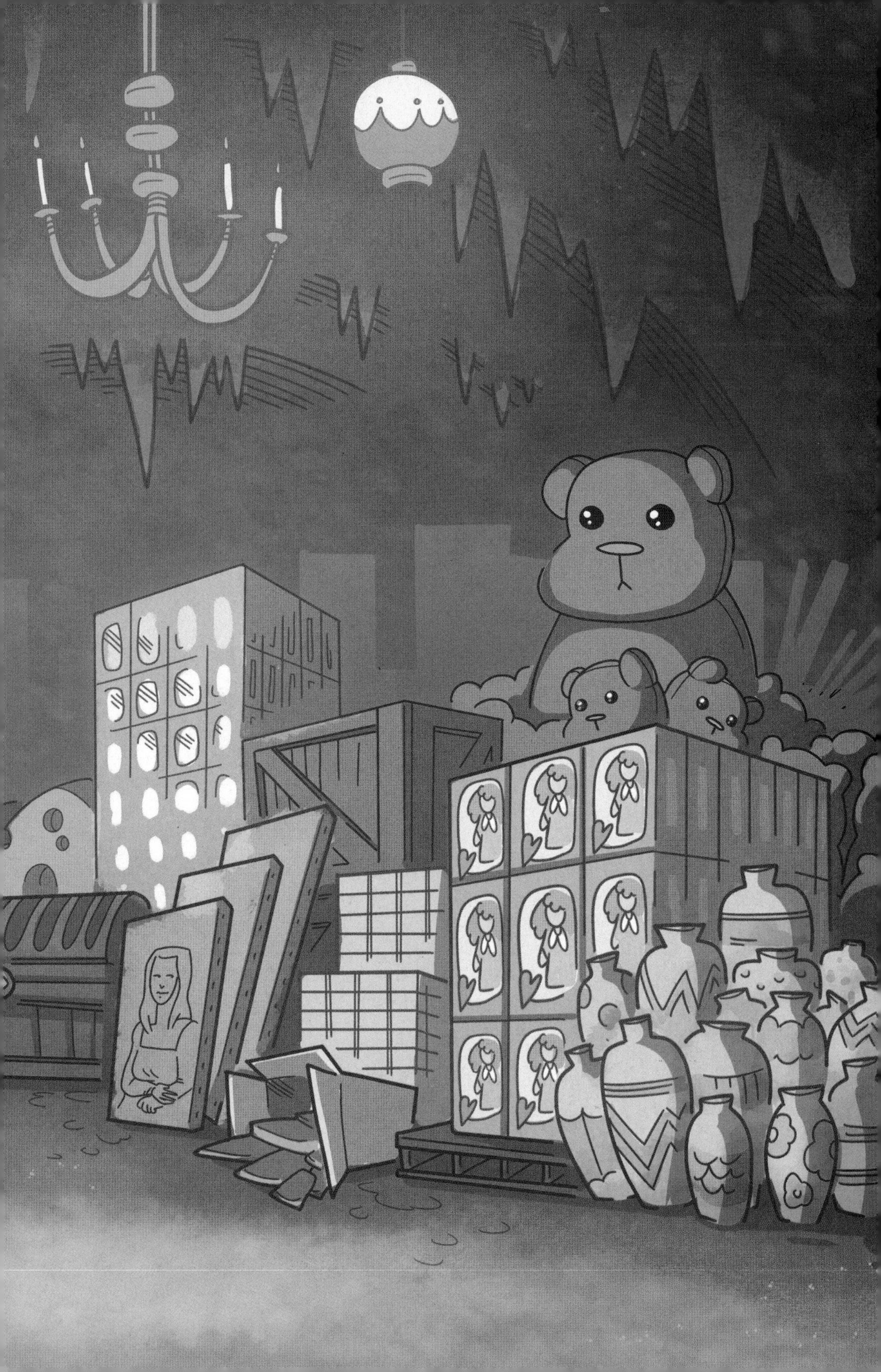

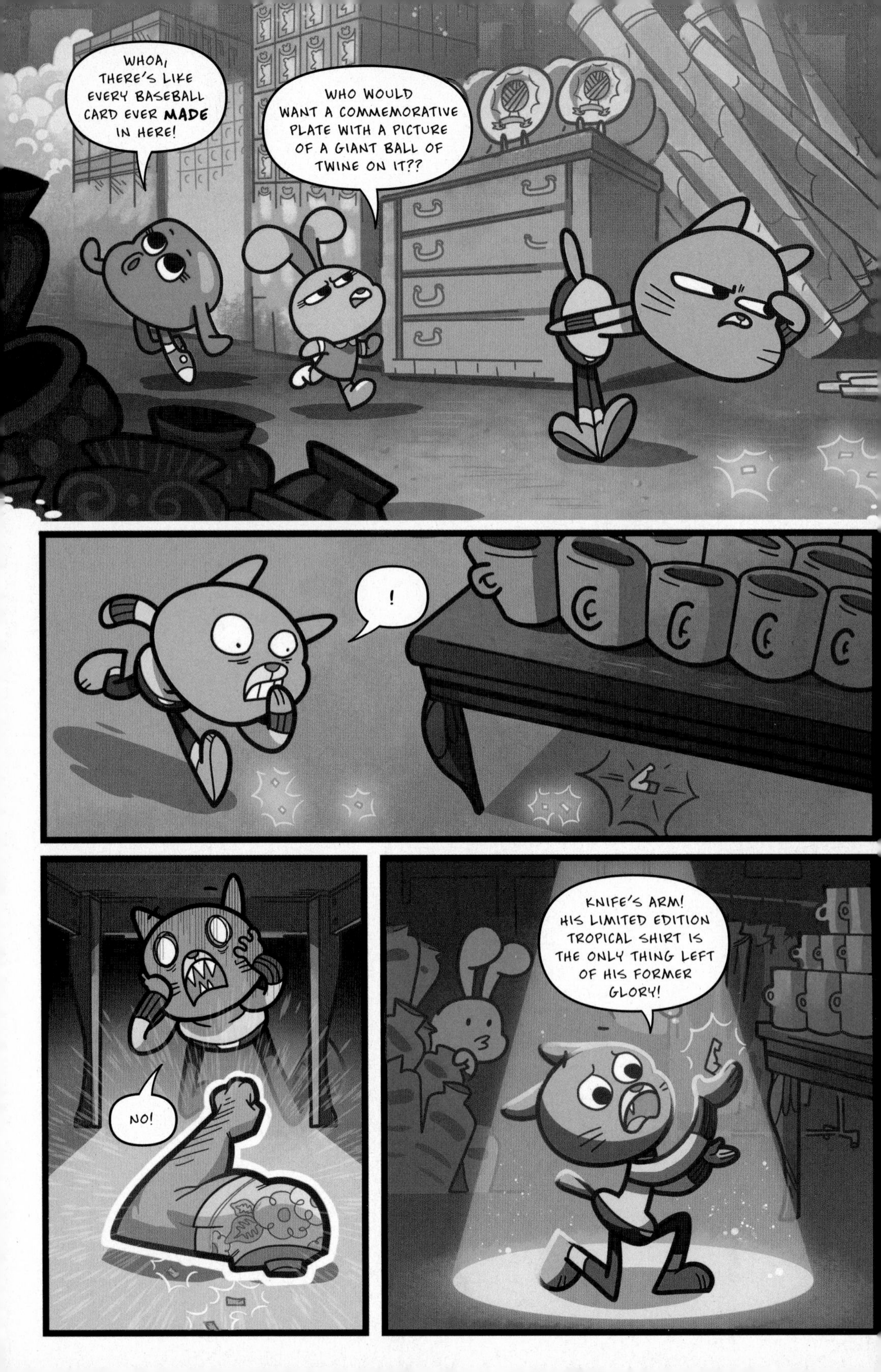
WHOA, THERE'S LIKE EVERY BASEBALL CARD EVER MADE IN HERE!
WHO WOULD WANT A COMMEMORATIVE PLATE WITH A PICTURE OF A GIANT BALL OF TWINE ON IT??
!
NO!
KNIFE'S ARM! HIS LIMITED EDITION TROPICAL SHIRT IS THE ONLY THING LEFT OF HIS FORMER GLORY!

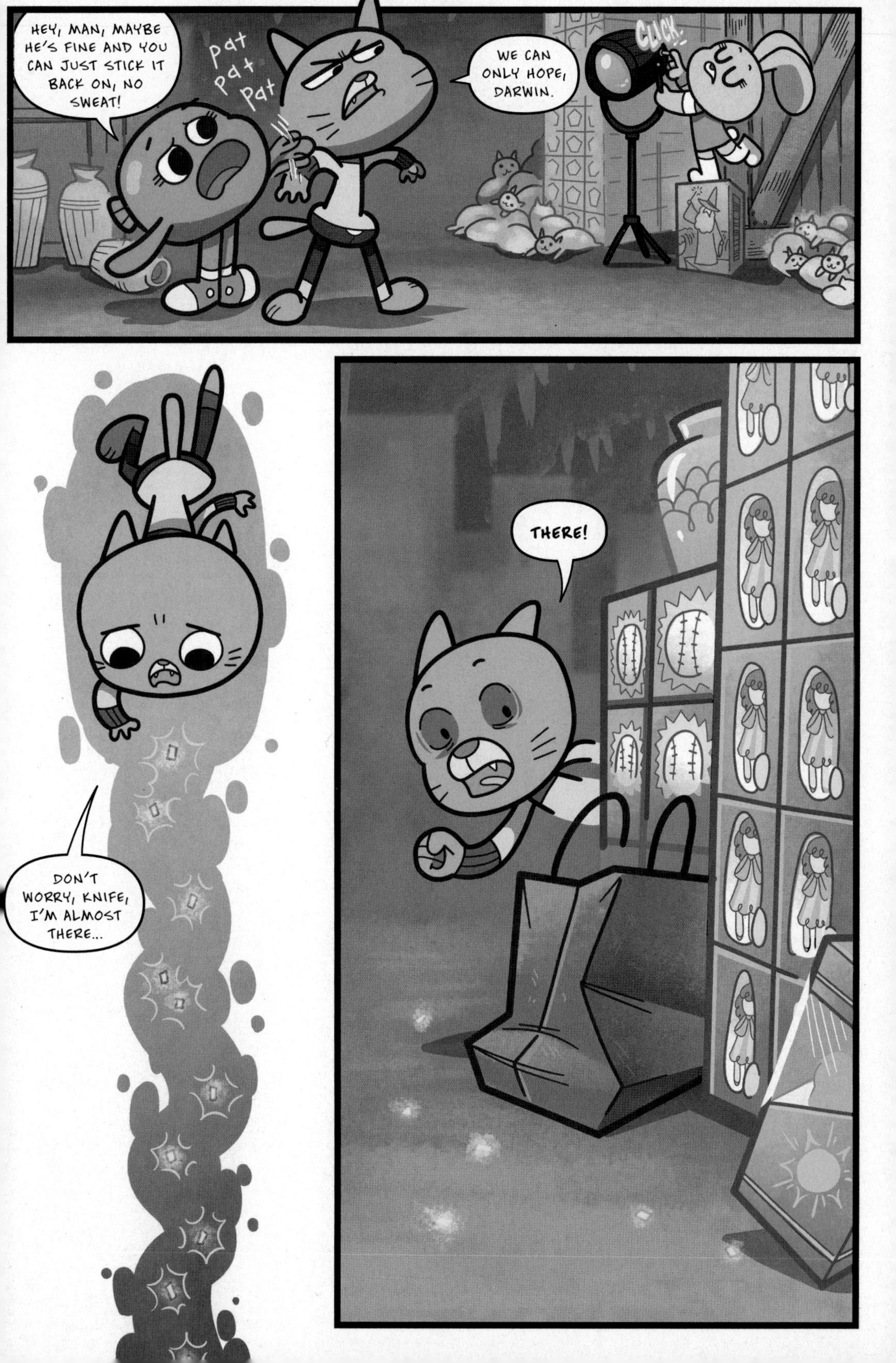
HEY, MAN, MAYBE HE'S FINE AND YOU CAN JUST STICK IT BACK ON, NO SWEAT!
pat pat pat
WE CAN ONLY HOPE, DARWIN.
CLICK!
DON'T WORRY, KNIFE, I'M ALMOST THERE...
THERE!

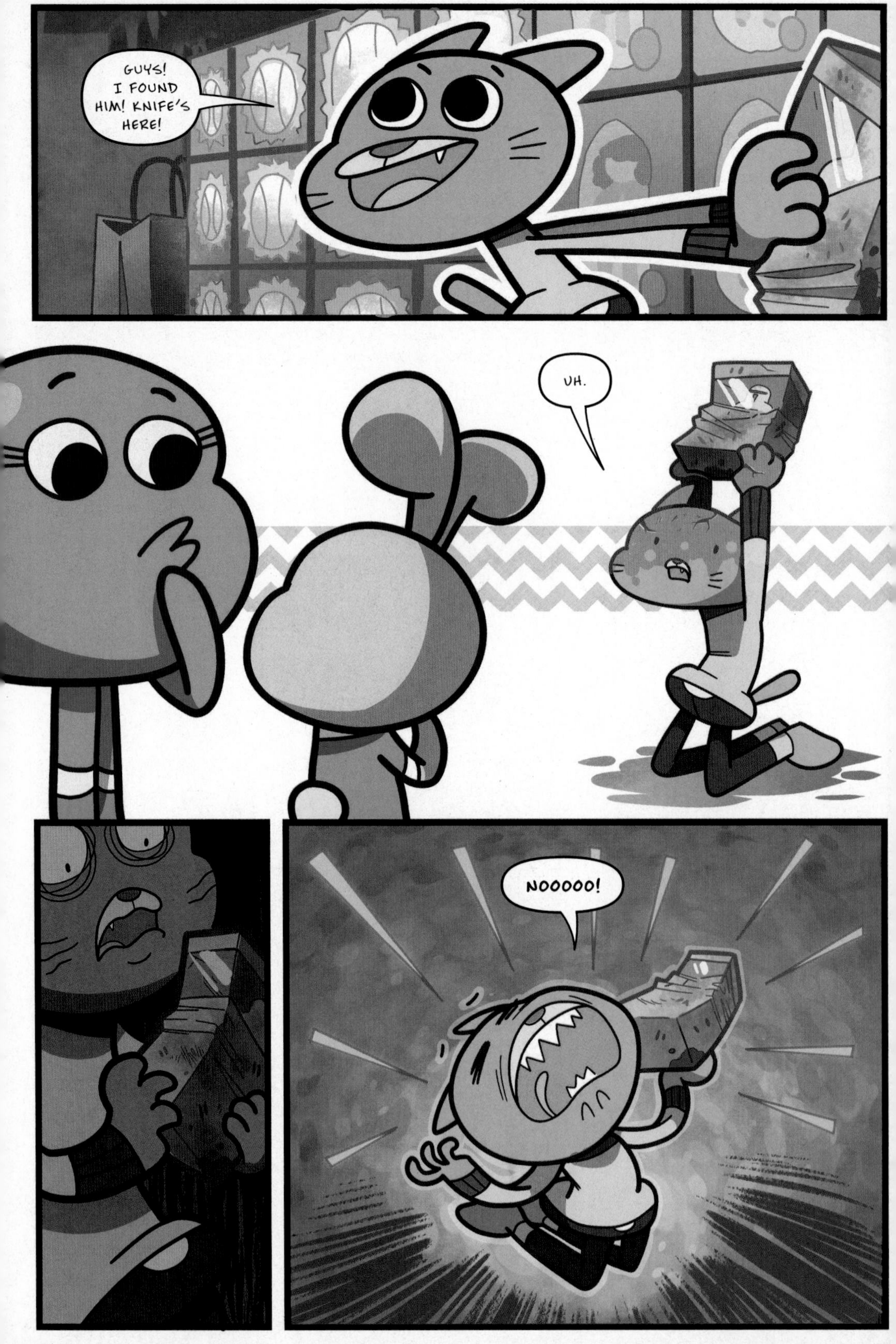
GUYS! I FOUND HIM! KNIFE'S HERE!
UH.
NOOOOO!

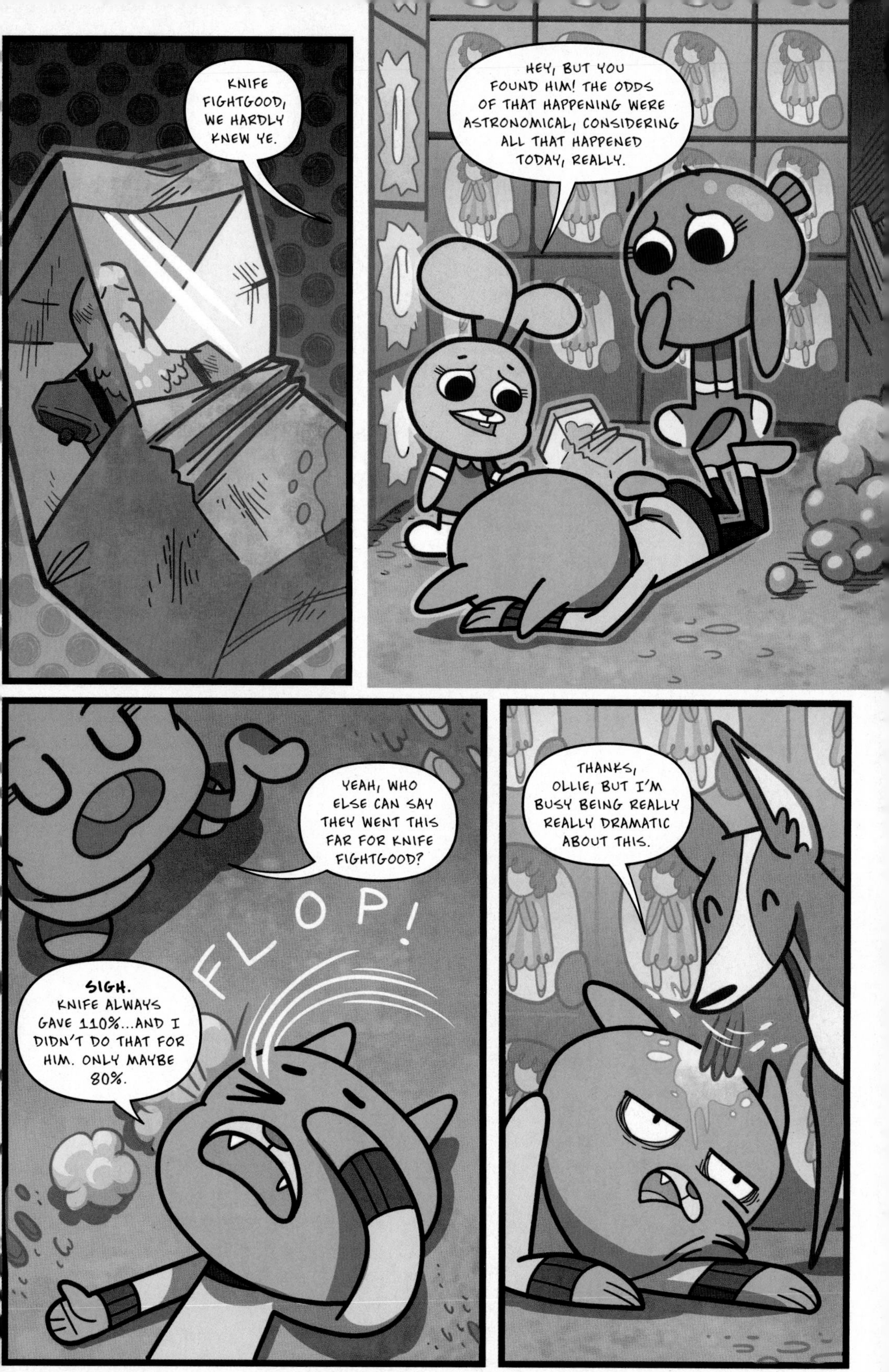
KNIFE FIGHTGOOD, WE HARDLY KNEW YE.
HEY, BUT YOU FOUND HIM! THE ODDS OF THAT HAPPENING WERE ASTRONOMICAL, CONSIDERING ALL THAT HAPPENED TODAY, REALLY.
YEAH, WHO ELSE CAN SAY THEY WENT THIS FAR FOR KNIFE FIGHTGOOD?
FLOP!
SIGH. KNIFE ALWAYS GAVE 110%...AND I DIDN'T DO THAT FOR HIM. ONLY MAYBE 80%.
THANKS, OLLIE, BUT I'M BUSY BEING REALLY REALLY DRAMATIC ABOUT THIS.

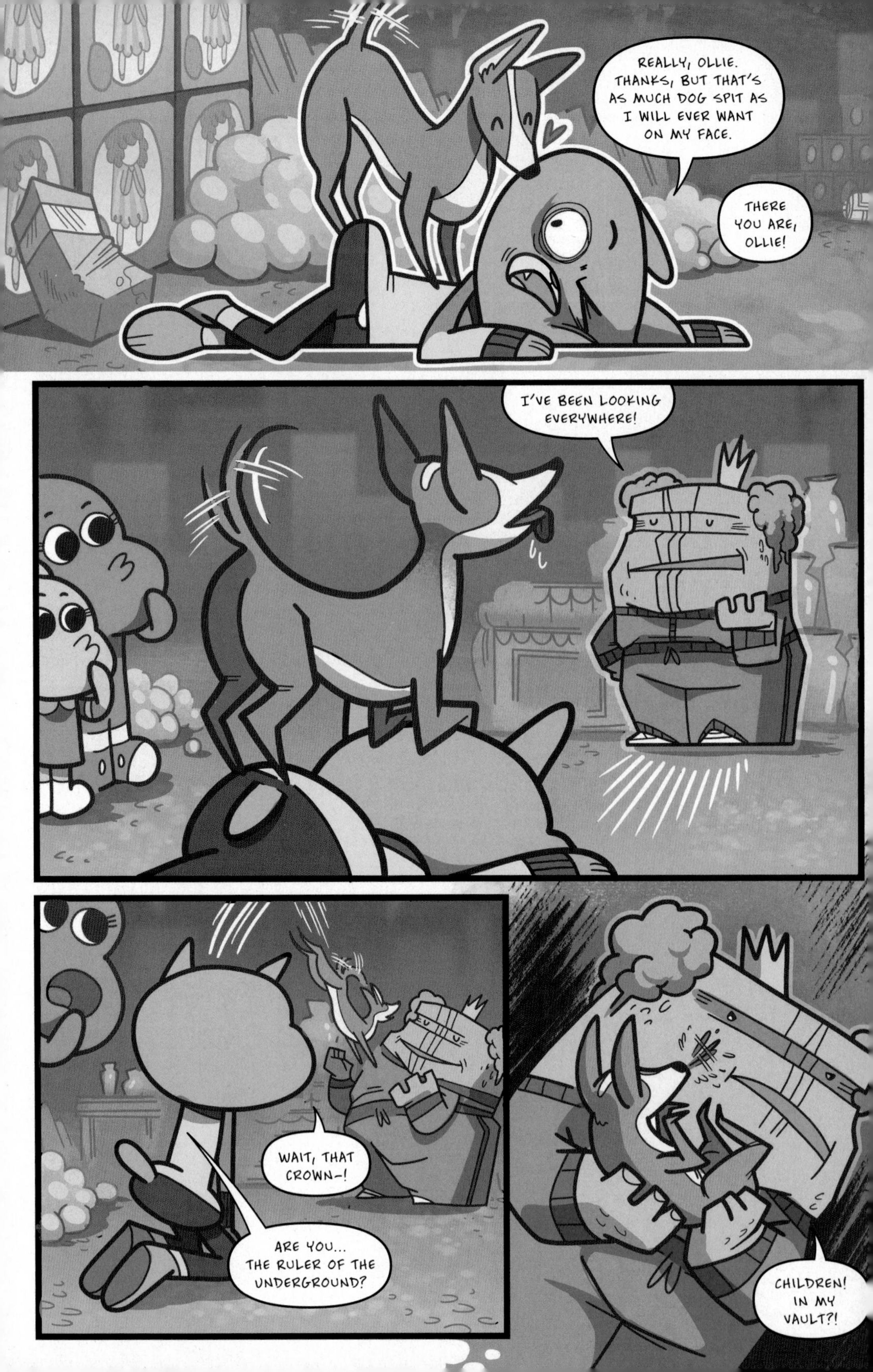
REALLY, OLLIE. THANKS, BUT THAT'S AS MUCH DOG SPIT AS I WILL EVER WANT ON MY FACE.
THERE YOU ARE, OLLIE!
I'VE BEEN LOOKING EVERYWHERE!
WAIT, THAT CROWN-!
ARE YOU... THE RULER OF THE UNDERGROUND?
CHILDREN! IN MY VAULT?!

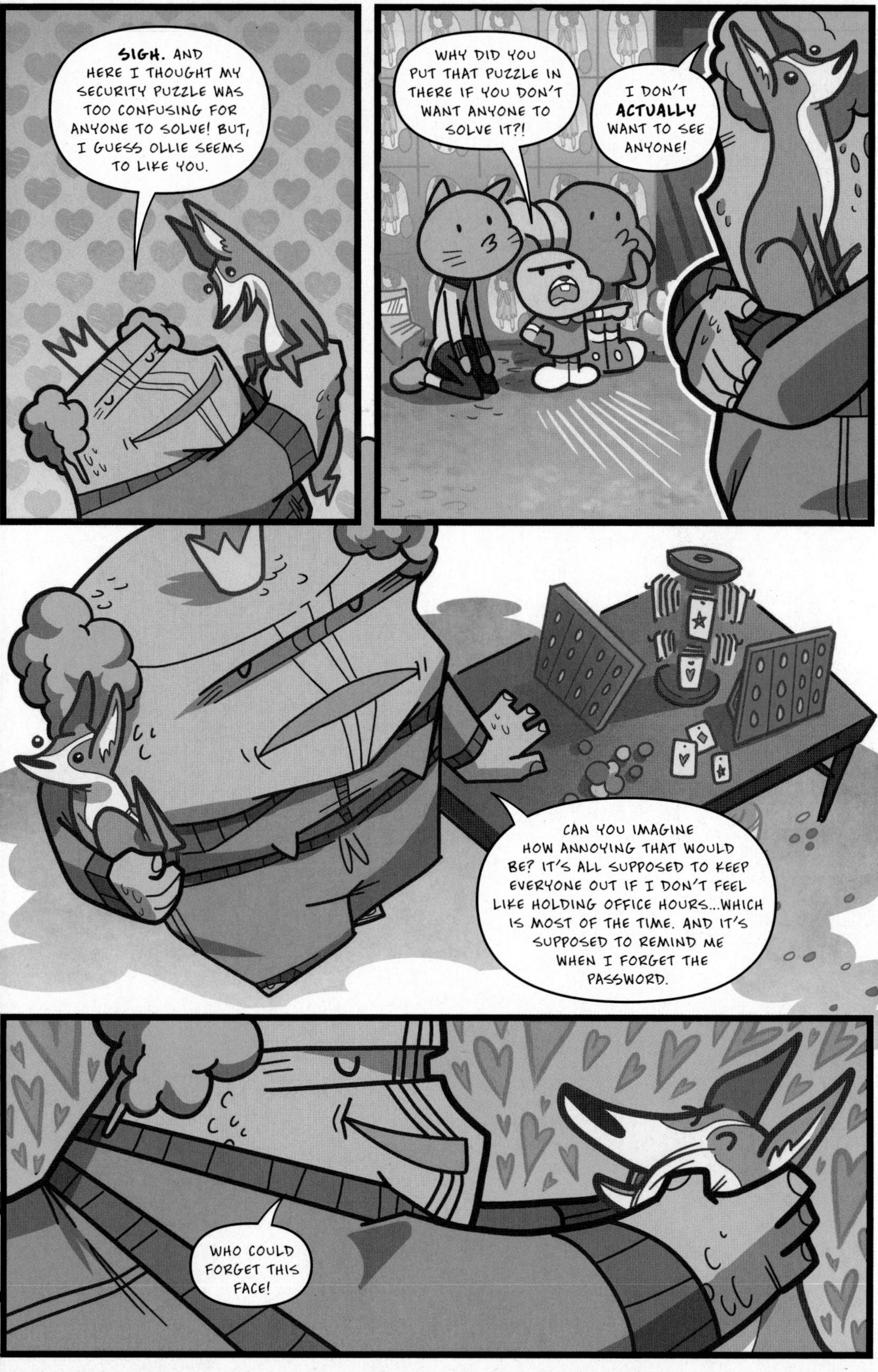
SIGH. AND HERE I THOUGHT MY SECURITY PUZZLE WAS TOO CONFUSING FOR ANYONE TO SOLVE! BUT, I GUESS OLLIE SEEMS TO LIKE YOU.
WHY DID YOU PUT THAT PUZZLE IN THERE IF YOU DON'T WANT ANYONE TO SOLVE IT?!
I DON'T ACTUALLY WANT TO SEE ANYONE!
CAN YOU IMAGINE HOW ANNOYING THAT WOULD BE? IT'S ALL SUPPOSED TO KEEP EVERYONE OUT IF I DON'T FEEL LIKE HOLDING OFFICE HOURS...WHICH IS MOST OF THE TIME. AND IT'S SUPPOSED TO REMIND ME WHEN I FORGET THE PASSWORD.
WHO COULD FORGET THIS FACE!

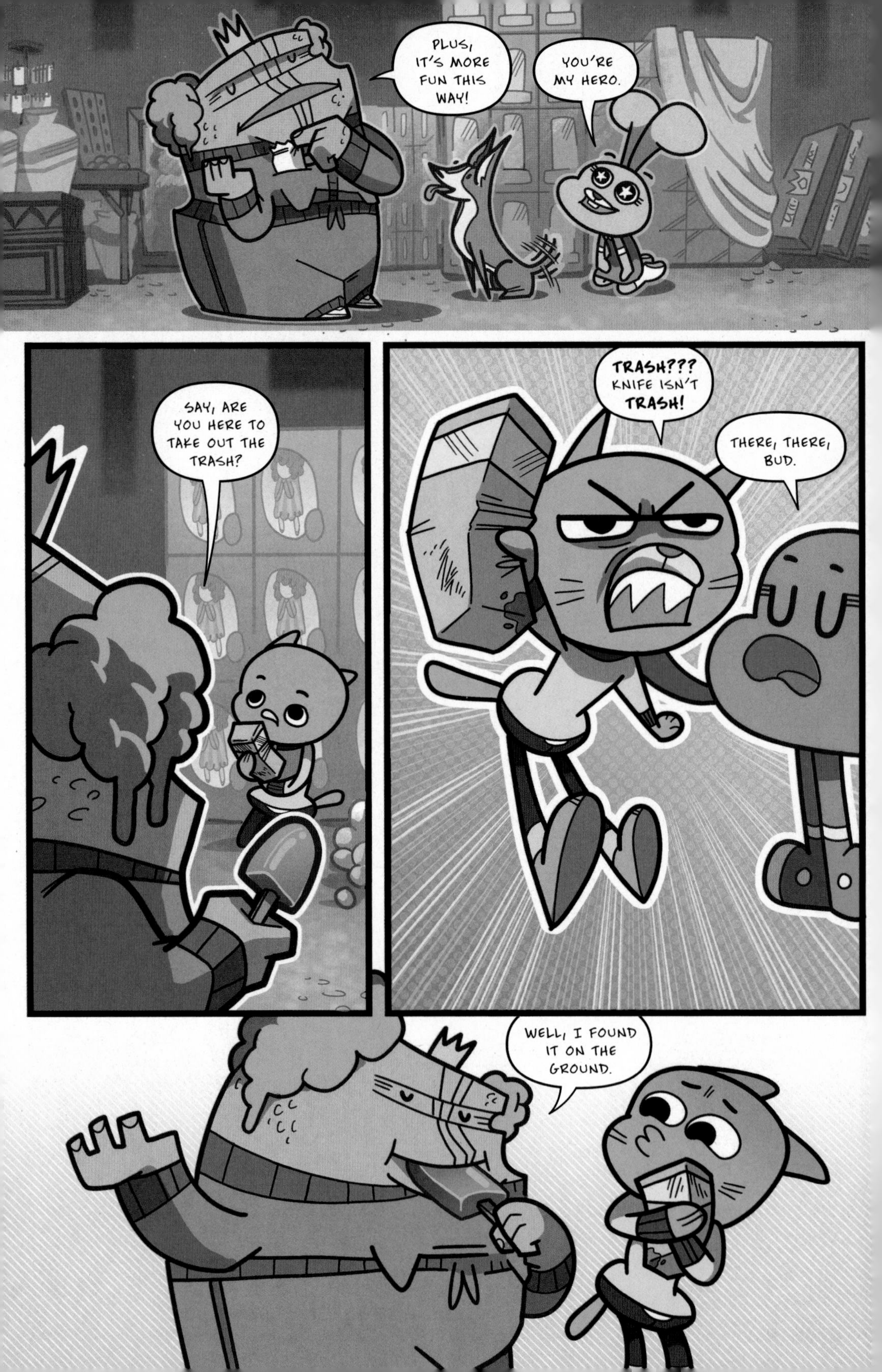
PLUS, IT'S MORE FUN THIS WAY!
YOU'RE MY HERO.
SAY, ARE YOU HERE TO TAKE OUT THE TRASH?
TRASH??? KNIFE ISN'T TRASH!
THERE, THERE, BUD.
WELL, I FOUND IT ON THE GROUND.

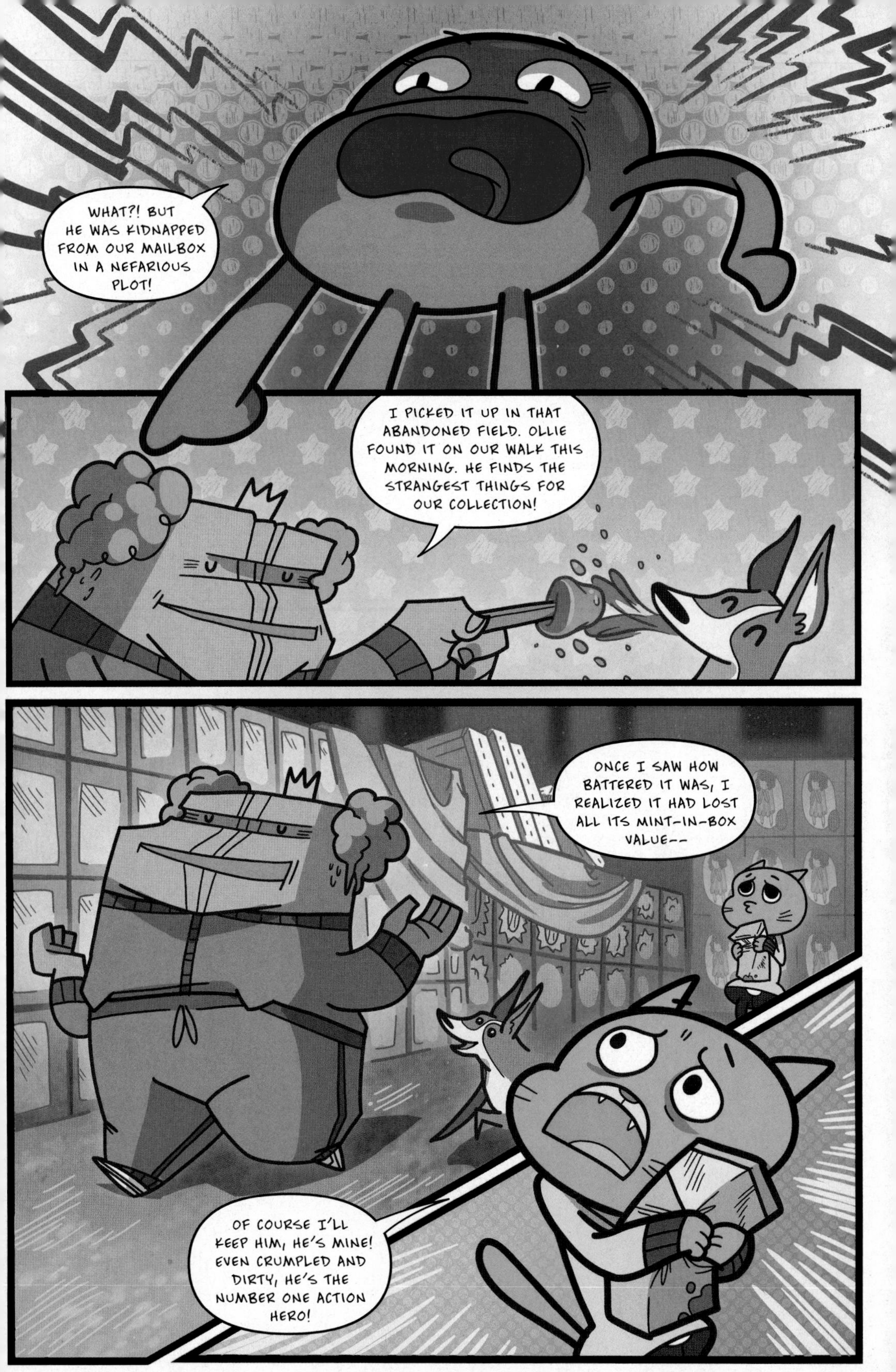
WHAT?! BUT HE WAS KIDNAPPED FROM OUR MAILBOX IN A NEFARIOUS PLOT!
I PICKED IT UP IN THAT ABANDONED FIELD. OLLIE FOUND IT ON OUR WALK THIS MORNING. HE FINDS THE STRANGEST THINGS FOR OUR COLLECTION!
ONCE I SAW HOW BATTERED IT WAS, I REALIZED IT HAD LOST ALL ITS MINT-IN-BOX VALUE--
OF COURSE I'LL KEEP HIM, HE'S MINE! EVEN CRUMPLED AND DIRTY, HE'S THE NUMBER ONE ACTION HERO!

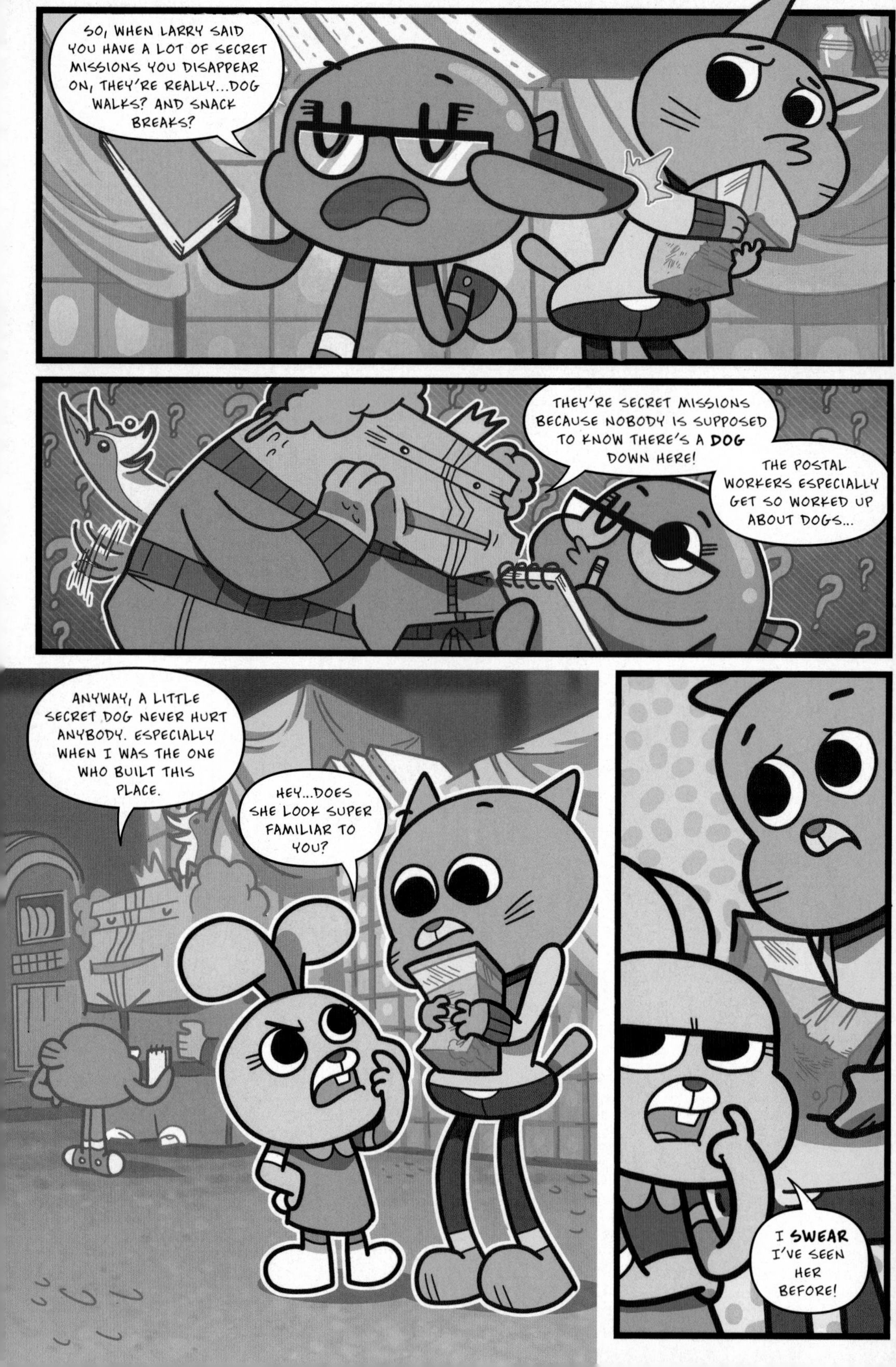
SO, WHEN LARRY SAID YOU HAVE A LOT OF SECRET MISSIONS YOU DISAPPEAR ON, THEY'RE REALLY...DOG WALKS? AND SNACK BREAKS?
THEY'RE SECRET MISSIONS BECAUSE NOBODY IS SUPPOSED TO KNOW THERE'S A **DOG** DOWN HERE!
THE POSTAL WORKERS ESPECIALLY GET SO WORKED UP ABOUT DOGS...
ANYWAY, A LITTLE SECRET DOG NEVER HURT ANYBODY. ESPECIALLY WHEN I WAS THE ONE WHO BUILT THIS PLACE.
HEY...DOES SHE LOOK SUPER FAMILIAR TO YOU?
I **SWEAR** I'VE SEEN HER BEFORE!

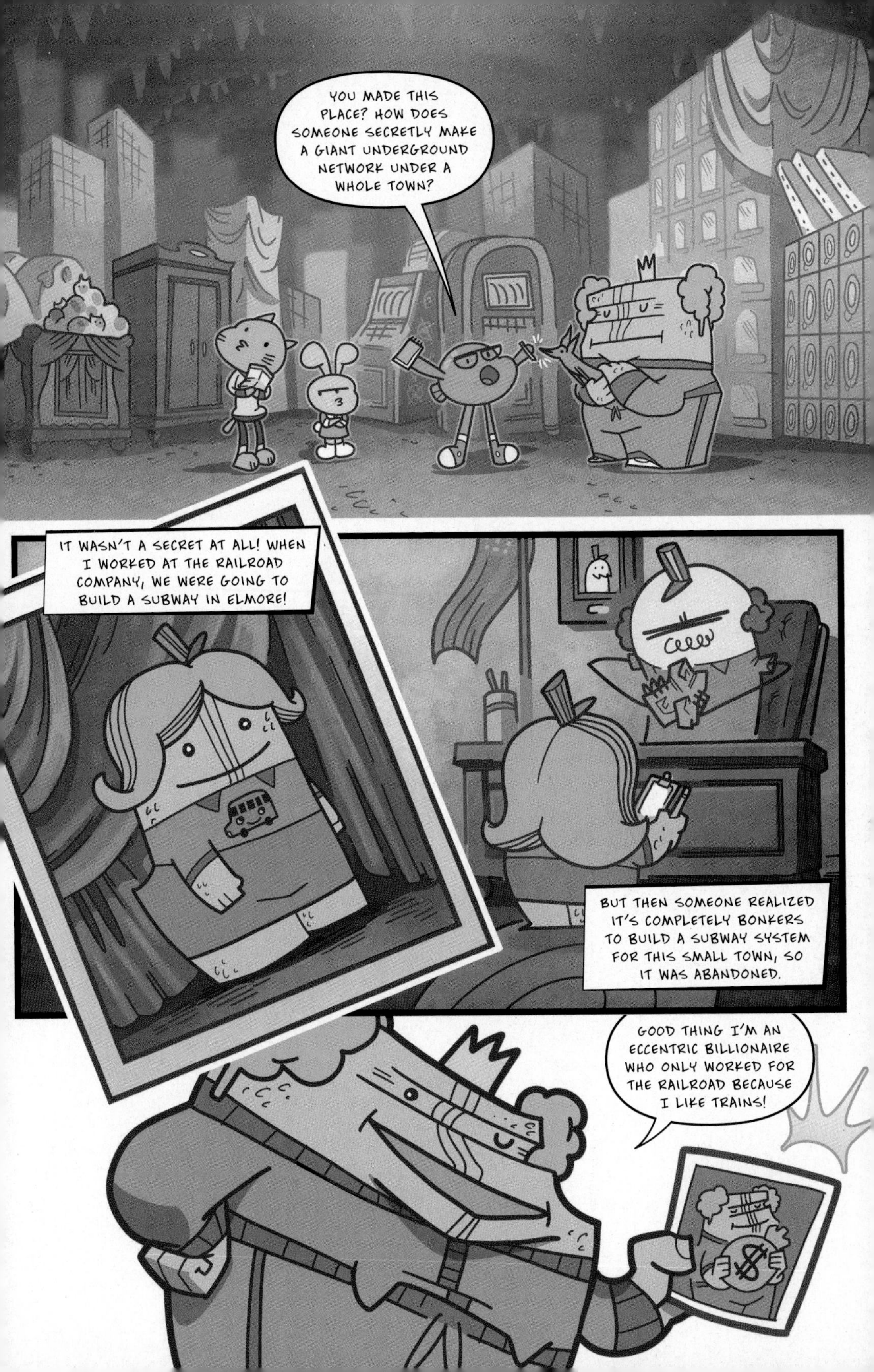
YOU MADE THIS PLACE? HOW DOES SOMEONE SECRETLY MAKE A GIANT UNDERGROUND NETWORK UNDER A WHOLE TOWN?
IT WASN'T A SECRET AT ALL! WHEN I WORKED AT THE RAILROAD COMPANY, WE WERE GOING TO BUILD A SUBWAY IN ELMORE!
BUT THEN SOMEONE REALIZED IT'S COMPLETELY BONKERS TO BUILD A SUBWAY SYSTEM FOR THIS SMALL TOWN, SO IT WAS ABANDONED.
GOOD THING I'M AN ECCENTRIC BILLIONAIRE WHO ONLY WORKED FOR THE RAILROAD BECAUSE I LIKE TRAINS!

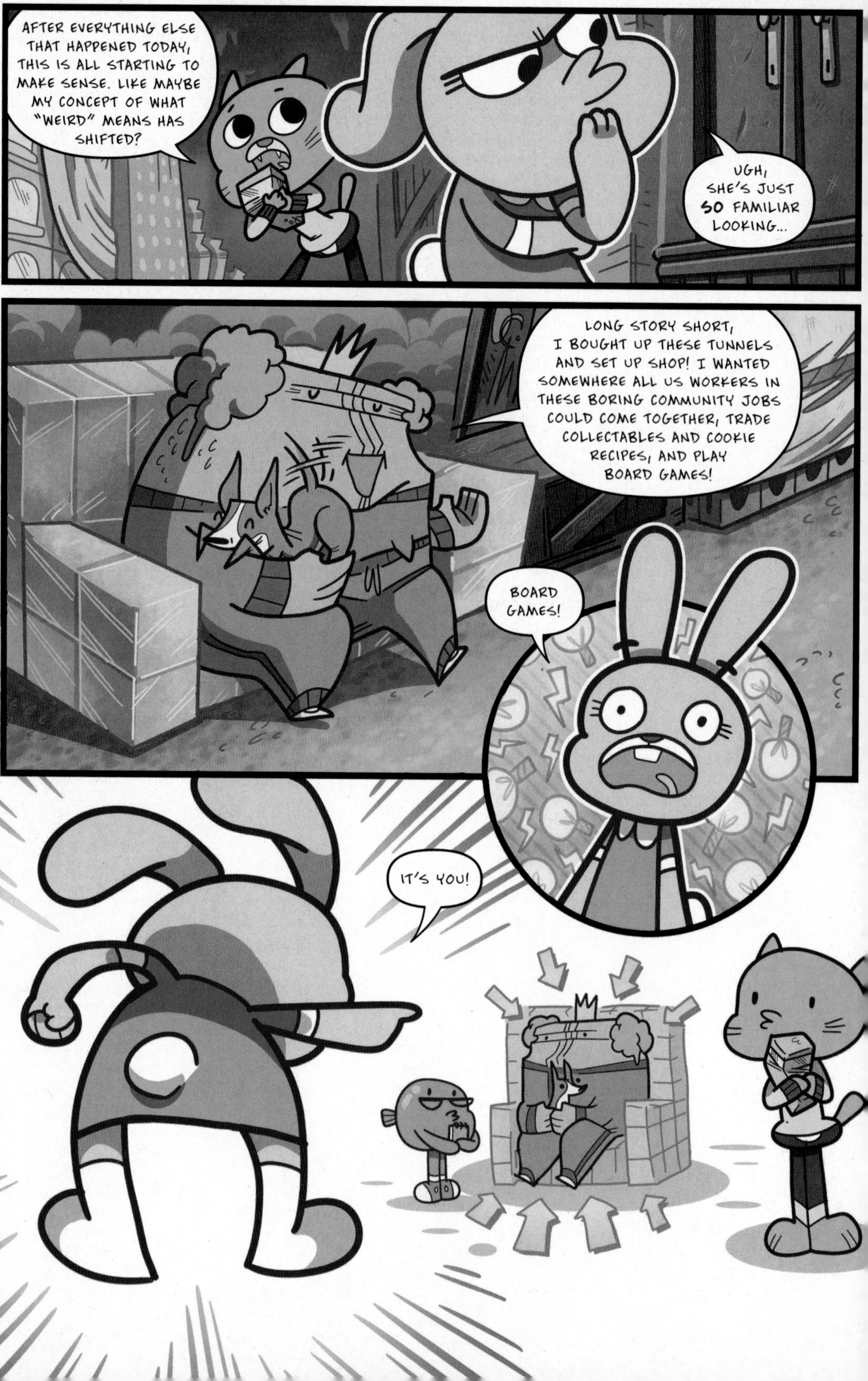
AFTER EVERYTHING ELSE THAT HAPPENED TODAY, THIS IS ALL STARTING TO MAKE SENSE. LIKE MAYBE MY CONCEPT OF WHAT "WEIRD" MEANS HAS SHIFTED?
UGH, SHE'S JUST **SO** FAMILIAR LOOKING...
LONG STORY SHORT, I BOUGHT UP THESE TUNNELS AND SET UP SHOP! I WANTED SOMEWHERE ALL US WORKERS IN THESE BORING COMMUNITY JOBS COULD COME TOGETHER, TRADE COLLECTABLES AND COOKIE RECIPES, AND PLAY BOARD GAMES!
BOARD GAMES!
IT'S YOU!

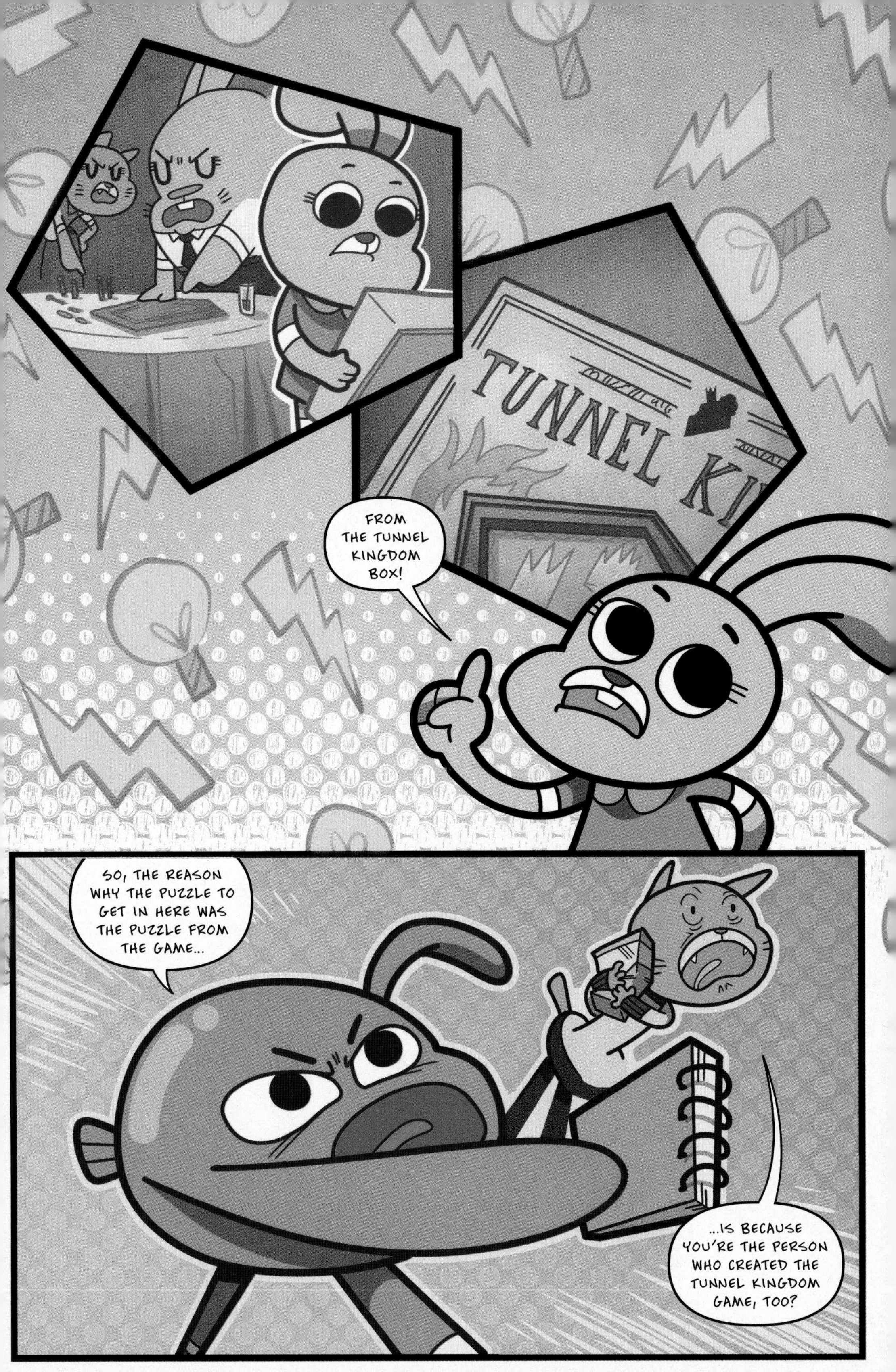
TUNNEL KI
FROM THE TUNNEL KINGDOM BOX!
SO, THE REASON WHY THE PUZZLE TO GET IN HERE WAS THE PUZZLE FROM THE GAME...
...IS BECAUSE YOU'RE THE PERSON WHO CREATED THE TUNNEL KINGDOM GAME, TOO?

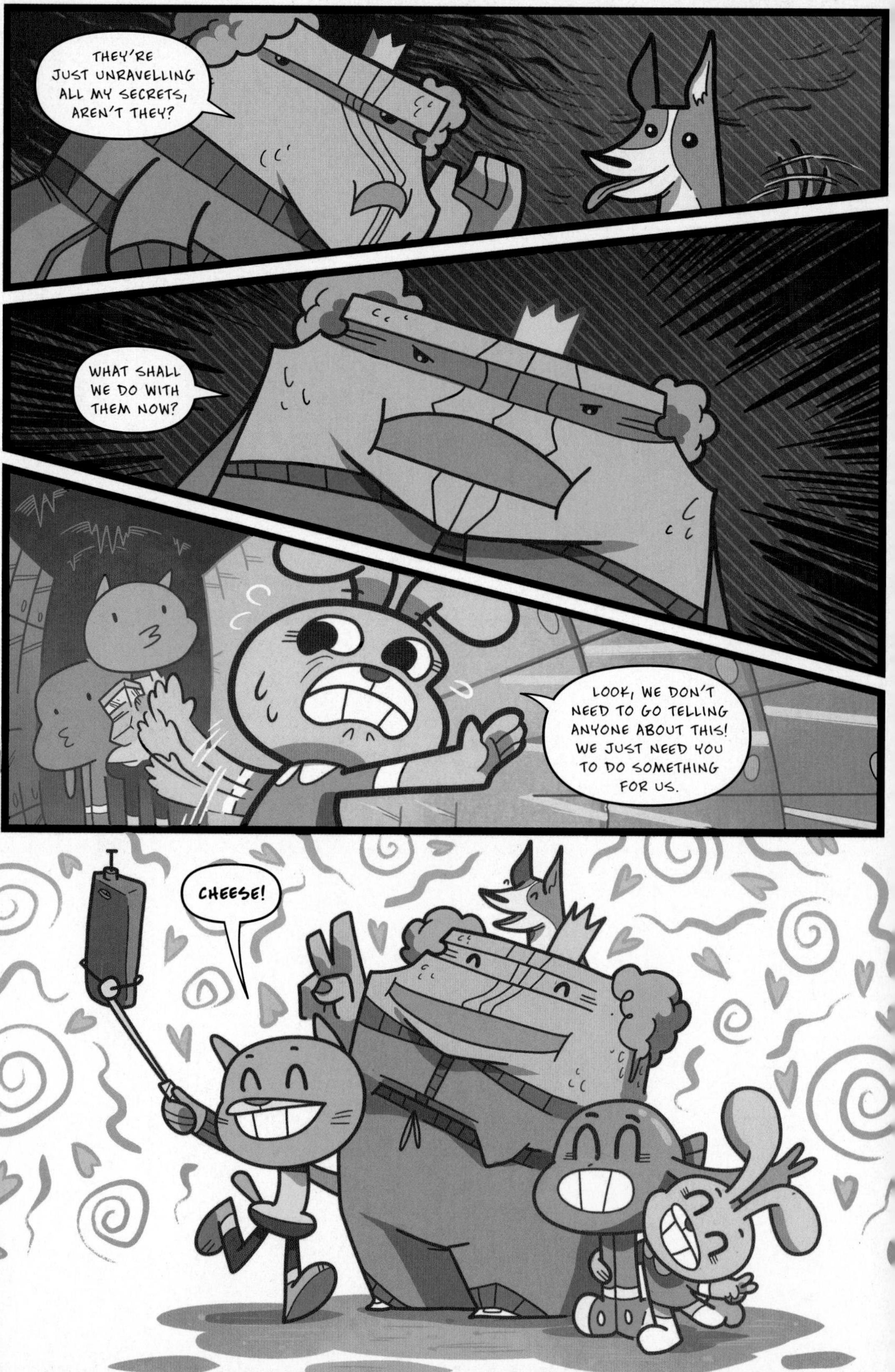
THEY'RE JUST UNRAVELLING ALL MY SECRETS, AREN'T THEY?
WHAT SHALL WE DO WITH THEM NOW?
LOOK, WE DON'T NEED TO GO TELLING ANYONE ABOUT THIS! WE JUST NEED YOU TO DO SOMETHING FOR US.
CHEESE!

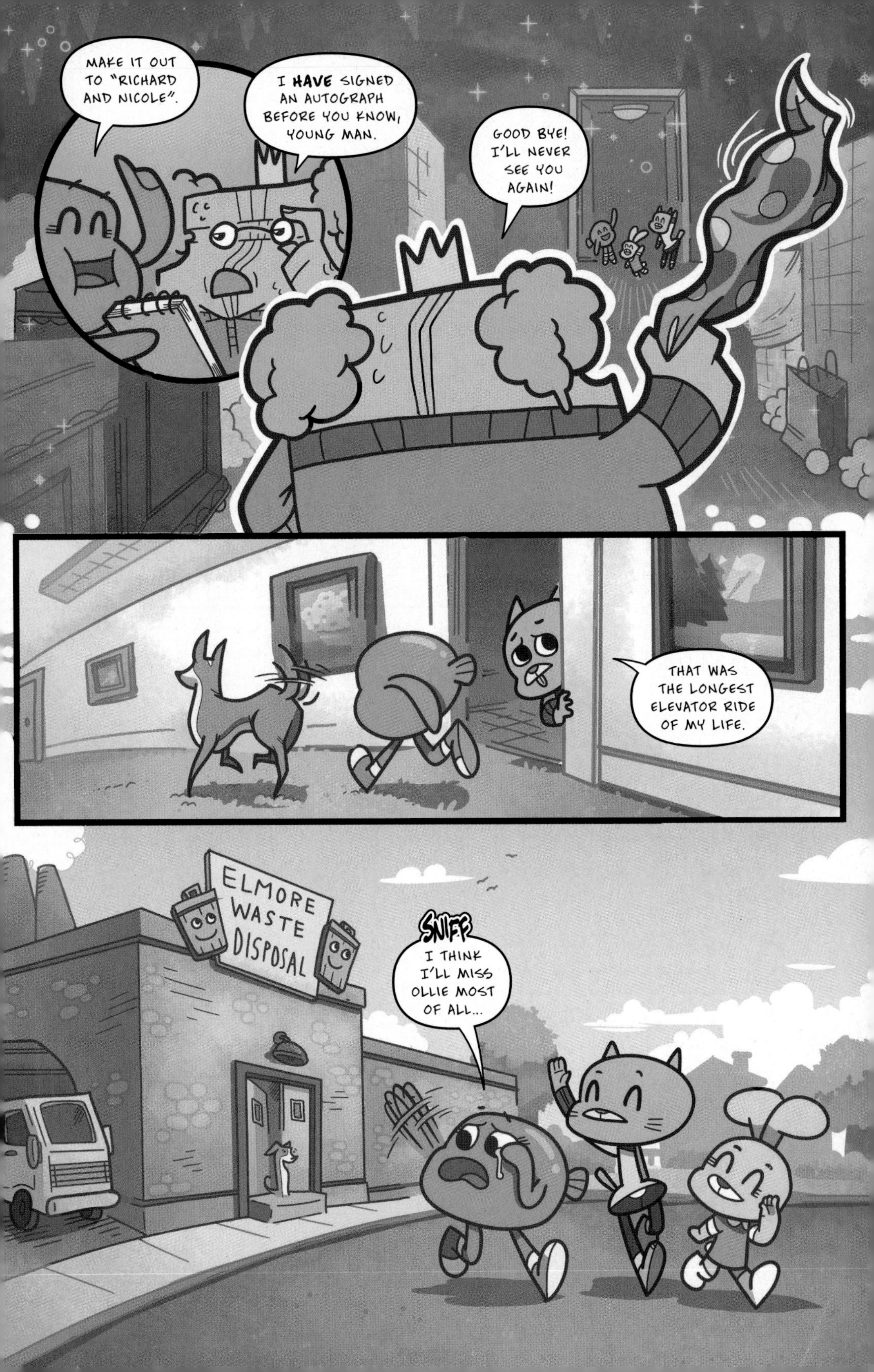
MAKE IT OUT TO "RICHARD AND NICOLE".
I **HAVE** SIGNED AN AUTOGRAPH BEFORE YOU KNOW, YOUNG MAN.
GOOD BYE! I'LL NEVER SEE YOU AGAIN!
THAT WAS THE LONGEST ELEVATOR RIDE OF MY LIFE.
ELMORE WASTE DISPOSAL
SNIFF
I THINK I'LL MISS OLLIE MOST OF ALL...

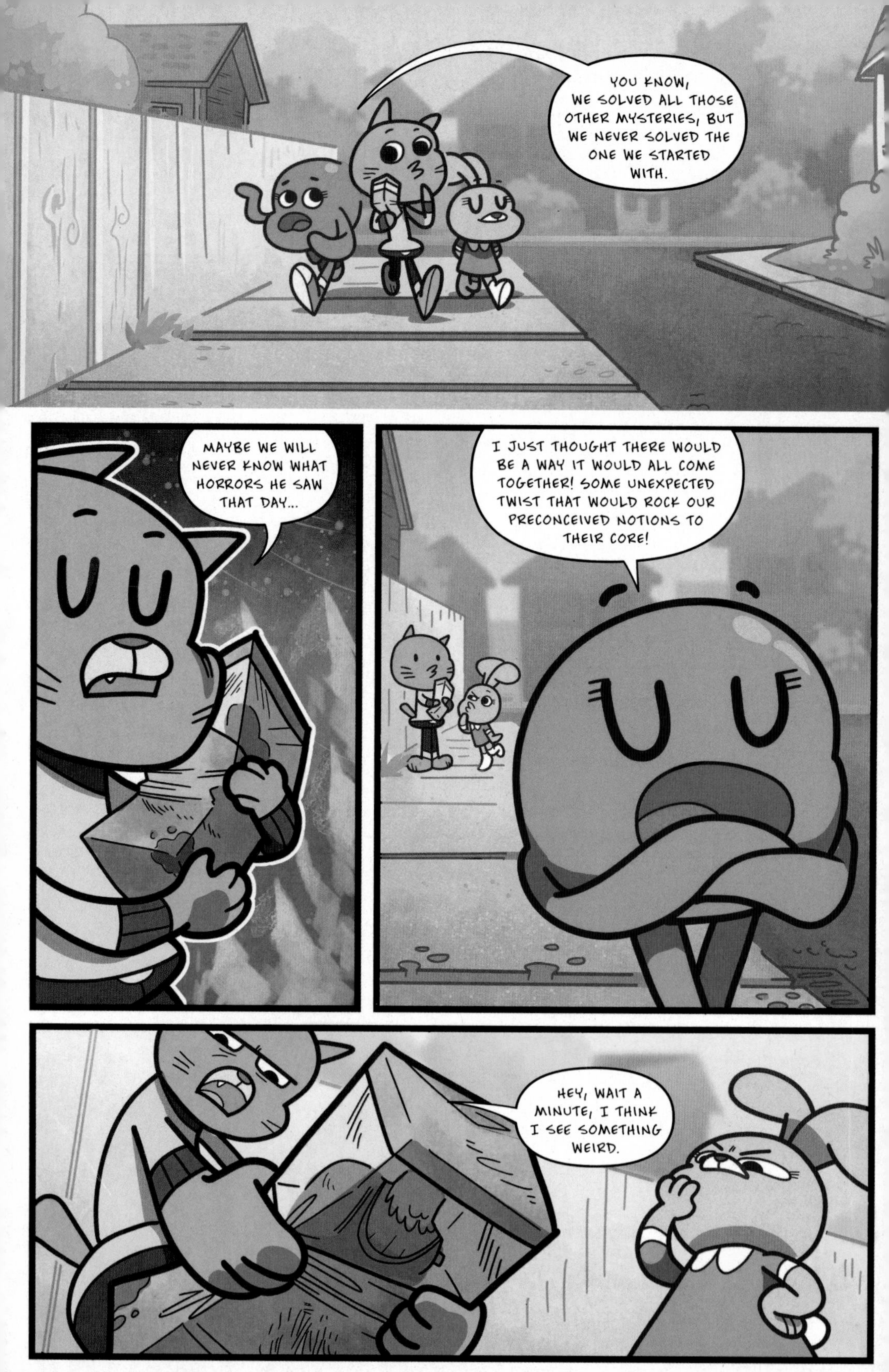
YOU KNOW, WE SOLVED ALL THOSE OTHER MYSTERIES, BUT WE NEVER SOLVED THE ONE WE STARTED WITH.
MAYBE WE WILL NEVER KNOW WHAT HORRORS HE SAW THAT DAY...
I JUST THOUGHT THERE WOULD BE A WAY IT WOULD ALL COME TOGETHER! SOME UNEXPECTED TWIST THAT WOULD ROCK OUR PRECONCEIVED NOTIONS TO THEIR CORE!
HEY, WAIT A MINUTE, I THINK I SEE SOMETHING WEIRD.

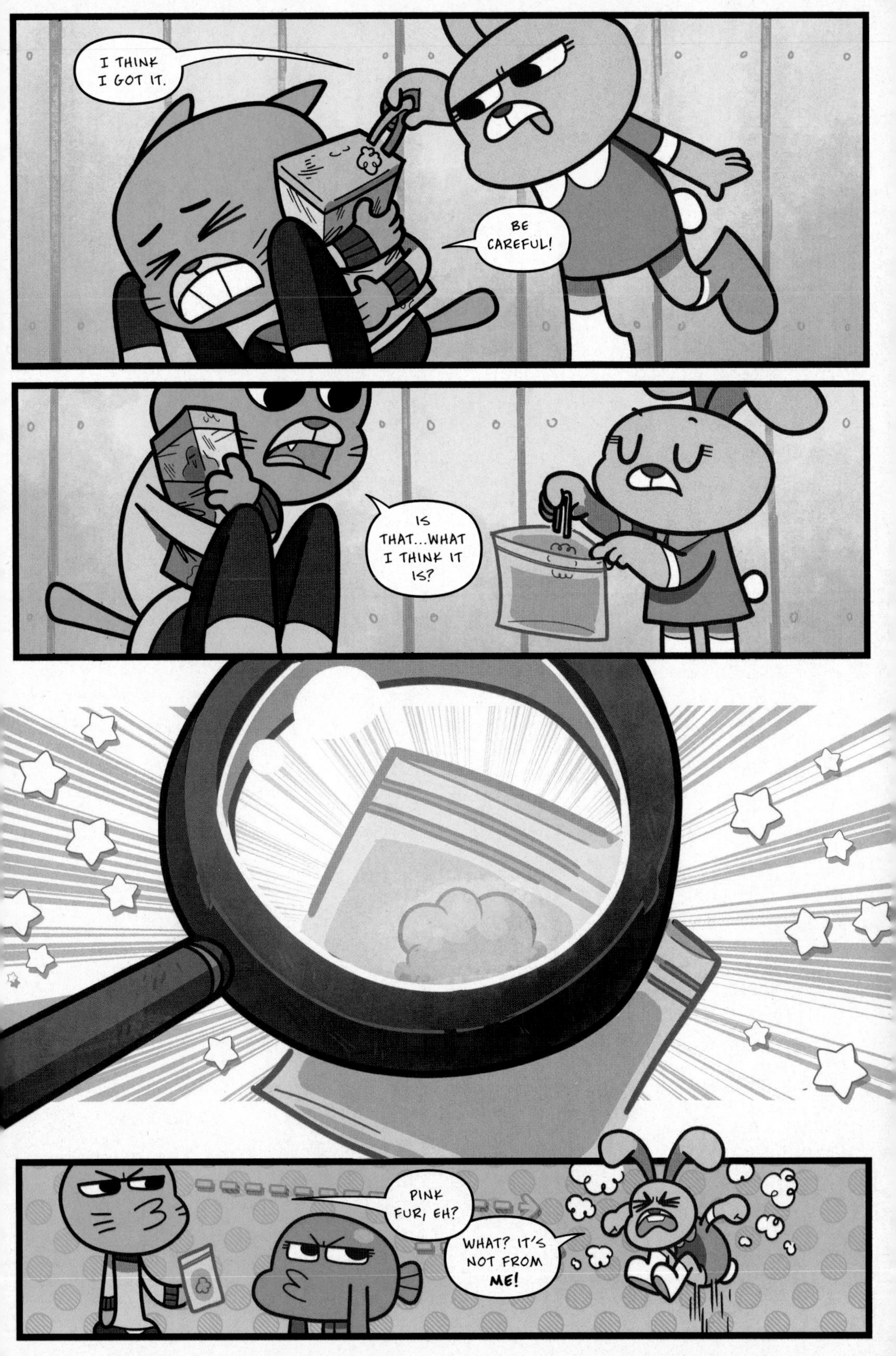
I THINK I GOT IT.
BE CAREFUL!
IS THAT...WHAT I THINK IT IS?
PINK FUR, EH?
WHAT? IT'S NOT FROM **ME!**

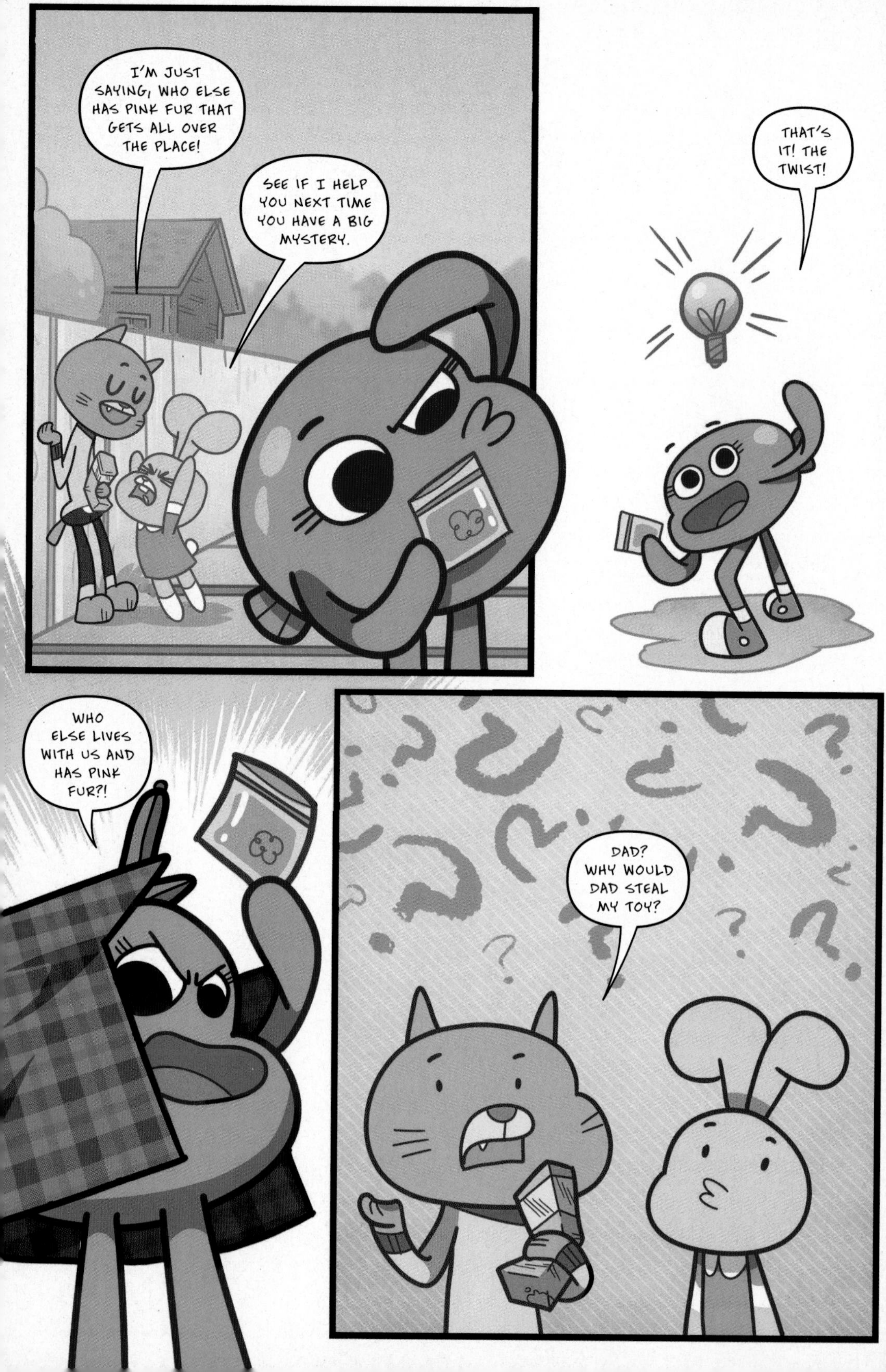
I'M JUST SAYING, WHO ELSE HAS PINK FUR THAT GETS ALL OVER THE PLACE!
SEE IF I HELP YOU NEXT TIME YOU HAVE A BIG MYSTERY.
THAT'S IT! THE TWIST!
WHO ELSE LIVES WITH US AND HAS PINK FUR?!
DAD? WHY WOULD DAD STEAL MY TOY?

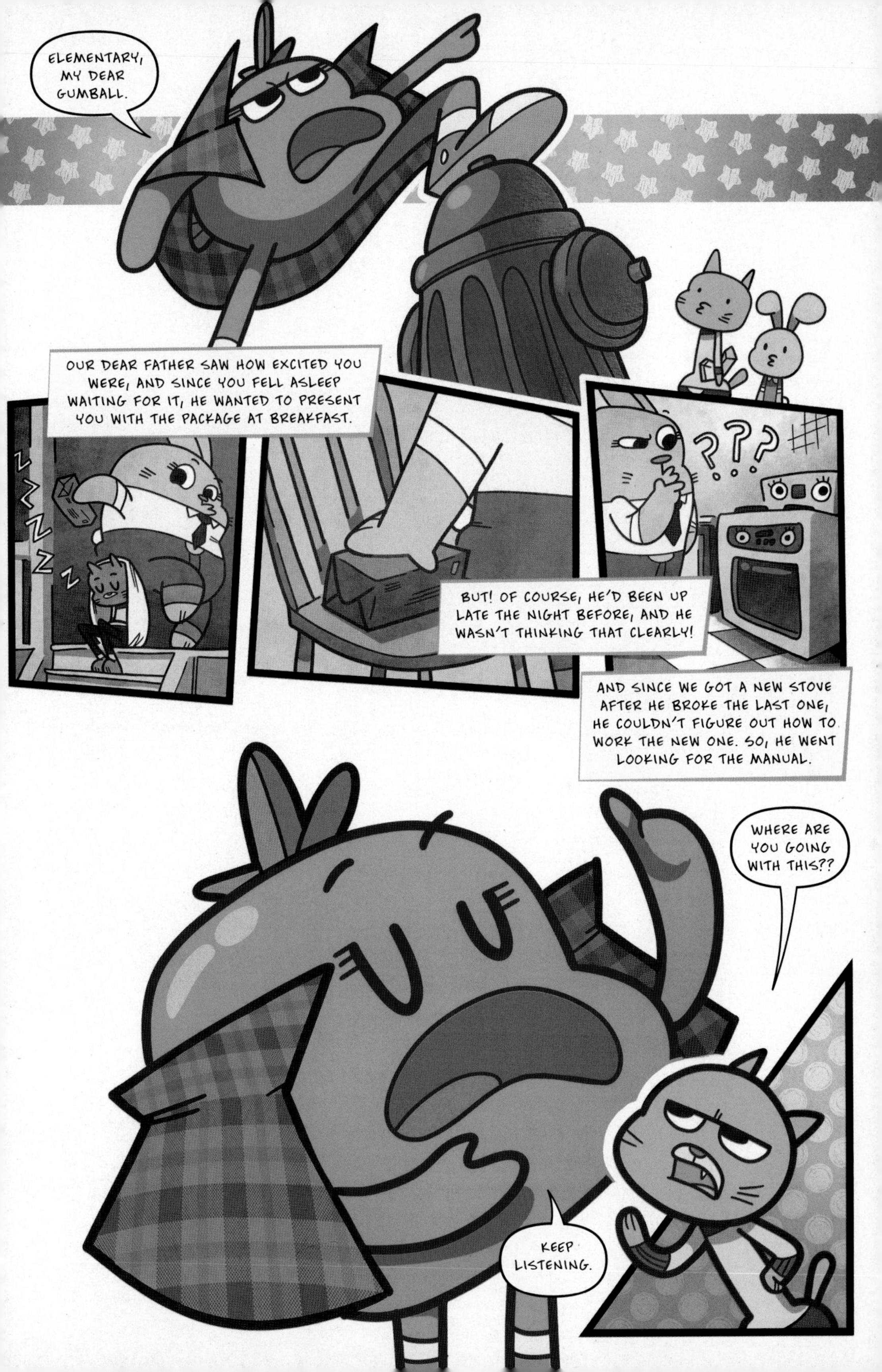
ELEMENTARY, MY DEAR GUMBALL.
OUR DEAR FATHER SAW HOW EXCITED YOU WERE, AND SINCE YOU FELL ASLEEP WAITING FOR IT, HE WANTED TO PRESENT YOU WITH THE PACKAGE AT BREAKFAST.
Z Z Z Z Z
BUT! OF COURSE, HE'D BEEN UP LATE THE NIGHT BEFORE, AND HE WASN'T THINKING THAT CLEARLY!
???
AND SINCE WE GOT A NEW STOVE AFTER HE BROKE THE LAST ONE, HE COULDN'T FIGURE OUT HOW TO WORK THE NEW ONE. SO, HE WENT LOOKING FOR THE MANUAL.
WHERE ARE YOU GOING WITH THIS??
KEEP LISTENING.

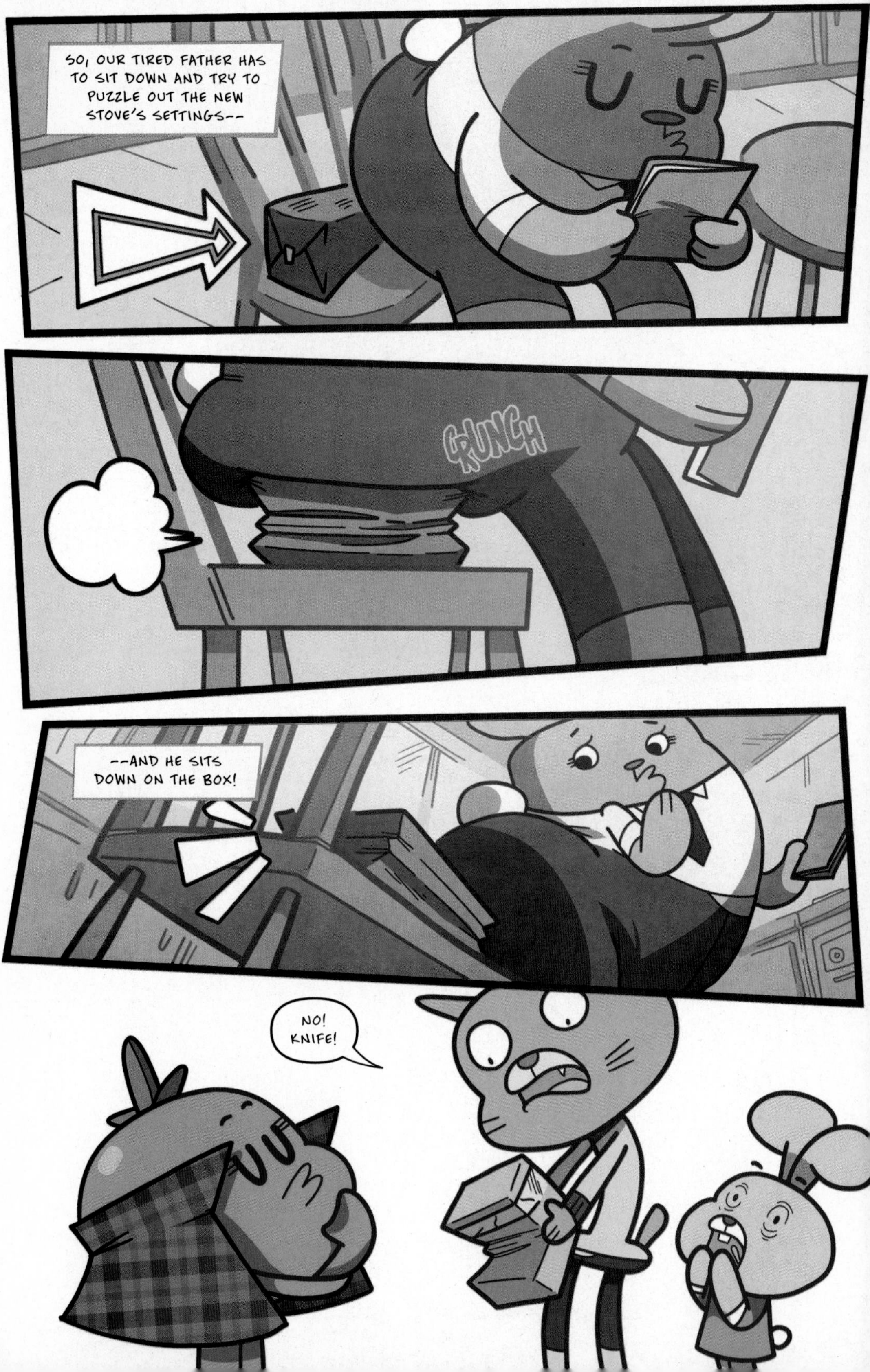
SO, OUR TIRED FATHER HAS TO SIT DOWN AND TRY TO PUZZLE OUT THE NEW STOVE'S SETTINGS--
CRUNCH
--AND HE SITS DOWN ON THE BOX!
NO! KNIFE!

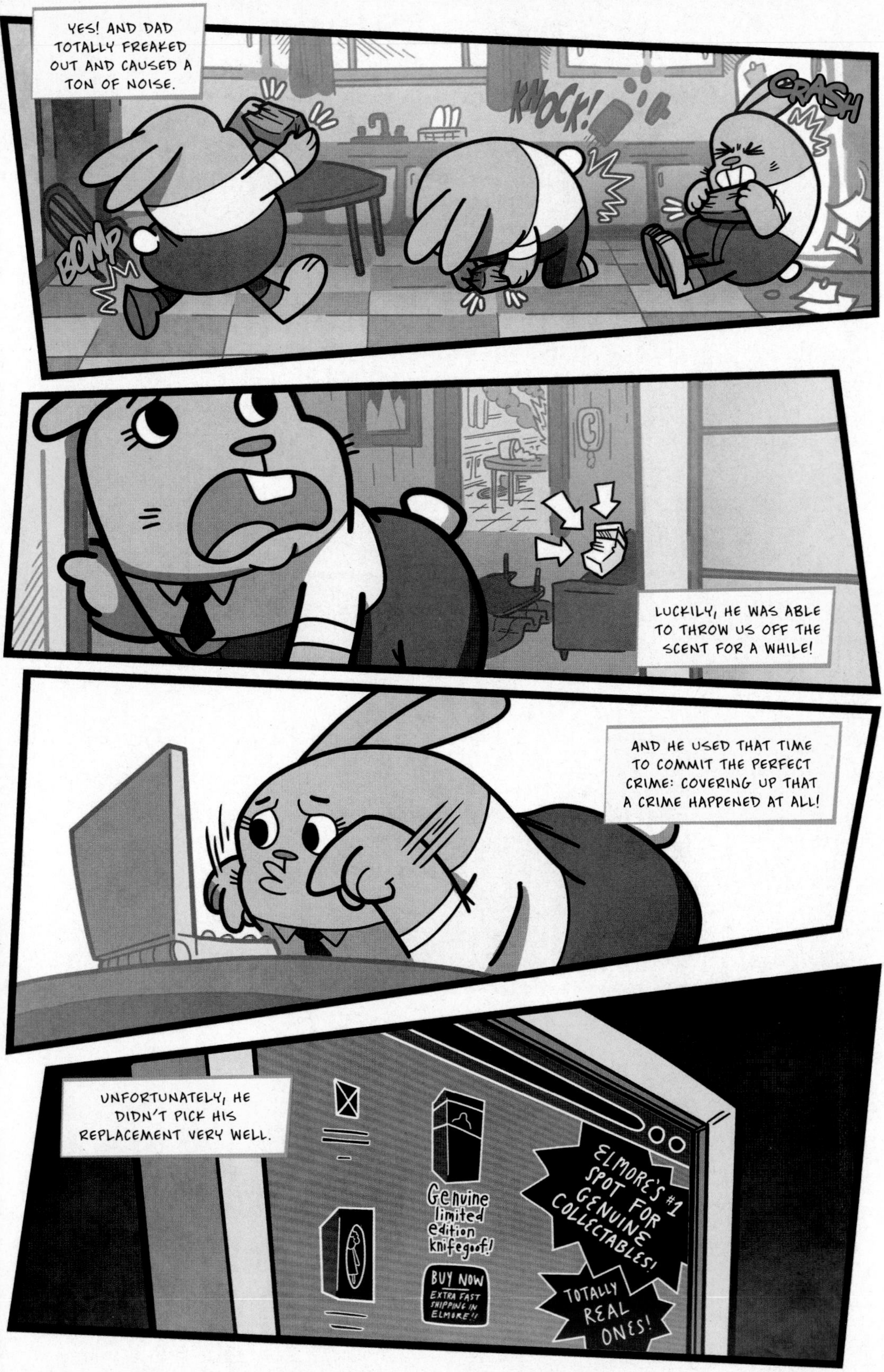
YES! AND DAD TOTALLY FREAKED OUT AND CAUSED A TON OF NOISE.
KNOCK!
CRASH
BOMP
LUCKILY, HE WAS ABLE TO THROW US OFF THE SCENT FOR A WHILE!
AND HE USED THAT TIME TO COMMIT THE PERFECT CRIME: COVERING UP THAT A CRIME HAPPENED AT ALL!
UNFORTUNATELY, HE DIDN'T PICK HIS REPLACEMENT VERY WELL.
Genuine limited edition knifegoof!
BUY NOW
EXTRA FAST SHIPPING IN ELMORE!!
ELMORE'S #1 SPOT FOR GENUINE COLLECTABLES!
TOTALLY REAL ONES!

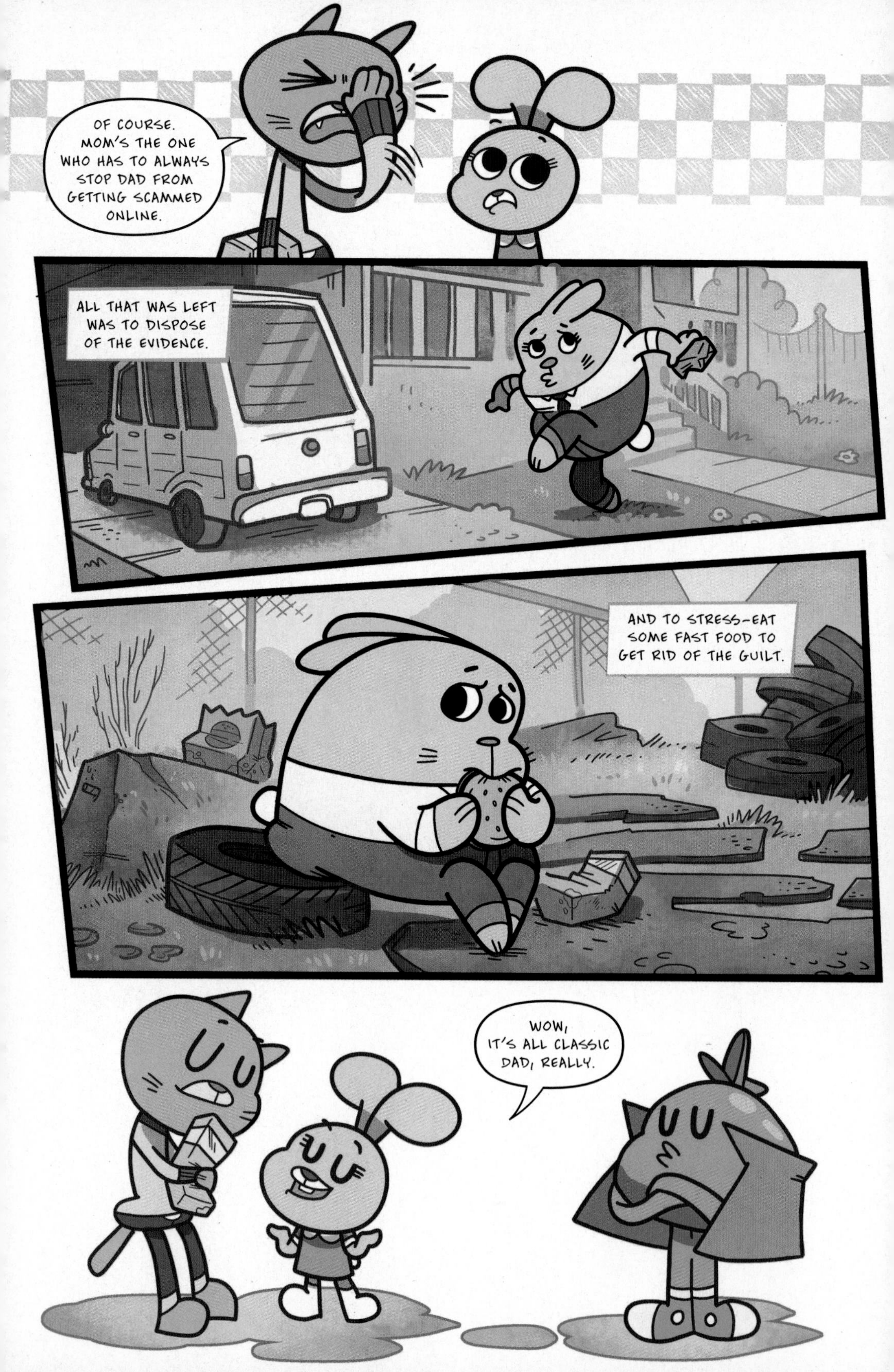
OF COURSE. MOM'S THE ONE WHO HAS TO ALWAYS STOP DAD FROM GETTING SCAMMED ONLINE.
ALL THAT WAS LEFT WAS TO DISPOSE OF THE EVIDENCE.
AND TO STRESS-EAT SOME FAST FOOD TO GET RID OF THE GUILT.
WOW, IT'S ALL CLASSIC DAD, REALLY.

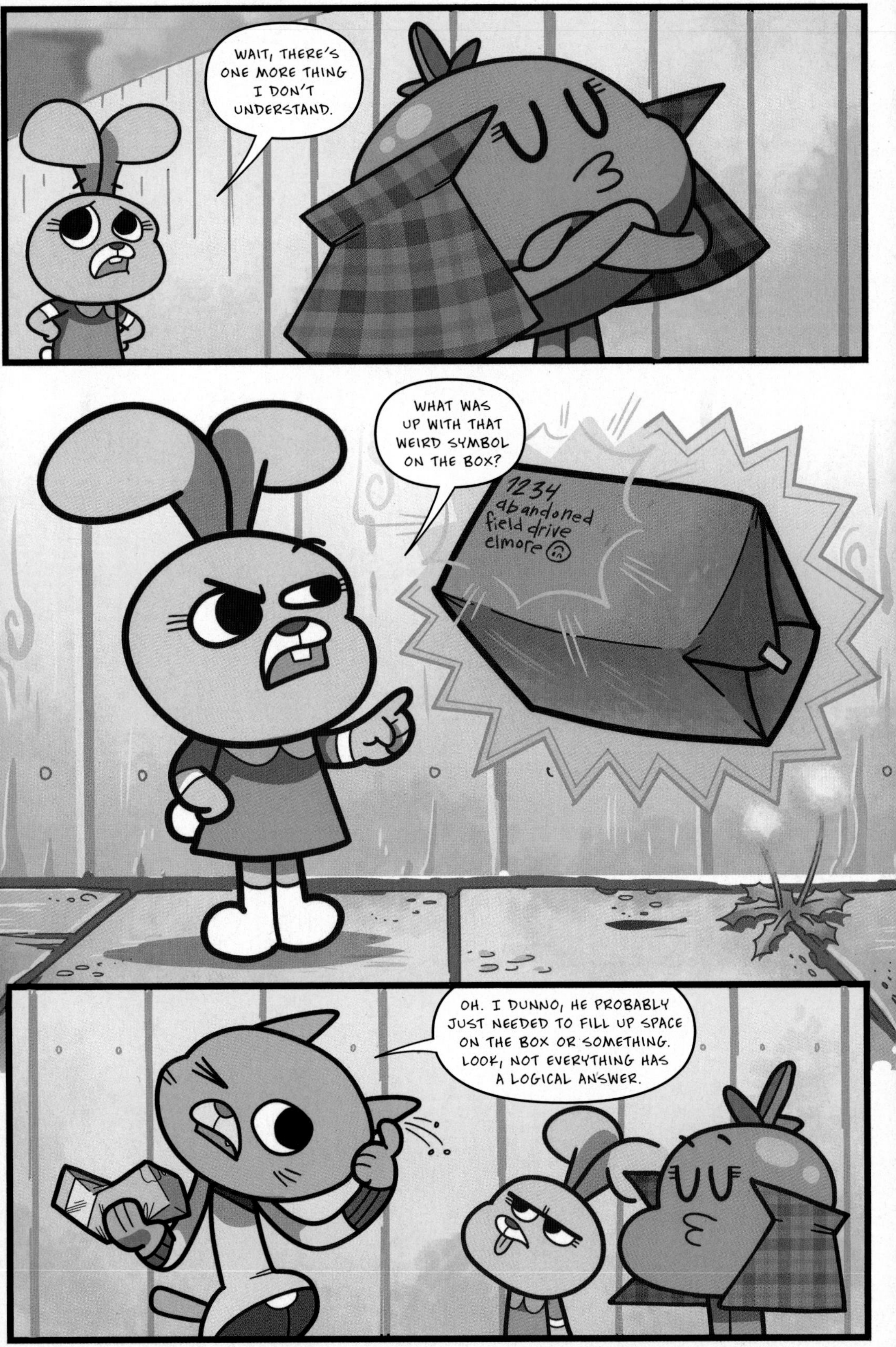
WAIT, THERE'S ONE MORE THING I DON'T UNDERSTAND.
WHAT WAS UP WITH THAT WEIRD SYMBOL ON THE BOX?
1234 abandoned field drive elmore
OH. I DUNNO, HE PROBABLY JUST NEEDED TO FILL UP SPACE ON THE BOX OR SOMETHING. LOOK, NOT EVERYTHING HAS A LOGICAL ANSWER.

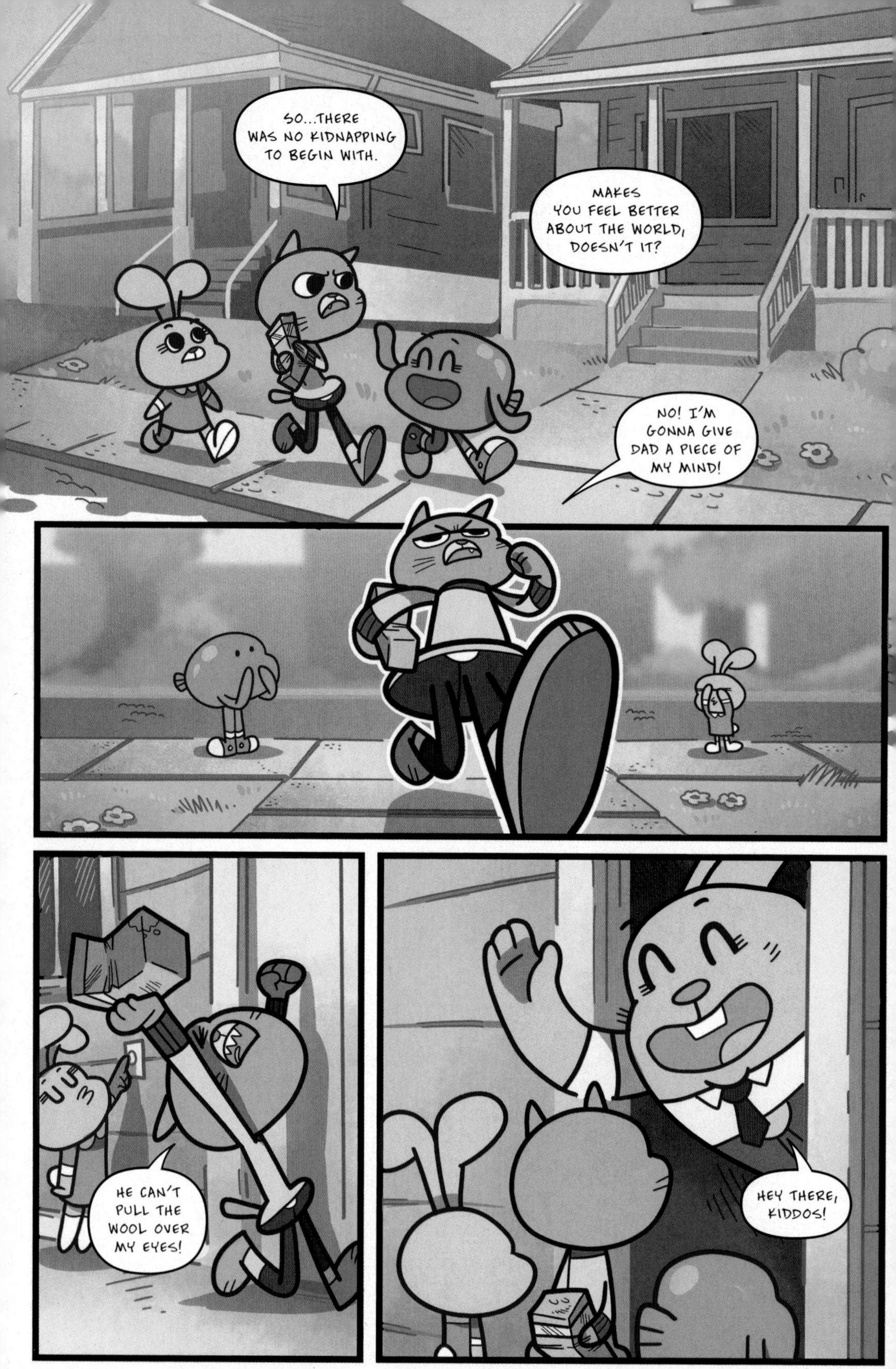
SO...THERE WAS NO KIDNAPPING TO BEGIN WITH.
MAKES YOU FEEL BETTER ABOUT THE WORLD, DOESN'T IT?
NO! I'M GONNA GIVE DAD A PIECE OF MY MIND!
HE CAN'T PULL THE WOOL OVER MY EYES!
HEY THERE, KIDDOS!

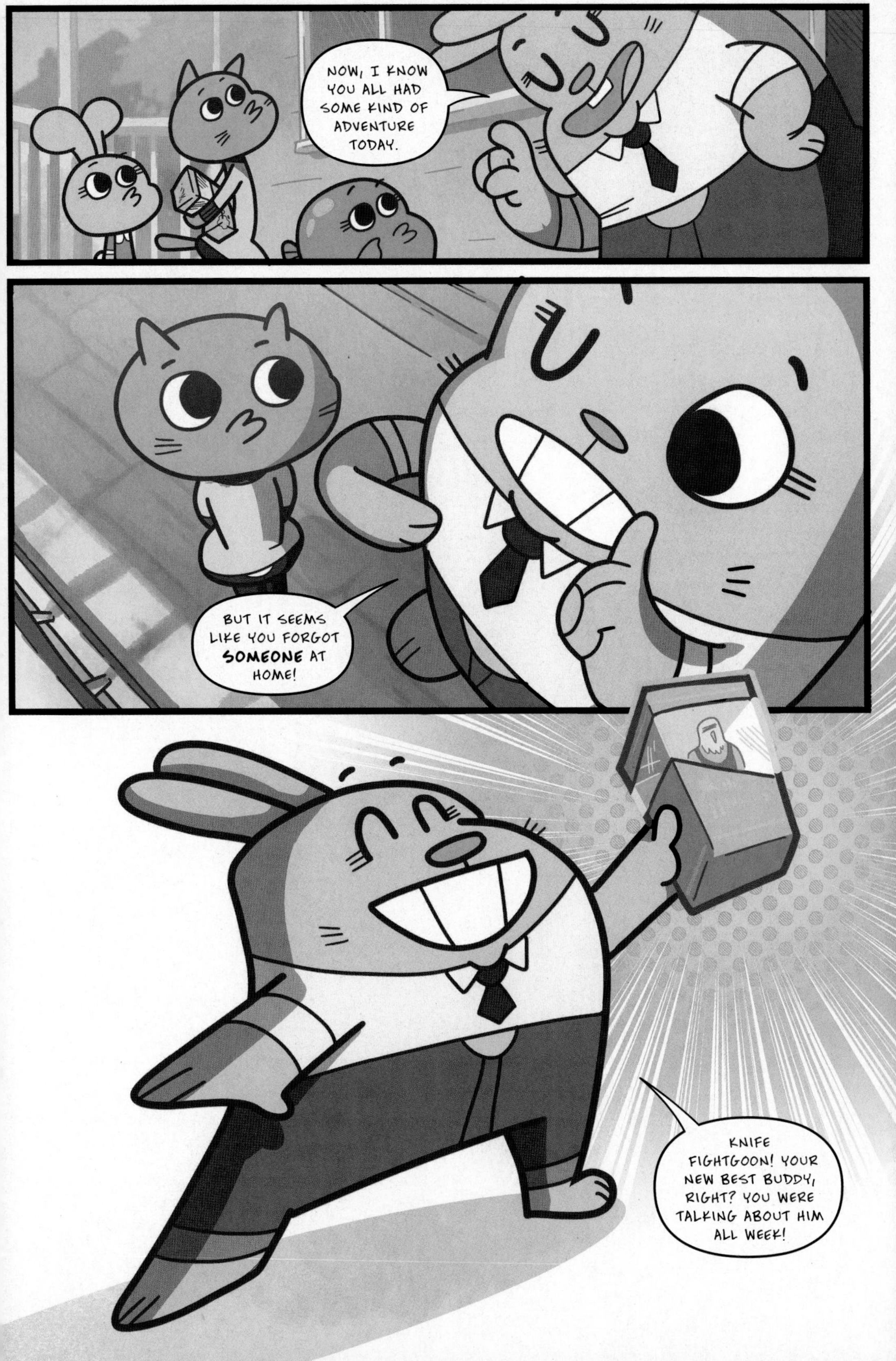
NOW, I KNOW YOU ALL HAD SOME KIND OF ADVENTURE TODAY.
BUT IT SEEMS LIKE YOU FORGOT **SOMEONE** AT HOME!
KNIFE FIGHTGOON! YOUR NEW BEST BUDDY, RIGHT? YOU WERE TALKING ABOUT HIM ALL WEEK!

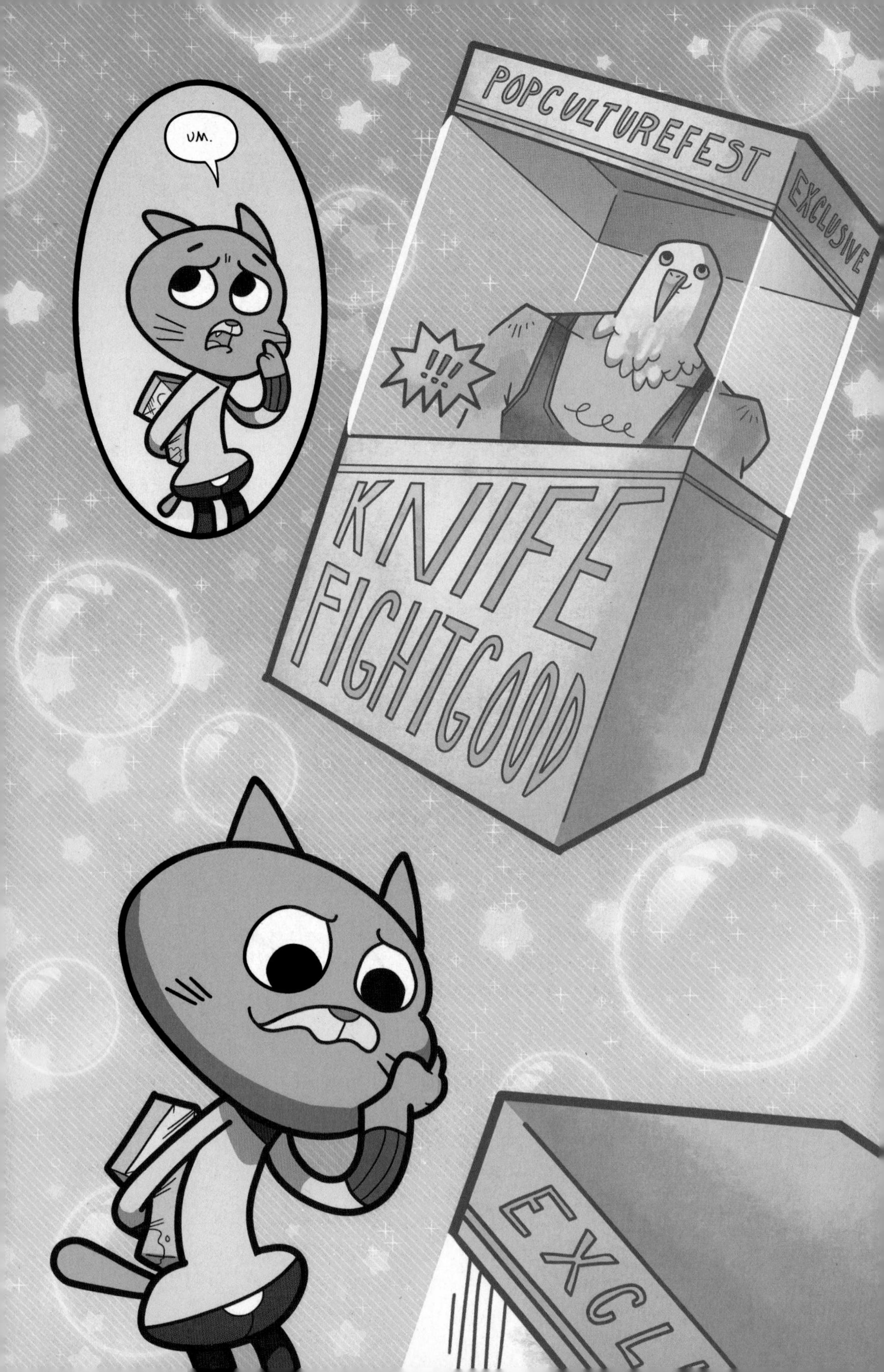
UM.
POPCULTUREFEST
EXCLUSIVE
!!!
KNIFE FIGHTGOOD
EXCL

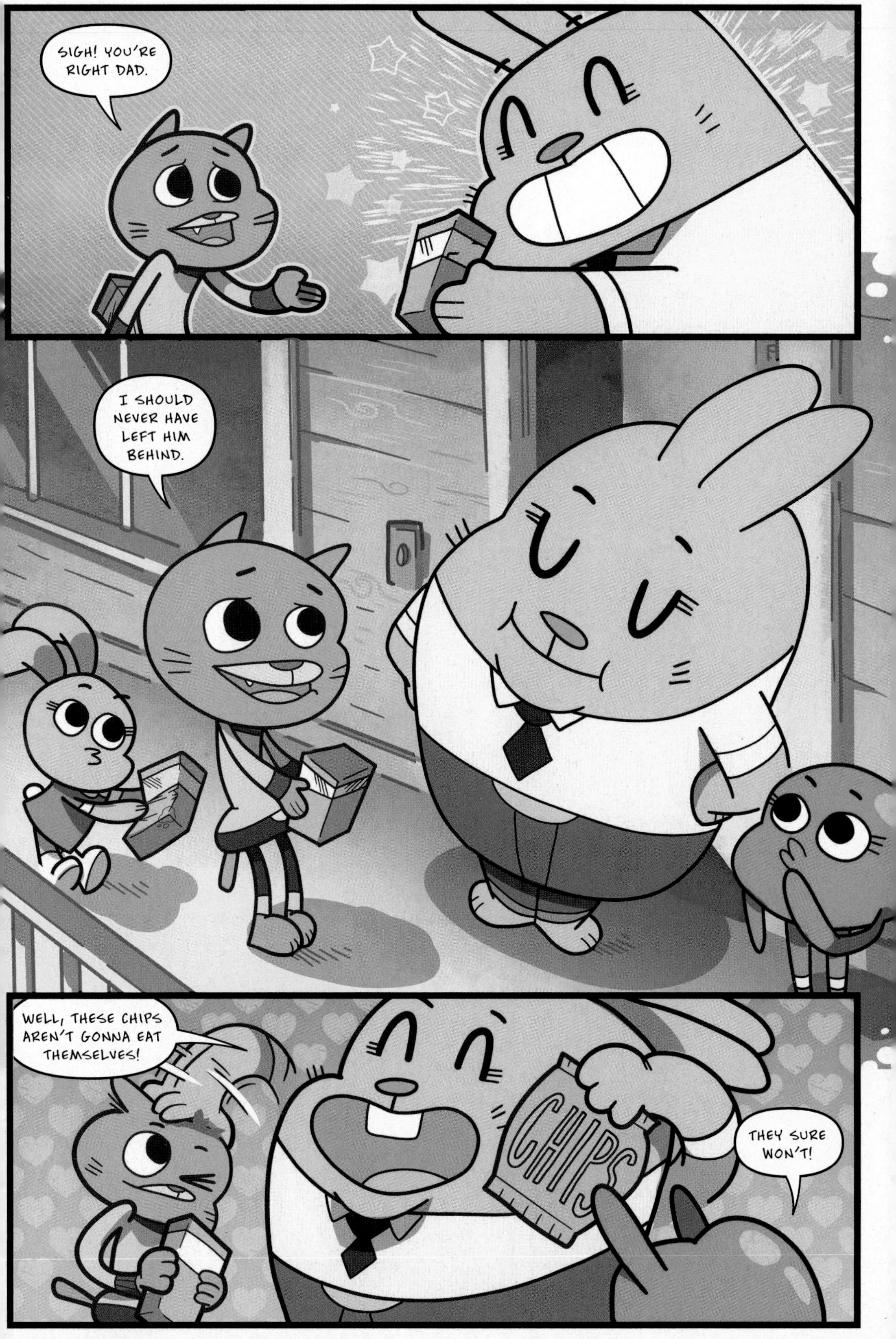

SIGH! YOU'RE RIGHT DAD.
I SHOULD NEVER HAVE LEFT HIM BEHIND.
WELL, THESE CHIPS AREN'T GONNA EAT THEMSELVES!
CHIPS
THEY SURE WON'T!

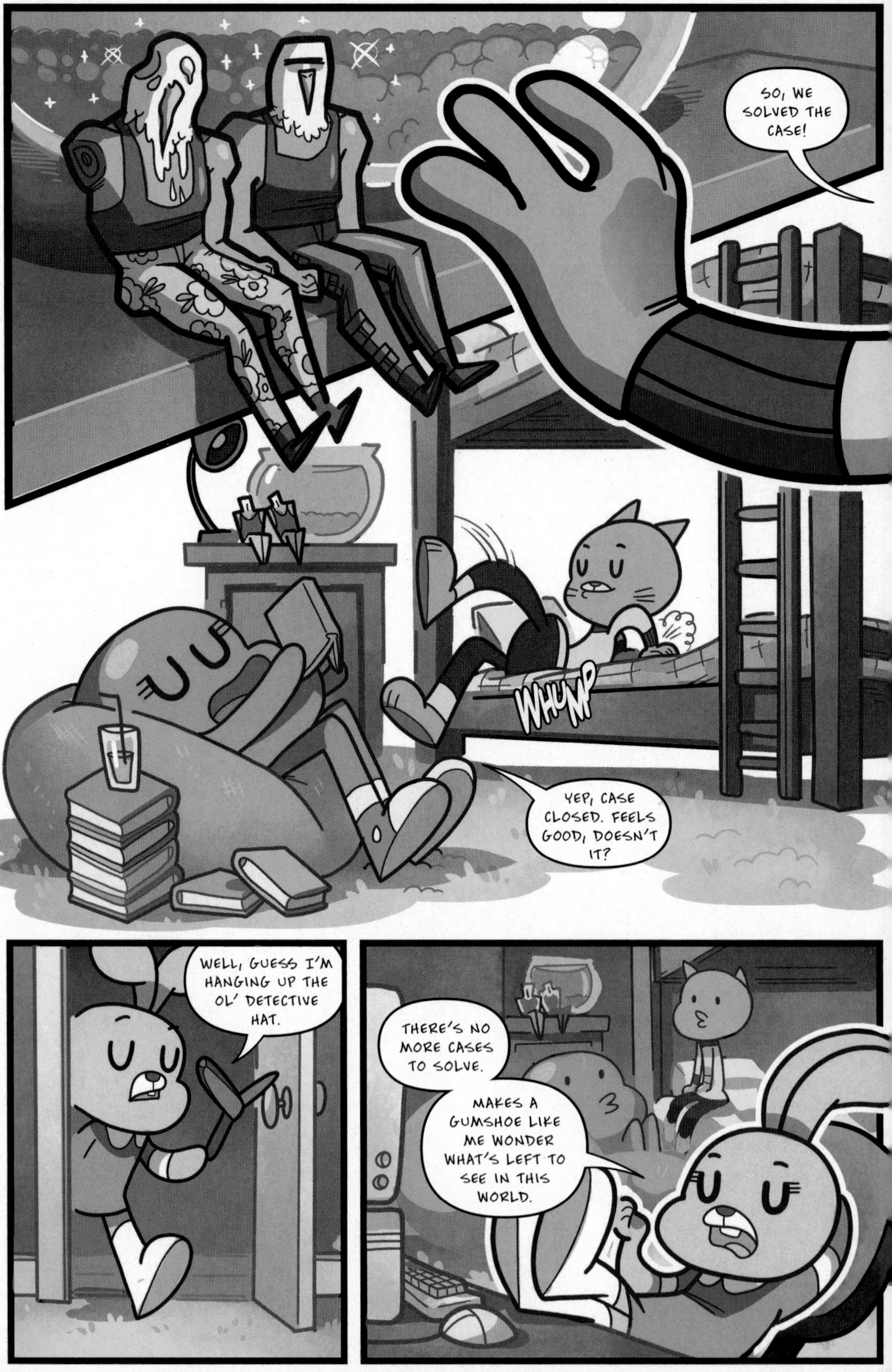
SO, WE SOLVED THE CASE!
WHUMP
YEP, CASE CLOSED. FEELS GOOD, DOESN'T IT?
WELL, GUESS I'M HANGING UP THE OL' DETECTIVE HAT.
THERE'S NO MORE CASES TO SOLVE.
MAKES A GUMSHOE LIKE ME WONDER WHAT'S LEFT TO SEE IN THIS WORLD.

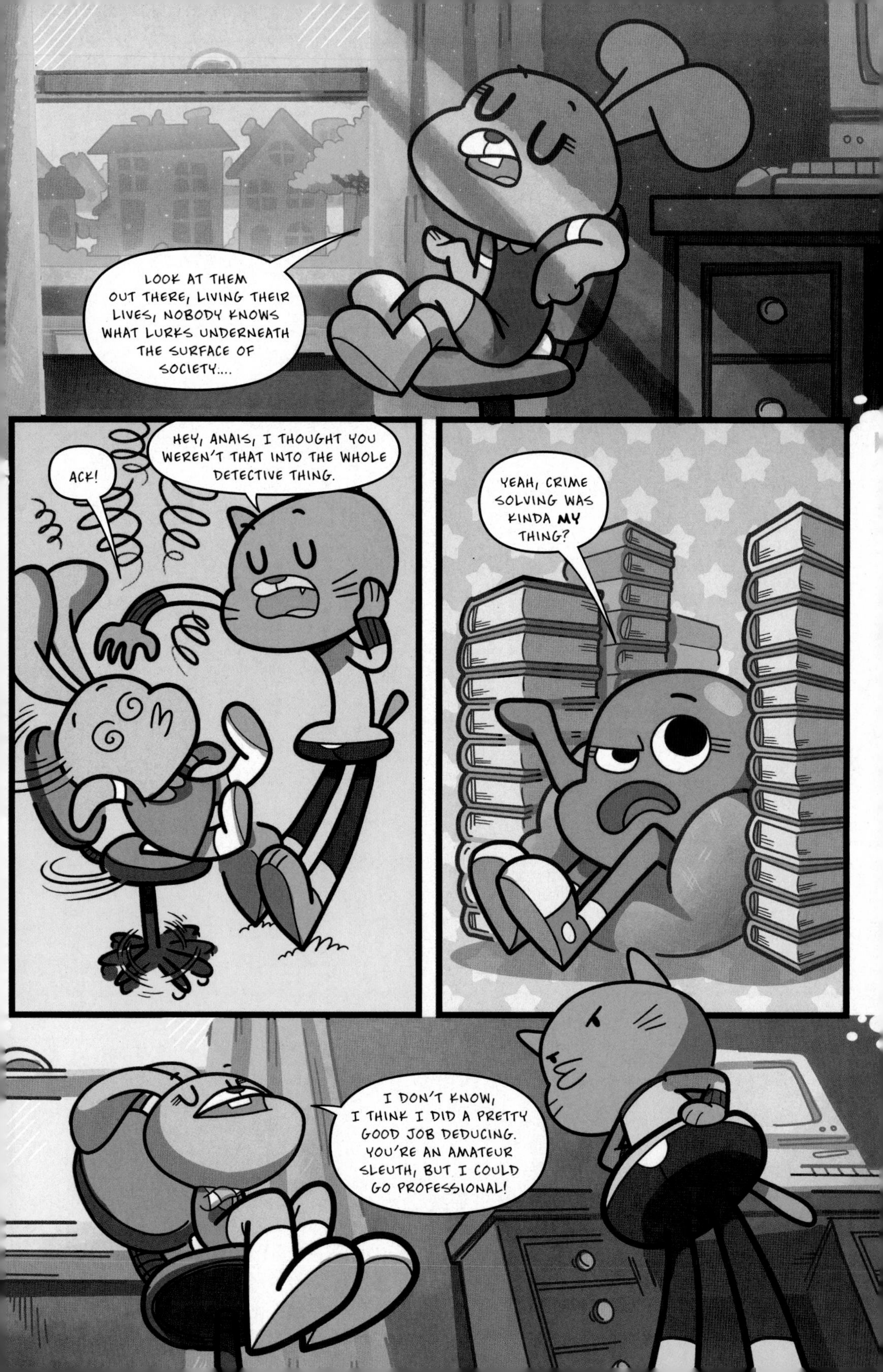
LOOK AT THEM OUT THERE, LIVING THEIR LIVES, NOBODY KNOWS WHAT LURKS UNDERNEATH THE SURFACE OF SOCIETY....
HEY, ANAIS, I THOUGHT YOU WEREN'T THAT INTO THE WHOLE DETECTIVE THING.
ACK!
YEAH, CRIME SOLVING WAS KINDA **MY** THING?
I DON'T KNOW, I THINK I DID A PRETTY GOOD JOB DEDUCING. YOU'RE AN AMATEUR SLEUTH, BUT I COULD GO PROFESSIONAL!

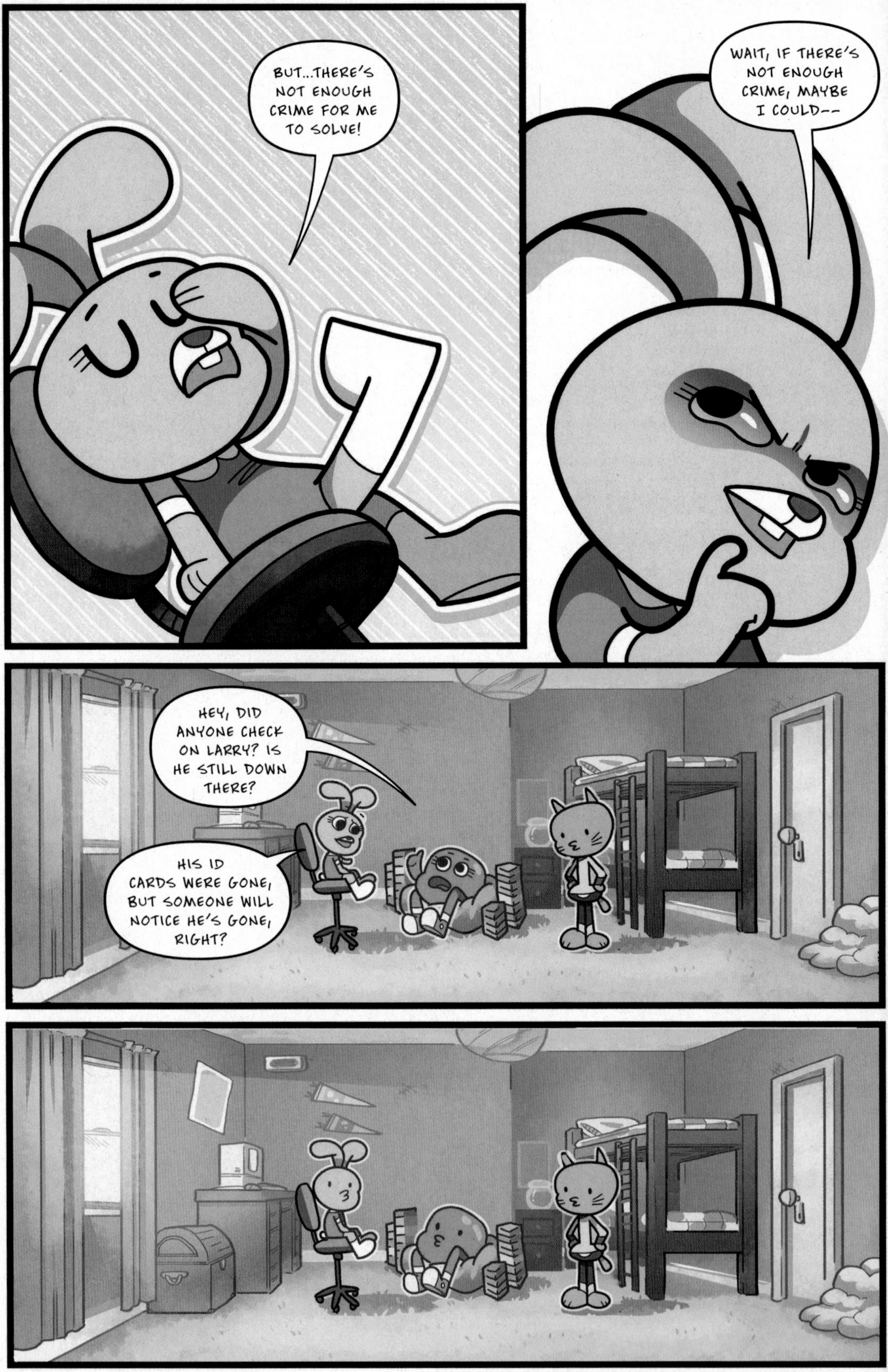
BUT...THERE'S NOT ENOUGH CRIME FOR ME TO SOLVE!
WAIT, IF THERE'S NOT ENOUGH CRIME, MAYBE I COULD--
HEY, DID ANYONE CHECK ON LARRY? IS HE STILL DOWN THERE?
HIS ID CARDS WERE GONE, BUT SOMEONE WILL NOTICE HE'S GONE, RIGHT?

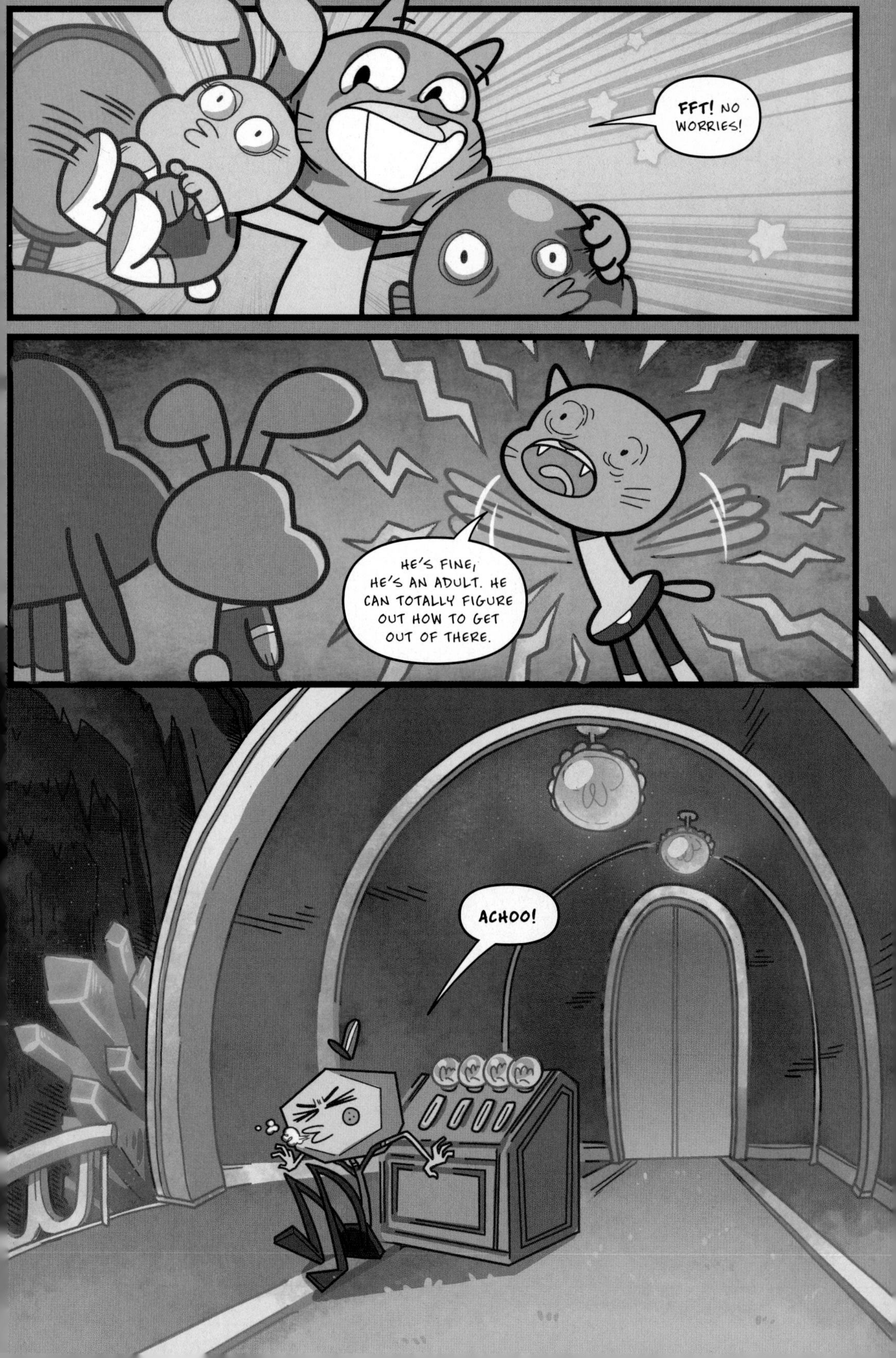

FFT! NO WORRIES!
HE'S FINE, HE'S AN ADULT. HE CAN TOTALLY FIGURE OUT HOW TO GET OUT OF THERE.
ACHOO!

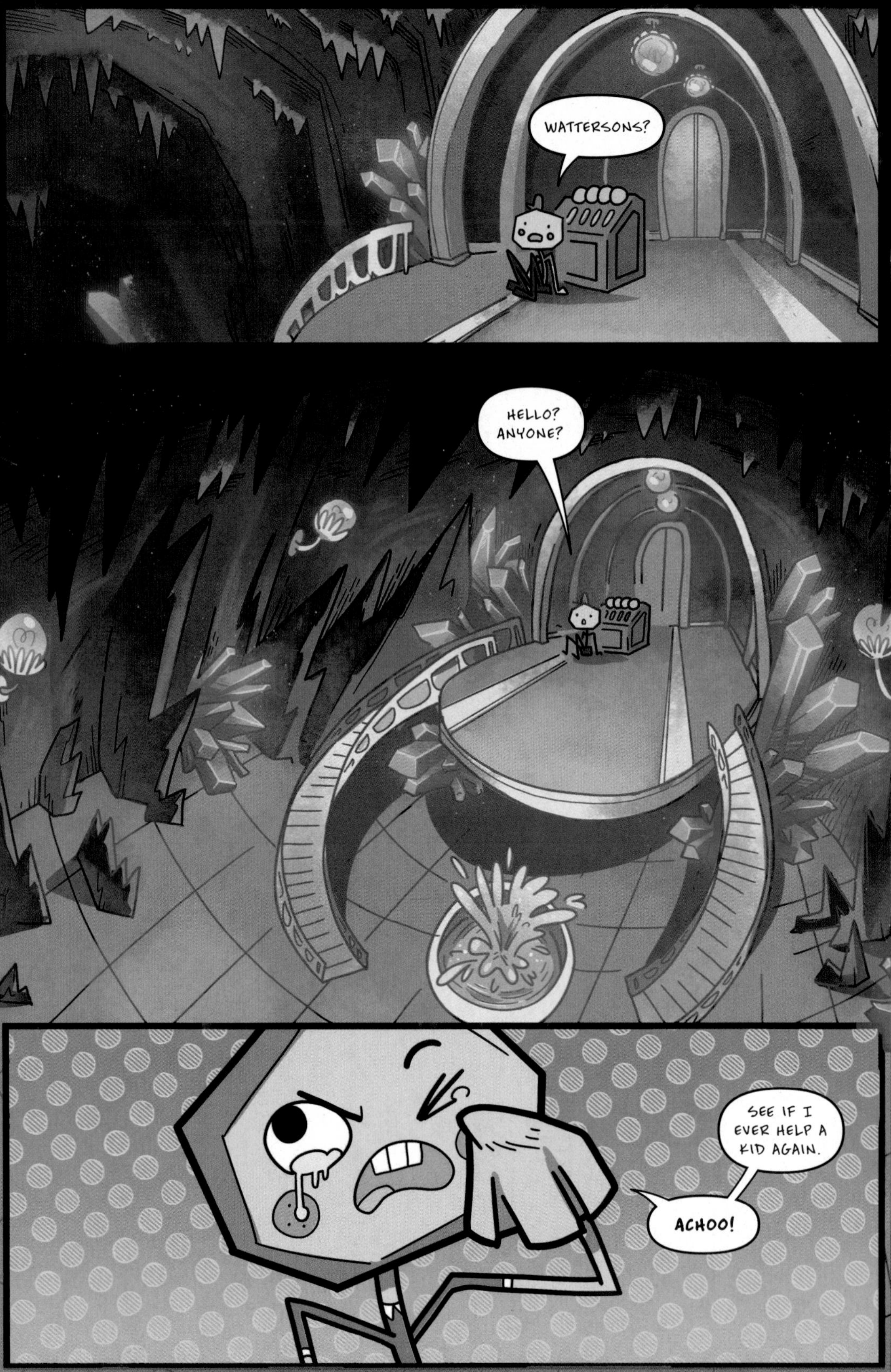
WATTERSONS?
HELLO? ANYONE?
ACHOO!
SEE IF I EVER HELP A KID AGAIN.

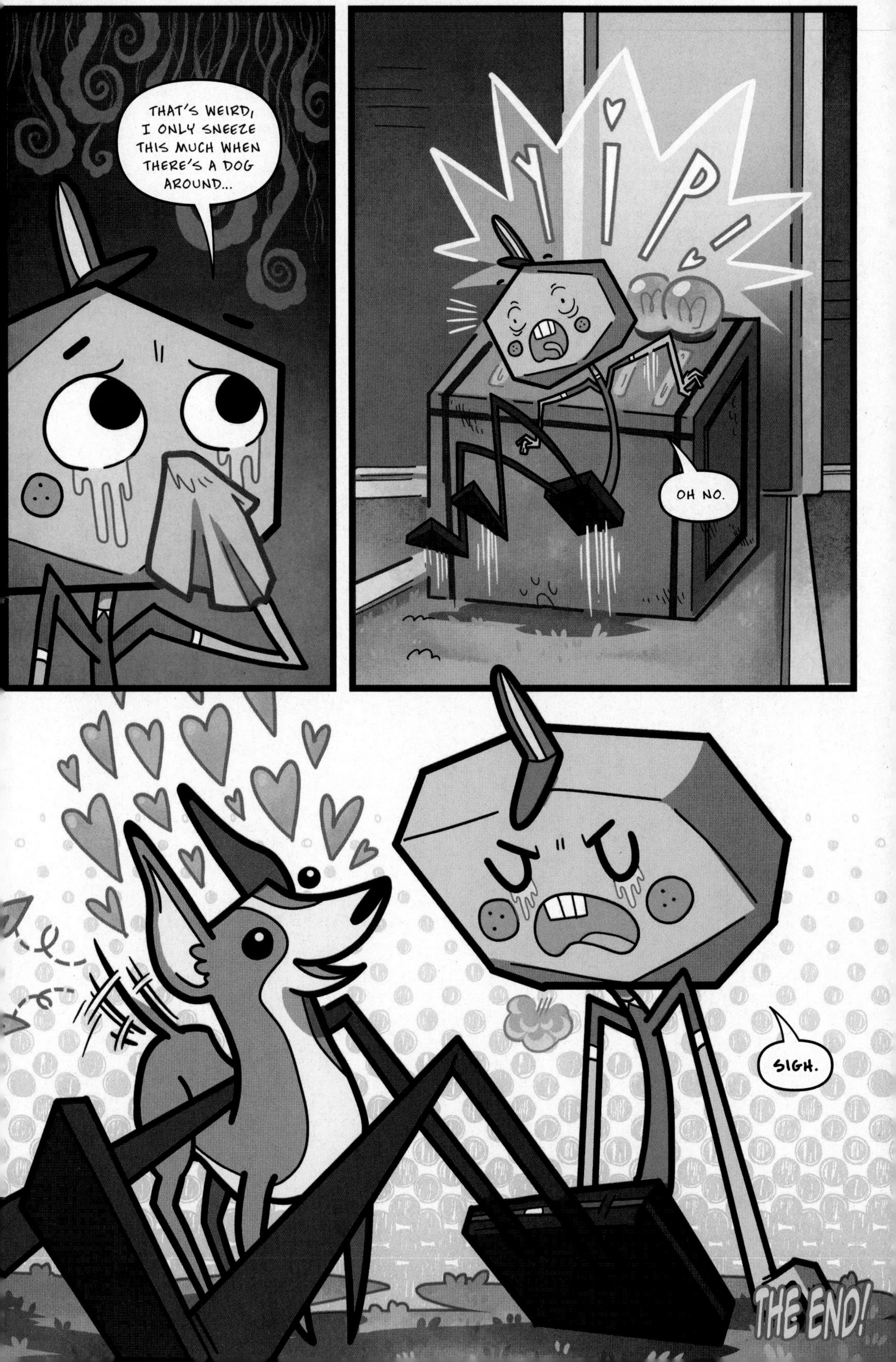
THAT'S WEIRD, I ONLY SNEEZE THIS MUCH WHEN THERE'S A DOG AROUND...
YIP!
OH NO.
SIGH.
THE END!

DISCOVER
EXPLOSIVE NEW WORLDS

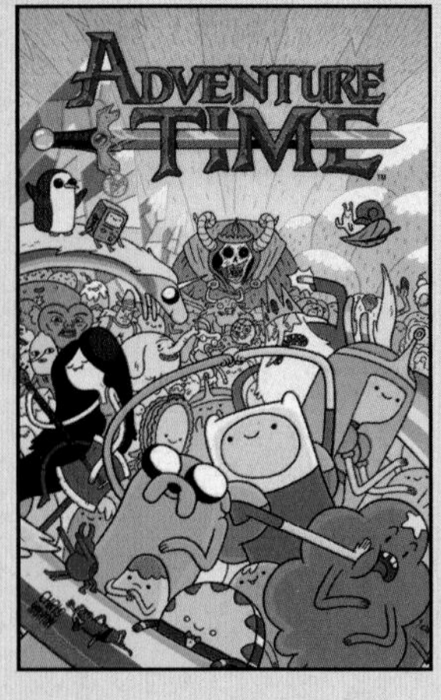
ADVENTURE TIME

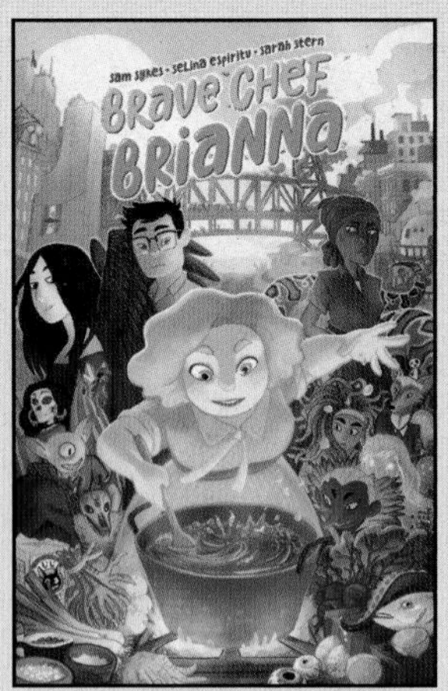
sam sykes · selina espiritu · sarah stern
Brave Chef Brianna

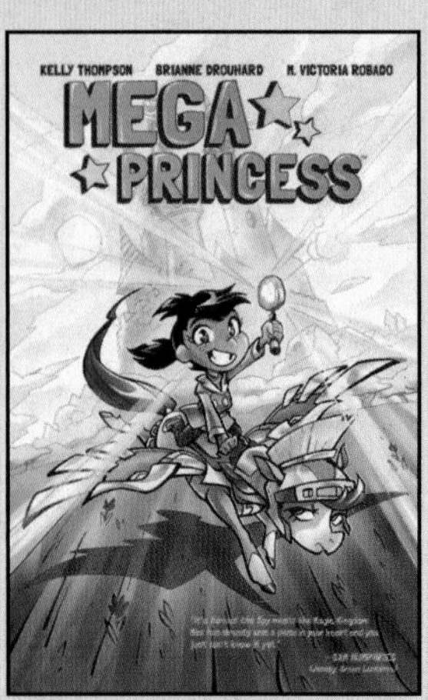
KELLY THOMPSON BRIANNE DROUHARD M. VICTORIA ROBADO
MEGA PRINCESS

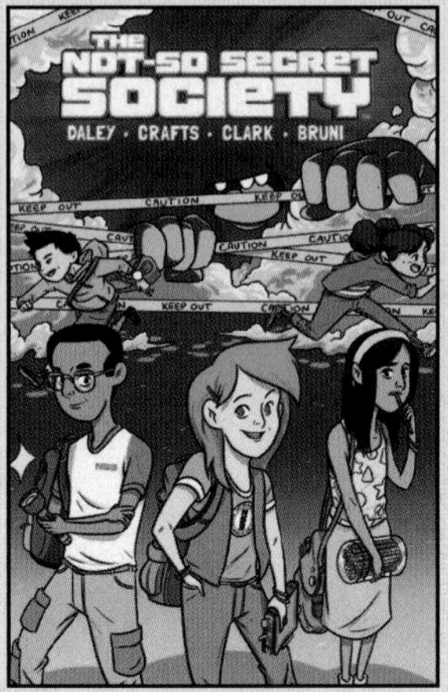
THE NOT-SO SECRET SOCIETY
DALEY · CRAFTS · CLARK · BRUNI
KEEP OUT
CAUTION

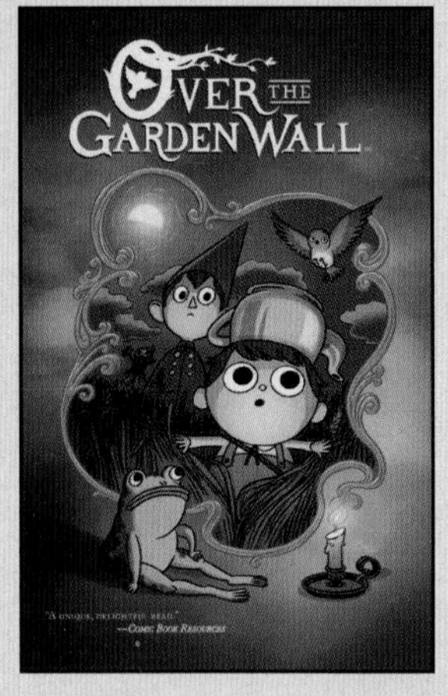
OVER THE GARDEN WALL

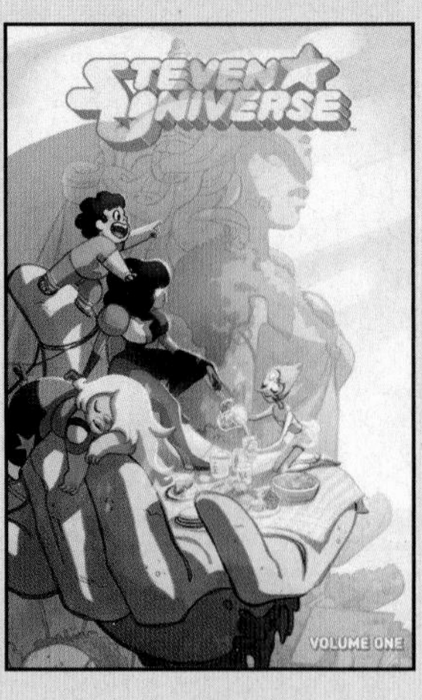
STEVEN UNIVERSE
VOLUME ONE

AVAILABLE AT YOUR LOCAL COMICS SHOP AND BOOKSTORE
To find a comics shop in your area, call 1-888-266-4226
WWW.**BOOM-STUDIOS**.COM

kaboom!™

Adventure Time
Pendleton Ward and Others
Volume 1
ISBN: 978-1-60886-280-1 | $14.99 US
Volume 2
ISBN: 978-1-60886-323-5 | $14.99 US
Adventure Time: Islands
ISBN: 978-1-60886-972-5 | $9.99 US

The Amazing World of Gumball
Ben Bocquelet and Others
Volume 1
ISBN: 978-1-60886-488-1 | $14.99 US
Volume 2
ISBN: 978-1-60886-793-6 | $14.99 US

Brave Chef Brianna
Sam Sykes, Selina Espiritu
ISBN: 978-1-68415-050-2 | $14.99 US

Mega Princess
Kelly Thompson, Brianne Drouhard
ISBN: 978-1-68415-007-6 | $14.99 US

The Not-So Secret Society
Matthew Daley, Arlene Daley, Wook Jin Clark
ISBN: 978-1-60886-997-8 | $9.99 US

Over the Garden Wall
Patrick McHale, Jim Campbell and Others
Volume 1
ISBN: 978-1-60886-940-4 | $14.99 US
Volume 2
ISBN: 978-1-68415-006-9 | $14.99 US

Steven Universe
Rebecca Sugar and Others
Volume 1
ISBN: 978-1-60886-706-6 | $14.99 US
Volume 2
ISBN: 978-1-60886-796-7 | $14.99 US

Steven Universe & The Crystal Gems
ISBN: 978-1-60886-921-3 | $14.99 US

Steven Universe: Too Cool for School
ISBN: 978-1-60886-771-4 | $14.99 US